SECOND SISTER

CHAN HO-KEI

*Translated from the
Chinese by Jeremy Tiang*

HEAD
of ZEUS

First published in Taiwan in 2017 by Crown Publishing Company
First published in the UK in 2020 by Head of Zeus, Ltd
This paperback edition first published in 2020 by Head of Zeus Ltd

9 7 5 3 1 2 4 6 8

A catalogue record for this book is available from
the British Library.

ISBN (PB): 9781788547130
ISBN (E): 9781788547109

Printed and bound in Great Britain by
CPI Group (UK) Ltd, Croydon CR0 4YY

Head of Zeus Ltd
5–8 Hardwick Street
London EC1R 4RG

WWW.HEADOFZEUS.COM

SECOND
SISTER

Also by Chan Ho-Kei

The Borrowed

SECOND
SISTER

CONTENTS

PROLOGUE

WHEN NGA-YEE LEFT her flat at eight that morning, she had no idea her whole life would change that day.

After the nightmare of the last year, she was sure better times were ahead if they just gritted their teeth and clung on. She firmly believed that destiny was fair, and if something bad happened, something good must naturally follow. Unfortunately, the powers that be love playing cruel jokes on us.

A little after six that evening, Nga-Yee dragged her exhausted body homeward. As she walked from the shuttle bus stop, her mind busily calculated whether there was enough food in the fridge to make dinner for two. In just seven or eight years, prices had risen alarmingly while wages stayed the same. Nga-Yee could remember a pound of pork costing twenty-odd dollars, but now that barely got you half a pound.

There was probably a few ounces of pork and some spinach in the fridge, enough for a stir-fry with ginger. A dish of steamed eggs on the side would complete a simple, nutritious dinner. Her sister Siu-Man, who was eight years younger, loved steamed eggs, and Nga-Yee often served this soft, silky dish when the cupboard was almost bare—a fine meal with chopped scallions and a dash of soy sauce. Most important, it was cheap. Back when their finances were even tighter, eggs got them through many a difficult moment.

Although there was enough for that night, Nga-Yee wondered if she should try her luck at the market anyway. She didn't like leaving the fridge completely bare—her upbringing had left her wanting a backup plan at all times. Besides, quite a few vendors dropped their prices just before closing, and she might pick up some bargains for the next day.

Ooo-eee-ooo-eee.

A police car sped past, the siren piercing Nga-Yee's thoughts of discounted groceries. Only now did she notice the crowd at the foot of her building, Wun Wah House.

What on earth could have happened? Nga-Yee continued walking at the same pace. She wasn't the sort of person who liked joining in the excitement, which was why many of her secondary school classmates had labeled her a loner, an introvert, a nerd. Not that this bothered her. Everyone has the right to choose how to live their lives. Trying to fit in with other people's ideas is pure foolishness.

"Nga-Yee! Nga-Yee!" A plump, curly-haired, fiftyish woman waved frantically from among the dozen or so onlookers: Auntie Chan, their neighbor on the twenty-second floor. They knew each other to say hello, but that was about it.

Auntie Chan sprinted the short distance toward Nga-Yee, grabbed her by the arm, and dragged her toward the building. Nga-Yee couldn't make out a word she was saying, apart from her own name—sheer terror made her voice sound like a foreign language. Nga-Yee finally began to understand when she picked out the word "sister."

In the light of the setting sun, Nga-Yee walked through the crowd and was finally able to make out the horrifying sight.

People were huddled around a patch of concrete about a dozen yards from the main entrance. A teenage girl in a white school uniform lay there, tangled hair obscuring her face, dark red liquid puddling around her head.

Nga-Yee's first thought was, Isn't that someone from Siu-Man's school?

Two seconds later she realized the still figure on the ground *was* Siu-Man.

Her little sister was sprawled on the cold concrete.

All the family she had in the world.

Instantly, everything around her turned upside down.

Was this a nightmare? If only she were dreaming. Nga-Yee looked at the faces around her. She recognized them as her neighbors, but they felt like strangers.

"Nga-Yee! Nga-Yee!" Auntie Chan clutched at her arm, shaking her violently.

"Siu . . . Siu-Man?" Even saying her name out loud, Nga-Yee couldn't connect the object on the ground with her little sister.

Siu-Man ought to be at home right now, waiting for me to cook dinner.

"Move back, please." A police officer in a neatly pressed uniform pushed through while two paramedics knelt by Siu-Man with a stretcher.

The older paramedic held his hand beneath her nose, pressed a couple of fingers to her left wrist, then lifted an eyelid and shone a penlight at her pupil. This took just a few seconds, but Nga-Yee experienced every one of these actions as a series of freeze-frames.

She could no longer feel the passing of time.

Her subconscious was trying to save her from what would happen next.

The paramedic straightened and shook his head.

"Please step back, clear the way please," said the policeman. The paramedics walked away from Siu-Man, looking somber.

"Siu . . . Siu-Man? Siu-Man! Siu-Man!" Nga-Yee pushed Auntie Chan aside and dashed over.

"Miss!" A tall police officer moved quickly to grab her by the waist.

"Siu-Man!" Nga-Yee struggled futilely, then turned to beseech the officer, "That's my sister. You have to save her!"

"Miss, please calm down," said the policeman in a tone that suggested he knew his words would have no effect.

"Please save her! Medics!" Nga-Yee, all color drained from her face, turned to implore the departing ambulance crew. "Why isn't she on your stretcher? Quick! You have to save her!"

"Miss, are you her sister? Please calm down," said the policeman, his arm around her waist, trying to sound as sympathetic as possible.

"Siu-Man—" Nga-Yee turned back to look at the broken figure on the ground, but now two other officers were covering her with a dark green tarp. "What are you doing? Stop that! Stop that now!"

"Miss! Miss!"

"Don't cover her, she needs to breathe! Her heart is still beating!" Nga-Yee leaned forward, her energy suddenly gone. The policeman was no longer holding her back, but propping her up. "Save her! You have to save her! I'm begging you . . . She's my sister, my only sister . . ."

And so, on this ordinary Tuesday evening, on the empty ground in front of Wun Wah House, Lok Wah Estate, Kwun Tong District, the normally voluble neighbors fell silent. The only sound among these cold apartment buildings was the heartbroken weeping of an older sister, her sobs rushing like the wind into each person's ears, filling them with a sorrow that could never be wiped away.

CHAPTER ONE

1.

"Your sister killed herself."

When Nga-Yee heard the policeman say these words in the mortuary, she couldn't stop herself from blurting out, her speech slurred, "That's impossible! You must have made a mistake, Siu-Man would never do such a thing." Sergeant Ching, a slim man of about fifty with a touch of gray at his temples, looked a little like a gangster, but something about his eyes told her she could trust him. Calm in the face of Nga-Yee's near hysteria, he said something in his deep, steady voice that silenced her:

"Miss Au, are you *really* certain your sister didn't kill herself?"

Nga-Yee knew very well, even if she didn't want to admit it to herself, that Siu-Man had ample reason to seek death. The pressure she'd been under for the last six months was much more than any fifteen-year-old girl should have to face.

But we should start with the Au family's many years of misfortune.

Nga-Yee's parents were born in the 1960s, second-generation immigrants. When war broke out between the Nationalists and Communists in 1946, large numbers of refugees began surging from the Mainland into Hong Kong. The Communists emerged victorious and brought in a new regime, cracking down on any opposition, and even more people started arriving in the safe haven of this British colony. Nga-Yee's grandparents were refugees from Guangzhou. Hong Kong needed a lot of cheap labor and rarely turned away people who entered the territory illegally, and her grandparents were able to put down roots, eventually getting their papers and becoming Hong Kongers. Even then, they led difficult existences, doing hard manual labor for long hours and low wages. Their living conditions were terrible too. Still, Hong Kong was going through an economic boom, and as long as you were prepared to suffer a little, you could improve your circumstances. Some even rode the wave to real success.

Unfortunately, Nga-Yee's grandparents never got the chance.

In February 1976 a fire in the Shau Kei Wan neighborhood on Aldrich Bay destroyed more than a thousand wooden houses, leaving more than three thousand people homeless. Nga-Yee's grandparents died in this inferno, survived by a twelve-year-old child: Nga-Yee's father, Au Fai. Not having any other family in Hong Kong, Au Fai was taken in by a neighbor who'd lost his wife in the fire. The neighbor had a seven-year-old daughter named Chau Yee-Chin. This was Nga-Yee's mom.

Because they were so poor, Au Fai and Chau Yee-Chin didn't have the chance for a real education. Both started work before coming of age, Au Fai as a warehouse laborer, Yee-Chin as a waitress at a dim sum restaurant. Although they had to toil for a living, they never complained, and they even managed to find a crumb of happiness when they fell in love. Soon they were talking of marriage. When Yee-Chin's father fell ill in 1989, they wed quickly so at least one of his wishes could be fulfilled before he died.

For a few years after that, the Au family seemed to have shaken themselves free of bad fortune.

Three years after their marriage, Au Fai and Chau Yee-Chin had a daughter. Yee-Chin's father had been an educated youth in China. Before his death, he'd told them to call their child

Chung-Long for a boy, Nga-Yee for a girl—"Nga" for elegance and beauty, "Yee" for joy. The family of three moved into a small tenement flat in To Kwa Wan, where they lived a meager but contented existence. When Au Fai got back from work each day, the smiling faces of his wife and daughter made him feel that there was nothing more he could ask for in this world. Yee-Chin managed the household well. Nga-Yee was bookish and well-behaved, and all Au Fai wanted was to earn a little more money so she could go to university one day rather than having to get a job halfway through secondary school as he and his wife had had to do. Academic qualifications were now necessary to get ahead in Hong Kong. In the 1970s and '80s you could get a job as long as you were willing to work hard, but times had changed.

When Nga-Yee was six, the god of fortune smiled on the Au family: after years on the waiting list, it was finally their turn to get a government flat.

In land-scarce, overpopulated Hong Kong, there wasn't enough subsidized government housing to meet demand. Au Fai got the notification in 1998 that they'd been allocated a unit in Lok Wah Estate, just in the nick of time. In the wake of the Asian financial crisis, Au Fai's company had done a big restructuring, and he was one of the workers let go. His boss helped him find a position elsewhere, but his wages were much lower, and he struggled to pay Nga-Yee's primary school tuition. The letter from the Housing Authority was manna from heaven. Their new rent would be less than half of what they were currently paying, and if they were frugal, they might even be able to start saving.

Two years after moving into Wun Wah House, Chau Yee-Chin was pregnant again. Au Fai was delighted to be a father twice over, and Nga-Yee was old enough to understand that becoming an elder sister meant she'd have to work hard to help share her parents' burden. Because his father-in-law had left only one name for each sex, Au Fai was stuck for a second girl's name. He turned to their neighbor, a former schoolteacher, for help.

"How about calling her Siu-Man?" the old man suggested as they sat on a bench outside their building. "Siu as in 'little,' and Man as in 'clouds colored by twilight.'"

Au Fai looked to where the old man was pointing and saw the setting sun turning the clouds a dazzling array of hues.

"Au Siu-Man . . . that's a nice-sounding name. Thanks for your help, Mr. Huang. I'm too ignorant to have ever come up with something so beautiful on my own."

Now that there were four in the household, the Wun Wah flat began to feel a little cramped. These were designed for two to three people and had no internal walls. Au Fai put in an application to move somewhere larger. They were offered places in Tai Po or Yuen Long, but when the couple talked it over, Yee-Chin smiled and said, "We've gotten used to living here. Those places are so far away. You'd have a nightmare commute to work, and Nga-Yee would have to change schools. This place might be a bit of a squash, but do you remember how much smaller our wooden hut was?"

That's the sort of person Chau Yee-Chin was, always content with her lot. Au Fai scratched his head and couldn't think of a single argument, although he still hoped to give his daughters their own rooms before they started secondary school.

He couldn't have known that he wouldn't live to see it.

Au Fai died in a workplace accident in 2004. He was forty years old.

After the 1997 financial crisis and the SARS outbreak in 2003, Hong Kong's economy was in the doldrums. In an effort to cut costs, many employers outsourced operations or started hiring on short-term contracts, thus avoiding the burden of employee benefits. A big company would hire a small one to carry out certain operations, and the small company farmed the job out to even smaller ones. After each of them had taken their cut, the workers' wages were much lower than before, but in this precarious climate they had to no choice but to quietly accept what they were given. Au Fai made the rounds of these contractors, jostling with the other laborers for the few available jobs. Luckily, he'd been at the warehouse long enough to have acquired a forklift license, which gave him the edge when it came to distribution or dockside jobs. With the latter, it wasn't goods he was moving, but cables. The mooring lines used by the cargo ships were too thick and heavy to be secured by hand and had to be hauled by forklift. To maximize his income, Au Fai was working two jobs at once, moving goods at a Kowloon warehouse as well as unloading ships at Kwai Tsing Container Terminals. He wanted to earn as much as he could while he still had the energy. He knew his strength wouldn't last forever, and the day would come when he wouldn't be able to work his body this hard even if he wanted to.

One drizzly evening in July 2004, the manager of Kwai Tsing Dock Number Four noticed that a forklift was missing. Au Fai had been driving toward Zone Q13, and there his coworkers found a post that had been badly scraped along one side. The shreds of yellow plastic on the ground next to it were immediately recognizable as part of the forklift, which Au Fai had accidentally driven into the water, ending up pinned between the vehicle and its prongs, both of which were half buried in the seabed twenty feet deep. By the time they hauled the forklift out with a crane, Au Fai was long dead.

Nga-Yee was twelve when she lost her father, and Siu-Man was four.

Even though Yee-Chin was heartbroken at her beloved husband's passing, she didn't allow herself to sink into grief, for her daughters were now completely dependent on her.

According to labor law, the family of anyone killed at work ought to receive sixty months' wages in compensation, which Yee-Chin and her daughters could have lived on for a few years. Sadly, the Au family's bad luck struck again.

"Mrs. Au, it's not that I don't want to help, but this is all the company can offer you."

"But Ngau, Fai worked hard for Yu Hoi for so many years. He left the house when it was still dark and didn't get home till the girls were in bed. He hardly ever got to see his own daughters. Now I'm a poor widow with two fatherless girls. We don't have anyone to help us. And you're saying we can only have this tiny bit of money?"

"The company isn't much better off, to be honest. We might have to close our doors next year, and if that happens, we couldn't even give you this small sum."

"Why would the money come from you? Fai had worker's insurance."

"Fai's claim . . . It seems there's a problem with it."

Ngau had been at the company longer than Fai, and he'd met Yee-Chin a few times, so the Yu Hoi boss Mr. Tang asked him to have a "chat" with her. According to him, the firm had indeed arranged worker's insurance for Au Fai, but when the insurance company got an adjuster to look into the case, they denied the claim. The accident took place after Au Fai's shift ended, and there was no way to prove he'd been operating the forklift for work purposes. Besides, they'd found nothing wrong with the vehicle, and they couldn't rule out the possibility that Au Fai had simply passed out.

"I heard they even wanted to pursue damages for the forklift, but the boss said you shouldn't kick a man when he's down. Fai worked hard for our company, and even if the insurance company won't honor the claim, we have to do something for him. So the company is offering this small sum as a condolence. We hope you'll accept it."

When Yee-Chin reached out to take the check, her hands wouldn't stop trembling. The words "pursue damages for the forklift" had filled her with such rage, she could have burst into tears, but she knew Ngau was just passing on what he'd been told. This money—the equivalent of three months of Au Fai's wages—would be a drop in the bucket.

Yee-Chin sensed that the boss was hiding something, but she didn't see any way to fight back. She had to accept the check and thank Ngau.

Yee-Chin hadn't worked full-time since the children were born, had only helped out now and then at a Laundromat to earn a bit of pocket money. Now she had no choice but to go back to waiting tables at a dim sum restaurant. Although the cost of living had skyrocketed in the ten years since she'd last done this, her wages were about the same as before. Realizing there was no way she and her daughters could survive, she was forced to take a second job. Three days a week, she worked the night shift at a convenience store, getting off work at six a.m. and sleeping barely five hours before heading to the restaurant.

Quite a few neighbors urged Yee-Chin to quit her jobs and go on welfare, but she refused. "I know I'm only earning a bit more now than I would on welfare, and I could take care of Nga-Yee and Siu-Man full-time if I stopped working," she would say, smiling sweetly. "But if I did that, how will I ever teach my girls to stand on their own two feet?"

Nga-Yee noticed and remembered every time she said such things.

Losing her father was a big blow for Nga-Yee. She was just starting secondary school, and Au Fai had promised that after her final exams, the whole family would take a three-day trip to Australia to celebrate—but he was ripped away from them before this could happen. Nga-Yee had always been an introverted child, but she became even more withdrawn. Yet she didn't give in to despair—her mother's example showed her that no matter how cruel reality was, you had to be strong. With work taking up all of Yee-Chin's time, Nga-Yee had to be in charge of the housework: cleaning, food shopping and cooking, and taking care of her four-year-old sister. Before turning thirteen, Nga-Yee was already adept at all these chores, and she understood how to scrimp and save. Every day after school she had to turn down social invitations and miss extracurricular activities. Her classmates called her odd and a loner, but she didn't mind. She understood where her responsibilities lay.

In contrast, Siu-Man's development didn't seem affected by her father's death.

Sheltered by her mother and elder sister, Siu-Man had a fairly normal childhood. Nga-Yee sometimes worried that she was spoiling her, but one sight of Siu-Man's innocent smile and she'd decide it was perfectly natural to adore her little sister. Now and then Siu-Man would get too mischievous, and Nga-Yee would have to put on a stern face and scold her. Yet when Nga-Yee got stressed and burst into tears—after all, she was only a secondary school student—it was Siu-Man who comforted her, stroking her face and murmuring, "Sis, please don't cry." There were times when Yee-Chin got home late at night to find her daughters curled up together in bed, having made up after an argument.

It wasn't easy for Nga-Yee to get through five years of secondary school, but she survived, even managing to get some of the highest exam results in her year. She did well enough to get into a sixth-form college, and her form teacher thought she'd have no problem winning a place at a top university. Yet no matter how her teachers tried to persuade her, she refused to be swayed, insisting that she was ready to get a job. This was a decision she made the year her father died: no matter how well she did in her exams, she would give up her shot at a university education.

"Mom, once I start work, we'll have two wages coming in, and you can take it a bit easier."

"Yee, you've worked so hard and done so well. Don't give up now. You don't have to worry about money. At worst, I can find a third part-time job . . ."

"Enough, Mom! You'll wreck your health if you keep going like this. It's been such a struggle paying my tuition for the last couple of years, I can't let you go on worrying."

"It's just another two years. I heard that universities have some sort of assistance plan, so we won't need to worry about tuition."

"They're called student loans, Mom—I'd still have to pay them back after I graduated. Starting salaries aren't great for degree holders these days, and arts students like me don't have many jobs to choose from. I'd probably wind up making loan repayments out of my tiny salary. There'd be hardly anything left over. Another five years of you supporting all of us, and then probably another five or six when I couldn't contribute much. You're forty, Mom. Do you really want to keep working this hard till you're fifty?"

Yee-Chin had no response. Nga-Yee had been rehearsing this speech for almost two years now, so it was a pretty watertight argument.

"If I get a job, everything changes," Nga-Yee went on. "First, I can start earning now, not in five years. Second, I won't be in debt to the government. Third, I can get some work experience while I'm still young. And most important, as long as we both work hard, by the time Siu-Man finishes secondary school, we'll have saved enough that she won't have to worry about any of this, but can focus on her studies. Maybe we'll even be able to send her to an overseas university."

Nga-Yee had never been one for making speeches, yet these heartfelt words came out smoothly and persuasively.

Yee-Chin gave in to Nga-Yee in the end. After all, looking at the matter objectively, she'd made many good points. Still, Yee-Chin couldn't help feeling sad. Did it make her a bad mother that her elder daughter was sacrificing her future for the sake of the younger?

"Mom, trust me, this will all be worth it."

Nga-Yee had it all planned out. Between housework and taking care of her sister, the only hobby she could fit in was reading. As they had no money, most of her books came from the public library, where she now hoped to find a job. And sure enough, she successfully applied for the position of library assistant at the East Causeway Bay branch, making her an employee of the Hong Kong's Leisure and Cultural Services Department.

Although Nga-Yee was working for the government, she wasn't considered a civil servant, and thus got none of the associated benefits. In order to cut costs, the Hong Kong government, like many private businesses, cut permanent staff in favor of contract employees, usually for one- or two-year terms, after which the job naturally came to an end without any hassle or payout. Thus, in times of economic downturn, there could be "natural attrition" of payroll, while contracts could be renewed if there was money to spare, with the employer retaining complete control. In addition, the government outsourced some jobs, so it was entirely possible that someone stacking shelves at a public library might actually be working for a contractor, on even worse terms than the contract employees. When Nga-Yee learned all this, she couldn't help thinking of the way her father was treated, and seeing him in some of the library's old security guards.

Still, Nga-Yee wasn't discontented. Her position was low-ranking, but she took home about ten thousand Hong Kong dollars a month, which greatly improved the Au household's situation. Yee-Chin was able to give up her second job, easing her burden after years of toil. She continued working at the dim sum restaurant, but got to spend more time at home and gradually took back the task of raising Siu-Man. Nga-Yee's shifts kept changing, so she didn't have a definite schedule and as a result spent less time with her sister. To start with, Siu-Man would seize on her exhausted sister as soon as she got back from work, gabbling away about any and everything, but eventually she seemed to accept the fact that her sister was busy and stopped pestering her. Nga-Yee's family slowly became normal. She and Yee-Chin were no longer constantly worried about making ends meet. After all their suffering, they finally had a taste of something better as their once-chaotic lives settled into regularity.

Unfortunately, this respite lasted only five years.

The previous March, Yee-Chin had fallen at the restaurant and broken her right thighbone. When Nga-Yee got the news, she took the rest of the day off and hurried to the hospital, not expecting to receive even worse news when she got there.

"Ms. Chau didn't break her bone in the fall—she fell because her bone snapped," the consultant said. "I suspect she may have multiple myeloma. We need to do more tests."

"Multiple what?"

"Multiple myeloma. It's a form of blood cancer."

Two days later, as Nga-Yee waited with trepidation, the diagnosis arrived. Chau Yee-Chin had late-stage cancer. Multiple myeloma is an autoimmune disease in which a mutation of the plasma cells causes bone marrow cancer in many places in the body. If detected early, patients might survive another five years or more. With proper treatment, some even make it past a decade. But in Yee-Chin's case, it was too late for chemotherapy or stem cell transplants. The doctors thought she had six months.

Yee-Chin had noticed her symptoms—anemia, joint pain, weakening muscles—but attributed them to arthritis and exhaustion. Even when she sought treatment, the doctor hadn't seen anything other than normal degenerating cartilage and inflamed nerves. Multiple myeloma mostly strikes older men, rarely a woman in her forties.

To Nga-Yee, her mom had always seemed as resilient as Úrsula Iguarán, Buendía's wife in *One Hundred Years of Solitude*, and sure to reach a healthy old age. Only when she looked closely at her mother did she realize with a start that this woman of almost fifty was no longer young. All those years of backbreaking labor had eaten away at her, and now the creases around her eyes looked as deep as cracks on tree bark. Holding her mother's hand, she shed silent tears while Yee-Chin remained self-possessed.

"Nga-Yee, don't cry. At least you got through secondary school and have a job. If I leave now, I won't have to worry about the two of you."

"No, no, don't . . ."

"Yee, promise me you'll be strong. Siu-Man is delicate, you'll have to take care of her."

As far as Yee-Chin was concerned, death wasn't something to be afraid of, especially as she knew her husband was waiting for her on the far shore. The only thing tethering her to this world was her two daughters.

In the end, Yee-Chin didn't make it as long as her doctors predicted. Two months later, she was gone.

Nga-Yee held back her tears at her mother's funeral. In this moment she completely understood how her mother had felt when sending off their dad—no matter how sad she was, how heartbroken, she had to stay strong. From now on, Siu-Man would have no one to rely on but her.

In Siu-Man, Nga-Yee saw herself a decade ago: hollow-eyed, grieving her father's death.

That said, Nga-Yee suspected that their mother's death was hitting Siu-Man harder. Nga-Yee had always been quiet, while Siu-Man was the talkative one. Now Siu-Man grew silent and withdrawn. The contrast was so great, she seemed like an entirely different person. Nga-Yee remembered how lively their family dinners used to be, with Siu-Man chatting animatedly about school—which teacher embarrassed himself saying the wrong thing at assembly, which teacher the student aide snitched to, what pointless fortune-telling game people were playing. These happy moments might as well have taken place in a different world. Nowadays Siu-Man shoveled food into her mouth, barely looking up, and if Nga-Yee didn't make the effort to start a conversation, Siu-Man would just say "I'm full" and leave the table. She'd retreat into her "room"—when Nga-Yee started work, Yee-Chin had rearranged the furniture to give her daughters a little privacy, carving out two little nooks with bookshelves and wardrobes—to tap blankly at her phone.

I should give her some time, thought Nga-Yee. She didn't want to force her sister to do anything, especially at the awkward age of fourteen. It would only make matters worse. Nga-Yee was sure that before too long, Siu-Man would find her own way out of this depression.

And indeed, after about half a year, Siu-Man returned to her former self. Nga-Yee was glad to see her sister smiling again. Neither of them could have imagined that fate had an even worse calamity in store.

2.

A little after six p.m. on November 7, 2014, Nga-Yee got an unexpected phone call and hurried with a heavy heart to Kowloon Police Station. An officer led her to an office in the Criminal Investigation Department, where Siu-Man, in her school uniform, was sitting on a bench in the corner, next to a female officer. Nga-Yee rushed over to hug her, but Siu-Man didn't respond, just allowed her sister to wrap her arms around her.

"Siu-Man—"

Nga-Yee was about to start asking questions when Siu-Man seemed to come to herself and clutched her sister tightly, pressing her face into Nga-Yee's chest, shedding tears like rain. After sobbing for ten minutes, she seemed to calm down.

The lady officer said, "Miss, you don't have to be scared. Your sister's here now. Why don't you tell us what happened?"

Seeing a flicker of hesitation in her sister's eyes, Nga-Yee grabbed Siu-Man's hand and squeezed it in silent encouragement. Siu-Man glanced at the policewoman, then at the statement form on the table with her name and age already filled in. Letting out a breath, she began to speak in a small, unsteady voice about the events of an hour ago.

Siu-Man was studying at Enoch Secondary School on Waterloo Road in Yau Ma Tei, close to other elite prep schools such as Kowloon Wah Yan College, True Light Girls' College, and ELCHK Lutheran Secondary School. Enoch's exam results weren't quite as good as these posh schools, but it was still considered one of the better mission schools in this district and was also known within educational circles for its emphasis on the internet, tablet computers, and other high-tech teaching innovations. Each morning, Siu-Man took a bus from Lok Wah Estate to Kwun Tong station, then another half hour's MTR ride to Yau Ma Tei. Enoch's classes ended at four p.m., but she sometimes stayed back at the library to do her homework. And so, on November 7, she headed home a little later than usual, leaving the school around five.

That September, mass protests had risen up in response to proposed electoral reforms, and the government had escalated the situation by sending in the riot police. Huge numbers of disgruntled citizens poured out into the streets, occupying the main roads of Admiralty, Mong Kok, and Causeway Bay, paralyzing part of the city. With the roads blocked and buses rerouted, many people switched to using the Mass Transit Railway, causing massive congestion, particularly at rush hour, when platforms got so crowded that two or three trains would come before you were able to squeeze on. It was even worse in the cars—never mind grabbing a handrail, you'd be hard-pressed even to turn around. Commuters were squashed like sardines, back-to-back or chest-to-chest, even standing on tiptoe, swaying forward or back as the train sped up or slowed down.

Siu-Man got on at Yau Ma Tei station and found herself a space in the fourth car, pressed against the left-hand door. On the Kwun Tong line, Mong Kok and Prince Edward are the only two stations where the doors open on the left, so after those stops, Siu-Man was effectively boxed in. This was her usual spot. She got off at the terminus, and this way she could stay put rather than having to step aside at each station to let other commuters on and off.

According to Siu-Man's statement, something went wrong as the train pulled out of Prince Edward station.

"I . . . I felt someone touching me . . ."

"Touching you where?" asked the policewoman.

"My—my ass," Siu-Man stammered. She'd been clutching her schoolbag, facing the door, and hadn't seen who was behind her, but she felt a hand groping her. She looked around, seeing lots of ordinary faces. Apart from a few foreigners chatting among themselves, a stout, yawning office worker, and a curly-haired woman talking loudly into her phone, everyone else had their heads down, staring at their screens. Never mind how crowded the train, they weren't willing to miss a single second of social media, chat, or movie streaming.

"At . . . at first I thought I was mistaken . . ." Siu-Man's voice was as thin as a mosquito's hum. "The train was so full, maybe someone was just taking their phone out of their pocket and accidentally touched me. But then a while later, I felt—aah . . ."

"He touched you again?" asked Nga-Yee.

Siu-Man nodded, agitated.

As the policewoman asked more questions, Siu-Man blushed furiously and continued her account. She'd felt the hand passing slowly across her right buttock, but when she made a frantic grab for it, there were too many people in the way and she couldn't reach it in time. There was no way to turn around, so she twisted her neck as far as she could, thinking she would glare at the pervert to warn him off, but once again she had no idea who'd done it. Was it the man in a suit right behind her, the bald geezer next to her, or someone out of her line of vision?

"Didn't you call for help?" said Nga-Yee, regretting the words as soon as they left her mouth. She didn't want to sound like she was blaming her sister.

Siu-Man shook her head.

"I—I was scared of causing trouble . . ."

Nga-Yee understood. She'd once seen a girl screaming and grabbing her attacker after getting groped on a train, but it was the victim everyone looked at with disgust, and the culprit yelled at her, sneering, "You think you're a supermodel or something? Why would I touch *your* tits?"

Siu-Man was silent for a few minutes, then pulled herself together and slowly started speaking again. The policewoman wrote everything down. Siu-Man told them how she'd started to panic, then the hand suddenly pulled away. Just as she was breathing a sigh of relief, she felt it lifting the skirt of her school uniform and stroking her thigh. She felt a wave of nausea, as if cockroaches were skittering across her skin, but it was still too crowded for her to move, and all she could do was pray he didn't reach any higher.

Of course, her prayers weren't answered.

The perv went back to her ass, squirmed beneath her knickers, and started inching toward her private parts. Too terrified to move, all she could do was frantically pull her skirt back down, trying to keep him from going any farther.

"I—I don't know how long he was touching me . . . I just kept begging him in my head to let me go." Siu-Man trembled as she spoke. Nga-Yee's heart hurt at the sight. "Then the lady saved me."

"Lady?" said Nga-Yee.

"Several public-spirited onlookers helped to stop the molester," explained the policewoman.

As the train pulled into Kowloon Tong, a woman's loud voice cut through the car. "You! What do you think you're doing?" It was the middle-aged woman Siu-Man had noticed chatting noisily on her phone.

"When the lady shouted, the hand suddenly went away," Siu-Man said shakily.

"I'm talking to you! What were you just doing?"

The woman was shouting at a tall man two or three passengers away from Siu-Man. He looked about forty, with waxy yellow skin, protruding cheekbones, a flat nose, and thin lips. There was something shifty in his eyes. He wore a dull blue shirt, which made his pallor even more stark.

"Are you talking to me?"

"Yes, you! I said, what were you just doing?"

"What was I doing?"

The man looked a little anxious. The train came to a halt at Kowloon Tong, and the doors opened on the right-hand side.

"I'm asking you, pervert. Did you touch this girl?" The woman nodded at Siu-Man.

"You're crazy!" The man shook his head and tried to leave with the departing passengers.

"Not so fast!" The woman pushed through the crowd and caught hold of his arm before he could get away. "Girl, did this man just touch your ass?"

Siu-Man bit her lower lip, her eyes wandering, uncertain whether she ought to tell the truth.

"Don't be scared, girl. I'll be your witness! Just tell me!"

Filled with fear, Siu-Man nodded.

"You're both insane! Let me out!" screamed the man. The other passengers were starting to notice what was going on, and someone pressed the emergency button to let the conductor know.

"I saw it with my own eyes! Don't deny it! You're coming with us to the police station!"

"I—I just bumped into her by accident! Look at her. You think I'd bother touching her ass? If you don't let go of me, I'll have you charged with illegal detention!" The man shoved the woman aside and tried to leave the train, but among the onlookers was a strapping chap in a muscle shirt who reached out and stopped him.

"Sir, whether you did it or not, you'd better go to the station and clear this up," he said, a little threateningly.

Amid the commotion, Siu-Man huddled in her corner, feeling the eyes of the other passengers on her, some with pity, others out of curiosity or prurience. The way some of the men looked at her made her uncomfortable—as if they were asking, "So you were groped? What was that like? Are you ashamed? Did you enjoy it?" Her legs wobbled. She crumpled into a heap on the ground and started sobbing.

"Hey, don't cry, I'll take care of you," boomed the woman.

The loud woman, the strapping man, and another lady who looked like an office worker accompanied Siu-Man to the police station to make a statement. According to the first woman, everyone else on the train was busy looking at their phones, so she was the only one who'd noticed Siu-Man seeming flustered. Then at Shek Kip Mei station, as people moved out of the way, she glimpsed the schoolgirl's skirt being lifted and her ass being groped. As soon as she raised the alarm, quite a few passengers had started filming with their phones. These days, there are literally cameras everywhere.

The man they detained was named Shiu Tak-Ping. He was forty-three, the owner of a stationery shop in Lower Wong Tai Sin. He denied the charge, insisting that he'd bumped into Siu-Man by accident, that she was making a big thing out of it because they'd had a small argument earlier. His version of events was that Siu-Man had visited the station kiosk at Yau Ma Tei and taken such a long time to pay that a line started to form. Shiu Tak-Ping had been right behind her and snapped at her to hurry up. She'd been angry with him for that, and when she saw him again on the train, she decided to get her revenge with a false accusation.

The police questioned the convenience store cashier and confirmed that there had been an unpleasant encounter. The cashier recalled that Shiu Tak-Ping had lost his temper badly and, even after Siu-Man left, had gone on grumbling, "Young people today are all wasters. They'll ruin Hong Kong, causing trouble for no reason." This didn't prove that Siu-Man had a grudge against him, however, and Shiu Tak-Ping's actions certainly seemed to indicate guilt: he'd spat out insults and then tried to flee the scene, and Kowloon Tong wasn't even his stop—his home and his shop were in Wong Tai Sin.

"Miss, please read this over and make sure there isn't anything you don't agree with," said the policewoman, placing the statement in front of Siu-Man. "If there are no problems, sign at the bottom."

Siu-Man picked up the ballpoint pen and signed her name uneasily. This was Nga-Yee's first sight of a police witness statement. Above the signature line was the declaration "I understand that knowingly making a false statement to the police is a crime, and I am liable to prosecution if I do so." This sounded serious. Nga-Yee hardly ever had to sign any legal documents, and here was Siu-Man, still a child, taking on the responsibility of putting her name to such a hefty document.

As the case worked its way through the legal system, a few small news items showed up, referring to Siu-Man only as "Miss A." One reporter tried to cause a splash by revealing that Shiu's stationery store carried racy magazines, some of which centered around Japanese schoolgirls, and that Shiu was a photography enthusiast; sometimes he and his fellow shutterbugs would book a model for a shoot, and the article hinted that he had a particular interest in underage girls. A public indecency case like this wasn't given a great deal of space, however, and hardly any readers would have paid attention. After all, such incidents happened every day, and at that point, all the newspapers and magazines were focused on the Occupy movement and other political news.

On February 9, the first hearing was held, and Shiu Tak-Ping was formally charged with indecent assault. He pleaded not guilty, and his lawyer requested an adjournment, arguing that the "widespread media coverage" had made it impossible for him to receive a fair trial, but this was denied. The judge scheduled a trial to begin at the end of the month, and Nga-Yee received a notification summoning Siu-Man to the court, where she would be permitted to testify by video link or from behind a screen. Nga-Yee was anxious for her sister, who would have to stand there all alone being questioned by Shiu's lawyer, who was sure to be ruthless in asking her about every little detail of the crime and her personal life.

As it turned out, Nga-Yee needn't have worried.

When the trial began on February 26, Shiu Tak-Ping abruptly changed his plea to guilty, which meant that no one would be called on to testify. All that remained was for the judge to read through the psychiatric evaluation and other materials in order to pass sentence. On March 16, Shiu was sent to prison for three months, although taking his guilty plea and remorse into account, he would serve only two months, starting immediately.

Nga-Yee thought this would be the end of the matter, so Siu-Man could forget about this awful event and slowly go back to normal. Instead, a month after Shiu began his sentence, a nightmare began that would eventually bring her sister to the end of the line.

On Friday, April 10, a week before Siu-Man's fifteenth birthday, a post appeared on Popcorn, a local chatboard:

POSTED BY kidkit727 ON 10-04-2015, 22:18
Fourteen-Year-Old Slut Sent My Uncle to Prison!!

I can't take it anymore. I have to stand up for my uncle. My uncle's 43. He lives with my aunt in Wong Tai Sin and owns a stationery shop. He works so hard every day, just to earn a living for his family. He doesn't have much education—he quit school after Secondary Three—but he's an upright guy. He used to be a cashier at the shop, and he was so honest and polite, the previous boss let him take over when he retired. I've never heard my uncle tell a lie, his prices are fair, and all the neighbors would tell you the same. But a fourteen-year-old slut said he did something he didn't, and now he's in prison.

This was last November, on the Kwun Tong MTR. A fourteen-year-old schoolgirl accused my uncle of grabbing her ass. He didn't! This girl just wanted revenge! Earlier, my uncle stopped at the Yau Ma Tei convenience store for cigarettes. He was standing behind this girl, I think she was buying a phone top-up card, but when she tried to pay, she didn't have enough money. She took forever scrabbling around in her bag for change, while the line behind her grew longer and longer. Finally, my uncle shouted, "Hurry up, all these people are waiting for you. Just move aside if you can't afford it." She swung around and started screaming, so of course my uncle said something like she must be badly brought up, and who knows what kind of parents she had. She just blanked him. People say barking dogs don't bite, and this bitch is an excellent example. She didn't say a word the whole time my uncle was scolding her, but got her revenge later on when she falsely accused him.

He didn't do anything, so of course he couldn't confess, but all the newspaper reports were biased against him. My uncle and aunt got a rough ride. My uncle likes taking photographs—his only hobby. They don't have much money, so he only has cheap or secondhand equipment. He stocks photography magazines in his shop, and sometimes he gets together with like-minded friends to take pictures of landscapes or figures. The papers made it sound like he was a pedo shooting naked girls. Oh, please! There are dozens of photo books in my uncle's shop. The reporters found the one or two that had girls in school uniforms, and made that into a big thing. Those photo sessions only took place once or twice a year, but they made it sound like some monthly orgy.

My uncle was worried these stories would influence the judge. He knew it was stupid of him to run away when that slut accused him. The lawyer told him because he'd tried to flee, and the plaintiff was under sixteen, it was less likely the court would believe him. At least if he pleaded guilty, they might reduce his sentence. Otherwise, he'd "force" the girl to relive the whole experience on the stand, the judge would think he had no remorse, and he'd end up spending even longer in jail. My uncle stood firm for a while, but finally gave in. My aunt isn't well, and he was worried she'd find it hard being all alone. He thought it was better to get it over with quickly. Ever since those nonsense stories in the papers, people came to the shop every day to point and whisper at my aunt. My uncle loves her so much, he decided to bow in the face of injustice and go to prison.

How could such a good and loving man have ever touched a girl on the MTR?

There are quite a few holes in this case:

(1) My uncle is five foot ten, and that girl is barely five foot three. That's a whole seven inches difference. She said my uncle lifted her skirt to touch her ass. Wouldn't he have to reach down quite far to do that? Yet no one else noticed?

(2) Of course my uncle wanted to get away. Wouldn't you? Imagine some weird, nasty-looking person accuses you of something you didn't do, would you just stand there and take it? Everything in Hong Kong is upside down and back to front these days—there's power, but no justice. The law doesn't mean anything anymore, you can say that black is white and people agree. How could he be sure anyone would believe him?

(3) The police said this was a serious case because the victim was under sixteen. So why not collect evidence right

away? If what she said was true, there'd be cloth fibers under his fingernails, and sweat from his fingers on the underpants. Did they test for DNA?

Most importantly, my uncle isn't stupid enough to take this kind of risk. He could lose his family, his career and his whole life, and for what? Some plain-looking underage girl?

My uncle pleaded guilty to put an end to the whole thing. I was going to go along with it and let this blow over, then today I got some news that made me angry all over again.

A friend of mine dug up some dirt about this fourteen-year-old girl. It seems everyone at her school knows she's a bitch who likes to make trouble. She might seem all nice on the surface, but actually she's scheming behind everyone's back. She stole someone's boyfriend, then dumped him when she got bored. That's why she has no friends. None of her classmates want anything to do with her. Outside of school, she was hanging out with scumbags and drinking, maybe even taking drugs and sleeping around, who knows.

According to a classmate, she was brought up without a dad. When her mom died last year and there was no one to keep her under control, she got even worse. The way I see it, she's taking out her unhappiness on everyone around her. After her stunt on the MTR, she gets to play the pitiful little victim and get everyone's sympathy. But what did my uncle ever do wrong? So he has to sacrifice his and his family's happiness for her selfish desires?

I'm sorry, uncle. I know you want this whole thing to go away, but I can't keep quiet any longer!

Less than a day after this rant was posted, it became the most popular item on the site, and soon it was going viral on Facebook and other social media. The Umbrella Movement was making many people suspect that the police were abusing their powers and using too much force, or even that they were in cahoots with the triads. When they tried to keep order, the protesters said they were totalitarians suppressing the people's rights. In this atmosphere, many people on Popcorn took the side of the anonymous poster. It fitted their narrative: justice hadn't been served, the police had been lax in their duties, which meant that Shiu Tak-Ping must be innocent. They threatened "Miss A" and said they would expose her. A few days later someone posted a picture of Siu-Man on that thread, along with her full name, school, and address. It's illegal to reveal information about an underage victim, so the mods swiftly deleted the post, but not before many people had screenshotted the photo and info, deleting a word or two to get around the law: "this slut Au ___ Man from E___ School in Yau Ma Tei" or "a fourteen-year-old whore from Lok ___ Estate __ Siu-Man." They posted awful things about her and even photoshopped her face onto all sorts of humiliating pictures.

Nga-Yee loved reading books, but she was practically illiterate when it came to the internet. She didn't have any friends, so social media and chatboards were like foreign countries to her. She had to learn how to use email because of her job at the library, but that was about it. That's why she hadn't heard about the post until three days after it appeared, when one of her colleagues told her on the Monday. Only then did she realize why Siu-Man had spent all weekend at home, looking distracted. Their dusty home computer was a low-cost model, installed along with the internet. There were a lot of residents in their estate, so the providers offered a cheap monthly internet fee. This happened a couple of years after Nga-Yee started work, when their finances weren't as tight, and Yee-Chin hadn't been able to resist the salesman's urging that this would "help your daughter do even better at her studies." In fact, the black desktop hardly ever got used. Instead, when Siu-Man started secondary school, she bought herself a cheap smartphone and used their home Wi-Fi.

By the time Nga-Yee had read through the whole thing on her colleague's tablet, she was fuming. Those slanderous words "taking drugs" and "sleeping around" were awful enough, but when she calmed down, she realized how serious this was. Beginning to panic, she had no idea what to do. Should she call her sister? But Siu-Man would be in class. She phoned the school and asked to speak to Siu-Man's form teacher, Miss Yuen. As it turned out, Miss Yuen had been told about the rumors by the other teachers, and they'd set up a committee to deal with the problem.

"Don't worry, Miss Au. Siu-Man seemed fine in class today. I'll keep an eye on her, and we'll arrange for her to speak with a social worker," said Miss Yuen.

After work, Nga-Yee went home prepared to comfort her sister—even if she wasn't sure exactly what to say—but Siu-Man's response surprised her.

"I don't want to talk about it, Sis," she said expressionlessly.

"But—"

"I'm exhausted from today. All those teachers talking at me. I've had enough."

"Siu-Man, I just want to—"

"No! I don't want to talk about it! Don't bring it up again!"

Siu-Man's attitude shocked Nga-Yee. She couldn't remember the last time her sister had lost her temper.

After reading the post, Nga-Yee was certain that Shiu Tak-Ping's nephew was telling a pack of lies. He must be trying to cover up his uncle's behavior, and he didn't care how many falsehoods that took or how he had to harp on those weak arguments to make Mr. Shiu look innocent. He was even happy to trash Siu-Man to make his uncle look better. To borrow a line from his post, wasn't he sacrificing Siu-Man's happiness for his uncle's selfish desires? Yet when Nga-Yee got home and faced Siu-Man's strange behavior, she couldn't help having her faith shaken a little. Of course she didn't think her little sister was capable of making up lies to hurt someone, but those other things he said about her—might they be even one percent true?

Like a seed falling from a tree, doubt took root in her heart without her noticing, and it would grow larger and larger.

Apart from the original post, Nga-Yee lost sleep over many of the follow-up comments.

Her colleagues taught her how to navigate bulletin boards and social media, and each night, after Siu-Man went to bed, she'd quietly turn on that old computer and carefully read each new post. Nga-Yee had heard her share of nasty comments over her solitary behavior in secondary school, so she understood that most human beings had a dark side, but she was shocked by the scale and brutality of the attack. The commentators seemed to morph into a giant monster that devoured rationality.

—Fuck! Everyone in Hong Kong should shun this lying liar. She's just trying to look pathetic for the judge
—Would you want to fuck something with a face like that?
—Nothing special, but I would
—She's a whore, you could have her for three hundred
—I wouldn't have her if you paid me three hundred. She's a public toilet
—Scum like her should be euthanized

Nga-Yee was stunned to see her sister becoming a target of public abuse and objectification from a bunch of strangers. They'd never met Siu-Man, but they spoke as if they knew her intimately, projecting their imagination onto her and wielding it as a cudgel. These posts were full of filthy language, as if speaking from the other end of a fiberglass cable was an excuse to be lewd and disgusting, even about an underage girl. To put it another way, it was precisely because Siu-Man was underage that they thought the law would favor her, so they had to redress the balance in the interest of "fairness."

There were also quite a few people playing detective, along with "psychologists" analyzing Siu-Man's motives for making this false accusation and therefore diagnosing what syndrome or personality disorder she must have. Occasionally someone would come along and try to present the other side of the story, but they were inevitably rudely rebutted, and the discussion would devolve into personal attacks and meaningless arguments.

Nga-Yee felt as if she were looking at human nature at its most naked, splayed before her in the most unattractive posture.

And Siu-Man had innocently gotten swept up in this fray.

For the next two weeks, an uneasy atmosphere filled their home. The post brought media attention back to this case on a much bigger scale than before. Reporters came to their door a few times, but Siu-Man refused to speak to them. Some also went to Wong Tai Sin and tried to speak to the prisoner's wife, with the same result—Mrs. Shiu was avoiding journalists, which meant the stationery shop was closed for business. The newspapers and magazines covered this story from many different angles, some agreeing that it was a miscarriage of justice, others criticizing this behavior as a form of bullying. Yet whether they were pro or anti, it didn't change the fact that Siu-Man was now a public figure. As she made her way to and from school every day, people pointed at her and whispered.

There was nothing Nga-Yee could do to relieve this pressure.

She thought of taking Siu-Man out of school for a while, but the girl hated that idea. She wanted to live her life as normally as possible rather than allowing it to be disrupted by "this nonsense." Nga-Yee felt powerless, but she didn't want to look weak in front of Siu-Man, so she pushed aside her jumbled emotions and smiled broadly as she tried to cheer her sister up. There were quite a few times after the incident when Nga-Yee had to hide in the toilets at work so no one saw her crying.

By May, there were fewer newspaper stories, and trolls were losing interest too. Siu-Man gradually started talking and behaving like her old self, although she'd lost a lot of weight and there was something unstable in her eyes. Nga-Yee decided that if her sister had been strong enough to get through the last three weeks, she'd surely be able to deal with whatever came next. Siu-Man had had the right idea: carrying on as usual was the best medicine.

But she was wrong.

Just as Nga-Yee thought everything was going back to normal, Siu-Man stepped from the window of their twenty-second-story flat.

Nga-Yee couldn't believe that her sister would commit suicide. Things had slowly started to calm down, their lives settling back into their regular tracks rather than spinning out of control.

"Siu-Man wouldn't kill herself! Someone must have broken in and pushed her—" Nga-Yee now said to Sergeant Ching.

"We have ample evidence to show she did this herself."

That afternoon, their neighbor Auntie Chan had a builder around to fix her front door, and they both saw Siu-Man arrive home at ten past five, definitely alone. At around eight minutes past six, the moment of Siu-Man's fatal leap, two residents of On Wah Building, directly opposite Wun Wah House, saw the whole thing. It was sunset, when many older people liked to sit and look out into the street. These two noticed Siu-Man open the window, clamber out onto the sill, and jump. One of them was so terrified, he fainted, while the other started screaming for someone to call the police. Both were certain that no one was behind Siu-Man when she stepped out. To clinch it, surveillance had captured Siu-Man's final moments. The footage exactly matched the eyewitness testimony.

Nga-Yee already knew that there were no signs of a struggle in their flat. When she opened the front door, everything looked exactly as it always did—apart from Siu-Man's absence. This was real life, not a novel or some cunning murder disguised as a suicide. That sort of thing didn't happen, or even if it did, it wouldn't happen to an ordinary fifteen-year-old girl.

The only strange thing was that she hadn't left a note.

"In fact, quite a few people don't leave suicide notes. Sometimes it's because they acted on the spur of the moment and didn't have time," said Sergeant Ching slowly. "Miss Au, your sister's been under a tremendous amount of stress for months now. I've seen many cases like this. Please trust the police to investigate thoroughly. Given all the controversy surrounding your family, we'll definitely leave no stone unturned."

Nga-Yee understood perfectly well that any fifteen-year-old girl might end up being driven to suicide by the relentless pressure, but she still couldn't accept that Siu-Man had killed herself over anonymous bullying. This was the death of a thousand cuts, strangers slicing away at Siu-Man's flesh, slowly torturing her to death.

Nga-Yee longed to seek justice from every single person on the internet who'd had a part in this, but of course that wasn't possible. No matter how hard she tried, she'd never be able to get to every one of them.

"But what about whoever wrote that blog post? That's who killed her! Shiu Tak-Ping's nephew! He's a murderer!" Nga-Yee yelled.

"Please try to control yourself, Miss Au," said Sergeant Ching. "I understand you're upset and angry, but there's very little the law can do in this situation. You say this person is a killer, but the most you might be able to do is bring a civil suit against him for libel. All he did is write some words. Right now what you need is psychological support. I'll put you in touch with a volunteer organization that provides grief counselling. Hopefully you'll feel better soon."

What he said made sense, but Nga-Yee couldn't take any of it in. She turned down his offer, but to shut him up, she accepted some pamphlets from the organization, and her heart filled with hatred and helplessness.

In the weeks after Siu-Man's death, Nga-Yee arranged her last rites. She hadn't expected her experience of booking her mother's funeral the year before to come in handy this soon. Hardly anyone came to Siu-Man's wake, though there were plenty of reporters lurking outside. More than once, Nga-Yee was stopped and asked, "How do you feel now?" "Do you have any thoughts about your sister's suicide?" "Do you think netizens are the real killers?" and other tactless questions. One magazine's story had the headline FIFTEEN-YEAR-OLD GIRL COMMITS SUICIDE: ADMISSION OF GUILT, OR ACCUSATION? with a pixelated headshot of Siu-Man in a corner of its cover. When Nga-Yee saw it at a newsstand, it was all she could do not to rip the entire stack to shreds.

As far as Nga-Yee was concerned, the media was just as bad as the people on the internet. If netizens were "the real killers," then those reporters who'd hounded Siu-Man in the name of "the people's right to know" were their accomplices.

Yee-Chin's funeral the year before had been quite well attended. Throughout the day, her bosses and colleagues from the dim sum restaurant, the neighbors she'd shot the breeze with, old friends from back in To Kwa Wan, and even Au Fai's coworker Ngau all showed up to pay their respects. By contrast, only a handful of people showed up for Siu-Man. What left Nga-Yee most baffled was that by evening, not a single one of her classmates had appeared, only her form teacher Miss Yuen.

Could Siu-Man really have been so unpopular?

Nga-Yee recalled the post claiming that she hadn't had a single friend at school.

Impossible. Siu-Man was so animated and full of chatter, she couldn't have been isolated. Sitting in the family section of the hall, Nga-Yee grew more and more uneasy. It wasn't the thought of Siu-Man being friendless, but the idea that the poster might have been speaking the truth.

Fortunately, at half past seven, Nga-Yee's worries were eased when two figures in school uniform showed up: a short-haired girl leaning on the arm of a boy.

They walked up to the altar and bowed. Nga-Yee noticed that their eyes were red from crying. She thought she'd seen them before—hadn't they brought Siu-Man home last Christmas Eve, when she got sick at a party? Their mother had stayed up all night nursing her. The young couple didn't say a word to Nga-Yee, just nodded at her before leaving. One other student turned up later on, and that was it. It was Thursday night, and perhaps her classmates couldn't stay up late with school the next day, so they'd just sent a couple of representatives.

After the funeral and cremation, with Siu-Man's ashes resting in an urn by their parents,' Nga-Yee's grief welled up all over again. For the last two weeks she'd been running around, making arrangements, and hadn't had time to think about anything else. Now that everything was over and she was back in the empty flat, she felt hollowed out and stricken. She stared blankly at every corner of her home, as if she could still see her family there: Siu-Man playing with her rag doll on the rug by the sofa, her mother preparing a meal in the kitchen, her father by Nga-Yee's side, his resonant voice calling something out to his wife.

"Siu-Man . . . Mom . . . Dad . . ."

That night, Nga-Yee drifted into sleep, clinging to memories of happiness despite their poverty.

A few days later she got a letter taking away even this last oasis.

The Housing Authority informed Nga-Yee that she'd have to move out of Wun Wah House, leaving this flat and all its memories.

"Miss Au, I'm sure you understand, we're just following the rules," said a manager at the Housing Authority headquarters in Ho Man Tin. She'd made an appointment to voice her protests in person and was now sitting in a meeting room there.

"I—I've lived in this flat since I was little. Why do I have to move?"

"Let me be frank with you, Miss Au," said the manager, shuffling some papers. "You're all alone now, and Wun Wah House is for families of two or three people. According to our regulations, single-person households are restricted to flats of two hundred square feet or smaller. You're currently underoccupying your flat; we'll find you a new place more suitable for your needs."

"But this—this is my home! I need to stay here to remember my family!" said Nga-Yee. "They're all dead now, and you want to chase me away? Do you have to be so inhuman?"

"Miss Au," said the manager in his neat suit and gold-rimmed glasses, looking directly into her eyes. "I have a lot of sympathy for your situation, but do you know how many families we have on our waiting list? If we don't find them flats as quickly as possible, they'll be stuck in cramped, unsuitable lodgings. You called us inhuman, Miss Au, but couldn't I just as easily say you were being selfish by clinging to your home when other people need it more?"

Nga-Yee's face turned red, then white. She had no response.

"Look, Miss Au, we're offering you another three months in this flat, and you'll be able to choose your new place from a list we provide you." Each time the manager opened his mouth, her name was the first thing that came out of it, as if to emphasize that the problem lay with her. "Although these other places might be farther off, perhaps Yuen Long or North District in the New Territories, they're all newly built, so the facilities are much better than Lok Wah Estate. We'll let you know if anything comes up, Miss Au, and please keep us informed if you decide to travel outside Hong Kong."

It was clear that this was the end of the interview.

Nga-Yee rose to her feet helplessly. Just as she was about to walk away, the manager took off his glasses and said, "Miss Au, don't think I'm some highly paid civil servant. I worry about paying my rent too. These days, private flats sell for millions, even the ones someone died in. The housing situation here is terrible. The only way to live is to take what you can get, even if it's not what you wanted. Just be a bit more flexible, and you'll be fine."

All the way home, Nga-Yee seethed at the manager's final words. He was telling her to give up hope and accept her fate.

Her father's accident, her mother's illness, her sister's suicide— these things were her fate, and there was no avoiding them.

Nga-Yee sat on the bus, not realizing how forbidding her expression looked: crinkled brows, red eyes, teeth clamped tightly together, as if she were about to blow apart from the strain of holding in a monstrous injustice.

I will not accept my fate!

Nga-Yee couldn't forget how she'd felt speaking to Sergeant Ching in the morgue. A complicated mixture of pain, bitterness, and resentment.

The killer is the person who wrote that post! He's the reason Siu-Man killed herself! I need to confront Shiu Tak-Ping's nephew —these were the thoughts swirling around in Nga-Yee's mind.

She didn't know what she would accomplish by meeting this person—or rather, she didn't know what would happen if she met him. Would she scream at him for being a cold-blooded killer? Force him to kowtow before Siu-Man's grave and beg for forgiveness? Beat him up? Insist that he die in reparation, a life for a life?

No matter what, this was all Nga-Yee wanted. It was how she would resist her fate, an ineffectual protest against cruel reality.

She remembered that her colleague Wendy had a relative, a Mr. Mok, who'd opened a detective agency. She'd mentioned it the year before while they were sorting through a box of old detective novels in the library. Now Nga-Yee called him at the agency and asked if he might be interested in taking this case, and how much he would charge. It was a simple enough task, finding out the name of Shiu Tak-Ping's nephew, as well as where he went to work or school and what he looked like. That's all she'd need to ambush him and say what she needed to say. A run-of-the-mill case, perhaps easier than usual because Shiu Tak-Ping had been in the media so much recently.

"This sort of job usually costs three thousand dollars per day plus expenses, and takes me five or six days, so that'd be twenty thousand total. But seeing as you're Wendy's colleague, Miss Au, and I'm sympathetic to your situation, I'll give you a discount: two thousand per day. So you should count on spending twelve thousand or so," said Mr. Mok, a man in his fifties, at their first meeting. Although Nga-Yee had spent a fair bit on her mother's and sister's funerals, she'd saved up more than $80,000 for Siu-Man's university education, and she had no use for the money now. She agreed right away.

Four days later, on the evening of June 5, Mr. Mok phoned Nga-Yee and asked to meet. He had something to report.

"Miss Au," said the detective solemnly after his assistant had served their coffee and gone back out, "I ran into a spot of bother during my investigation."

"Was it . . . money?" Mr. Mok had seemed honest, but now Nga-Yee wondered if this was a prelude to his fee going up.

"No, no, you've misunderstood." He chuckled. "Let me say first of all, I personally carried out this investigation rather than having my employees do it. I'm tired of trailing cheating spouses and jumped at the chance to be part of a meaningful investigation. For the past few days, my assistant and I have been sniffing around the Shius' home in Wong Tai Sin. Actually, I found this out on day two, but I took another two days to make absolutely sure."

"You found Shiu Tak-Ping's nephew?"

"Well, that's the problem." Mr. Mok took a stack of documents and photographs from his bag as he spoke. "Shiu Tak-Ping doesn't have any siblings—he's an only child."

"Yes?" She didn't quite understand.

"That means he can't have a nephew or a niece," said Mr. Mok, pointing at the pictures. "Shiu Tak-Ping's father died four years ago, and he currently lives with his wife and seventy-year-old mother on the tenth floor of Lung Gut House, Lower Wong Tai Sin Estate. Not only does he not have any siblings, his only cousin emigrated to Australia many years ago and doesn't have any children—though even if he did, Shiu wouldn't technically be their uncle."

Nga-Yee gaped at Mr. Mok. "So who wrote the post?"

"I don't know, and Shiu Tak-Ping's family doesn't know either."

She stared at him, unable to speak.

"I got talking to a neighbor who knows old Mrs. Shiu well, and apparently they have no idea what's going on." Mr. Mok shrugged. "I'm not sure why anyone would pretend to be Shiu's nephew and write such a screed. I'd thought it might be the work of Mrs. Shiu or his mother, but if it were either of them, surely they'd take advantage of the interest from the press to put in a good word for Tak-Ping—yet they've continued to refuse interviews."

"Mr. Mok . . . in that case, could you help me find out who kidkit727 is?" Nga-Yee said, staring at the photographs and documents.

"That might be difficult." Mr. Mok sighed. "This is a traditional detective firm, and we aren't really equipped to ferret out someone hiding on the internet. At most, we could pick up surface clues from the words. I spent a bit of time looking into the chatboard, but I found something strange—this kidkit727 has only posted this one thing on Popcorn, and the account was created that day. There were no more log-ins after that. It seems this account existed for the sole purpose of propping up Shiu Tak-Ping's reputation. But Miss Au, I can only speculate."

"Mr. Mok, if you want me to increase your fees, I'm willing—"

"It's not that," he interrupted. "It truly isn't about the money. To be honest, I'm not going to charge you any more, because the investigation was a failure. I have made a reputation in this business for being trustworthy. I'll do everything I can for a case, but if I'm not getting any further, I won't take one dollar more. Though I'm afraid I won't be able to return your four-thousand-dollar deposit. I don't mind not being paid, but I can't ask my assistant to work for free."

"But . . ." Nga-Yee stared helplessly at the detective, then at the papers on his desk. A sense of powerlessness welled up in her chest and spread through her limbs. She felt as if nothing she did would ever be any good. The words of the man from the Housing Authority came back to her mind: *The only way to live is to take what you can get.*

"Don't be sad, Miss Au," said the detective, handing her a tissue. Only then did she realize that tears were pouring down her cheeks.

"Must I—Must I just accept my fate?" she said, blurting out what was in her heart.

Mr. Mok seemed to stop himself from speaking. Finally he shook his head and took a business card out of the box on his desk. He scribbled on it with a ballpoint pen, then thrust it in her direction a little hesitantly.

"What's this?" she asked.

"If you really want to find out who wrote that post, Miss Au, you should look up the person who lives at this address."

"That's his name? N?"

"Yes. He specializes in high-tech cases. He's a little odd and might not take you on as a client. And even if he does, I don't know what he'd charge."

"He's a private detective too?"

"You could call him that." Mr. Mok smiled wryly. "He's not licensed, though."

Nga-Yee frowned. "Not licensed? But is he . . . reliable?"

"Miss Au, when you come up against a problem you can't solve yourself and you need someone to investigate, who do you call?"

"I call . . . you?"

"Right, you call a detective." Mr. Mok smiled tightly again. "But have you ever thought who us detectives call when we encounter a case that stumps us?"

Silent a moment, Nga-Yee looked down at the business card. "You call N?"

Mr. Mok grinned. She'd got it right.

"Once again, I don't know if he'll take your case, but it might help if you show him this card."

Nga-Yee picked up the card, not sure what to believe. Could this N be as good as Mr. Mok said he was? Still, he wasn't telling her to accept her fate, but giving her another way to fight back. She was grateful for that much.

Mr. Mok walked her to the door. "There's something I forgot to mention earlier, Miss Au."

"What?" she said, turning to look at him.

"I thought of one other possibility—that the person who wrote this post had some other motive in mind that doesn't have anything to do with Shiu Tak-Ping. His real target could have been your little sister. Perhaps he had no interest in helping Shiu clear his name, but rather in destroying your sister's reputation. That could be why a complete stranger would pretend to be Shiu's nephew. It would make him sound more believable, as if he were standing up for justice, when actually he just wanted to put pressure on your sister until her spirit broke."

Mr. Mok's words were like an icy knife slicing straight through Nga-Yee's soul. She felt cold waves racing up her back.

"And if that's what happened," said Mr. Mok, "this would be a case of murder."

Tuesday, May 5, 2015

!!!

The devil is dead!!!! 20:05 ✓

The devil is dead!!!!!!!!!

? 20:06

Au Siu-Man!!!! She killed herself!!!!!!

http://news.appdaily.com/hk/20150505/realtime/a72nh12.htm 20:07 ✓

Breaking News: Fifteen-Year-Old Jumps to Her Death at Lok Wah Estate

Now what? 20:07 ✓

Answer me!!! 20:12 ✓

don't worry 20:12

they won't trace it to us 20:14

Really?? But we killed her!!!! 20:14 ✓

how did we kill her? all we did was make certain facts public 20:16

stop thinking nonsense 20:18

where are you now 20:23

i'll come find you 20:25

CHAPTER TWO

1.

Nga-Yee stood outside a six-story tenement building on Second Street in Sai Ying Pun, staring at the house number in confusion.

One fifty-one . . . is this the place?

She glanced again at the handwritten address on the business card, then at the numbers by the front door, so faded they were almost illegible. The building must have been at least seventy years old. Its outer wall was a dilapidated gray, which she suspected might have started out white. The gutter was coming off the porch roof, and there were no mailboxes. A plain doorway led to a staircase that reached up to the darkness of the first floor. The building had no name—just 151, though the bottom half of the 5 had been more or less rubbed away.

It was eleven o'clock, the morning after Nga-Yee's meeting with Mr. Mok. She had followed the address on the card, making her way to Sai Wan on Hong Kong Island. She'd expected to find a commercial building, but when she walked out of the Sai Ying Pun MTR station and down Second Street, there were only run-down tenements. But of course, Mr. Mok had said N was unlicensed, so he could hardly run his firm from a gleaming skyscraper.

Even so, this building was far from what she'd imagined.

It didn't look habitable by human beings, not because of the worn exterior, but the reek of abandonment that filled the place. All the windows except on the top floor were tightly shut, and none had air-conditioning units, unlike the mud-yellow five-story building right across the street, with units of different sizes and brands on all floors, and laundry racks draped with T-shirts, trousers, and sheets. Number 151 looked as if no one had lived here for years, the sort of place that might be taken over by vagrants, delinquents, junkies—even ghosts. The only sign that it wasn't abandoned was the intact windows—and the front door hadn't been boarded up.

Are they going to tear this down and start over? she wondered.

She looked around, wondering if she'd got the address wrong. Second Street was a slightly curved road in the old quarter of Sai Ying Pun. There were new, tall buildings at either end, but along the stretch that Number 151 was on, it was all historical tenements. Apart from one paper goods store and two hardware stores, the dozen or so other shops in the area had their shutters drawn, though she couldn't tell if they were empty or just closed for the day. There were hardly any pedestrians on this street, which was barely wide enough for two lanes of traffic, though a black van was parked just a few yards from Nga-Yee, blocking one of the lanes. Bustling Queen's Road West, just a couple of streets away, was completely different. Had Mr. Mok written down the wrong street or number? Perhaps he'd meant First or Third Street, an easy mistake.

As Nga-Yee hesitated, wondering whether she should walk into the murky stairwell or turn tail and look elsewhere, loud footsteps got her attention. A woman in a dark blue dress was clumping down the stairs.

"Beg—Beg your pardon, is this 151 Second Street?" Nga-Yee asked.

"That's right," the woman answered. She was about fifty. She looked Nga-Yee up and down while Nga-Yee took in her red plastic bucket filled with cleaning products, rubber gloves, brush, and dustpan.

"Do you live here? I wanted to ask if the sixth floor—"

"Are you looking for N?"

So this *was* the right address.

"That's right—sixth floor," said the woman, glancing at the card in her hand and giving a friendly smile. "Only one apartment on each floor, you'll see it right away."

Nga-Yee thanked the woman and watched as she walked away toward Water Street. If this resident—was she a cleaning lady?—knew N, it must be the right place. Her heart in her mouth, she climbed the murky stairwell. She had no idea whether N would be able to help her or not, but this place was giving her the creeps. As she approached each corner, she fully expected some horrifying creature to jump out at her.

Having slowly made her way up five flights, she arrived at the sixth floor. The landing had an ordinary white wooden door with a metal gate before it. There was nothing on the door or the gate—not a PRIVATE DETECTIVE sign nor the usual effigy of the door god or the red banner proclaiming "Come and go in peace." A black doorbell was mounted on the wall, the old-fashioned kind, like something from the 1960s or '70s.

After double-checking that the sign on the wall said 6, Nga-Yee pressed the doorbell.

Tak-tak-tak-tak-tak-tak. An old-school ring.

She waited ten seconds, but there was no sign of movement.

Tak-tak-tak-tak-tak-tak. She tried again.

Another half a minute. The door remained tightly shut.

Could he be out? But then a faint rustling noise came from within the flat.

Tak-tak-tak-tak-tak-tak-tak-tak-tak. She kept her finger on the buzzer so the maddening noise kept going like a machine gun.

"Stop that!" The white door abruptly opened a crack, revealing half a face.

"Um, hello. I'm—"

The door slammed shut.

Nga-Yee gaped. Everything went quiet. She pressed the bell again, unleashing another racket.

"I said stop that!" The door opened again, showing a little more of the face this time.

"Mr. N! Please wait!" she cried.

"Never mind 'please,' I'm not seeing anyone today!" said the man, pushing the door shut.

"Detective Mok sent me!" Nga-Yee blurted out frantically before the door could fully close.

The words "Detective Mok" actually seemed to have an effect. The man paused, then slowly opened the door again. Nga-Yee took out Mok's business card and passed it to him through the gate.

"Damn it! What stupid business is that bastard Mok throwing my way this time?" The man took the card and opened the gate to let Nga-Yee in.

Now that she was inside, Nga-Yee got a proper look at him, and what she saw was not what she expected. He looked about forty, neither tall nor well built. A regular, normal guy, a bit skinny. His messy hair looked like a tumbleweed, and his bangs fell past his brows to a pair of lethargic eyes that seemed rather at odds with his aristocratic nose. There was stubble all over his face, and combined with his grimy, creased gray T-shirt and fraying blue-and-white-checked cropped trousers, the overall effect was of someone who slept in a doorway. Nga-Yee grew up on a government housing estate and had seen lots of these unkempt figures around. Auntie Chan's husband used to look like that. Every day she'd stand, arms akimbo, and yell at him for being so useless while Uncle Chan ignored her and drank more beer.

Nga-Yee looked away from the man and received yet another shock. Two words popped into her mind: "rat's nest."

Random objects were piled by the door—newspapers and magazines, clothes and shoes, cardboard boxes of all sizes. Past the entrance, the living room was just as chaotic. Two bookcases took up the far wall, both untidily stuffed with books. On the round table in front of them were three wooden caskets about the size of shoe boxes, crammed with wires, extension cables, and electronic components Nga-Yee had never seen before. All the chairs around the table were covered with stuff, including an old computer terminal, yellowing and upside down.

On the left side of the living room was a desk, just as messy as the rest of the place: papers, stationery, books, empty beer bottles, snack bar wrappers, and two laptops were scattered across its surface. In front of it, two dark green armchairs faced each other, on them an electric guitar and a pink suitcase. Between the armchairs was a coffee table, the only item of furniture that wasn't covered in trash. Shelves on either side of the desk held an ancient-looking sound system, every available space filled with CDs, vinyl records, and cassette tapes. On the lowest shelf were the electric guitar's amp and cables tangled like a ball of wool, a whole clump of them on the ground. To the right of the shelves was a three-foot-high potted plant standing in front of a large window. Although the broken venetian blind was half lowered, harsh sunlight managed to force its way in, illuminating a thick layer of dust over all the furniture and surfaces, not to mention the stains on the floorboards.

What kind of famous detective would look like a tramp and live in a dump like this? Nga-Yee almost spoke the thought out loud.

"Ex-excuse me, are you Mr. N? I'm—"

"You, sit down. I just woke up," said the man, ignoring her question. He yawned, and walked barefoot to the bathroom off the vestibule. Nga-Yee looked around, but there was nowhere to sit, so she hovered awkwardly by the sofa.

The sounds of flushing and running water came from the bathroom. Nga-Yee poked her head out, saw that the bathroom door was open, and swung around to face the other way. A door beside the bookshelf was ajar. Through the gap, she could see an unmade bed, with boxes, clothes, and plastic bags scattered around it. The place gave Nga-Yee the creeps. She wasn't a clean freak, but this whole flat could fairly be called a rubbish heap. It was only because this was the top floor and the ceiling high that it didn't feel completely suffocating.

The other reason for her discomfort was now walking out of the bathroom.

"Why are you standing there like an idiot?" said the disheveled man, scratching his armpit. "Didn't I tell you to take a seat?"

"Are you Mr. N?" Nga-Yee asked, hoping he'd say "The detective is out, I'm just his roommate."

"Call me N. I don't like being Mister anything." He waggled the business card she'd given him earlier. "Isn't that what Mok wrote here?"

N tossed the guitar off the armchair and plunked himself down. He glanced at Nga-Yee, indicating with his eyes that she should move the suitcase. She did as he asked. It was so light, it must have been empty.

"Why did Mok tell you to find me? You have five minutes to explain." N was lounging back in the armchair, looking completely uninterested in her. He yawned again.

He seemed so full of himself, Nga-Yee was tempted to walk out and leave this disgusting place.

"My . . . My name is Au, I want to hire you to help me find someone."

Nga-Yee gave a quick summary of everything that had happened—Siu-Man being groped on the MTR, the accused changing his plea to guilty, the Popcorn post claiming there'd been a miscarriage of justice, internet bullying, reporters swarming, and finally her sister's suicide.

"I asked Mr. Mok to help me find Shiu Tak-Ping's nephew, so I could confront him . . . but he discovered that Mr. Shiu has no siblings, and therefore no nephews." She pulled Mr. Mok's report from her handbag and handed it over. N glanced at the first page, flicked through the rest, and dropped it on the coffee table.

"Given Mok's abilities, I'd say he got as far as he could with this," N sneered.

"Mr. Mok doesn't have the technological know-how to find a person's identity from an internet post, so he told me to speak to you." Nga-Yee wasn't happy about N's dismissive tone. After all, Mr. Mok was a good person who'd tried to help her.

"I don't take cases like this," said N bluntly.

"Why not? I haven't said how much I'm willing to pay . . ."

"It's too easy, so I'm not taking it." He stood up, ready to see her out.

"Too easy?" She stared at him, unable to believe this.

"So easy, super-easy," said N, deadpan. "I don't take boring cases. I'm a detective, not a technician. I've never taken on low-level cases that just require me to follow the steps to find the answer. My time is precious—I'm hardly going to waste it on a garbage case like this."

"Gar—garbage case?"

"Yes, garbage—it's boring and meaningless. This sort of thing happens every day. People are always looking for the real identity of someone or other online so they can take revenge for some trivial thing. If I took cases like this, I'd be no better than a customer service hotline. Mok's getting sentimental again. I've told him before not to send dog shit my way. I'm not his cleanup crew."

Nga-Yee had been keeping her temper under control, but this little speech made her explode. "You—you *can't* do it, that's why you're finding excuses to say no!"

"Oh, you want to get emotional?" N smiled at her outburst. "I could solve a case like this with my eyes shut. It's simple. Every bulletin board server keeps a record of IP addresses. It would take me a few minutes to get into the back end of Popcorn and download the file I need. Then I'd drop the IP address into a database, do a reverse search for the ISP, look at the log-in history of the ISP, and work out the client computer's actual location. You think the police have any trouble tracking down people who disseminate sensitive material or organize political rallies online? It's nothing to them. And if even they can do it, I can too."

Nga-Yee had no idea what a server or an ISP were, but N's methodical explanation convinced her that he knew what he was doing. This made her even angrier. If this was so easy, then helping her track down kidkit727 should take hardly any effort, yet he was still turning her down.

"If it's so simple, I'll just find someone else," she snapped, trying to get the last word.

"You've got it wrong, Miss Au," said N smugly. "This task is simple *to me*. As far as I'm aware, there are about two hundred hackers in Hong Kong who could break into the Popcorn server, but probably fewer than ten who could do it without leaving any trace. Good luck if you're setting out to find one of those ten—oh right, it's nine, because I've already turned you down."

Only now did Nga-Yee realize that N was one of those hackers she'd heard about, individuals who lurked in the darkness of the internet, making astronomical sums just by tapping their fingers. E-criminals who extorted money from celebrities by invading their privacy and blackmailing them.

Nga-Yee shivered, now terrified of this unprepossessing man, yet that's what made him the perfect person to help her. In order to find an explanation for Siu-Man's death, she pushed her anger aside, stiffened her resolve, and pleaded her case again.

"Mr. N, please help me. I'm at the end of my rope. If you turn me down, I don't know where I'd go," she said. "I'll go down on my knees if you like. I can't stand the thought of Siu-Man dying at the hands of some unknown person . . ."

"Okay," he said, clapping his hands.

"Okay?"

"Your five minutes is up." He walked over to the desk and pulled on the red hoodie that was hanging over the back of the chair. "Please leave. I'm going out for some breakfast now."

"But—"

"If you don't go, I'll call the police and say a madwoman broke into my flat." He was in the vestibule, stepping into his flip-flops. He opened the front door and gate and nodded toward the exit.

Nga-Yee had no choice but to grab the documents off the coffee table, stuff them back into her handbag, and leave. She stood on the landing, not knowing what to do. N sauntered past her without a glance and headed down the stairs.

Watching him disappear, Nga-Yee's sense of helplessness resurfaced. She descended the gloomy stairwell, her heart sinking a little with each floor. Mr. Mok had warned her that N might not take her case, but she hadn't expected him to be so rude. Nga-Yee believed that no matter how hard she struggled, she wouldn't be able to escape what destiny had in store for her. All this humiliation N heaped on her was surely a warning from fate.

The Housing Authority manager's instruction to *be a bit more flexible* came back to her.

When she emerged from the gloom into the street, the bright sunlight jolted her out of her thoughts. As she held her hand up to shield her eyes, urgent footsteps sounded nearby.

"You . . . oh!"

Right in front of her eyes, two man grabbed hold of N. The taller one was young and strapping. His arms were thicker than Nga-Yee's thighs, and he had a dragon tattooed on his left wrist. The shorter one wasn't as scary looking, but his golden hair was shaved at the sides and his T-shirt was tight, giving him the distinctive look of a triad gangster.

The tattooed man pinned N's hands, then wrapped an arm around his neck, pressing on his windpipe so he couldn't scream for help. Blondie punched him a couple of times in the stomach, ran over to their parked black van, and opened the door for Tattoo to heft him in.

Nga-Yee didn't know what to do—her brain was in a fog. In any case, she didn't have much time to think about it.

"Hey, D, that chick looks like she's with him," said Blondie.

"Get her too!" yelled Tattoo. Before she could run, Blondie caught her wrist.

"Let me go!" she screamed.

He clapped a hand over her mouth and yanked her hard. She stumbled and would have fallen, but Blondie held her upright as he shoved her into the van.

"Let's go!" roared Tattoo as soon as Blondie slammed the door.

Nga-Yee understood what was happening—Tattoo and Blondie were probably from some triad that had a problem with N, and she was just collateral damage. She struggled hard, but Blondie pressed down on her shoulder and pushed his knee into her thigh, immobilizing her. She glared at him, only to meet his murderous gaze.

At least N was in the van with her. He probably encountered many situations like this. Surely he had great fighting skills, like Lee Child's Jack Reacher, and would be locked in battle with Tattoo . . .

"*Gakkk . . .*"

N was hunched over in his seat, clutching his stomach and dry-retching. There was a row of seats against either wall. Tattoo sat next to N on one of them, looking as startled as Nga-Yee. Both were having the same thought: N was kind of pathetic.

"*Gakk . . .* dammit . . . did you have to hit so hard?" N spat something that might have been bile, or just saliva. He slumped back, his face pale. Tattoo and Blondie—who was still clinging to Nga-Yee—exchanged glances, uncertain how to deal with this. Generally speaking, their captives would try to break free at this point, and they'd respond with fists or weapons.

"You're N? Our Brother Tiger wants to have a word with you," said Tattoo, apparently having tried and failed to find something more threatening to say.

N didn't reply, just slowly stuck his hand into the left-hand pocket of his hoodie. Tattoo immediately pounced, grabbing his wrist and growling, "You'd better not try anything, or I'll—"

"Fine. I won't touch it," said N, holding his hands up. "You can get it for yourself."

"What?" Tattoo had no idea what he was talking about.

"*Gak* . . . the thing in my pocket. Please reach in and take it."

"Heh, trying to bribe us?" Tattoo leered. He was thinking of something that happened from time to time—people would offer him cash to let them go. He was never stupid enough to accept. If word got back to his triad boss, it wouldn't end well for him.

Tattoo reached into N's pocket and pulled out a white envelope. It was too thin to be cash—at most, it had a sheet or two of paper in it. He turned it over, and his face changed, as if he'd seen a ghost in broad daylight.

"What . . . what's this?" he yelped.

"What's wrong?" asked Blondie, loosening his grip on Nga-Yee.

"I asked you what this is!" Tattoo cried anxiously, ignoring Blondie and grabbing N by the collar.

"*Gakk* . . . a letter for you," said N calmly, dry-retching a little more.

"I don't mean that! How do you know my name?" Tattoo pulled the collar tighter around N's throat.

Nga-Yee glanced at the envelope, which had "Ng Kwong-Tat" written on it in blue ballpoint.

"Open it, and you'll find out," N replied.

Tattoo shoved N back into his seat and ripped open the envelope. A photograph slid out. Nga-Yee and Blondie couldn't see it, but they watched as the color drained from Tattoo's face and his eyes widened.

"You—"

"Don't try anything," N said.

Tattoo had been about to lunge at N again, but he froze at those words.

"I had that photo ready, so of course that means I came fully prepared. Even if you buried me in concrete and dropped me into Hau Hoi bay, my associates will make sure that everyone sees that picture."

"What's going on, D?" asked Blondie, letting go of Nga-Yee.

"Nothing! Nothing at all!" Tattoo frantically stuffed the photo and envelope into his trouser pocket.

Blondie looked dubiously at N and his gang elder.

"I have one for you too," said N, producing another envelope and handing it to Blondie, who gaped to see his name written on it. He opened it, and his face turned pale. Nga-Yee leaned over for a look. It was another photo: Blondie in a brown armchair, eyes shut, a beer bottle in his right hand. He looked sound asleep.

"You bastard!" Blondie was completely ignoring Nga-Yee now. Across the narrow space of the van, he reached out to clutch N by the throat. "How did you get into my apartment? When did you take that picture? Tell me or I'll kill you!"

Tattoo pulled Blondie away, while Nga-Yee looked on in confusion. Why was this gangster now helping N?

"*Gakkkk* . . ." N wretched. "You youngsters get so worked up nowadays. Always screaming about beating this, killing that." He rubbed his throat and went on. "Wong Tsz-Hing . . . or would you prefer your nickname, Blackie Hing? I guess it doesn't matter. And never mind when I broke into your pigsty of a home, stood over you while you were asleep, and took your picture. What you should be worried about is that I did it without you noticing. I was *this* close, and you were defenseless. Have you stopped to think whether that beer you guzzle every day actually is beer? If anyone's done anything to the bread you eat? And as for the, uh, goods you keep in your toilet cistern, might someone have replaced them with ordinary headache pills?"

"You!" Blondie was still trying to strangle N.

"If you lay a finger on me, you could have nine lives and that wouldn't be enough to save you." All of a sudden N's expression turned lunatic, and he came up close to Blondie's face, staring directly into his eyes. "I could gouge out your eyes while you're asleep. Dig out your kidneys. Put brain-eating parasites in your drinking water so they empty out your skull. Don't think you have balls just because you got in some fights for your boss. You'll never be as hard as me. You could kill me now, but I guarantee your life after that won't be worth living, not for a single second."

In those few seconds N had gone from being at the mercy of these thugs to threatening them himself. Tattoo and Blondie looked fearful, as if they were suddenly lost, unable to control the situation. Nga-Yee was impressed.

"Oh, and I've got something for your driver. Hey, Mr. Yee!" N yelled toward the cab. "Drop me off at the noodle stall on Whitty Street; otherwise I can't be sure a mysterious accident won't take place at Saint Dominic Savio Kindergarten in Tsuen Wan."

The driver slammed on the brakes so suddenly that Nga-Yee almost fell to the floor.

Looking petrified, the driver swung around to glare at N, sputtering with incoherent rage. "You . . . you . . . If you dare to touch my daughter—"

"Why wouldn't I dare?" N said, expressionless once more. "Mr. Yee, you have a perfectly good job. Do you really need to help scum like these two for extra cash? If you get into trouble, you'll drag your wife and daughter down with you. The smart move would be to turn this vehicle around right now. Delay even one second, and there may be nothing I can do."

The van was near Shun Tak Centre on Connaught Road West, Sheung Wan. The driver looked anxiously at Tattoo, who muttered, "Do as he says."

Five minutes later they were back in Sai Ying Pun and dropped off near Whitty Street. On this short ride, Nga-Yee had felt a strange tension in the vehicle. She didn't fully understand what was happening. She was one of the victims, but now she felt she somehow had the upper hand. Tattoo and Blondie didn't say another word, just stared uneasily at N, as if he—and perhaps Nga-Yee too—would turn into vicious monsters if they took their eyes off them.

As N got out of the van, he reached into his pocket and handed a third envelope to Tattoo, saying, "Take this."

Tattoo hesitated. "What's this?"

"It's for your boss," said N. "You're returning empty-handed, aren't you? Just bring that back, and hand it to Chang Wing-Shing. Not only will he not blame you, you'll never bother me again."

Tattoo looked skeptical, but reached out for the letter. N held on to it for a moment.

"I'm warning you, though. Don't read it." He smirked. "Curiosity will cost you a lot. You can't afford to gamble with your shitty lives."

Tattoo and Blondie froze. N let go of the letter, slammed the door without a second glance, and banged the rear of the van to tell the driver to move off.

Nga-Yee watched the van speed away, still unsure of what she'd just witnessed.

"Mr. N—" she began, but didn't know what to ask next.

"Why are you still hanging around? I told you, I'm not taking your case. Please take your business elsewhere!" N frowned, looking annoyed with her. For a moment his response made her wonder if she'd dreamed the whole thing.

"No. I—I just wanted to know, what on earth was all that about?" Nga-Yee shivered, remembering the moment she'd been dragged into the van.

"Do you have shit for brains? Isn't it obvious? Those gangsters came to pick a fight with me," said N breezily.

"Why would they do that? Did you do something to them?"

"Not to them. Some idiot corrupt businessman lost some money and asked them to take revenge on me. Brother Tiger—Chang Wing-Shing—is the new head of the Wan Chai Triad. He hasn't been in the job long enough to know his limits—"

"Then why did they let us go?" Nga-Yee interrupted.

N shrugged. "Everyone has a weakness. As long as you can find your opponent's, you can pretty much do what you like."

"What weakness? What was in the photo you showed that tattooed man?"

"He's sleeping with his boss's wife. I have a picture of them in bed."

Nga-Yee stared at him in shock.

"How did you get that?" She paused, then thought of something even more peculiar. "No, wait—they were most surprised to see their names written on the envelopes. Did you already know they were coming to kidnap you?"

"Naturally. Before the triads do anything, they'll lay the groundwork first, just like detectives follow suspects and scope out a location. That's called reconnaissance. They've spent almost a week casing my neighborhood. I'd be stupid not to have spotted them."

"But how did you know their names? You even dug into their backgrounds and broke into their houses to take those photographs? Weren't they just regular gangsters, the sort you see everywhere?"

"What were you saying just fifteen minutes ago, young lady?" N smiled sardonically. "It's easy as pie for me to find a person's identity. I can do it without breaking a sweat. As for the rest, that's a trade secret, and I'm not going to tell you."

"Since you already knew their weaknesses, why let them take you at all? Why not just scare them off right away?" Nga-Yee was still shaken by the encounter.

"You have to let your opponents get a little ahead of themselves, make them think they're in control. That way, you'll have more impact when you strike, and cause more damage. Don't you know that you need to give a little ground before you move in for the kill?"

"But—"

"Don't you get tired of asking questions? I've said everything I want to say. This is the end of our time together. Thank you for coming. Goodbye." N walked into the noodle shop.

"Hi, N! I haven't seen you for a whole week!" called out a man who looked like the proprietor.

N laughed. "I've been busy."

"The usual?"

"No—I'm not too hungry. Just got punched in the stomach. I'll have a bowl of clear wonton soup."

"Heh, those idiots don't know what they're getting into, daring to take you on."

Nga-Yee stood outside the shop, hearing the easy banter. N looked like a completely different person from the sly, ruthless man she'd seen in the van. The restaurant was small, its ten seats all taken now that it was lunchtime. Nga-Yee didn't know if she should follow him in, but after a while she realized that lingering here could only bring more disappointment, and she walked down Whitty Street to the MTR station.

As she got on the train, all she felt was regret.

He could definitely help me find the person who caused Siu-Man's death—the thought refused to leave her head. Seeing how

easily N had got them out of danger—remaining so many steps
ahead of the gangsters, ferreting out their secrets before they'd
laid a finger on him. With such godlike powers, surely he could
find kidkit727 and uncover his motive.

Each day that went by without her knowing what happened
would be another thorn in her heart.

More than that, she had a duty to find out the truth.

2.

For the next week, Nga-Yee went to Sai Ying Pun every day.
Her shifts were irregular, so sometimes she went before work,
sometimes after. She tried to see N again, but no matter how long
she pressed the doorbell, there was no answer. At first she wasn't
sure if he happened to be out, but on the third day, when loud
music started playing inside the flat, she knew he was ignoring
her. She banged hard on the door, but the volume went up in
response. She waited outside for half an hour, and that whole
time, the same English song played on a loop. She gave up and
walked back down the stairs, the tune still ringing in her ears. N
was making fun of her. The first line of the song was "You can't
always get what you want."

Nga-Yee worried that if N kept trying to drive her away with
loud music, eventually his downstairs neighbors would notice,
and she'd be accused of harassing him. Maybe they'd even call
the police. In order to keep out of trouble, she stayed outside
from then on, but there was no sign of N. She looked up at the
sixth-floor window as she waited, but day or night, whether the
window was open or shut, whether the lights were on or off, she
never caught so much as a glimpse of him.

This was taking up two or three hours of her days, but she
wasn't going to give up. Eventually she'd catch him. As for what
she'd say, she hadn't thought that far ahead.

The evening of June 12, she rushed to Second Street after work and continued to watch this pot that never boiled. It was raining heavily, and her trousers were soaked through, but she stood clutching her umbrella, huddled by a streetlamp and gobbling down the McDonald's burger she'd bought for dinner, never taking her eyes off the entrance to number 151. She was off the next day, and just as she was contemplating staying there all night, never mind the weather, her phone rang. She awkwardly fished the ten-year-old Nokia out of her bag. An unidentified number.

"Hello?"

"Please stop loitering outside my flat, it's unsightly."

"Mr. N—How did you get my number?" she stammered.

"Trade secret."

"Mr. N, please hear me out." She decided to let the question of the phone number slide. "I'm begging you, I'll give you anything you want, just find this one name for me. This is the only thing I'll ever ask you for, please . . ."

"You can stop your nonsense. I'm taking your case."

"Please think about it, Mr. N, I'll—what?"

"Come upstairs. Let's see if you can afford it." N hung up.

Nga-Yee was shocked and overjoyed in equal measure. She wolfed down the rest of the burger and ran straight up to the sixth floor. Before she could ring the doorbell, N had opened the door and was ushering her in. He looked exactly the same as before: a mess. There was a little less stubble on his chin, though, so at least he'd shaved at some point.

"Mr. N—"

"N," he snapped, shutting the door. He had the grumpy expression of a boss giving an order.

"Of course, whatever you say." Nga-Yee knew she was bowing and scraping, but by now she'd given up every scrap of dignity. "N, you're willing to help me find kidkit727?"

He walked over to the desk and sat down. "Let's see if you can pay my price."

"How much?" Nga-Yee asked, agitated. Leaving the sodden umbrella in the vestibule, she walked over to him.

"Not much, just $82,629.50."

Nga-Yee paused. This was a lot of money, but if he was trying to scare her off, why not go straight to a million or ten million? That would definitely be beyond her reach.

And why such a specific sum?

Just as Nga-Yee started to feel that something wasn't right, an image flashed into her mind.

"Isn't that—"

She'd made a withdrawal from an ATM that morning, and the balance on the screen was . . .

"You—How did you—" She stopped herself. It was clear that N had hacked into her bank account. She felt completely naked, as if this vulgar man could see every inch of her.

She knew how Blondie and Tattoo felt seeing their names on those envelopes.

"Will you pay?" said N, leaning back in his chair.

"Yes!" Nga-Yee said without hesitation. Now that he'd changed his mind, she wanted to seize the opportunity before his mood shifted again.

N grinned and stuck out his right hand. "All right, let's shake on it. This isn't a legit business, so don't expect a contract or anything."

Nga-Yee stepped forward and took his hand. Although he was scrawny, his grip was firm. She felt strength pulsing through his hand, and she grew even more certain he'd find the person who'd caused Siu-Man's death.

"No deposit. I want the whole amount up front before I start work," he went on.

"Fine," said Nga-Yee quickly.

"And I want it in cash."

"Cash?"

"Yes, or bitcoin," he said, gesturing for her to sit by the desk. "But I'm guessing you have no idea what that is."

Nga-Yee shook her head. She'd heard that word on the news, but didn't know what it meant.

"Do you want the exact amount in cash, even the coins?" she asked.

"Yes. I won't accept it if it's short even one penny."

"I understand." Nga-Yee nodded. "But—"

"But what? If you're not happy, the deal's off."

"No. I just wanted to ask why you changed your mind."

"Do you know why I chose this as my fee, Miss Au?" he asked.

Nga-Yee shook her head.

"Because I wanted to make sure that this case was the most important thing in the world to you. You agreed right away. I've had a lot of people come to me, but when I demand their entire life savings, most of them immediately back out. If they won't even go that far, but they expect me—an outsider—to put myself at risk—"

"So . . . these last few days, you were testing me?"

"Do I look like a Good Samaritan?" N snorted. "I'm willing to take your case because it turns out that this is a lot more interesting than I'd first thought. Of course, if you'd valued your money more than getting an answer, I wouldn't have helped, no matter how fascinating it was."

She was baffled. "It's interesting?"

"Yes, very. If it was just a question of tracking someone down the way I described, I wouldn't touch it, even if you stood in the street so long you started to rot and mushrooms grew on you." N shoved an empty peanut packet and two beer bottles aside and opened a laptop computer, turning the screen to face Nga-Yee. On it was the Popcorn "Fourteen-Year-Old Slut" post.

"These are the Popcorn log-in details for that day, with every user's location." N clicked on another window and brought up rows and rows of dense type in a spreadsheet.

"You . . . you've already done it for me?"

"Young woman, let's get this clear. I didn't do anything for you. I was just bored," he said. "Even if I'd found this person's name, age, address, job, and a family tree going back eighteen generations, I'd still have no intention of telling you."

Nga-Yee stayed silent, though she was mentally cursing him. She'd just have to put up with this a bit longer.

"This is kidkit727's IP address"—N pointed at a string of numbers—"212.117.180.21."

"What's IP?"

N eyed her as if she were some sort of rare animal.

"You don't know what an IP address is?"

"I don't understand computers."

"Primitive," N sneered. "It stands for Internet Protocol address. To put it simply, it's the serial number that tells us where someone is when they go online. Just like when you go to the bank or the doctor, you get a queue number. When you connect to the internet, the service provider allocates a unique number to you. When you surf the net, play online games, or chat, that all happens through this number."

"Bulletin boards too?"

"I just said, everyone who goes online gets one of these numbers. If you want to post on a bulletin board, the server—I mean, the 'machinery' of the board—will make a note of everyone's IP address. Which means you can do a reverse search on any post to find out which computer it came from. Do you understand now?"

Nga-Yee nodded urgently. "So you know where kidkit727 posted that from?"

N smiled wryly. "Steinsel, a town in the central region of Luxembourg."

"Europe?" Nga-Yee was taken aback. "Isn't kidkit727 in Hong Kong?"

"This fellow's pulling a little trick on us." N pointed at the IP address string on the screen. "This is a relay." He used the English word.

"A relay?"

"In Chinese we'd call it a transfer station. If you want to hide your identity on the internet, the simplest and most effective method is a relay, which connects you to an overseas computer. That computer then makes the connection, which registers as coming from that other computer rather than your true location."

"So we just need to find everyone who used the computer in Luxembourg on that day, and we'll know kidkit727's actual IP address?"

N raised an eyebrow. "You're quick on the uptake. Yes, you're right, that would work in theory, but not in this case."

"Why not?"

"Because I've checked, and I'm certain this fellow used more than one relay. This Luxembourg IP has appeared in my files many times. It's a common relay point, and it belongs to the Tor network, or, in Chinese, 'The Onion Router.' "

"Onion?"

"The name comes from the network's fundamental principles. I won't go into too much detail, but essentially this is a huge, anonymous network. Quite a few people use it only to access the dark web, those underground sites for things like porn or selling drugs, but Tor was invented mainly so people could cover their digital tracks. The easiest way to use Tor is an independent software called an Onion Browser. This automatically jumps between thousands of relays around the world, so even if I hacked this Luxembourg server and got the records for that day, and if I checked every single IP address of that relay, I ought to be able to find whether the user was in America, France, Brazil, or wherever. I'd have to do this over and over many times before I'd have a chance of finding the actual location. And if a single relay doesn't have recoverable records, the trail ends there. You might as well search for a needle at the bottom of the ocean."

Nga-Yee felt deflated.

"Having hit a wall with the IP address, I tried searching for other clues. Kidkit727 only registered their account on the day the post went up." N pointed at a line on the screen. "The email address associated with the account is rat10934@yandex.com—yandex.com is a free Russian email service that doesn't need phone verification to set it up. I'm sure this was just a burner account."

N moved his finger along the kidkit727 line, stopping farther along the grid.

"More significantly, this kidkit727 very carefully wiped away another piece of information. When a user accesses a website, the browser sends a string of characters that reveals what device is being used—known as the user agent—so the other computer knows if you're on Microsoft or Apple, a smartphone or a tablet, or even which version of a browser you're using. For instance, Windows NT 6.1 is the name of the seventh version; OPiOS stands for Opera, the Apple iOS browser; and so on. But in the Popcorn records, there's only one character where kidkit727's user agent ought to be."

Nga-Yee looked at the box for HTTP_USER_AGENT. All the others were long, complicated strings of letters and numbers, as N had said, but on the line for kidkit727, there was only an X.

"X?"

"I've never seen such a short user agent. This must have been hand-coded by the user. Some browsers allow their users to change this string of characters to hide the device or browser they're using. Tor is one of them."

"Wait—you said 'one of them.' Does that mean he might have used another one?"

"Miss Au, you still don't understand." N leaned back, his fingers interlaced on the desk. "Whether or not he used Tor, this person obviously covered his tracks. Kidkit727 registered as a Popcorn user only on the day the post appeared, and he logged in only once, to post it. There's no record of any subsequent activity. What's more, he used a relay to do all this, so there's no trace of what browser or device he was on. That's a near-perfect erasure of his identity. If all he wanted was to defend Shiu Tak-Ping, why go to such lengths? He's saying 'I'm aware this post will get a lot of attention, and people might come sniffing around, but I don't want anyone to know who I am.'"

Nga-Yee finally understood what N was getting at. She couldn't believe it.

"The person who wrote this post knew exactly what it would lead to. He must have some sort of background in IT," N said. "Now the only question is, was this mystery person truly trying to prove Shiu Tak-Ping's innocence, or was this a campaign of internet harassment targeted at your sister?"

Thursday, May 21, 2015

I'm home. 21:41 ✓

Dad asked why I was so late. I said was studying with friends. 21:43 ✓

He thought I was with you. 21:44 ✓

Am I a murderer? 21:51 ✓

what nonsense is this 21:53

it was her own choice to jump 21:53

nothing to do with anyone else 21:54

people who make up false accusations like that deserve to die 21:55

Are you sure no one will know it's us? 22:00 ✓

not this again 22:01

there's no way 22:02

just trust me, i know what i'm doing 22:03

even if the police get involved they won't find anything 22:04

Okay. 22:05 ✓

But there's one more thing I need to tell you. 22:06 ✓

CHAPTER THREE

1.

"Hey, Nam, the boss is watching."

At Ma-Chai's warning, Sze Chung-Nam hastily stuffed his phone back into his pocket.

"You keep looking at your phone. Flirting with some girl?" Ma-Chai cackled.

Chung-Nam shrugged, not denying it.

They were on the fifteenth floor of Fortune Business Center in Mong Kok. Chung-Nam was at a computer, like his coworkers —all four of them. GT Technology Limited consisted of five employees and their boss, squashed into the six hundred square feet of their open-plan office and conference room. The boss didn't have his own room—but then Jack Dorsey, the CEO of Twitter, didn't even have a desk of his own. According to him, anywhere could be a workspace as long as he had a laptop.

Of course, their boss, Lee Sai-Wing, was nowhere near Dorsey's league—just a crappy knockoff. Mr. Lee had big dreams of taking their company international, but his talent, vision, and motivation simply weren't up to the task. He'd taken over his family business, a textile factory in Mainland China, but after several years of losses he sold it and set up a tech firm in Hong Kong.

GT Technology Ltd. was about a year old; its core business was a chatboard called GT Net. Chung-Nam and Ma-Chai, the most tech-savvy of the employees, were in charge of setting up and maintaining the site. The others were Thomas, the graphic designer; Hao, board moderator and customer service officer; and Joanne, a recent college grad who was Mr. Lee's personal assistant. Not long after joining the company, Chung-Nam had begun to suspect that Joanne's relationship to Mr. Lee might be more "personal" than "assistant."

Hao, a couple of years older than Chung-Nam, was more blasé. "Sure, the boss has a quarter century on her, but they're both single. No harm, no foul. Anyway, it's nice to have a babe in the office."

Chung-Nam agreed but was still unhappy. Joanne was no supermodel, but she was young, and the only woman in the office. Naturally he'd been interested, until finding out from Hao that their boss had got there first. In fact, Mr. Lee had made his move only a month after Joanne started working there. So Chung-Nam had backed off—he wanted to keep this job.

In the last half year, even with such a small staff, by combining the best elements of social media and chatboards, GT Net had become the territory's hottest new website. The biggest section was Gossips Trading, which had its own e-currency—G-dollars. Unlike other paid sites, payment was based on ratings and the number of hits. Like the stock market, there were winners and losers—anything to do with celebrities usually exploded, while duller items plummeted or sometimes went for free.

"Have you two finished testing the video streaming?" Mr. Lee asked, walking up just as Chung-Nam put away his phone.

"More or less. We'll be able to release the beta next week," said Ma-Chai. At the moment, GT supported images, but videos had to be posted via a third-party platform such as YouTube or Vimeo, which meant that users were able to bypass the payment process.

"This is top priority. Get it done soon."

Although GT had been online a few months, there were still many ongoing improvements. Early on, Mr. Lee had named three key elements: secure payment, a deep search engine, and video streaming. Only the third now remained to be completed.

Chung-Nam was most proud of the search engine, his brainchild. If you looked up a certain male celebrity, for instance, it would also bring up gossip about every woman he'd ever been linked to. In a world where everyone got fifteen minutes of fame, anything as mundane as a restaurant argument or a lover's tiff on the bus could be filmed and uploaded to GT. Once logged, it would become an indelible, searchable item. With the rise of the "human flesh search engine," in which people's real-world identities would be exposed after an online mob went searching for them, everyone was afraid of their privacy being infringed upon. Yet this trend could also be weaponized, and those who understood the rules of the game could profit from it.

"Don't worry if you need more manpower. If all goes well, we'll be expanding soon," said Mr. Lee, slapping Chung-Nam on the shoulder. "I have a meeting now. Show me the streaming prototype tomorrow."

As soon as he was gone, Ma-Chai scooted over. "Why did Lee say not to worry about manpower? Did we come into some money?"

"Don't you know who he's meeting?"

Ma-Chai shook his head.

"It's some new program from the Productivity Council. They line up blind dates for venture capitalists and local tech start-ups."

"Oh, like 9GAG got twenty million a few years back?"

"Twenty mil would be great," said Hao, who happened to be walking by. "We'd be able to move into a better office and hire more mods."

"The world is full of VCs with more money than they'll ever spend. Maybe one or two will be stupid enough to send twenty mil our way." Chung-Nam grinned. "Of course, whether they'll ever get it back is another matter."

"Ha, so you think GT has no value?" said Hao, pulling a chair over to sit next to them.

Chung-Nam glanced at Joanne, the boss's eyes and ears, making sure she was too busy on the phone to eavesdrop. "It's not profitable, and too easily replaceable. Right now we issue G-dollars for free, so of course people are happy to spend them. Once we start charging cash, who's going to pony up? Besides, there's no way to keep the hot gossip exclusive—everything will end up on Popcorn in less than a day."

"That's up to you guys." Hao shrugged. "Lock the videos so they're hard to share, and people will fork over their G-dollars. It's no different from paying for an entertainment magazine."

People who didn't know how to code always thought it was so easy, Chung-Nam reflected. In fact, it would be near impossible to keep any video from being downloaded and reposted on YouTube.

"This might work even without encryption," Ma-Chai piped up. "Before Apple started iTunes, people said it would never work, because of piracy—but plenty of people were willing to pay."

"I'm still not sure," said Chung-Nam. "If you want gossip, wouldn't you just go to Popcorn? It's free."

"We don't have enough penetration," said Hao. "Popcorn gets thirty million hits a month. If we got numbers like that, we'd make good money on ads alone."

"*If* we got numbers like that," said Chung-Nam.

"I'm with Nam," said Ma-Chai. "Popcorn's so far ahead, we could spend ten years trying and never catch up. Remember the fourteen-year-old girl who falsely accused that guy of assault? The story went viral only because it was posted on Popcorn."

"We can't help that they got there first," said Hao, spreading his hands. "But doesn't that show there's room for GT to expand? Think about it: the story first appeared on Popcorn, but if we'd been the ones who doxxed her, people would still have registered and paid up to find out her real name."

Ma-Chai frowned. "She killed herself, bro. That's really how you want to earn a buck?"

"My dear, innocent Ma-Chai," said Hao. "Money is money, there's no good or bad about it. If you earn a profit on the stock market, you're taking it from other investors. Does that make it dirty money? So you believe in karma. How do you know that girl's suicide wasn't exactly what she deserved? Every single thing you code could lead to a tragedy someday. Are you going to take responsibility for that? As long as it doesn't break the law or get us sued, we should take the money that's on the table. Hookers drum up business on the Popcorn 'adult friends' board—does that make Popcorn a pimp? This city's about survival of the fittest—fleece or get fleeced. Good deeds don't get rewarded these days. Nothing matters in Hong Kong except capitalism and the market."

"But it's different when it comes to people's lives . . ." Ma-Chai hesitated, uncertain how to form his thoughts into sentences. "What do you think, Chung-Nam?"

"Mmm, you both have a point," Chung-Nam said diplomatically. "The girl chose to kill herself. If you want to blame someone else, why not say the whole of society was at fault? Anyway, let's talk about that when it happens to us. The main thing now is to finish building our platform."

Hao pouted, as if to say "You coward, sitting on the fence," and went back to his seat. Ma-Chai swung back to his keyboard, and lines of code began flying across his monitor again.

Neither of them saw Chung-Nam smiling darkly to himself.

How could they have guessed the girl's actual killer was right in front of them?

2.

Ever since getting out of jail, Shiu Tak-Ping had taken to wearing a cap every time he left the house. By pulling the brim down low, he mostly managed to avoid eye contact.

He'd been home a month now, but hadn't returned to the stationery shop—his wife was holding down the fort. The schoolgirl had killed herself ten days before he was released, and naturally the journalists were swarming again. The only way to avoid those piranhas was to stay in the apartment.

Luckily, the press lost interest after a month or so, and now he only had to deal with nasty looks from his neighbors. He went out occasionally for lunch, but never at peak times. He also stayed away from his regular cooked food stall at Lower Wong Tai Sin Estate and walked a little farther to Good Fortune Restaurant on Tai Shing Street. In the past, he'd looked around as he strolled, paying particular attention to skimpily dressed women, but now he kept his eyes firmly fixed on the ground ahead.

"Tofu and roast pork rice, and a hot milk tea," he said to the waitress.

He looked around to see if there was anyone he recognized. The incident had shown him people's true natures. They'd once smiled and haggled in his shop, but now they turned around when they saw him in the street or, worse, shouted foul things as he hurried past. The shop had lost half its customers, and with the rent going up, finances were tight. His wife complained so much when she got home each day, he could feel calluses forming on his ears.

Tak-Ping scanned every face in the restaurant, gratified to find none of them familiar.

Glimpsing a camera at the next table, he thought for a moment that the paparazzi had caught up with him, then realized he must be mistaken—this was an old-fashioned twin-lens reflex. No journalist would be using such an antique.

The camera was so unusual, he couldn't take his eyes off it, even after the waiter brought his tea.

"Excuse me," said the man abruptly.

"Wh—What?"

"Could you pass the sugar?" He pointed at the bowl on Tak-Ping's table.

Tak-Ping did as he asked, still gawking.

"Thanks." The man took the bowl and stirred a couple of spoonfuls into his coffee. "You're into photography?"

"I am. Is that a Rolleiflex 3.5F?"

"No, 2.8F."

Tak-Ping was astounded. Rollei was a well-known German brand, and the 3.5F a fairly common model—you could get one for a few thousand Hong Kong dollars. The 2.8F was much rarer, though, and one in good condition could set you back a healthy five-figure sum.

"Have you used a twin-lens before?" the man asked.

Tak-Ping shook his head. "Too expensive. All I can afford is a Seagull 4B." This was a Shanghai brand that cost only a few hundred.

"Forget it." The man smiled. "Seagulls look all right, but their pictures are lifeless."

"A friend was selling a used Rolleicord last year for fifteen hundred. I almost got it," said Tak-Ping.

"That's not bad. Why didn't you?"

"Wife said no." Tak-Ping grimaced. "Women. She nags if I so much as buy extra film."

"Film? Aren't you on DSLR?"

"No. All I have at the moment is a Minolta X-700 and a couple of lenses."

"Oh, that's all right." The man nodded. "But it's all about digital these days. I use both."

"Single-lens digitals are too expensive."

"You can pick up secondhand ones cheaply online," said the man. "Want me to give you a website?"

Tak-Ping shook his head. "It's fine. I don't really understand chatboards or whatever. Anyway, I heard you need a powerful computer to go digital. I don't have that kind of money."

"Only if you're doing a lot of editing. Don't you have a computer at home?"

"Yes, but we hardly ever use it. Got it a few years ago with our cable. I only use it for chess and PPS videos. Do you really not need a powerful computer?"

"If you're just storing and viewing photos, any old model will do," said the man. "You'll have to install a couple of programs once you've bought your camera. Know anyone good with computers?"

"Um, maybe, if it's not too difficult." Tak-Ping was thinking of a couple of friends who shared his interests, though he hadn't got in touch after being released—he didn't know if he was still welcome. The thought was daunting. "Never mind. My wife will give me hell if I buy another camera."

"Ah. Well, nothing to be done."

Their food arrived, interrupting their conversation. They ate in silence, and Tak-Ping decided not to linger after the meal.

"I'll be off, then," he said.

"Right, bye." The man nodded and took another mouthful of coffee.

As he walked home, Tak-Ping couldn't stop thinking about the camera. For the first time since his release, his footsteps felt light and he was able to keep his mind off his family, the schoolgirl, and prison. He decided to treat himself—either to a digital camera or a cheaper Seagull.

Let the wife complain if she likes, he thought. In this world, you have to go with the flow and take your pleasures where you can find them.

3.

"Shiu Tak-Ping is a bastard," N announced as he opened the door.

He'd agreed to take Nga-Yee's case on Friday evening. The following morning, she'd gone to the bank to clear out her account. The teller kept asking if she was the victim of some scam, and she had to smile and repeatedly assure him that she knew what she was doing. In fact, she had wondered if this was any different from handing money over to a con man. What if N said he hadn't found anything? There'd be nothing she could do. Still, she handed the notes and coins over. He said he'd call if there was any news, then started herding her toward the door less than a minute into their meeting. It was only when she got home that she realized she had no way of getting in touch with him. Trying to calm down, she told herself he'd surely call soon. In her head were the competing voices of the bank clerk saying, *I hope you're not being cheated, Miss*, and Mr. Mok describing N as *an expert*.

After handing her savings over to N, Nga-Yee was left with only the hundred-dollar note she'd had in her purse, her Octopus transit card with about fifty dollars on it, and a little over ten dollars in loose change. She'd been grocery shopping the day before, so she had enough food for the moment, but it was still two weeks till payday. Even if she lived on instant noodles, her daily commute would cost twenty dollars a day, and she could hardly stop going to work. And there were the water and electric bills. She regretted never getting a credit card, but her mom's warning—not to spend money she didn't have—had sunk in too deep.

When she went for her library shift on Saturday afternoon, she asked her coworker Wendy for a loan to tide her over. This surprised Wendy, who knew that Nga-Yee was usually careful with money. When Wendy asked why, Nga-Yee said something vague about unexpected expenses.

"Okay, here's eight hundred. You can pay me back next month," said Wendy, pulling out all the hundred-dollar bills from her wallet.

"Thanks, but five hundred will do."

"Don't worry, I know you're good for it. If something's wrong, you know you can tell me."

Wendy had transferred to the Central Library from the Sha Tin branch two years earlier. She was a warm, chatty person, about five years older than Nga-Yee. Nga-Yee found her a bit overfriendly, and always found an excuse when Wendy organized an office outing for a meal or a movie. Yet it was Wendy's friendliness that had prompted Nga-Yee to ask her for help. Her concern, coupled with the bank clerk's questions that morning, left Nga-Yee feeling like one of those foolish scam victims on *Crimewatch*, which made her more anxious about N's progress. She kept checking her phone in case she'd missed a call from him.

After three days, she finally lost patience.

On Tuesday, June 16, she went back to Sai Ying Pun, ready to demand a progress report, but she hesitated at the corner of Second Street.

Am I being an idiot? What if I annoy him so much he stops the investigation and fobs me off with some excuse? Even though she was a paying customer, she had a strange fear of him, like a frog seeing a snake and instinctively recognizing it as a natural predator.

She'd been standing there for ten minutes, unable to gather the resolve to keep walking, when her phone rang.

"You might as well come up, now you're here, or someone might mistake you for a stalker and call the police," N said, and hung up.

Nga-Yee looked around wildly. She was nowhere near number
151, and there was no way N could have seen her from his window. She hurried to his building and up the five flights of stairs.

"Shiu Tak-Ping is a bastard," he said, opening the door to her.
"But he's not kidkit727."

"What?" She'd expected him to grumble that she was hassling
him, not to give her actual information about the case.

"Shiu Tak-Ping had nothing to do with that post." N managed to clear enough space in the mess for her to perch on the
couch. "Mok's report said that Shiu had no idea who did it,
but he's the main person mentioned in the post, so I had to see
for myself."

"You mean you met him? Couldn't you just find out what
you needed to know on the internet?"

"There are some things it's simpler to ask in person."

"You saw Shiu Tak-Ping? And asked him yourself? Surely he
wouldn't tell the truth."

"People are strange creatures, Miss Au. Once you get them
to let down their guard, they'll say more to a stranger than to
their own family." N put the camera on the table in front of her.
"I followed him for two days; then yesterday I pretended to be
a photography fan and struck up a conversation."

"What—so you went up to him and said, 'Are you kidkit727?'"

N laughed. "Don't be silly. We chatted about cameras."

Nga-Yee picked up the twin-lens reflex and studied it. "And
just like that, you worked out that he had nothing to do with
kidkit727?"

"First of all, Shiu Tak-Ping, his wife, and his mom know nothing about computers or the internet. He said he didn't do anything online except play chess and watch PPS videos; I verified
that against the browsing history of his home broadband and all
their cell phones. None of those three would have the first idea
how to scrub a digital footprint from a chatboard. I also asked

if any of his friends were computer experts, but that didn't turn up anything either."

Nga-Yee was silent, listening attentively.

"Second, Shiu's politics are at odds with what's expressed in that post," N continued. "If the mastermind really was him or someone he was close to, it would have been written differently."

"Political stance?"

"Shiu once campaigned for a pro-establishment candidate—the poster is still up in the stationery shop. And the clerk at the Yau Ma Tei convenience store said that Shiu complained that young people today are all 'wasters causing trouble for Hong Kong.' It's clear that he leans to the right." N moved the laptop from his desk to the coffee table. It was still open to the Popcorn chatboard. "Yet this post was clearly written by a libertarian, and a young one at that, one who uses trendy resistance slogans. For instance, 'Everything in Hong Kong is upside down and back to front these days—there's power, but no justice. The law doesn't mean anything anymore, you could say that black is white, and people would agree,' or talk about 'bowing in the face of injustice.' A conservative would never say such things—at the very least, they'd have left out the politically loaded phrase 'power but no justice.' Birds of a feather flock together. I don't believe Shiu would have anyone around him with such opposite views, yet close enough to write this screed on his behalf."

"Okay, but even with these two points, aren't there always exceptions?" Nga-Yee retorted. "For all we know, Shiu might just happen to have met a computer expert, and they clicked, so he asked him to help clear his name. The phrases and whatnot might be part of the plot."

"Fine, let's suppose kidkit727 is a brilliant deception, created by someone whose thought processes are as thorough as mine, so they know how to embed a fake personality within the words. Someone with enough self-restraint to stop after a single post rather than keep fanning the flames," N said smugly. "Yet this genius was stupid enough to strike while Shiu was still in prison, and the situation was most difficult to control?"

"Difficult to control?"

"Imagine you're Shiu Tak-Ping. Would you ask your computer expert friend to post while you were stuck inside, unable to do anything as your wife and mom came under siege from reporters? Or would you wait till you were out and could speak directly to the TV cameras."

Only now did Nga-Yee understand what N was driving at.

"Shiu Tak-Ping's relationship with his wife isn't as loving as that post suggested, but he's not enough of an idiot to hurt his stationery business. That shop was the family's only source of income, and his wife was running it while he was inside. Trying to claim innocence while he was still in jail doesn't seem worth the effort. He missed out on his fifteen minutes of fame—by the time he was released a month later, the media had lost interest. His cunning friend kidkit727 was surely aware of that." N paused a moment. "And most important, after your sister killed herself, Shiu came in for even more criticism and hatred. If he really was responsible, he'd have been hurting himself as well as her."

The mention of Siu-Man sent a wave of sadness through Nga-Yee. "So you're saying my sister was the target?" she said, trying to stifle the pain.

"Yes, that's the most likely scenario. Of course, we have no concrete evidence, so we can't rule out any theories right now."

"If Shiu really has nothing to do with kidkit727, why doesn't he just tell that to the press?"

"What would he say?" N chuckled. " 'Actually, I don't have a nephew, but a mysterious stranger defended me online and tried to lessen my guilt.' That would just muddy the waters and make the press and public hound him even more."

Nga-Yee thought about this. It made sense.

"Speaking of which, now that I've met Shiu, there are some parts of the post I don't understand." N was no longer smiling as he sat with his hands clasped over his chest.

"You mean—"

"What it says about Shiu Tak-Ping is accurate in some ways and exaggerated in others." N gestured at the camera in Nga-Yee's hands. "It's correct that he enjoys photography and only owns secondhand cameras. I've been to his shop, and there are indeed quite a few photo books on sale, although I don't know whether he got rid of the ones focusing on attractive young women. It's clear from the range on offer that Shiu's interest is genuine. And he was happy to chat about old camera models with me, a complete stranger, so we know this wasn't just a front. By the way, you should put that down. It's borrowed, and it's worth twenty-five grand. You can't afford to damage it."

Nga-Yee was so startled she almost dropped the camera. Hastily but gingerly she returned it to the coffee table.

"The post is wrong about his marriage, though," N went on, leaning against the desk. "It claims that he went to jail to calm things down—he loved his wife so much he didn't want to put her through any more trouble. That's all bullshit. Ever since Shiu got out, he's been hiding at home rather than going to work at the shop, because he's afraid people will give him a hard time. No guts. His wife is left to take on the whole burden of supporting the family, and not only is he completely ungrateful, he even complained to me, someone he'd just met, that she wouldn't allow him to buy a camera."

"So why is half of it false?" asked Nga-Yee. "Whoever wrote this must have known Shiu, to have written the true portion."

"Have you looked closely at it? Don't you think it reads a particular way?"

"What way?"

"Like a lawyer defending a client in court."

Nga-Yee stared.

"Emphasizing the good, hiding the bad. Showing the client in the best possible light, while working hard to distort subjective things like the state of his marriage. After all, if Mrs. Shiu says, 'We're a loving couple,' how would the other side prove otherwise? That's pretty much something you're expected to say when you testify in court. I suspect that the poster is connected to Shiu's defense lawyer in some way, although the lawyer himself wouldn't be foolish enough to get directly involved—it wouldn't help his client." N pulled a sheet of paper from the pile on his desk. "That's Martin Tong. He's made a bit of a name for himself in the profession. Organizes community talks on legal advice and does pro bono work. He's not going to put his glossy reputation at risk by stooping to dirty tricks. That would hurt his brand."

"Even if he didn't do it himself, he might still be involved?"

"You're right, but it isn't easy to cross swords with a lawyer." N shrugged. "I'll keep looking into that, but there's another line of inquiry I'm more eager to follow."

"What's that?"

"Your sister."

A chill went through Nga-Yee.

"Don't you want to go there, Miss Au?" said N indifferently. "From the evidence we have, it's most likely that this post was written to hurt your sister, either because of a personal grudge or because the writer genuinely believed she'd wronged Shiu Tak-Ping and wanted to get justice for him. I'll need to know everything there is to know about Au Siu-Man: what circles she moved in, her private life, her thoughts, and any enemies she might have had."

"Siu-Man was only fifteen. What enemies could she have had?"

"You're far too naive," N sneered. "Girls of fourteen or fifteen these days have far more secrets than us grown-ups, and their social networks are incredibly complex. With social media and instant messaging, it's easy for kids in their early teens to enter the adult world. In the old days, working girls were dependent on their pimps, but these days they have apps for finding clients. Some of these girls don't know what they're getting into—they imagine that being an escort means going out with someone in public and holding their hand. Then they get tricked into bed, maybe photographed or filmed, which makes them a target for blackmail. They can't ask for help or they might get arrested for prostitution, so they put up with it. All the while, their families assume that any strange behavior is teenage angst. The post said that your sister drank, took drugs, and sold her body. Can you look me in the eye and say for certain that Siu-Man wasn't that kind of girl?"

Nga-Yee met his gaze and started to speak, but then she remembered how only a handful of Siu-Man's classmates had expressed their condolences, and she couldn't get the words out. It was only after Siu-Man's death that she'd realized she hadn't understood her sister all that well. She often got back late because of her library shifts, and she had never wondered whether Siu-Man came straight home after school or, on the few occasions she'd returned later, if she'd actually been studying at the library as she claimed. Had Siu-Man gotten into bad company while Nga-Yee wasn't paying attention? Were there secrets she'd felt she couldn't share with her sister? Could she have used this window of time to carry out illicit activities for pocket money?

When Siu-Man died, a seed of doubt had been planted in Nga-Yee's heart. Without her noticing, this had now grown into a poison vine wrapping itself around her soul, devouring her faith.

Seeing Nga-Yee pull back, N didn't press the issue, but said in a softer tone, "Miss Au, if you want to find the person pulling the strings, you'll have to dig into your sister's past. There may be some things you don't want to discover. Do you understand?"

"Yes," said Nga-Yee without hesitation. "No matter what, I want to find the person responsible for Siu-Man's death."

"All right, then I'll need you to go home and see if your sister kept a diary or any kind of notebook. Oh, did she have a computer?"

"No, just a smartphone."

"I'll need to see that. People have their phones on them all the time. You can understand a person completely just by looking at their phone."

"Don't you want to come and have a look at our place?"

"I've already spent two days tailing Shiu Tak-Ping, Miss Au. You don't get to tell me what to do. I'm not your personal assistant." N went back to his desk and sat in his office chair. "Call this number if you need to get hold of me, though I can't promise I'll answer. Leave a message if it's important, and I'll call you back when I have time."

He handed her a piece of notepaper with eight digits scrawled in pencil.

As soon as she took the number, he gestured at the door to indicate their meeting was over. Nga-Yee still had more questions, but she'd seen enough of N by now to know that asking them would get her nothing but another tongue-lashing. On the way home, she mused that he might speak harshly, but he hadn't tried to stonewall her with "the investigation is ongoing." Instead, he'd discussed the case seriously with her. Mr. Mok was absolutely right—he was a real eccentric.

I guess I have to trust him, she said to herself, looking at the note in her hand.

In order to save on travel, Nga-Yee took the tram, ferry, and bus rather than the more expensive MTR. These days, she was allowing herself the subway only on her commute to work, when she needed to be on time. It didn't matter if it took her a little longer to get home. It was after ten by the time she arrived back at Wun Wah House.

She turned on the lights and, not even stopping to change her clothes, walked around the bookshelf that divided Siu-Man's "room" from the rest of the apartment. She hadn't touched Siu-Man's things since her death, so everything was exactly the way it had been: a little desk, a loft bed above a bookcase and a wardrobe. As a child, Nga-Yee had sorted through her late father's possessions with her mother; then, when her mom died, she'd wept while packing away her clothes. Yet when it came to Siu-Man, she hadn't been able to bring herself to do the same. Siu-Man's form teacher, Miss Yuen, had phoned at the end of May to say that Siu-Man had left some books in her locker, would Nga-Yee come by to pick them up? Nga-Yee had said she was too busy, and she kept putting it off, thinking that seeing Siu-Man's things might be too much for her to handle.

Now Nga-Yee went through the desk drawers and bookcase, but there was nothing like a diary, just makeup, accessories, and a couple of kawaii stationery packs and washi tape. The shelves had only her homework books and a few fashion magazines, and her schoolbag contained only textbooks. Nga-Yee went through every inch of the wardrobe, but there was nothing there either.

Why doesn't she even have a planner? Nga-Yee wondered, being the sort of person who wrote everything down on paper, before it hit her. "Of course, the phone!"

Which led to the next problem: the phone was nowhere to be found.

Nga-Yee clearly remembered that Siu-Man always kept her bright red cell phone at the top right corner of her desk, where the charger was. The charger was empty. She rummaged through the bedding, but it wasn't there.

Thinking more carefully, Nga-Yee realized that she hadn't seen the phone since Siu-Man's death.

Reaching for her own phone, Nga-Yee dialed her sister's number, but it went straight to voice mail. Of course, after more than a month, the battery must have run out.

Unless . . . the phone went out of the window with her . . .

Nga-Yee had so far resisted thinking about the actual moment of Siu-Man's suicide, but now she had to consider this possibility. Yet no, she realized—it would have landed near her and been found by the police, who'd surely have returned it to Nga-Yee.

Where was it, then? Could it be at school?

She reached for the note and dialed the eight digits.

"You have reached the voice mailbox for 61448651. Please leave a message after the tone," said a robotic voice.

"Hello, hello, it's Au Nga-Yee. I did what you said, but I couldn't find a diary, and the phone's missing too. Um . . . Maybe you should come see for yourself?" she stammered, and hung up.

She searched again, just to be sure. Siu-Man's wallet and keys were there; it was just her phone that was missing.

Nga-Yee slept even more badly than usual. She kept worrying about the cell phone, and N never called back. When her alarm clock went off the next morning, she felt as if she'd been up all night. She went to work as usual, but kept making mistakes checking books in and out. Finally, to stop the tide of complaints, the manager took her off the counter and put her on shelving instead.

She called N after lunch but got his voice mail again.

He still hadn't called by that evening.

"Hello, this is Au Nga-Yee. Could you call me back when you get this?" This came out a little exasperated. What was the point of giving out a phone number if you were never going to pick up?

There was nothing that night, but she woke at seven the next day to find a text message in her in-box: "Are you blind? Make sure you've searched the whole apartment, moron."

This had arrived at 4:38 a.m. Wide awake now, Nga-Yee resentfully thought that N was underestimating her. Since Siu-Man's death, she hadn't been able to sit with her thoughts, so had endlessly distracted herself with housework. She'd cleaned every inch of the flat, apart from Siu-Man's things. If the phone was on a kitchen shelf, by the TV, or even under a sofa cushion, she'd definitely have spotted it. She almost texted back an angry response but managed to calm down.

She was at work till eight, after which she decided to go back to N's place and drag him back by force if necessary, to prove she hadn't missed anything. But just as she was about to board the tram that would take her to the west of Hong Kong Island, she thought of something else.

There was one place she had avoided looking at too closely: the window Siu-Man had jumped from. It was next to the washing machine, and every time Nga-Yee did laundry during the last month, she imagined Siu-Man leaning against the machine, stepping onto the folding chairs next to it, pushing the window open, and leaping out.

Could she have been holding her phone right up to the last moment?

She hurried home, gathered her courage, and went into the laundry area, forcing herself to search.

When she knelt down and put her face on the ground, she saw it.

Siu-Man's phone was under the washing machine.

Nga-Yee reached for it, but her hand wouldn't fit. Looking around, her eye landed on some metal clothes hangers. Hands shaking, she quickly unfolded one and hooked the wire under the machine.

There it was: a cat charm dangling from it, a crack across the screen where it hit the ground. Nga-Yee pressed the power button, but nothing happened. Her heart sank. Had it broken when it fell? Dashing over to Siu-Man's desk, she was trembling so badly it took three attempts to plug it into the charger.

Ping.

The screen lit up, and a "charging" symbol appeared. Nga-Yee let out a sigh of relief. Looking back at the window, she wondered how the phone had landed there in the first place. Had Siu-Man dropped it? But it would have taken some force for it to slide so far under the machine. Had she thrown it? Or had it been kicked in there by accident? Had it slipped between the machine and the wall?

What had Siu-Man been doing just before she died?

Nga-Yee had no idea, and she gave up trying to work it out. The main thing was, she had the phone. As it charged, she hit the power button again. The screen lit up with the service provider's logo, then a grid of nine circles. She slid her fingertip across them, but "password incorrect" flashed up. After a few attempts, she gave up and let it charge.

N's a hacker. He'll be able to get in, she thought.

Her initial impulse had been to rush over to N's with the phone, but as the excitement faded, she realized it was too late to set out now. She'd have to get a taxi back, which would be expensive. Besides, what if she hurried over only to have him toss it in a corner? She decided to wait till after work the next day, when she'd be able to stand over him as he hacked the password.

"I've found Siu-Man's phone. I'll bring it over after work tomorrow," she texted when he failed to answer her call yet again.

That night, Nga-Yee dreamed of Siu-Man. She was sitting on the couch, engrossed with her phone as usual. Nga-Yee said something to her, and she replied, but when Nga-Yee woke up, she couldn't remember what they'd talked about.

All she remembered was Siu-Man's smiling face.

In the morning, she wiped the traces of tears from her eyes, washed up and got dressed, put the charged phone into her bag, and left for the library.

"You've been so distracted lately, Nga-Yee," Wendy said to her in the break room at lunchtime. "Are you really all right?"

"Yes. I'm just worried about something," she replied.

"Is it about the investigation? Hasn't my uncle found anything yet?" Wendy had no idea that the case had been passed on to a maverick hacker detective.

Nga-Yee hedged. "There's been some progress."

"If money's the problem, I can help out," said Wendy earnestly. Ever since Siu-Man's death, she'd been full of concern for Nga-Yee.

"You lent me eight hundred just a few days ago. That's enough."

"Is my uncle charging too much? My aunt's always been fond of me. I could ask her if he could lower his rate . . ." Wendy got out her cell phone, ready to Whatsapp Mrs. Mok right away.

As Wendy slid her finger across the keypad to unlock her phone, Nga-Yee froze. An image flashed into her mind: Siu-Man doing the same thing. For a second she thought this was from her dream the night before, but then she realized.

This was an actual memory of a moment she'd glimpsed: Siu-Man unlocking her phone.

Bottom left, middle left, top right, middle, top left.

She quickly pulled out Siu-Man's phone and entered the pattern she remembered. This time the password screen melted away.

Cracking the code did bring her a moment of happiness, but as soon as she saw the words on the screen, she felt her organs go into free fall and her scalp grow numb. When she clicked, what she saw next made her heart beat so much faster, she thought she might stop breathing.

"Wen-Wendy, please help me say I needed half a day off—" she stuttered, trying to steady herself.

"What's wrong? Nga-Yee, are you all right?"

"I—I need to leave and take care of something urgent. Pl—please just help me deal with—" She dropped the phone into her bag and, ignoring Wendy's cries, rushed out of the building.

Nga-Yee had never used a smartphone, but she'd clicked instinctively on the email icon, which brought up the most recent message:

From: kid kit <kidkit727@gmail.com>
To: Siu-Man <ausiumanman@gmail.com>
Date: May 5, 2015, 06:06 pm
Subject: RE:

Au Siu-Man,
Are you brave enough to die? Aren't you just up to your
usual tricks, trying to make people feel sorry for you?
Your classmates won't be fooled again. Scum like you
have no right to go on living.
        kidkit727

Thursday, May 21, 2015

There's something I haven't told you.   22:07 ✓

I emailed Au Siu-Man.

Will that be a problem?   22:07 ✓

possibly   22:09

how did you send it?   22:10

was it the way I taught you?   22:11

covering your tracks online   22:12

Yes.   22:15 ✓

that's okay then   22:16

don't worry   22:17

CHAPTER FOUR

1.

"Everyone, listen up! Make sure you dress properly tomorrow! Tidy your desks and get rid of any personal items by today. If your desktop wallpaper is some porno chick, change it. I'll check tomorrow morning, and if I see anything that makes the company look bad, I'll dock five hundred dollars from your pay!"

Mr. Lee had taken a phone call and was now standing in the middle of the GT Technology office, screaming at his employees. Although he seemed flustered, it was clear to all that underneath it was excitement.

"What's up, boss?" asked Hao.

"A VC is coming tomorrow! A foreign one—just joined the Productivity Council's program, and they're interested in us. They might want to invest!" Mr. Lee shouted. Ma-Chai and Sze Chung-Nam stopped coding and turned to face him.

"Is anyone in the world really such an idiot?" whispered Ma-Chai to his friend.

"Which country is the VC from?" asked Chung-Nam.

"No pressure, but it's SIQ from America!"

Chung-Nam, Hao, and Joanne jumped at that name, though Ma-Chai and Thomas didn't react.

"Is SIQ famous, Chung-Nam?" asked Ma-Chai.

"Thomas is a print designer, I can forgive him not knowing. But you're supposed to be a programmer—shouldn't you know what's going on in the field?" Chung-Nam frowned. "SIQ is America's number one investor in internet technology. They're as famous as Andreessen Horowitz."

"Andrewhat Whatowitz?"

No point talking to such an ignoramus. Chung-Nam snapped, "Anyway, they have a lot of money and foresight." He understood the reason for their boss's anxiety: having SIQ Ventures come visit was a once-in-a-lifetime opportunity. The name was the initials of its founders: Szeto Wai, Satoshi Inoue, and Kyle Quincy. In 1994, while still at UCLA, the computer wunderkind Satoshi had come up with a new method of compressing images, allowing more images to be transferred at the same time even if bandwidth was limited. This changed the whole trajectory of the internet. He and his classmate Szeto Wai set up a software company, Isotope Technologies, in Silicon Valley, coming up with new algorithms for transferring pictures, videos, and music. Next, they took on the encryption of wireless communication, filing hundreds of patents. Thanks to Szeto Wai's business acumen, Isotope's patented technologies were used in every major company's hard- and software. This placed Szeto and Satoshi within the ranks of Silicon Valley's most influential talents before they'd even turned thirty, not to mention earning them more than a hundred million dollars. In 2005 they partnered with Kyle Quincy to form SIQ, a VC investing in new small- and medium-scale tech enterprises. Just as Andreessen Horowitz got a huge return on its investment in Facebook and Twitter in just a few years, SIQ was able to turn its seed investment of four hundred million American dollars into almost three billion.

Although GT wasn't remotely in the same league as Isotope, Mr. Lee had unrealistic hopes that he could acquire the same sort of wealth and reputation as Satoshi and Szeto. Chung-Nam had a sense of his boss's aspirations, and he sneered at the idea of someone who'd waited till he was in his forties to sell off his family business, a textile mill, and start all over again in IT. Such a person was hardly going to become a tech mogul. As a matter of fact, Chung-Nam had an ambition of his own: to set up a business and become the next Jack Ma or Larry Page.

At least I have a science background, unlike that loser Lee Sai-Wing, he thought to himself.

After college, Chung-Nam found a job in a small company with the intention of using that as a stepping-stone to greater things. With his strong credentials, he could have gone somewhere bigger, but he was aware of his own limitations, and he knew it would be harder to catch the attention of the higher-ups and gain promotion in a larger outfit. He refused to struggle in silence for decades and taste success only in middle age. GT had fewer than ten employees, making it easier to suck up to the boss, as well as giving him many more opportunities to shine.

Soon, for instance, he would come face-to-face with the key figures of SIQ.

He had no interest in helping the despicable Mr. Lee persuade SIQ to invest, but for his own sake, he would still go all out. If he left a good impression, he might have a chance to work with them himself and win a chunk of seed money for his own business. He'd once heard of a local investor who met an entrepreneur for coffee and decided on the spot to pour millions of American dollars into his business. In the tech world, VCs were willing to spend big on the right talent or idea, and as long as he was able to convince them of his ability, a poor guy could transform himself into a mogul. This, Chung-Nam thought, was the opportunity he'd been waiting for.

"Huh, the boss actually managed to get a meeting with SIQ," said Hao to Chung-Nam in the elevator after work. "I guess some people are born lucky. He ran his dad's textile mill into the ground, but he just has to reach out his hand and money drops into it . . . I bet Ma-Chai says this is a reward for his good deeds or something."

Chung-Nam didn't believe in cosmic justice. For many years now, he'd watched unscrupulous bastards pull dirty tricks and get rewarded while nice guys got bullied. Although he never said so out loud, he despised the weak, but society forced everyone to be a "good person," so he went along with it. The hypocrisy of these rules was obvious. Government ministers and tycoons used morality as a smoke screen, and the law was just a tool for them to gain even more advantage and keep regular folk down. Good deeds weren't rewarded; it was every man for himself. If there really were such a thing as retribution, the things he'd done would have been punished long ago, but in fact he only saw people who'd done even worse steadily scaling the ladder. God helps those who help themselves, he thought.

At nine the next morning, the GT staff were ready for the visitors—even though they weren't expected till eleven. Thomas, who normally dressed casually, looked uncomfortable in a suit that didn't quite fit, and he had to keep tugging at the collar so he could breathe. Joanne was in a white blouse and black skirt, much more somber than her usual outfits. Although Mr. Lee was fairly lax when it came to their dress code, Chung-Nam felt that as a software engineer, he ought to dress like a professional. If he went around looking like a nerd, that's all he'd ever be.

"Nam, my English is terrible. If the SIQ guys ask me anything, you have to help me," said Ma-Chai, whose normal clothes screamed "nerd." He'd been working for only a couple of years, and like many computer science students, his humanities grades hadn't been great, with English as his weakest subject.

"Don't worry. If they ask tech questions, I'll take over." Chung-Nam put on the expression of a dependable older colleague, and Ma-Chai nodded, reassured. Chung-Nam had been intent all along on speaking to the SIQ people, not giving his younger coworkers a chance to butt in. Although they had the same job title, Chung-Nam had never seen Ma-Chai as anything other than someone to be used. If anything ever went wrong, he'd be the first to throw Ma-Chai under the bus.

In contrast to the usual relaxed atmosphere, the next two hours passed in dead silence. Everyone was far too tense for idle chatter. Chung-Nam was in no mood to work. His programming tool was open on his screen, but his eyes kept drifting to the little clock in the corner, calculating to the second how far away eleven o'clock was.

When the door buzzer sounded, everyone sat up straight and Mr. Lee jumped to his feet. Seeing this, Joanne stood, too, and scurried to the main door. GT might be small, but it would never do to have the boss open the door.

Chung-Nam, Ma-Chai, and Hao kept their eyes fixed on their computer screens, but they pricked up their ears. At the main door, Joanne greeted the visitors in English, only to get a reply in Cantonese.

"We have an eleven o'clock appointment with Mr. Lee Sai-Wing," said a crisp female voice.

"This—this way," stammered Joanne, switching back to Cantonese.

As footsteps entered the office, Chung-Nam couldn't resist turning to look. Walking next to Joanne was a striking woman in her twenties, petite with brown hair, her features suggesting both Asian and Western heritage. Like Joanne, she was in a suit, although with trousers instead of a skirt, which gave her an air of capability. She had no bag, just a dark gray iPad, which added to the neatness of her appearance. She was pretty enough that Chung-Nam's eyes lingered on her for a few moments, until the man behind her grabbed his attention.

He looked about ten years older than Chung-Nam and was in a dapper gray suit, his black tie contrasting nicely with his white pocket square. Behind a pair of rimless glasses, his eyes radiated confidence. With his sharp eyebrows and floppy hair, he looked like Richard Gere in *Pretty Woman*—the Asian version, of course.

Chung-Nam wasn't drawn to his handsomeness, though. He looked familiar somehow.

"Good morning. I'm Kenneth Lee, from GT Technology," said Mr. Lee, going over to shake the attractive duo's hands.

"Hello," said the Eurasian woman, gesturing at the man beside her. "This is Szeto Wai of SIQ Ventures."

Mr. Lee's jaw hit the ground, and Chung-Nam almost leaped into the air with excitement. Now he realized where he'd seen this man: he'd found an old photo of him on a foreign IT news website. Szeto Wai and Satoshi Inoue stayed out of the limelight, leaving Kyle Quincy to face the press. A decade ago, when Isotope was founded, they'd taken some media interviews, and the photos sparked some witty comments. Satoshi was a typical nerd, living in T-shirt and shorts, while Szeto Wai, who was about the same age, dressed like an old fogy in a stiff suit. Standing next to each other, they looked like a businessman and his teenage son.

Looking closely at Szeto Wai, Chung-Nam was certain that this was indeed the man he remembered from the photo. He'd never expected SIQ to send its number two man to visit a tiny firm of only five employees,

"Mr. Sze—Szeto Wai, it's n—nice to meet you," Mr. Lee stuttered in English, though he was so nervous he actually said, "Night to miss you."

"Feel free to speak Cantonese," said Szeto. His accent was a little off, but every word was clear. "My mom's from Hong Kong, and I went to primary school here. I haven't forgotten my Cantonese."

"Oh, uh, great to see you. I've heard good things," said Mr. Lee, even more flustered as they exchanged business cards. "Mr. Szeto . . . as in *the* Mr. Szeto?"

"That's me. The job title isn't fake, you know." He smiled, pointing at the card. "Everyone asks me that when I do a site visit."

"For—forgive my presumption," said Mr. Lee, getting into even more of a tangle and forgetting the flattering opening speech he'd prepared. "I didn't expect the famous Mr. Szeto to come in person. Welcome to our humble office."

"I happened to be in Hong Kong visiting friends. I've handed over a lot of the business to Kyle and moved to the East Coast. I don't do much except short video conference calls with them. This semiretired lifestyle gets boring, though, so when an interesting project comes along, I like to get personally involved." Szeto grinned. "In the internet age, a company's size doesn't necessarily correlate with its potential. When I set up Isotope with Satoshi, there were only four of us. Small firms can end up much more profitable. To be honest, I prefer lean outfits to those huge companies with hundreds of people. When it comes to talent, it's all about quality, not quantity."

"We're honored to have you here. Let's go into the conference room, and I'll tell you more about our services and prospects." Mr. Lee gestured for the visitors to follow him.

As the higher-ups filed in, Hao darted over to Chung-Nam and whispered, "My god, they sent in the big guns! Is that really the founder of SIQ?"

"Yes. I've seen his photo." Chung-Nam opened a browser and searched for Szeto's and Satoshi's names. The first result was that image of the nerd and the gentleman.

"Click on their company website, let's have a look," said Ma-Chai, pointing at one of the links.

Chung-Nam clicked, and the SIQ Ventures home page filled his screen. There was nothing snazzy about this. The main page consisted of a series of posts and images, covering all sorts of topics: the direction social media was taking, examples of collaborations between Silicon Valley and the American military, the future of virtual reality, the ups and downs of the video game market, and something about quantum computing that even Chung-Nam couldn't decipher.

"Why's there a tab for Portfolio? Do we need to see samples of their work?" said Hao, jabbing at a corner of the screen.

"I think they mean investment portfolio." Chung-Nam clicked, and sure enough, the browser filled with a long list of firms, their CEOs' names, and links to their home pages. He recognized a number of them as web companies.

"Let's have a look at Team," urged Ma-Chai, pointing at the next tab.

There were fewer employees than Chung-Nam had expected —forty-odd head shots popped up on this page. Of course, these could have been only a portion of the higher-ranked staff.

"There, Szeto Wai." Chung-Nam moved the mouse over to the picture of a man in a suit. Most of the people in the other photos were dressed much more casually. Many of the men weren't even wearing ties.

With a click, the door of the conference room opened. Hao leaped back to his own seat, and Ma-Chai swiftly bent over his keyboard. Chung-Nam hit alt-tab to return to his programming screen. After all that, the only person who stepped out was Joanne, who'd been sent to get coffee for the visitors.

Ma-Chai and Hao stayed at their desks after Joanne went back in, but Chung-Nam wanted to find out more about Szeto Wai. Clicking on Szeto's picture brought up his LinkedIn profile, but there was nothing particularly interesting in his work history, so Chung-Nam went back to the SIQ site.

As he scrolled, he scolded himself for his carelessness. When Mr. Lee said yesterday that they'd be getting a visit from SIQ, he'd rehearsed answers for any tech questions he might be asked in English, but he hadn't thought to look up SIQ and make sure he knew more about the company than Mr. Lee did, thus making an impression on their guest. Luckily, it wasn't too late—he could seize the moment to take in as much information as possible.

After he'd spent almost twenty minutes looking up SIQ's investors and familiarizing himself with its staff roster, the conference door opened again, and he hastily minimized the browser.

"Mr. Szeto, allow me to introduce some of our outstanding employees," said Mr. Lee, rubbing his hands together and trotting over to their desks. "This is our director of technology, Charles Sze, and next to him is our chief software engineer, Hugo Ma."

Chung-Nam was slightly thrown at being introduced in this way. It's true, his English name was Charles, but he hardly ever used it, except maybe with certain women. And he'd had no idea that Ma-Chai was also called Hugo. More than the Western names, though, it was the job titles that left him on the verge of laughter. They were the only two programmers in the place. Even with such lofty titles, weren't they still responsible for everything down to the lowliest tasks?

"Good to meet you." Chung-Nam and Ma-Chai shook hands with Szeto Wai. Chung-Nam noticed that his sleeve was monogrammed with his surname, his cufflinks silver inlaid with black enamel.

Mr. Lee went on to introduce Thomas and Hao to Szeto, by the equally grand titles of art director and customer experience designer.

"I'm interested in your systems," said Szeto, turning back to Chung-Nam and Ma-Chai. "For example, could GT's server handle a hundredfold increase in user numbers? Have you considered parallel data processing? You'll be offering video streaming soon, which will be a big strain on your server and database and will have a domino effect on the customer experience."

"We're prepared for that," said Chung-Nam. "When a user uploads a video, the program will chop it into thirty-second segments, which will reduce the pressure on the server and also prevent other users from using an external plug-in to download the entire video."

Chung-Nam went on to explain GT's streaming and encryption systems. Although Ma-Chai had actually been responsible for designing these, Chung-Nam was afraid he'd steal the limelight, so didn't let him get a word in. Next, Szeto asked about the mechanics of G-dollar trading, what their keyword search algorithms were, how the system placed a value on each item of gossip, and so on. Chung-Nam answered each question with aplomb.

"Charles is our most outstanding employee. His tech skills are definitely up to the task of expanding GT," Mr. Lee interjected as soon as there was a pause in Szeto's rapid-fire questioning.

"I'll be frank, Kenneth," said Szeto, smiling and shaking his head. "Charles is clearly talented and very familiar with your system, but when it comes to GT's core business of buying and selling information, I still have some reservations . . . or I should say it's not quite what I expected. I don't think this model will be profitable in the long term."

Mr. Lee froze. He worked hard to keep his smile in place, but the stiffness of his lips and his wandering eyes betrayed his feelings. Stammering a little, he said, "Th—that's not all we have to offer. We're pr—preparing to expand our range of services."

"Such as?" asked Szeto.

"Um—"

"Such as packaging G-dollars and information trading like financial products," said Chung-Nam abruptly.

Szeto looked interested. "Oh?"

Mr. Lee nodded frantically. "Yes, yes, that's right."

"Could you say more about that?"

"Well, uh . . ." Once again, Mr. Lee fell silent.

"We're still designing this, and of course it's proprietary information, so we can't say too much at the moment," said Chung-Nam. "But I can reveal that by treating the buying and selling of information like the stock market, we'll be able to provide futures and options. The twenty-first century is the age of information explosion, and GT's future depends on being able to keep information locked down so it becomes a product that can be traded."

"Mmm, that makes sense." Szeto stroked his chin.

Mr. Lee's head bobbed up and down like a pestle in a mortar. "Right, right—that's the direction we're expanding in, though it's still early days, so I didn't say anything in my report just now."

"In that case, could you give me a brief proposal?" Szeto turned to look at Mr. Lee. "I'm happy to sign an NDA—that's not a problem. I guarantee I won't breathe a word to any third parties about your proprietary information."

"Well, let's see—"

"We'll need some time to put this together," Chung-Nam interrupted yet again. "How long will you be in Hong Kong, Mr. Szeto?"

"No rush." He smiled. "I'm spending a whole month here and won't be heading back to the States till mid-July. As long as you get it to me before I leave, that's fine."

Chung-Nam nodded and smiled, then glanced at Mr. Lee, who was attempting an ingratiating smirk. Everything Chung-Nam had just said was completely improvised—GT had no plans of this sort whatsoever. He'd realized that the only way to grasp this golden opportunity was a Hail Mary pass, and he was happy to spout utter nonsense as long as it gave him a chance to meet Szeto again and continue impressing him. He wondered if he'd gone too far and revealed his ulterior motives. On the other hand, Americans seemed quite proactive, and Szeto surely wouldn't think any less of Chung-Nam for seizing the moment.

"Let's call it a day, seeing as we're going to meet again," said Szeto, taking one last look around the room. "Your office is very clean. I didn't expect that either."

"We tidied up because we knew you were coming," said Mr. Lee awkwardly.

"Tech companies shouldn't be too neat. Back when Satoshi and I were developing software in our college dorm, our room was a disaster zone. Satoshi could code only if he had rock music blaring, so he kept turning the volume up as far as it would go. We fought over it hundreds of times." Szeto grinned.

"Don't you like rock, Mr. Szeto?" asked Mr. Lee.

"I'm more of a classical guy," said Szeto, waving his right hand like a conductor. "The Hong Kong Philharmonic has a concert tomorrow with the famous Chinese pianist Yuja Wang—in fact, that's one of the main reasons I decided to vacation here."

"The Hong Kong Philharmonic . . . I can't say I've heard of them. Can you really earn a living playing classical music in Hong Kong?" Mr. Lee asked woodenly.

"Of course!" Szeto chuckled. "The Hong Kong Phil is one of the most famous in Asia—it has quite a few world-class musicians. At the same time, the conductor, Jaap van Zweden, is Dutch; the principal guest conductor, Yu Long, is from Shanghai; and the concertmaster, Jing Wang, is Chinese-Canadian. There does seem to be a shortage of local talent."

Szeto Wai's words planted an idea in Chung-Nam's head, but he kept his face blank as Mr. Lee and Szeto chattered away. After another ten minutes of small talk about Hong Kong's delicious food, scenery, and weather, Chung-Nam had gleaned quite a bit of information: Szeto was staying at a service apartment in Wan Chai, he had nothing else on his plate apart from GT, and the Eurasian woman with him was his personal assistant, Doris.

"Let's leave it here." Szeto stood up. "Great to meet all of you. When you have the report ready, get in touch with Doris and she'll set up a meeting time. Looking forward to working with you."

Szeto Wai shook everyone's hand again, and he and Doris left.

"Whoo!" After Mr. Lee and Joanne had seen the visitors off, everyone let out a sigh of relief, as if they'd all been holding their breath the whole time.

"Char—I mean, Chung-Nam, those 'financial products' you mentioned—do you have any idea what they might look like?" asked Mr. Lee, loosening his tie.

"Of course not. That was just the first thing that popped into my mind." Chung-Nam shrugged.

"In that case . . . Hao, you'll spend the next two weeks helping Chung-Nam put this proposal together."

"Huh? Why me?" Hao yelped.

"Because you're our customer experience designer," Mr. Lee chuckled. "Chung-Nam, it's on your shoulders whether our company gets this investment or not. The stakes are high, so don't mess this up. Ma-Chai will take over all your projects so you can focus on this proposal. If there's anything urgent, make sure you hand it over to Ma-Chai in the next day or two."

"Okay."

Chung-Nam rolled his chair over to Ma-Chai's desk and prepared to talk him through the work, only to find Ma-Chai scrolling through SIQ's website.

"What are you looking at that for?" he asked.

"I noticed something earlier," said Ma-Chai.

"What?"

"Satoshi Inoue isn't in their organizational chart." Ma-Chai moved the mouse, scrolling the page this way and that. Satoshi's picture was nowhere to be seen, not in tech nor investment.

"I guess that's just the business side. Satoshi's strength is software development. He probably doesn't like interacting with people."

"That may be true. I enjoy coding, but if you asked me to be a consultant, my skin would crawl," said Ma-Chai.

"Close that. I need to tell you about these modules I'm compiling."

As Chung-Nam ran through the work with Ma-Chai, his mind was on something else: how to win over Szeto Wai and get onto SIQ's Portfolio page.

This was a once-in-a-lifetime opportunity, and only a complete mediocrity would let it pass by. He recalled how his classmates and professors had rolled their eyes at him and teased him for being ambitious and impractical. Here was his chance to show them all.

2.

Tak-tak-tak-tak-tak-tak-tak-tak-tak. Nga-Yee jabbed at the doorbell like a madwoman, but apart from the sharp ringing inside the apartment, nothing stirred. When she was finally convinced that N was out, rather than just ignoring her, she got out her phone and called the number he'd given her. Again, it went straight to voice mail.

"This . . . This is Nga-Yee. I've found something important. Um, it's important. Uh. Please come back soon."

Having left that garbled message, Nga-Yee sat down on N's doorstep, scarcely noticing how filthy the ground was. The stairwell was dark, but she didn't have time to be scared. Her mind was too occupied with that awful email she'd found on Siu-Man's phone. On the bus to Sai Ying Pun, she hadn't looked at the phone once—partly because she was afraid of deleting the email by accident, partly because she couldn't face the truth: before killing herself, Siu-Man had been in touch with the person who'd written the post and started the cyberbullying.

Are you brave enough to die? The first line of the message might as well have been an invisible hand pushing her out the window.

The longer Nga-Yee sat thinking in the gloom, the more agitated she grew. It was as if the murder weapon were hidden in her handbag, as if a cloud of evil were emanating from that red phone and would swallow her whole.

Distracted, she pulled her sister's cell phone from her purse. By the time she realized what she was doing, she'd already entered the password. Because she hadn't closed the email earlier—in fact, she had no idea how—the first thing that flashed up were those poisonous words. At least this time she was prepared, able to stay calm enough to look closely and try to understand the interface. She jabbed at the screen the way she'd seen other people do, accidentally tapping on a circle with a 5 in it.

The message expanded, and she understood that 5 meant the number of emails between the first and last one. In other words, Siu-Man had had a dialogue with this person before her death.

Despite her lack of experience with anything but the library's outmoded email program, Nga-Yee was getting the hang of this. She tapped on the first message.

From: kid kit <kidkit727@gmail.com>
To: Siu-Man <ausiumanman@gmail.com>
Date: May 5, 2015, 05:57 pm
Subject: (no subject)

Au Siu-Man,
I've been watching you. Don't think people will feel sorry for you because you're fifteen. I'll expose your true face to the world, and everyone will know how hideous you really are. You haven't been punished enough. I'll make sure you never smile again.
    kidkit727

That was the first message. Kidkit727 had initiated the exchange. Breathing rapidly, Nga-Yee read the words helplessly.

I have to keep calm, she said to herself. Panicking wouldn't help. Only by keeping her cool would she be able to scrutinize every detail for clues to find the killer.

Of course, she didn't know whether this message came from the actual culprit. She remembered N saying that on the Popcorn board, kidkit727's email address was some Russian company staring with a Y. Although this was a different address, its contents were very similar to that post—exactly the same venomous tone.

When Nga-Yee noticed the time stamp, she felt dizzy—5:57 p.m. on May 5.

Ten minutes before Siu-Man killed herself.

From: Siu-Man <ausiumanman@gmail.com>
To: kid kit <kidkit727@gmail.com>
Date: May 5, 2015, 06:01 pm
Subject: RE:

Who are you?
Why do you have my email?
What do you want?

Nga-Yee could sense Siu-Man's terror even in those few short lines. And now, six weeks later, she could only watch from the sidelines as her little sister, all alone, tried vainly to battle the figure hiding in the shadows.

From: kid kit <kidkit727@gmail.com>
To: Siu-Man <ausiumanman@gmail.com>
Date: May 5, 2015, 06:01 pm
Subject: RE:
Attachments: IMG_6651.jpg

Au Siu-Man,
Are you scared? So you can get scared too? Heh heh.
You ought to be scared, because I'm about to make this photo public. You'll be a disgrace to your classmates, and everyone around you will know the post I wrote was all true.
    kidkit727

That last sentence made it clear that this was no copycat, but the instigator of the wave of cyberbullying. Distracted by this, Nga-Yee forgot to wonder what the "photo" was, so she was unprepared for the attachment that confronted her when she scrolled down.

There was Siu-Man, on the tiny screen.

The picture was taken somewhere dark, maybe a karaoke lounge or nightclub. On a low table were several beer bottles and glasses, packets of instant coffee, two bowls of peanuts, a dice cup, and a microphone. Nearby were cigarettes, a lighter, and a little black box.

But Nga-Yee barely noticed this; her attention was on the two people in the frame: Siu-Man, not in her school uniform, and a spiffily dressed older teenage boy with dyed red hair. They were on a couch. The boy had both arms wrapped around her, and his lips were close to hers. His hands were all over her, one wedged in her armpit, reaching toward her breast. Siu-Man's eyes were half shut, and she was smiling vaguely as she looked at something behind the camera. Her expression was somewhere between intoxicated and seductive.

It shocked Nga-Yee to see her sister hanging out with such a slimeball. She and their mother had often warned Siu-Man against predatory guys, and she'd never shown any signs of rebelliousness. And here, on her face, was a womanliness Nga-Yee had never seen.

Suddenly she recalled a line from kidkit727's post: *Outside of school, she was hanging out with scumbags and drinking, maybe even taking drugs and sleeping around, who knows.*

Impossible! Impossible! Nga-Yee kept repeating to herself, trying to rid her mind of these filthy images.

There was no way to tell when the photo was taken, though Siu-Man was in cold-weather clothes. Last winter or the one before? Had her sister been thirteen or fourteen? Impossible to say. The girl in the picture was unquestionably Siu-Man, but

Nga-Yee felt as if she were looking at a stranger. Trying to rid herself of these uneasy thoughts, she went on to the next email.

From: Siu-Man <ausiumanman@gmail.com>
To: kid kit <kidkit727@gmail.com>
Date: May 5, 2015, 06:02 pm
Subject: RE:

How do you have this photo?
It's not true!
It was an accident!

Nga-Yee felt a million warring emotions. This response was as good as an admission of guilt—Siu-Man *did* know that awful boy. But her mention of an accident suggested that there was more to the story. In any case, it was clear the sender meant to do her harm. Worst of all, it wasn't a threat—there were no demands, just a desire to hurt her helpless sister.

From: kid kit <kidkit727@gmail.com>
To: Siu-Man <ausiumanman@gmail.com>
Date: May 5, 2015, 06:02 pm
Subject: RE:

Au Siu-Man,
Whatever we do, the gods see. I can answer to anyone
on heaven or earth for what I've done, but can you? You
only know how to make up stories and falsely accuse
other people.
    kidkit727

That was unexpected. Nga-Yee had thought the sender was malicious, but this message seemed to stake out the moral high ground, as if Siu-Man were being punished only in the name of justice.

Could this person really have done all this because they believed Shiu Tak-Ping was innocent? Nga-Yee's head was spinning.

From: Siu-Man <ausiumanman@gmail.com>
To: kid kit <kidkit727@gmail.com>
Date: May 05, 2015, 06:04 pm
Subject: RE:

Do you want me to die?

Nga-Yee's eyes filled with tears. In context, these seemed like angry words in an argument, but she could sense the true meaning behind them. This was no retort to the barrage of abuse, but a final despairing cry for help as Siu-Man stood on the brink of a precipice.

From: kid kit <kidkit727@gmail.com>
To: Siu-Man <ausiumanman@gmail.com>
Date: May 5, 2015, 06:06 pm
Subject: RE:

Au Siu-Man,
Are you brave enough to die? Aren't you just up to your usual tricks, trying to make people feel sorry for you? Your classmates won't be fooled again. Scum like you have no right to go on living.
    kidkit727

This was the first message Nga-Yee had read, and also the last one Siu-Man saw in her life.

Reading this exchange left Nga-Yee exploding with hatred for the culprit. If the tone of that final email had been even slightly different, if it had said something else, Siu-Man might have been saved. Or if it had arrived a little later. If Nga-Yee had been home, she'd have noticed something wrong, Siu-Man might have cried on her shoulder and let it all out, and the danger would have passed. But this demon hadn't given her a chance to breathe. Just as she was at her most psychologically fragile, he'd cruelly twisted the knife.

No right to go on living. The words were branded on her pupils, stabbing every one of her nerves.

"Hey, what are you doing here?"

Those gruff words brought Nga-Yee back to reality. She looked up, and there was N, disheveled as ever in a ratty T-shirt and cargo pants.

"Where were you? Why didn't you take my calls? Didn't I tell you I was coming over? Why didn't you wait for me?" She fired the questions so rapidly, he didn't have a chance to answer. She wasn't actually upset with him, but reading the messages had left her so enraged, she couldn't help but let her fury spew out.

"I got some lunch and went to the supermarket," said N, unflustered. He held up a shopping bag, holding it open so Nga-Yee could see that it was full of beer, frozen pizza, ham, snack bars, and instant ramen.

"I said I would come and see you after work! Why didn't you stay home? Why did you make me sit here and wait?"

"My god, it's only four in the afternoon. You don't get off work till seven today. How could I have known you'd be this early?" He shrugged off her rage.

She was about to retort when she realized that she'd never told him when her shift ended.

"Calm down, young lady," said N, taking advantage of her momentary pause. "You're all agitated, and you skipped out of work to come see me. I guess you've found something new?"

She thrust the phone at him. "During my lunch break I suddenly remembered Siu-Man's password. Then I read these messages—"

She traced the sequence in the air, and N's thumb mimicked her, unlocking the phone.

"Interesting." N grinned craftily. He stuffed the shopping bag into Nga-Yee's hands as if she were his servant and kept scrolling with his left hand while the right fished a heavy ring of keys from his pocket and unlocked the door.

"Put the groceries in the fridge," he said. His eyes remained fixed on the screen as he stepped over the threshold. His rudeness annoyed her, but she did as he said. The kitchen was much cleaner than she'd expected—at least it wasn't covered in used cartons and plastic bags like the living room—and the fridge was completely empty. He was probably the sort of person who ate every single scrap of food in the house before he went shopping.

Back in the living room, N was already at his desk, studying Siu-Man's phone intently.

"I don't suppose you know her Google password?" he asked abruptly.

Nga-Yee shook her head. "But you can read those messages. Why do you need the password?"

"This app has limited info. I'll be able to find out much more if I can get into her account on my computer." He set down the phone and turned on his laptop. His fingers danced lightning-quick across the keyboard.

"Can you hack into her account?" Nga-Yee asked.

"Of course I can, but you don't need a sword to kill a chicken." He pointed to a chair by the desk, indicating that she should sit, and he turned the screen ninety degrees so she could see it.

"Now that everyone's concerned about web security, quite a few services require two-factor authentication and make users change their passwords regularly. Yet there are still plenty of loopholes—maybe even more than before." N was on a browser Nga-Yee had never seen, pulling up the Google home page. "Services like Google and Facebook allow you to reset your password yourself rather than calling a help desk and waiting for days."

N clicked on Help, then selected Forgot Password from the drop-down menu.

"When users can't log in with their passwords, they need to verify their identities by other means, usually—"

Ding! Siu-Man's phone let out a crisp sound.

"—by text message." N showed Nga-Yee the screen, which had a six-digit number on it. He entered this into a box on the home page.

"Just like that?" Nga-Yee gaped.

"Yes. It's the same with Yahoo or Facebook or most other services. You just have to get hold of someone's phone, and you can become that person. The internet might seem convenient, but when everything's connected like this, you only have to find the weakest link to smash the entire chain."

N set up a new password for Siu-Man's account, then opened the string of messages. He clicked a few times, and a jumbled string of characters popped up on the screen. This happened four more times, until the screen was filled with unintelligible English words such as "DKIM-Signature" or "X-Mailer." Nga-Yee thought that this must be similar to the inner workings of Popcorn that he'd shown her last time. N spent a moment scrutinizing this alphabet soup, then smiled in satisfaction.

"You've found it, Miss Au."

"What?" She looked blank. "What do you see in this—this thing?"

"You have no idea what this 'thing' is, do you?" N gestured at the screen, which looked like lines of ants were crawling across it. "Emails don't just consist of the sender, the subject, and so on. There's also something called the header that records digital information only the software knows how to make sense of. The email client and the server will add extra data. There's a chance this will include the sender's IP address."

That phrase was an electric shock to Nga-Yee. She didn't know anything about computers, but her memory was good, and she hadn't forgotten what N had taught her.

"The culprit left his email address? It won't be somewhere in Luxembourg again—will it—" she stammered, almost biting her tongue in agitation.

N highlighted and expanded a section of the screen.

Received: from [10.167.128.165](1-65-43-119.static.netvigator
.com. [1.65.43.119])
By smtp.gmail.com with ESMTPSA id u31sm8172637pfa.81.2015
.05.05.01.57.23

"That's in Hong Kong." He beamed. Nga-Yee made out the
word "netvigator," which even she recognized as a local internet
provider.

"So we know the culprit's location?" Her eyes were wide, and
she had to stop herself from grabbing N.

"No. He might have loosened his grip a bit, but he wouldn't
be so stupid as to reveal his location."

"You've got his IP address, but you don't know where he is?
According to what you said before, that should be impossible."

"The four messages this guy sent came from three different
IP addresses." N highlighted three more sections:

Received: from [10.167.128.165](1-65-43-119.static.netvigator
.com. [1.65.43.119])
By smtp.gmail.com with ESMTPSA id u31sm8172637pfa.81.2015
.05.05.01.57.23

Received: from [10.191.138.91](tswc3199.netvigator.com.
[218.102.4.199])
By smtp.gmail.com with ESMTPSA id 361sm8262529pfc.63.2015
.05.05.02.04.19

Received: from [10.191.140.110](1-65-67-221.static.netvigator
.com.[1.65.67.221])
By smtp.gmail.com with ESMTPSA id 11sm5888169pfk.91.2015
.05.05.02.06.33

"The first two messages have the same address, but the third and fourth have different ones."

"So . . . he must be doing the same thing as before, using a proxy—" Nga-Yee said, dispirited.

"No. If that was it, we wouldn't just be seeing local IPs." N returned to the Google page. "It's quite common to jump from one IP address to another. Say you sent two emails from your laptop, one from home and one from the library. That would be two different IPs. The unusual thing here is three different IPs within ten minutes. I can think of only one situation where that would happen."

"What's that?"

"If he was in a moving vehicle, using different Wi-Fi networks along his route." N jabbed at the screen. "Let's say he was on the MTR. He could have gotten onto each station's Wi-Fi during the one minute his train was stopped there."

"These messages are short, but he couldn't have typed them in such a short amount of time, could he?" Nga-Yee wasn't sure what Wi-Fi was, but she remembered Siu-Man using something like that to get online at home.

"You don't need to be connected to read or write emails," N explained. "He could do that off-line and use the time at the station to send his messages and download new ones. That wouldn't take more than ten seconds."

"Can we find out which stations?"

"Yes." N turned the screen back, as if he didn't want Nga-Yee to see what he was doing next. "We have the date, time, and IP addresses, so we can work it out. Like I said before, that's how the police track down certain internet users. Of course, they go about it properly, by asking the providers to share their client records. My method is, ah, less orthodox."

Nga-Yee decided not to ask any more questions. This might well be illegal, and the less she knew about it, the better. After a few minutes N turned the screen back to face her.

"Yup, these are from MTR stations," he said blandly, as if it was completely natural that his guess would be right. "The first two are from Yau Ma Tei, the third from Mong Kok, and the last one is Prince Edward. He used a prepaid number to register, so we won't be able to trace him from that."

"Register?"

N scratched his head, seemingly annoyed at having to explain, but went on in the same level tone. "The Wi-Fi might be free, but you have to sign up for it first, either using your home plan or your cell phone number."

"So you don't need to enter any personal information if you have a prepaid number?" Siu-Man used one of those, but Nga-Yee had thought that was just because it was cheaper.

"That's right," said N, smiling mirthlessly. "Hong Kong's liberal that way—it's easy to get a burner. Plenty of other countries make you use your ID or credit card details. Here, those cards get shipped to the vendors in large quantities, and as long as you pay in cash, there'll be nothing tying you to the number."

"Even so," said Nga-Yee, looking earnestly at N, "the convenience store would have security cameras, wouldn't it? We may not have his ID, but we'd at least know what he looks like. If you could track down the number he registered with, find out where he bought the card, then locate the security footage—"

"Who do you think I am—God?" sneered N. "You're right, though. I could do all that if I wanted to. But there are many places selling these cards that don't have security cameras. The Apliu Street flea market, say."

"You haven't even tried. How do you know he got it from one of those places?"

N didn't reply, just reached out to open his desk drawer, from which he produced a black plastic box smaller than his palm. When he flipped it over, dozens of SIM cards no bigger than a fingernail tumbled onto the desk, a little heap of them.

"Because if it were me, that's what I would do." He scooped up a few and let them rattle around in his hand. "Just like you couldn't track me down from the number I gave you."

That's when Nga-Yee realized that he'd given her a burner, and he'd retire the number after this investigation was over. She was about to ask N why he bothered—after all, she already knew where he lived—but the answer came to her almost at once: he could easily move out of this rat's nest of a home and sever all ties with her at a stroke.

"Then—then let's not bother tracking down the number," she said, "and look at the station security footage. Like you said, we know where he was at what time, and we'll be able to trace his Octopus card from when he entered or left the station—" She'd heard that the police could find suspects this way, so surely N could do the same.

"Do you know how many commuters there are, Miss Au?" N swept the SIM cards back into their box. "Even if I could get hold of the footage, Yau Ma Tei, Mong Kok, and Prince Edward are the three busiest stations in Kowloon. How would we know who in the crowd was messaging your sister? Never mind that every station has surveillance dead zones, and there aren't any cameras on the trains. The culprit chose this method, rather than, say, going online anonymously in a coffee shop, precisely in order to avoid being recognized."

"Then . . ." Nga-Yee couldn't find a way to continue the sentence. She understood what he was telling her, but it was a bitter feeling to have the one clue she'd uncovered lead to a dead end.

"Anyway, this has all saved me a lot of time, so it should be easier to track down at least one of them," said N, putting the box of cards back into the drawer.

"One of them?"

"There are two people behind kidkit727—or maybe even three or four. But two is more likely."

"How do you know?"

"I'll cut straight to my conclusion," said N, still in that impassive tone. "Two people sent the emails and wrote that long post. I'm calling one of them Little Seven—after all, he calls himself kidkit727—while the other one registered with Popcorn as rat10934@yandex.com, so let's call him the Rat. Little Seven's probably the mastermind. He wrote the post and sent those emails to your sister, while the Rat just provided technical support. I deduced this from the difference between the way the Popcorn post and the emails were handled."

N took a sip from a mug on the desk and went on. "Although measures were taken on both platforms to evade detection, the latter took a more convoluted route. The Rat's tactic of registering on Popcorn using a burner phone and going through proxies was the most effective—even I couldn't trace anything back to him. Little Seven's use of station Wi-Fi to cover his tracks seems unnecessary. Why not just use proxies, like before? Or get online directly with that unregistered SIM? And why use a Gmail account? There are untraceable email providers that automatically erase all data at regular intervals. Anyone who knows how to use proxies would be aware of them. So I'm pretty sure kidkit727 is actually two people. They aren't regular collaborators, and all the secrecy tactics the Rat taught Little Seven were ones that someone without much technical knowledge could use. The prepaid phone number was probably obtained by the Rat. He only had to tell Little Seven the log-in details he'd used to register on the transit network, and instruct him to go online at the most crowded stations to avoid detection."

Even with Nga-Yee's lack of computer knowledge, she found this explanation easy to follow and persuasive.

"But why did you say this saved you time? Doesn't it make the investigation more complicated if there are more people involved?"

"No. Because all I have to do next is find out which of your sister's classmates uses an iPhone, and that will be our next suspect."

This made no sense. "Class-classmates?" Nga-Yee stuttered. "You think Little Seven is Siu-Man's classmate?"

"Very likely."

"How could you know that? Because the first two messages were from Yau Ma Tei station, near Siu-Man's school?"

"The location helped, but the most obvious clue was in the emails." N brought the first message up on the screen again.

"Was—Was this in the header thing again?"

N mock sighed and grinned at her. "Try using your eyes. It's in the second sentence."

"What about the second sentence?" Nga-Yee peered anxiously at the screen. *Don't think people will feel sorry for you because you're fifteen.*

"In the Popcorn post on April 10," N said, "the heading was 'Fourteen-Year-Old Slut Sent My Uncle to Prison,' but this email on May fifth says she's fifteen. Your sister's birthday was on April seventeenth, so her age did change between those two dates, but only someone close to her could have known that."

Nga-Yee was taken aback. He was right, the newspapers had referred to Siu-Man as "Girl A, 14" after the incident, and it was only after her suicide and the police statement that the reporters updated her age.

"Also, the second email says, 'You'll be a disgrace to your classmates.' That's a weird way to put it." N scrolled down. "Most people would have written something like 'a disgrace to your family' or 'a disgrace to your school.' But classmates? That suggests the sender saw themselves as one of that group. And this person knew when your sister's birthday was. That indicates they're likely to be in the same year, or even the same class."

"But—even if it's likely, we still can't be sure, can we?"

"Have you ever wondered about this person's motive?"

"Motive? To frighten Siu-Man, to make her suffer—"

"Those are objectives. I'm talking about the *motive* for sending these emails."

"Is there a difference?"

"Of course," said N, as if it were obvious. "Let me put it another way. Why would this person abruptly decide to send these threatening messages on May fifth? Why not wait a little longer, so the Rat could help find a more covert way?"

Nga-Yee hesitated. She hadn't considered this.

"I reckon the answer's simple." N pointed at the screen. "Little Seven got caught up in the heat of the moment and rushed to send out the messages without waiting for help. You can tell from the last sentence of the first email."

"'I'll make sure you never smile again'?"

"People unwittingly reveal a lot of extra information from what they say. Little Seven must have hated your sister—for personal reasons or because Shiu Tak-Ping had been wronged. And Siu-Man had been feeling low for a while?"

"Yes. She'd been depressed ever since our mom died last year . . . And every time she seemed to perk up a bit, something would happen to bring her down again."

"That makes sense. Little Seven wanted your sister to suffer and found satisfaction in her despair. 'You haven't been punished enough. I'll make sure you never smile again.' That word 'again' means they must have seen your sister smile and look unworried. Little Seven didn't like that and couldn't resist the urge to send her a threat right away, to make sure she didn't have a single moment of peace."

"You think that's the reason?" asked Nga-Yee in disbelief.

"The most malicious motives can arise out of the most banal reasons." N shrugged, as if this was commonplace to him. "In fact, as far as targeting your sister goes, these emails are much cruder and more pointless in their content and tactics than the Popcorn post. As for that photo attachment, it's child's play."

The mention of the picture made Nga-Yee doubt her sister all over again, but she couldn't understand why N just said what he'd said.

"Child's play? Isn't it an obvious threat to Siu-Man?"

"Let me ask you, Miss Au, where's the threat?"

"Siu-Man is being accused of hanging out with unsavory characters, and this hints that her character is bad, so she must have been lying about Shiu Tak-Ping—"

"So she's canoodling with some guy. So what?" N grinned. "Most adults would think that's no big deal. If Little Seven was trying to discredit your sister, wouldn't they have gone for something more scandalous, like the photos I threatened those secret society goons with? A picture like this—you could make it public and no one would care."

"Maybe the culprit had other photos in reserve."

"That would make sense if this had been posted online. That's how blackmail works, like squeezing toothpaste—you start with the more innocuous ones, then move on to nude photos, sex tapes, and so on, escalating the threat. But this was sent directly to your sister, which means there was no reason to hold back. Quite the opposite—you'd open with your strongest move to shock your victim into submission. It's clear that this was the only picture Little Seven had."

Nga-Yee realized she'd been too caught up in the situation, seeing these threatening emails only as a big sister would. They'd arrived a whole month after the Popcorn post, and even if the sender hoped to revive the scandal, that might not have worked. N was right, this photo wasn't particularly inflammatory. If it had come out at the same time as the post, it might have reinforced the point, but it didn't actually add any new information. The online conversation had moved on, and making it public then probably wouldn't have gained much traction.

"So, to sum up, Little Seven knew your sister's birth date, knew she was depressed, and used this photo as a half-assed threat in a moment of agitation. All these clues point to someone about your sister's age who saw her every day. Most likely one of her classmates. We could even deduce that when the Popcorn poster said 'everyone at her school,' his source for that was Little Seven. I think that gives us plenty of reasons to narrow our field of suspects."

"So . . . when you said an iPhone user—"

"That's from the 'header thing.' " N smirked, pulling up the other screen.

X-Mailer: iPhone Mail (11D257)

"The iPhone's email app would have added that string, and 11D257 is the model number, which means the iPhone's operating system was iOS 7.1.2." N leaned back. "So we just need to see which of your sister's classmates have iPhones, and we'll have our suspects."

Nga-Yee already knew that N was no ordinary mortal, but she had to marvel at him all over again. He was the real deal. She'd been staring at these messages for hours, while he'd needed a few minutes to pick up the salient points. She thought once again of Mr. Mok's words and understood why a senior detective would have brought his insoluble problems to this unemployed drifter.

"In that case," said Nga-Yee slowly, trying to keep the admiration out of her voice—after all, she still loathed his arrogance —"you'll need to go check up on every single one of Siu-Man's classmates to see what kind of phones they have?"

N let out a bark of laughter. "I really can't make you out, Miss Au. Sometimes your brain seems to work quite fast, but other times you ask the most moronic questions. Have you forgotten what I told you—that there's a type of data known as the user agent?"

Nga-Yee recalled. When they'd been trying to find kidkit727's registration info on Popcorn, the user agent had been the chatboard's records of each client.

N opened a new browser tab and pulled up Enoch Secondary School's home page. "Your sister's school is enrolled in the

Education Bureau's e-learning assistance program and has plenty of resources for setting up systems and networks. They have several servers and provide chatrooms for every subject, every class, and every club. The students are encouraged to use them for communication."

He pressed a few keys and brought up a chatroom with a minimalist design in shades of gray. A few more clicks, and he'd opened a discussion.

"Take a look at this."

Group: Class 3B
Posted by: 3B_Admin
Subject: [Class Admin] Sweater Orders
Time: October 10, 2014   16:02:53

The following people haven't handed in their order forms yet.
Please get in touch with the student aide when you see this.
Au Siu-Man, Mindy Chang, Trixie Tse, Woo Yui-Kar

Nga-Yee's heart leaped when her sister's name appeared, but she tried to get a grip on herself and kept reading.

Posted by: AuSiuMan
Subject: Re: [Class Admin] Sweater Orders
Time: October 10, 2014   20:01:41

No sweater for me, thanks.
I'll get my form back to you Monday.

"Siu-Man—Siu-Man posted that?" Nga-Yee choked up. It was like seeing something her sister had left behind.

"Yes. This is her class discussion group." N didn't seem to notice how agitated she was, and he went on rather mechanically. "Enoch Secondary flaunts its use of IT, but it doesn't actually have an IT team on staff. All its software is developed and maintained by an external vendor. The school administrator who manages the system is an idiot. Probably the school couldn't be bothered to hire a specialist, so it put one of the clerks in charge. Only students and teachers ought to be able to see this group, but I hacked into it a few days ago, and now I have full access, including the back end."

N scrolled, and Nga-Yee felt a jolt as her sister's words disappeared. Yet another sudden departure. The screen now showed a densely packed spreadsheet.

"This shows all the data for this chat group, including deleted messages, who logged in when, posters' IP addresses and user agents, and so forth. A quick look through will tell us what sorts of phones most people had. Look, your sister's is here too."

He moved the mouse to highlight a line:

```
Mozilla/5/0 (Linux; U; Android 4.0.4; zh-tw; SonyST2LI Build/11.0
.A.0.16)
AppleWebKit/534.30 (KHTML, like Gecko) Version/4.0 Mobile
Safari/534.20
```

"I know from this that your sister posted using a Sony Android, model ST2li." He picked up Siu-Man's red cell phone and waved it at Nga-Yee. "If I wanted, I could add in a line of code that wouldn't affect the front end, so everyone who logs in after this would leave behind a more complete digital footprint. Enoch Secondary's end-of-semester exams just happen to finish today, and everyone will be coming online in droves to discuss their summer plans. Kids nowadays use their phones more than their computers, so if we're patient, they'll take the bait one by one."

"What if someone doesn't log on?"

N opened another tab to show a Twitter account with a smiling young woman as its avatar.

"Lots of young people are on social media—Facebook, Weibo, Instagram, and so on. They post everything that's happened to them, photos, videos, new friendships—all public property. They'd rather collect 'likes' than hang on to their privacy. I don't need to do any hacking to find out their personalities, social groups, lifestyles, even their hobbies." N clicked on the page. "This account, 'cute_cute_yiyi,' belongs to one of your sister's classmates, who posts on social media every day. She has a lot of garbage tweets and stupid pictures. A lot of people post unboxing videos or images when they get a new toy. For a fourteen- or fifteen-year-old, a new phone—especially one as expensive as an iPhone—would surely be worth bragging about."

"How did you find this classmate?"

"Before you came by today, I'd been investigating everyone connected to your sister." N pulled up his browser history to show the last thirty or forty websites he'd visited. "These all have something to do with her classmates. I'd been planning to look into her relationships with them, but now we can zoom in on a single detail: their phones."

So she could count on him after all, Nga-Yee thought.

"Did you find any classmates she was close to?"

"No. In fact, I hardly found anything to do with her. Her classmates posted a line or two of condolences, and that was it. Not even any photos."

"Huh?" Nga-Yee was startled by this. "She—she didn't have a single friend?"

"You're her big sister, Miss Au. Shouldn't you know that better than I do?" He shot her a look. "But it's no accident that I couldn't find any pictures."

"Why's that?"

"If I were her friend, I'd delete every image I had of her. Have you forgotten what happened when that post appeared on Popcorn?"

Nga-Yee froze, realizing what he was getting at. In the days after kidkit727's accusation went up, pictures of Siu-Man from her classmates' social media got spread around. When this happened, the school had urged its students to delete any posts or photographs that could be used against Siu-Man.

"Then . . . how long will it take you to find something?" she asked.

"You mean the suspect with the iPhone?" N stroked his chin. "There are about two hundred people in your sister's year. I'll probably be able to capture seventy percent of them through the chat groups. As for the other thirty percent, I'll have to go through them one by one, focusing on her past and present classmates. It's a long weekend tomorrow because of the Dragon Boat Festival, so they'll be free to go online tonight, and I'll start gathering info from their school server. I should have something for you by tomorrow morning."

"I'm off work tomorrow. I can stay here and wait for the list of names."

N looked perturbed by this response. "Hey, Miss Au, are you joking?" He sounded dubious. "I'm used to working alone, and I hate being supervised. I said I'd do this for you, and I won't go back on my word."

"No, no. It's not that I don't trust you—"

"Then go home and wait a day or two!"

"I only wanted to find out as soon as possible," she wheedled. "If I went home, I'd just sit around thinking of Siu-Man reading those horrible messages. I don't know what I'd do with myself."

N frowned and glared at her. They were both silent for a while. Nga-Yee clutched a corner of her blouse and tried to think of some way she could persuade him to let her stay, but whenever she looked up and met his gaze, she was afraid he'd yell at her as soon as she opened her mouth. No, worse than yelling, he'd bark out a curt refusal.

The next thing N said was completely unexpected.

"Fine, up to you. As long as you don't bother me. But if you break my train of thought, I'll kick you out."

Nga-Yee nodded. She stood and retreated to the sofa. "I'll sit here and wait."

N ignored her, reaching for the remote. The speakers began blaring psychedelic rock. Nga-Yee rarely listened to Western music, and she didn't recognize this rock group. She sat there for a while before she realized that she'd been staring at N. In order to keep from annoying him, she tried to distract herself with a novel she'd borrowed from the library, but she wasn't in the mood to read, and not a single word entered her brain. The book was Thomas Pynchon's *Inherent Vice*, set in 1970s California. If she'd gotten past the first few pages, she'd have realized how much N had in common with the main character, a rogue detective named Doc.

She kept flicking through the pages, looking up now and then at the silent N. After forty minutes of this, a familiar tune caught her attention.

"Not this again," she mumbled. It was the same song N had played loudly to chase her away, when he first refused his services. As the final note faded away, the psychedelic rock number came on again. The album was going to repeat.

Nga-Yee gradually lost herself in its hypnotic rhythm.

"Hey!"

Unexpectedly, N had called out to her. Her attention snapped toward him.

"What? Did you find something?"

"How could I? It's only been a couple of hours," he said grumpily. "I was going to ask, are you hungry?"

Nga-Yee glanced at the clock. It was past seven.

She nodded. "Mmm, a little."

"Good." He handed her a twenty-dollar note and a ten-dollar coin. "Go get me some takeout from Loi's."

She reluctantly accepted the money. She'd thought he was asking out of thoughtfulness, but in hindsight she realized that was naive of her.

"Loi's—is that the one near Whitty Street?"

"Yes. I'll have a large wonton noodles, reduced noodles, extra scallions, soup on the side, fried greens, no oyster sauce," he recited expressionlessly.

What a finicky order just for a bowl of noodles, she grumbled to herself.

Nga-Yee left the apartment, crossed Water Street, and walked slowly down Des Voeux Road West. Second Street was desolate in the twilight, but as soon as she turned onto Des Voeux, the city's hubbub engulfed her. Office workers hurried home as lovers canoodled at the tram stop, and the restaurants were filled with families having dinner. Supermarkets, discount clothing stores, electronic shops, barbers—the lights blazed away, and although it wasn't as crowded as Causeway Bay or Mong Kok, there was still plenty of life.

After ten minutes, she arrived at Loi's, which was less crowded than at lunchtime: there were only a couple of customers ahead of her.

"What would you like, Miss?" the man stirring the wok called out in a resonant voice as soon as she stepped inside.

"A large wonton noodles, reduced noodles, extra scallions, soup on the side, fried greens, no oyster sauce." She glanced at the handwritten menu on the wall. "And, um, a small wonton noodles." She'd be living on borrowed money for the rest of the month and so resigned herself to ordering the cheapest item.

"Soup on the side for the small wonton noodles too?"

"Uh—no need."

"It's better if you keep them separate, that way the noodles won't soak up all the liquid," said the boss, scribbling on his order pad with one hand and taking the money from Nga-Yee with the other. "You're seven or eight minutes away. That's enough time for a perfectly good bowl of noodles to be ruined."

She gaped at him. "How do you know how far I have to walk?"

"This is for N, isn't it? Not many people ask for extra scallions and fewer noodles."

"True, not many people are that picky," she said diplomatically.

"Not at all." The man chuckled as he started putting her order together. "These days, people always want *more* noodles. It's the same price for a reduced portion, so who would ever ask for that? They just throw away their leftovers. But N understands that getting rid of food is an insult to the chef, so he asks for only what he can eat. Not to brag, I might not make these noodles myself, but I get them fresh from an old-school noodle seller on Third Street every day. Same high quality, year after year. As for the wontons, I get the shrimp first thing every morning—"

As he chattered on about the superb wonton noodles, Nga-Yee's mind wandered. When she was here before, she'd seen the boss greeting N like a regular. If he knew exactly how many minutes she'd walked, he must know where N lived.

"Um, excuse me . . ." she interrupted. "Do you know N well?"

"Not particularly, though he's been a regular . . . six or seven years now."

"What kind of person is he?" The noodle seller seemed frank, so Nga-Yee thought it would be okay to ask him directly.

He looked her in the eye and smiled. "He's the most upright guy I've ever met."

Nga-Yee would never have imagined the word "upright" being applied to N. He was clearly a cunning hacker who enjoyed bossing people around and an arrogant asshole who defeated secret society gangsters by being even more despicable than they. There was nothing "right" about him, let alone "upright." If she *had* to say something good about him, Nga-Yee would have gone for "reliable"—though she was withholding judgment until he actually got her some results.

The food was ready, packed into five separate containers. The boss handed it over, and Nga-Yee headed back to N's place.

"Oh!" As she walked up the slope of Water Street, it hit her what the boss had meant by "upright."

He must have misunderstood, she thought resentfully. A young woman buying dinner for a scruffy bachelor, then trying to find out about his character. She must have looked like she was wondering whether to settle—or at least was contemplating an affair.

No wonder he looked at me like that. That meaningful laugh . . . Loi and N are friends, so of course he decided to help N out by praising him. When you can't say anything good about a man, "upright" is a safe choice.

Only now did Nga-Yee realize how rash she'd been, a single woman wanting to spend the night at the home of a disreputable bachelor. She hadn't had a single friend all through secondary school, let alone anything resembling a date. Even as an adult, she hadn't had much to do with men. There was no room in her life for love, the way there was for other girls. She'd been so busy taking care of her sister, working, and helping to keep the house together. Then her mother had gotten ill. All the people she cared for had left her one by one. She still didn't have many friends, just acquaintances from the library, where her coworkers were mostly women and married men. It was lonely.

Don't think too much, she told herself, shaking her head, trying to forget her impulsiveness and Loi's insinuations. She had to keep her eye on the goal: finding Siu-Man's killer. She would pay any price to make that happen. From the moment she'd seen Siu-Man lying in that pool of blood, she'd stopped caring about herself or her future.

In this complicated frame of mind, she climbed the stairs of 151 Second Street, finding N's security gate wide open. Pushing open the front door, she wondered if he'd taken advantage of her absence to go missing, but there he was at the desk, completely absorbed in the two monitors. Nothing had changed in the room, apart from the music—he'd put on a different CD.

She set the noodles down on a corner of his desk. He didn't thank her, just stuck out his palm. She paused for a moment, managed not to roll her eyes, and handed over a two-dollar coin. His order had cost twenty-eight dollars.

Bullshit that he's "upright," the little miser, she thought.

She went back to the armchair and gobbled her meal. The noodles, wontons, and soup were all delicious. She was surprised to find herself actually hungry—finding out about Siu-Man's torment might have killed her appetite for good. It was N who didn't touch his food, at least to start with—she heard him slurping his noodles only a full half hour later.

The speaker was blaring out a rock song. Nga-Yee's English was only so-so, and she couldn't make sense of the odd lyric she picked out: "Jesus," "crows," "revolution," "raccoon." She got out *Inherent Vice* and started reading distractedly. Time trickled on. She went to the kitchen for a glass of water and used the bathroom with its tricky latch. Then it was the wee hours of the morning, and still N hadn't finished. She was slumped across the armchair and armrest, her eyes half shut as she continued reading about Doc's feud with a cop named Bigfoot.

"Oh, I fell asleep . . ." Her eyes blinked open, and she realized she'd dozed off in the chair. When she was awake enough to focus on the wall clock, she was startled to see that it was past six in the morning. She'd slept a whole four hours, her book in her arms. The lights, music, and computer had been switched off, and the first rays of the sun were coming in through the window.

She quickly turned to the desk, but the chair was empty. A door on the other side of the room that had been open before was now shut. It must be N's bedroom. She was about to wake him and demand to know how the investigation was going, but decided that might be a bit too much.

I was just sitting there and still couldn't stay awake. I can hardly complain if he needs some sleep, she thought, and sat back down.

Her thoughts ran wild again. Once more she imagined what Siu-Man must have looked like reading those messages. The image of her sister with that unsavory guy flashed through her mind. How many secrets did Siu-Man have? When kidkit727 threatened to "expose" her, was that an empty threat? Did Siu-Man have a different personality away from her family? Aching all over from her night in the armchair and trying to get rid of these unhealthy thoughts, Nga-Yee stood and started pacing around the room.

Stuff was crammed into every corner. Even the positions of the trash bags hadn't changed from the time of her first visit. Nga-Yee liked things to be tidy, and because her mother was so busy with work, she'd been the one to keep their home spick-and-span. She wasn't a germaphobe, but mess got to her. N's apartment was starting to get on her nerves, and the worst offenders were the two large bookshelves in one corner.

What a shame, she thought, looking at the jumble of books. As a lifelong reader and professional librarian, it hurt her to see them being mistreated. Some were upright, some stacked on top of others, and the rest, bent and buckled, jammed into any available space.

She quietly recited the titles to herself, only to find that she couldn't understand most of them—she, who spent her days surrounded by books. They were mostly in English, with a few in Chinese or Japanese. *UNIX: The Complete Reference*; *POSIX Operating Systems Interface Standard*; *Network Security: Current Status and Future Directions*; *Public-Key Cryptography*; *Artificial Intelligence: A Modern Approach*. These might as well have been in an alien language. Even less comprehensible was an old volume with an orange cover, lying horizontally over some other books: *Department of Defense Trusted Computer System Evaluation Criteria*, with the American crest above it. There was a series with a design of wild animals on their spines, but when she pulled them out, thinking they might be zoology references, she found more alien words: *802.11 Wireless Internet Technology*; *Managing Unix.Linux in Python*; and so on. There was a snake on the last one. Could that be the python?

The whole place was a filthy mess. She looked around the room. The polystyrene containers from yesterday were still on his desk.

N emerged from his bedroom a little over an hour later, at eight precisely. The moment he opened the door, he froze at the sight before him.

"Au Nga-Yee! What have you done!" he roared as she ran a feather duster over the bookshelves. The cardboard boxes scattered around the room were lined up nearly against the wall, and the wooden boxes full of random electronic components had vanished. The books were neatly shelved. The junk was gone from his desk, and his stationery stood in an orderly row.

"What have I done?" She looked at N in surprise. His hair was even more disheveled than usual.

"Why did you touch my stuff?" he yelled. He strode over and pointed at the round table in front of the bookshelf. "Where are my spare parts?"

Nga-Yee took a step back and let him see what was at her feet: the three wooden boxes, stacked in the space between the bookshelf and the wall.

"There's just enough space to fit them in, so why not put them here?" she said.

"I use those all the time! If they're stuck in there, they'll be hard to get to."

"Don't bullshit me," she retorted. "There was half an inch of dust on those chargers and plugs. You don't use them at all."

He blinked, not having expected the hitherto unobservant Nga-Yee to have picked out this detail. But of course, a clean freak like her would have noticed.

"What about the stuff on my desk?" He stomped over to it.

"I threw out the trash," she said. "The collection point's all the way down on the first floor—no wonder you couldn't be bothered to do it yourself. It took me two trips just to—"

"I don't mean that," he snapped. "I had all kinds of evidence set out here! There was a packet from another case—"

"This one?" She reached under the desk and pulled out a cardboard box. Right on top of the assorted objects inside was an empty peanut packet in a clear plastic bag.

"You . . . didn't throw that away?" He was momentarily stumped.

"Of course not. I only got rid of the snack bar wrappers, beer bottles, and god knows how many days' worth of take-out containers," she said, sounding wounded. "I knew you were using this."

"How did you know?"

"First of all, it's in a plastic bag. Second, you don't have any peanuts here, only snack bars." She pointed at the kitchen. "If you ate peanuts, there'd have been some in the supermarket bag you made me unpack yesterday."

"Your explanation isn't good enough. What if I'd just felt like eating peanuts one day, and the empty packet was in a plastic bag ready to be thrown away?"

"Third, there weren't any peanut shells on your desk." She pointed at the packet. "These were unshelled. If you'd bought them for yourself, why would you have gotten rid of the shells but left the packaging? Is my explanation good enough now?"

Before he could find something else to needle her with, there was a sharp click from the kitchen.

"Oh, the water's boiled." Ignoring N, she went into the kitchen.

"So you just helped yourself to my . . ." He followed her in and watched as she poured the boiling water into a teapot.

"I was going to cook breakfast, but you don't even have eggs or bread here. So I'm making tea." She swirled the teapot gently. "I didn't expect you to have such good tea leaves—I could smell the fragrance as soon as I opened the tin. What kind of brand is Fortnum and Mason? I noticed it was made in the UK."

"Did you consider that the tea might also be evidence for another case?"

She looked startled for a second, but quickly realized that he was giving her a hard time.

"You wouldn't put something that important in the kitchen." She poured the tea into two cups. "Your teapot seems nice and clean. I guess someone gave it to you?"

"No. I bought it for myself." He picked up one of the cups and took a sip. "But I usually can't be bothered to make tea."

"You probably think it's too much trouble to wash up afterward."

They stood in the narrow kitchen, silently drinking their tea. Something about N seemed different at this moment. His expression had softened, and he wasn't as tense as usual.

But when he opened his mouth again, she knew she'd been mistaken.

"If you touch my stuff without permission again, I'll terminate the investigation immediately." He put down his cup and went into the bathroom. Nga-Yee held her teacup and wandered back to the living room, only to find that he hadn't shut the door. She averted her eyes and sat down on the armchair where she'd spent an uncomfortable night.

"Did you find anything?" she asked when he came back to the living room.

"I'm about to look now."

"Now?"

"I wrote a program to sort through the data while I slept. It looked at all the people I haven't investigated yet." He yawned. "I set it to go through all your sister's classmates' social media pages and make a note of any posts or comments that mention the words 'cell phone,' 'iPhone,' and so on."

"A computer can do that?"

"It's not as sensitive as the human brain, of course." N sat at the desk and turned on both computers. One screen showed a number of windows, all different sizes: some Facebook pages, some Enoch Secondary School chat groups, some with white letters pouring endlessly across a black background. As for the other screen, it was divided into four, like surveillance footage, and each square showed a different stretch of an MTR platform. Quite a few passengers were getting on or off a train, jostling one another, while a few others were leaning against the blue pillars on the platform or sitting on the benches, heads down and staring at their phones.

"Huh? So you're checking the MTR footage after all?" Nga-Yee yelped.

He pressed a key, and the screen changed. "Ignore that. It's from a different case."

Nga-Yee suspected that he didn't want to admit he was wrong, but it seemed mean to gloat. "So . . . did you find any suspects among Siu-Man's friends?"

"Let me just sort through this." He opened a spreadsheet and pasted some text from the black-and-white screen into it. Next, he opened some of the social media pages.

"You should thank your lucky stars that Androids are most popular in Hong Kong." He clicked on the spreadsheet. "In North America, almost half of these would be iPhones. Here, it's only a fifth. Of the 113 students in your sister's year at school, 105 have smartphones, and 18 of those are iPhones. The others have Samsung, Xiaomi, Sony, or Android brands."

N tapped at the keyboard and produced a list of eighteen names.

"One of these people was responsible for Siu-Man's death?" asked Nga-Yee.

"I won't say definitely, but I'm ninety percent certain that one of these people is kidkit727. Are any of them familiar to you?"

Nga-Yee stared at the list but could only shake her head.

"Did your sister ever mention a classmate's name? Maybe an English name or nickname? This person found so many different ways to target her, it must be someone she'd interacted with a fair bit. It would be natural for her to mention the name in passing."

"I . . . I don't remember."

"Did you talk to your sister at all? She must have talked about her classmates. You really can't recall a single name?"

Nga-Yee dug into her memory, but couldn't come up with anything. At the dinner table, Siu-Man had definitely talked about school, but she simply couldn't think of any names.

To put it more accurately, Nga-Yee had never been particularly interested in the minutiae of Siu-Man's daily life, so it went in one ear and out the other. It was mostly their mother who responded.

"Are there any pictures? I can't remember their names, but maybe if I saw what they looked like, that might jog my memory."

N sighed and moved the mouse. Going down the list of names, he opened one social media page after another, highlighting the pictures of fourteen- and fifteen-year-olds. None of them looked familiar. All of them, from the handsome jock to the girl dressed up in Japanese accessories, were strangers to her. It was N who gave a brief description of each person—what they'd done, whether they'd shared a class with Siu-Man—as if he and not she were the family member. Nga-Yee looked through more than ten pictures without a single glimmer of recognition.

"Next, we have . . . Violet To." This picture had been taken on campus: a long-haired, bespectacled, rather nerdy girl. "No social media, but there happens to be a picture of her on the school's extracurricular activities page."

"Oh, I think—I've seen her before." Nga-Yee wasn't good at remembering what people looked like, but there was something familiar about those square-framed glasses and the way they didn't go with the shape of her face, plus that ill-fitting blue sweater. "That's right. She's the girl I saw at Siu-Man's funeral."

"She came to the funeral?"

"Yes, around eight p.m. By herself," said Nga-Yee. "She came to offer her condolences. Surely she couldn't be the culprit?"

"Or she might have had an ulterior motive: she made sure you saw her there, because she was afraid of being found out."

Nga-Yee hesitated. It was difficult to imagine that this child could be the evil, shadowy kidkit727.

N made a mark next to Violet To's name and went on pulling pictures up on the screen, but none of the subsequent ones rang a bell with Nga-Yee.

"This is the last one," said N, indicating a Facebook page. The profile picture showed a boy and a girl in short-sleeved summer clothes, standing in front of a classroom blackboard. The boy had a square face and hair just a little longer than a crew cut, while the girl had short hair and an attractive face. "The girl is Lily Shu. She and Violet To were both in the same class as your sister for three years in a row. I guess they're . . . Miss Au? What's wrong?"

"They . . . they were at the funeral too. The girl looked devastated."

"They?" N jabbed at the boy. "Him too?"

Nga-Yee nodded.

"That's Chiu Kwok-Tai. He was in Siu-Man's class this year. Looks like Lily Shu's his girlfriend." N checked a browser window on the other computer. "He has a Samsung, not an iPhone."

"It's them, I'm sure of it. They came to our place once. Siu-Man wasn't feeling well, and they brought her home."

"They've been to your home?" N's eyebrows lifted slightly. This had caught his interest.

"Yes. It would have been—last Christmas Eve."

"Are you sure?"

"That should be right. Our mom told Siu-Man to be home by half past ten, but it got to eleven and she still hadn't shown up, and we couldn't reach her on the phone. We were starting to get worried when the doorbell rang. They said Siu-Man had started feeling unwell at the party, so they'd come to make sure she got home safely. My mom nursed her all night long." Nga-Yee felt a twinge of sadness as she remembered. "When I saw the girl at Siu-Man's funeral, I thought she must have been Siu-Man's good friend. But looking at this, she might be . . . might be—"

"Might be the cyberbully who drove your sister to her death?"

Nga-Yee said nothing, just stared at the photo, her face blank. What N said a minute ago about an ulterior motive could equally apply to this classmate.

"In any case, we should investigate the Shu girl. Whether or not she was the one who sent the messages, we'll definitely be able to learn more about your sister's school life through her."

"Are you going to tail her and Chiu Kwok-Tai?"

"Much simpler. I'm going to do what I did with Shiu Tak-Ping, and have a chat with them."

"But if she's the culprit, she's hardly going to admit it."

"You really are a moron." N laughed. "Have you been in touch with your sister's school? Or can you find an excuse to visit?"

Nga-Yee thought about it. "Siu-Man's form teacher said she left some textbooks in her locker and asked if I could go fetch them."

"Perfect." N turned back to the screen, glanced at the spread-sheet again, then reached for the old-fashioned push-button phone on his desk. "It's not nine o'clock yet, but I'm guessing Miss Yuen will be up already."

"You're going to phone Miss Yuen?" Nga-Yee turned to re-trieve her bag from the armchair so she could get Miss Yuen's number from her planner.

N waved to tell her not to bother, quickly keyed in a string of numbers, and hit the button for speakerphone.

"Hello?" came a rather hoarse voice from the speaker, after three rings.

"Good morning, is this Miss Yuen?" N's voice was warmer than Nga-Yee had ever heard it. He leaned toward the phone. "My name is Ong. I'm a friend of the Au family."

"Oh, hello, good morning."

"I'm very sorry to call this early."

"Not at all. On a weekday I'd already be at school by this time," she said politely. "What can I do for you, Mr. Ong?"

"It's about Siu-Man's textbooks. I believe she left some in school? I'm calling to see if I can fix a time to come get them."

"Ah, yes, some reference books. Miss Au never got back to me about them, and I didn't want to bother her . . . How is Miss Au?"

"She's all right, thanks for asking. It's just taken her a long time to accept what happened to Siu-Man. When she mentioned the textbooks, I thought there's no point in putting off dealing with them. After all, it must be almost the end of the semester."

"That's very kind of you, Mr. Ong. You're right. I'd like to make sure Siu-Man's possessions get back to her family as soon as possible. Where do you live? Let's fix a time and I'll bring them to you."

"It's kind of you to offer," said N, still in that friendly voice Nga-Yee couldn't believe was coming from his mouth. "But my work schedule is irregular. Rather than you trying to accommodate me, it's probably easier for me to come by the school. Would Monday morning work for you?"

"That's absolutely fine. Sorry to make you come all the way," said Miss Yuen. "Will you be coming on your own or with Miss Au?"

"On my own—" The words were scarcely out of his mouth when Nga-Yee rushed forward and grabbed the phone, pointing vigorously at herself with her other hand. It was clear what she meant: bring me along, or I'm not letting go. N grimaced, reluctantly nodded, and wrestled his hand free. "I would have come on my own, but perhaps Nga-Yee would want to see the place where her sister studied. Let me ask her. It may help ease her pain."

"All right, then. I hope Miss Au feels better soon. How about eleven thirty?"

"That's fine. Thank you. See you the day after tomorrow."

"See you then."

As soon as he hung up, Nga-Yee yelled, "Don't even think of leaving me out. I'm coming along."

"Stop being so suspicious." N was back to his surly voice.

"Well, that was a quick change," Nga-Yee joked. "Hey, I'm your client. Maybe you could try being polite to me, like you were with Miss Yuen."

"Being polite to you wouldn't help the investigation one bit, you idiot. Why would I bother putting in the effort? Besides, that wasn't politeness, it was social engineering."

"What?" Nga-Yee had never heard this phrase.

"All good hackers can do it. It means using social interactions to gain entry to a system. Chatting with someone till they give up their password, or tricking them into doing it. Maybe even making them do it for you." N smiled grimly. "The weakest link is always humankind. Computer systems will get more and more perfect as time goes on, but human frailty will never change."

Nga-Yee mulled this over. She wasn't thrilled at the idea of seeing human beings as objects to be used, but she understood that N was stating a fact. In a competitive society, people get divided into the users and the used. It was easy to join the ranks of the successful if you were adept at exploiting the weakness of others.

"By the way, how do you have Miss Yuen's number?" Nga-Yee asked.

"I've been looking into anyone your sister interacted with. Of course I got her number," he answered nonchalantly. "I forgot to mention it earlier, but this Yuen woman is a suspect—she has an iPhone too."

Nga-Yee stared at him. She couldn't imagine Siu-Man's teacher hounding one of her own students to death.

"Remember, Lily Shu might not be kidkit727. We're visiting the school to try our luck and see if any of the other seventeen—no, eighteen—suspects are worth investigating further. The worst thing you can do is go in with preconceived ideas. It's fine to have a hypothesis, but you have to remember that it may not be true. You should actually work hard to disprove your hypothesis rather than looking for evidence to prop it up."

Nga-Yee nodded. She'd once read a book on logic that used this example: it's not rational to conclude that "all crows are black" just because you've seen ten thousand black crows; a single white crow could overturn your thesis. Instead, you'd have to take the inverse—there are nonblack crows in the world—and show that it couldn't be true.

Of course, it would be near impossible to prove such a thing. Nga-Yee worried that this trip to the school might not turn up any compelling evidence.

There was no help for it. They'd just have to take it step-by-step.

"Could I have a list of the eighteen suspects?" Nga-Yee pointed at the spreadsheet. "I'll go through them when I get home and see if any of their names or faces spark a memory."

N eyed her sideways, as if to say, "You could look at them a hundred times, you won't find anything," but he hit print and, ten seconds later, handed her an A4 sheet.

"Is this all their online information—Facebook, Insta-whatever?" Nga-Yee ran her finger down a column. "These look too short to be web addresses."

"You are such a bother." N tapped a few more keys, and the printer spit out a second page. This was densely covered in print, with more than a hundred lines.

"So many?" Nga-Yee asked.

"The first list had shortened hyperlinks. These are the full addresses—even a primary school student would be able to fig-ure that out. I hope you're satisfied now, Miss Au?" N yawned. "I'll start my investigation at your sister's school at eleven thirty a.m. the day after tomorrow. If you want to join me, please be there on time. And now I must beg your ladyship to relieve me of your gracious presence, for I must retire to my bedchamber."

This sarcastic display of politeness was aggravating, but Nga-Yee didn't say anything. She had more questions, such as which of the eighteen suspects was most likely to be the culprit, or whether he'd found signs that any of them were close to Siu-Man, or if he could find out whether Siu-Man had actually done the bad things she was accused of in that post. She knew, though, that she wasn't likely to get more information out of him at this moment. Besides, he'd kept his word about getting her a list of suspects within a day, and she'd be seeing him again at the school. She decided to let it rest.

Nga-Yee walked down the stairs, realizing that despite her exhaustion, her mind was a little more peaceful now.

She stepped out onto the sidewalk just as a woman approached the building and seemed to recognize her. "Oh, hello—good morning." It took Nga-Yee a moment to recall their first meeting: right there, two weeks ago.

"Good morning." Nga-Yee smiled and nodded.

"You're the young lady who came to see N half a month ago, aren't you?"

"Yes, my name's Au. Do you live here?"

"No, no. I'm a cleaner. I work for N every Wednesday and Saturday." The woman held up her red plastic bucket, full of cleaning products. "You can call me Heung."

Nga-Yee thought that Heung couldn't be doing a good job, given what a disaster zone N's apartment was. But then N disliked anyone touching his trash, so perhaps she cleaned only his bathroom and kitchen.

"I won't keep you, Miss Au. Hope to see you another time." Heung smiled. Nga-Yee thought she must be in a hurry to get to her job, and quickly said goodbye.

There'd been something a little odd about Heung's demeanor, but Nga-Yee didn't give it much thought. When she got to the bottom of Water Street, it struck her.

A young woman, her hair messy, looking like she hadn't slept, leaving a bachelor's apartment a little after nine in the morning. It must have looked like . . . At the thought, Nga-Yee couldn't help burying her face in her hands.

Forget it, let people think what they like, she told herself. She had to concentrate on Siu-Man's case. Those faces—including Miss Yuen's—flickered before her eyes. They all looked ordinary, but one of them had a dark side that had caused someone's death. The thought made her shiver.

There was another question that made her uneasy.

Why had Siu-Man been targeted by such a person?

Did Siu-Man have another side, one that even her sister hadn't known about?

Thursday, May 21, 2015

don't worry   22:17

account is to a prepaid card,
can't be traced   22:19

                                    Okay.   22:20 ✓

what did you even write her
anyway?   22:24 ✓

                    I wanted to scare her. I said
                    I'd release the photo.   22:24 ✓

                    She was talking and laughing
                    that day, like nothing happened.
                    I was so angry.   22:25 ✓

                    I wrote those messages
                    to teach her a lesson.   22:25 ✓

you're fine, she's the one
in the wrong   22:26

snowflake like her kills herself,
that's her business   22:27

she got what she deserved   22:27

                    But isn't it illegal? Abetting
                    suicide or something?   22:30 ✓

if you're guilty, then she's
even more guilty   22:32

don't waste your sympathy
on her   22:33

CHAPTER FIVE

1.

Sze Chung-Nam stood in the crowded foyer of the Hong Kong Cultural Centre, taking in the scene around him.

It was a quarter past ten in the evening, and the Hong Kong Philharmonic Orchestra concert with Yuja Wang had just ended. Hong Kongers were often thought of as uncultured, yet quite a few people turned up for these events. Of course, it was impossible to say how many of them were actually there for the sake of art and how many wanted to seem sophisticated, using money to mask their lack of taste.

Chung-Nam was completely ignorant when it came to classical music. During the concert he'd sat through Brahms's Piano Concerto Number 2 in B-flat major and Debussy's *La Mer* without any sense of recognition. Only Ravel's *Boléro* had sounded a tiny bit familiar. In any case, all he cared about at the moment was finding Szeto Wai in the crowd.

The day before, when Szeto had mentioned that he'd be attending this concert, Chung-Nam immediately formed the plan of pretending to bump into him by chance. He also considered trying his luck near Szeto's service apartment, but it would be much easier to start a conversation here than out on the street.

Yet Szeto Wai was nowhere to be seen. Chung-Nam had booked his ticket on his phone the previous afternoon, not realizing that there would be more than a thousand people in the audience. By the day before, only the cheapest tickets had remained, and he'd ended up sitting on the highest level, all the way to one side, which meant he hadn't been able to see the stalls. He'd also tried spotting Szeto on his way in, but hadn't managed to find him in the sea of well-dressed socialites.

As soon as the concert was over, Chung-Nam rushed down to the ground floor, hoping to waylay Szeto by the exit. A rich man like Szeto would have bought expensive tickets, and Chung-Nam hadn't seen him in the balcony, so he must be in the stalls. Unfortunately, Chung-Nam wasn't familiar with the layout of the Cultural Centre, and by the time he found his way to the stalls exit, quite a few people had already come out into the foyer. His plan thwarted, he could only wander through the crowd, hoping to find his target in the chaos.

After fifteen minutes, he was still empty-handed.

About half the audience had departed, and Chung-Nam was ready to give up when he noticed a black-suited figure standing by a display board near the box office. Szeto Wai was happily chatting with a tall white man while an attractive woman in a low-cut red gown stood nearby.

Chung-Nam's eyes gleamed, and he perked up. Mentally rehearsing his talking points, he slowly walked over, pretending to be engrossed in the ballet performances advertised on the display board. He shot a few quick glances at Szeto's two companions. The fifty-something gweilo wasn't wearing a tie and looked like a business associate. As for the woman, Chung-Nam thought at first that she was Doris, but a closer look revealed someone else equally pretty. As he drew closer, he heard Szeto and the white man saying goodbye in English, the white man adding, "Be sure to look me up for a drink next time you're in Hong Kong."

"Hey, aren't you one of Kenneth's guys?" Szeto called out when Chung-Nam allowed their eyes to meet. Chung-Nam silently cheered—much better that Szeto spoke first. This made it look less deliberately engineered.

"Oh! It's Mr. Szeto—good evening." Chung-Nam put on a startled expression. "So this *was* the concert you mentioned yesterday. I was too embarrassed to ask."

Szeto Wai smiled. "You came looking for me?"

"No. A friend of mine loves classical music, so he made me come along. I'm afraid I don't know much about the orchestra," Chung-Nam lied smoothly. "I would have mentioned it yesterday, but what if this had been a bad concert? That would have been awkward."

"Ha, I see. And your friend?"

"He had a date with his girlfriend."

"It's a holiday, and your friend abandoned his girlfriend to come listen to classical music with you, a person who isn't interested in classical music?"

"I'm not uninterested, I just don't know much about it. My friend's girlfriend only listens to Eason Chan. Making her sit through two hours of classical music would probably kill her," Chung-Nam joked. This fictitious girlfriend was based on Joanne, who'd once said she felt that "concerts without pop stars" were a waste of money.

"Eason Chan the Cantopop singer? Didn't he once perform with some European orchestra? If he did it again, your friend could bring his girlfriend," said Szeto Wai, smiling.

"What did you think of the performance?" Chung-Nam asked.

"Yuja Wang's talent as a pianist is unquestionable, but for me the main point is how well she worked with the orchestra. Van Zweden conducted perfectly—he didn't let the piano steal the limelight, nor did the Philharmonic smother her. The Brahms is a difficult piece to get right, but this rendition could hold its own against any number of European orchestras. What did you think?"

"Oh, I'm just a beginner. I can't tell good from bad. But even someone like me can tell how well the orchestra and the soloist blended."

"Van Zweden is one of Holland's most famous violinists and conductors. Putting him in charge of the Hong Kong Phil pretty much guarantees good performances," Szeto went on volubly. "The Phil has a distinguished history of its own. Many Hong Kongers might not be aware, but it's been around for more than a century, even longer than the London Symphony Orchestra or the Philadelphia Orchestra. It was initially called the Sino-British Orchestra, then changed its name in 1957. It's had some famous international conductors. Maxim Shostakovich, the son of the famous Russian composer, was one."

As Szeto Wai chattered on, excitedly sharing his knowledge of classical music, Chung-Nam thought gleefully, He's taken the bait.

"Mr. Szeto, why don't we get a cup of coffee? I'd love to learn more from you." Chung-Nam nodded toward the Starbucks in a corner of the lobby.

Szeto looked a little startled, then smiled meaningfully. "I'm so sorry. I'm not going to have much free time tonight." He placed his hand on his female companion's back, slid it down toward her slender waist, and winked at Chung-Nam. The woman giggled awkwardly, but nestled obligingly against Szeto. Her bosom looked ready to spring free of her dress. Chung-Nam couldn't help glancing briefly at her cleavage, but, anxious not to leave a bad impression, he fixed his eyes firmly on Szeto's face, hoping he hadn't noticed.

Chung-Nam had been prepared for a refusal, and he had several excuses ready to persuade Mr. Szeto, but he hadn't anticipated this scenario. As he searched for a way to drag the conversation on a little longer, Szeto spoke first.

"Why don't we have dinner another time? I don't have much to do while I'm in Hong Kong."

Chung-Nam exulted—he hadn't even had to ask.

"Sounds good." Chung-Nam took a business card from his suit pocket and handed it over respectfully. "My cell phone number is on there."

Szeto pulled out a BlackBerry (hadn't Americans given up on BlackBerrys? Chung-Nam wondered—but perhaps that was just the tech bloggers exaggerating as usual) and quickly entered the digits. Right away, Chung-Nam's phone started ringing in his trouser pocket. "Now you have my number too. Let's meet next week."

Chung-Nam hadn't expected this to be so easy. He'd had all sorts of excuses ready to prize Szeto's number out of him, and in the end they hadn't been needed.

Szeto studied the card. "I remember you said your name was Charles, but that's not on here."

Chung-Nam rubbed his brow in embarrassment. "To be honest, I seldom use my English name. Even my boss just calls me Chung-Nam."

"Ha, then I'll call you Chung-Nam too." Szeto chuckled. "By the way, I have some questions about GT I'd like to ask you. Let's talk about it more when we meet again."

This was surprising. So Szeto had an angle too. What could he want to know? And why would he go to a regular employee rather than the boss, Mr. Lee?

"I—I can't give up any company secrets," he muttered. He didn't know if this was the right decision, but he could tell that a bold move was needed here.

"You seem like a smart person," said Szeto, shooting him an approving look. He'd chosen correctly.

Szeto and his female friend said goodbye. Alone in a corner of the Cultural Centre foyer, Chung-Nam finally broke into a smile.

The encounter had gone incredibly smoothly. Chung-Nam saved Szeto's phone number in his address book. This was the best-case scenario he'd imagined. It wasn't so far-fetched that Szeto would want to meet him privately. North Americans were friendly like that. Besides, as a "director of technology," he sounded worth talking to.

Everything's going according to plan. Now I just need to decide how to sell myself, he thought as he strode toward the main doors.

"Excuse me."

Just as Chung-Nam pushed open the glass door, a teenage girl happened to be coming in. Realizing that she was in his way, she murmured an apology and turned to use the other door. Chung-Nam glanced at her and abruptly thought of that schoolgirl, Au something.

Survival of the fittest, he thought.

His brain was still buzzing with dopamine from the successful meeting with Szeto Wai, and he was euphoric. He had no idea that the whole time he'd been talking to Szeto, a pair of eyes had been watching him from another corner of the lobby.

2.

Monday, 11:20 a.m. Nga-Yee stood at the gate of Enoch Secondary School in Yau Ma Tei, waiting for N.

She'd been scheduled to work that day, but had asked her supervisor to change her shift. He wasn't thrilled with her recent unreliability, but her record was good and her work usually impeccable, and he knew about her succession of family tragedies. He looked the other way and said to get herself sorted out as quickly as possible. Nga-Yee knew she couldn't keep pushing her tasks onto her coworkers, but right now all she could focus on was finding Siu-Man's killer.

She'd spent quite a bit of time over the weekend going through the web pages N had given her, but apart from the two students she'd seen at the funeral, Lily Shu and Violet To, the eighteen suspects were all strangers to her. Like a stalker, she even went through their oldest Facebook and Instagram posts, but as N had hinted, these didn't turn up a single clue.

Determined not to give up, she'd gone through all the other names on the spreadsheet. There was Chiu Kwok-Tai, who'd been at the funeral with Lily. Maybe N was wrong, and kid-kit727 wasn't an iPhone user. Many of the web addresses were made up of random strings of letters and numbers, and several times she got confused between the small letter *l* and capital *I*, or zero and *O*, and had to laboriously enter the whole thing two or three times before she got it right. Even so, that didn't lessen her determination.

Unfortunately, determination alone was no help at this moment.

She'd spent all of Saturday glued to the computer screen. She had to work on Sunday morning, but as soon as her shift ended, she was back at it. Yet, after visiting more than a hundred websites, she was none the wiser, and she hadn't seen her sister anywhere on her classmates' social media pages. At most, there were some cryptic messages that *might* be condolences. On Chiu Kwok-Tai's Facebook page, she read:

Kenny Chiu, May 21, 2015, 22:31
    See you again. I'd never believed in an afterlife, but now I pray that there is one. I hope you'll live well there. Goodbye.

Maybe it was just as N had said, and the school had ordered the students to delete anything connected to Siu-Man. Nga-Yee found it hard to believe that these fourteen- and fifteen-year-olds would have obeyed their teachers so unquestioningly, and besides, they were of the generation that lives online—surely one or two of them would have slipped up and missed a post?

It seemed more likely that Siu-Man had never been present at all. Kidkit727's words, *that's why she has no friends*, echoed in her ears like a demonic spell.

Of the hundred-plus addresses N had given her, some were chat groups rather than social media sites. Whenever Popcorn appeared on her screen, her heart sank. These were all responses to that initial accusation, and she'd read most of them two months earlier. Having to go through these nasty messages again caused her more pain.

Then she typed in what looked like an ordinary Popcorn link, but what came up took her breath away.

A picture of a young woman, half nude.

Unlike the previous comments, this was in Popcorn's adult section—where people came to discuss racier topics and could make adult friends (or "friends"). The rules stipulated that photos couldn't show genitals or feature anyone under eighteen, but while the former was easier to enforce, only the person posting the image could know for sure whether its subject was underage or not.

The subject of this thread was "Young and Tender: Local Schoolgirl with Sugar Daddy." There were five photos attached, showing a woman wearing nothing but white panties, kneeling by a bed. Her breasts were completely exposed, but her face was cut off above the chin. The first three images showed her striking various awkward poses to showcase her bosom; the fourth was taken from the back, with her panties lowered to mid-thigh, revealing her smooth buttocks; and the fifth, which Nga-Yee found most disgusting, featured a heavyset man whose head was near the girl's left breast, his tongue out as if about to lick her nipple. His face had been pixelated, apart from his mouth and tongue. From the angle of the photograph it seemed as if he'd had one arm around her while taking this selfie with the other hand. He was shirtless, and though he was shown only above the waist, it seemed likely that he was naked.

Everything went black before Nga-Yee's eyes—she couldn't bear the thought that her sister had done this. Sadness, anger, and revulsion jostled within her. Finally she calmed down and managed to look at the images again, only to realize she'd made a big mistake: Siu-Man was shorter than the girl in the pictures, her breasts weren't this large, and the hair was wrong too. Most important, having bathed her little sister every day when she was a child, she knew every mole and freckle on her body, and the markings on this woman's torso were different.

Nga-Yee let out a shaky breath and started wondering why N had listed this website. This was the only address that linked to the adult section of Popcorn. Perhaps this was one of Siu-Man's classmates, and the picture had something to do with a private grudge between them. When she looked at the background of the third photo, though, she saw a blue school uniform on the bed. This was nothing like the Enoch uniform, which was white.

Maybe that bastard's playing a prank on me, she thought, having wasted a half hour staring at the pictures. Then another possibility occurred to her: N had realized that she would go through his entire list thoroughly, and so included an embarrassing link to punish her. If she complained, he'd probably say this proved she should have stayed out of it and left the detective work to the professionals. In that case, continuing to look at these images and the other hundred web links would just play into his hands. She shut down the computer, left the virtual world that had completely absorbed her for the last two days, and realized it was already ten o'clock on Sunday night.

She dreamed about her sister again that night, a dream that shocked her into wakefulness. A tubby man with a pixelated face was groping Siu-Man in a nightclub while a group of men stood nearby watching, their faces obscured, taking pictures and videos with their phones. Looking winsome, Siu-Man let the large man do whatever he liked as she loosened her clothing, apparently enjoying his hands roaming over every part of her. As the man pressed himself onto her little sister and started to grind, Nga-Yee screamed. Siu-Man, lying on the couch without a stitch on, shot her an annoyed look, as if to say, "What's it to you?"

The next morning, fragments of the nightmare clung to her mind. Rather than dwell on them, she forced herself to be strong and set off to meet N at the school.

It seemed that fate had it in for her. As she was heading out, she found an aggravating letter in the mailbox.

The Housing Authority had sent her a moving notice, letting her know she'd been allocated a new apartment and summoning her to the admin department before July 7 to deal with the paperwork. Her new address would be Tin Yuet Estate, at Tin Shui Wai in the New Territories. She decided to ignore this for the moment. She had the right to turn down two offers, after all—though there was no guarantee the next two wouldn't be in even more remote locations.

The sky was gray and overcast, matching her mood. Although it kept threatening to rain, not a single drop fell. Now she stood at the school gate, looking up and down the street, hoping to see N appear. Instead, the only people in sight were an old lady who looked like she scavenged trash for a living, a man in a suit standing by the side of the road, and two older gents, probably retirees, chatting away as they ambled along. The four-star Cityview international hotel was across the road, but it wasn't checkout time yet, so only one tour bus was parked there, with no sign of the noisy Mainland tourists who would appear later.

Ten minutes went by, and she glanced at her watch to see that it was half past eleven. Just as she was cursing N for his lack of punctuality, a thought occurred to her: Could he have phoned Miss Yuen and changed the meeting time without telling her? She pulled out her cell phone and dialed his number.

A ringing sound came from her left. When she turned, there was N, walking slowly toward her, looking down at the old-style phone he'd used to call Miss Yuen.

"Impatient people never accomplish anything," he said, hitting the button to reject her call. Typical, that the first words out of his mouth would be an insult rather than an apology for his lateness.

"Why didn't you dress properly?" Nga-Yee said. She didn't have time for his rudeness, because his appearance was more of a concern. As usual, he was in cargo pants and a red hoodie, and although it was zipped up, she was pretty certain that under it would be his usual wrinkled T-shirt.

"I wore shoes," he protested, holding up a foot to show that he was in sneakers rather than his usual flip-flops. "This is very cool streetwear. You just don't have an eye for it."

"You told Miss Yuen you were my good friend. I don't want her thinking I date badly dressed men!"

"What's your problem?" He grinned nastily. "You think you'll ever see her again? Are you planning to become best friends? Who cares what she thinks of your taste in men?"

She couldn't think of a single rebuttal.

"There are a lot of morons today who only care how other people see them. They think the world revolves around them. Stop reading novels. Have a look at Richard Feynman's *What Do You Care What Other People Think?* or Yoshihiro Koizumi's *The Self-Obsessed Pig*," N sneered. "Don't forget, our objective today is to find some people who've been hiding on the internet. If it turns out that Miss Yuen is kidkit727, will you still care about her opinion of us?"

Nga-Yee kept her mouth shut.

"Let's go." N was already walking. "If you can't keep up, I'll investigate on my own. Oh, and remember, my name today is Ong."

They entered the school and told the desk clerk why they were there. He gave them visitors' passes and brought them to a classroom on the third floor of the central building, where Miss Yuen was waiting. As soon as Nga-Yee stepped in, the teacher stood and came to greet her.

"I'll do the talking," N murmured as Miss Yuen approached. Nga-Yee couldn't argue. Miss Yuen would have heard.

"Hello, Miss Au. Are you doing all right?" asked Miss Yuen. "And this must be Mr. Ong."

"Hi there," said N, having switched to a friendly expression, shaking hands warmly with the teacher. "Thank you so much for everything you did for our Siu-Man."

Nga-Yee was shocked, but she managed to keep her expression neutral. N had said "our" as if he were family. Once again, the speed with which he'd changed personalities astonished her. He was probably trying to annoy her, she thought. Now that she'd made it clear that she didn't want Miss Yuen to think they were an item, of course he was going to make himself out to be Siu-Man's future brother-in-law.

"Siu-Man was a good girl, but . . ." Miss Yuen trailed off, as if unwilling to bring up something so sad. "But let's not stand around talking. Please, come with me."

She led them to a small meeting room that was furnished with a square table and eight chairs around it. There was a drink machine in a corner of the room, from which she poured two cups of tea for the visitors.

"These are the books Siu-Man left in her locker," she said, placing a white plastic bag and a small notebook on the table. The bag looked like it held six or seven textbooks.

"Thanks," said N, reaching out to take them.

"And this is where her classmates wrote their condolences." Miss Yuen indicated the notebook. "She left us very suddenly, and her classmates found it hard to cope. We asked them to put their thoughts down here, in the hopes it would comfort them."

Nga-Yee flipped through the loose-leaf notebook and found almost the same phrases on every page: "I'll always miss you," "Rest in peace," "Condolences," and so on. Many of them were unsigned, and Nga-Yee wondered if they'd treated this as yet another piece of homework, to be done quickly and never thought of again. In the twenty-odd pages, only a couple of entries were longer than a few words. One of them caught Nga-Yee's eye:

"Siu-Man, I'm sorry. Please forgive my cowardice. Since you left, I can't stop wondering if it's our fault. I'm so, so sorry. May you rest in peace. I hope your family can recover from their grief."

No signature. There was no way to be sure, but Nga-Yee couldn't help wondering if this might be kidkit727. Would the culprit feel guilty about what happened to Siu-Man? But what did this "cowardice" refer to? Nothing about kidkit727's messages seemed cowardly.

As Nga-Yee went through the notebook, N said, "Thank you, Miss Yuen. I'm sorry it's taken us this long to come."

"Not a problem." She smiled and nodded. "I thought you probably needed more time."

"Thank you for your understanding." N bowed slightly. "I hope this hasn't caused you too much trouble. It can't be easy for the school to deal with something like this."

"We follow directives from the Education Bureau, so everything's under control." Miss Yuen looked sidelong at Nga-Yee. "We had already set things in motion during Siu-Man's incident on the MTR. When the accusation was posted in April, we set up a response team to deal with it. A handful of parents complained about our handling of the situation, but they don't know what's happening behind the scenes. The students have mostly calmed down. It's not been much trouble."

"The Popcorn post must have caused quite a stir," said N. "If you don't mind me asking—was the student body investigated to see if anyone here was responsible for the false accusations? After all, the school was affected too."

Nga-Yee was startled that N would cut straight to the chase like this, though she wanted to hear Miss Yuen's answer.

The teacher's face sank. "You're right, Mr. Ong. That post did cause quite a bit of harm. As educators, though, our main concern is our children's futures, and we have to think of them first. We couldn't afford to heighten the fear and unease. After Siu-Man's death, we brought the same attitude to counseling the students on their grief so as to rebuild their trust and sense of security."

"It's been hard on you. I'm sure the school's protocols are very thorough, but it's hard to be prepared for the unexpected, and there'll always be bad luck," said N, nodding. "Now, if I remember right, you teach Chinese?"

"Yes."

"I'd like to know what Siu-Man talked about in her composition homework. I don't mean her reasons for doing what she did, but it would help if we just knew what she was thinking at the time, and if there was anything on her mind we weren't aware of."

"I don't remember anything in particular . . ." Miss Yuen paused. "If you wait a moment, I'll go have a look. We keep the students' essays and publish the outstanding ones in the school magazine. The rest get returned at the end of term. I'm sure her writing will mean much more to you, of course."

"That would be great."

Miss Yuen left the room. Nga-Yee made sure she was gone, then turned to ask N what he wanted with Siu-Man's homework. As soon as she opened her mouth, he said, "Let's talk about this later." And so she sat in silence, studying her surroundings. When she saw the school crest on the wall, it suddenly sank in that her sister had been in this place almost every weekday for the last three years. She'd been alive here. Through the window of the meeting room, Nga-Yee could see a corridor in the other wing of this L-shaped building. A girl was skipping along in her white short-sleeved uniform, textbooks clutched to her chest, animatedly chatting with her companion. Nga-Yee imagined she could see Siu-Man's shadow trailing behind them.

But Siu-Man was no longer here.

In an instant, her nose twitched, and she found herself holding back tears. But she knew her purpose: to find her little sister's killer. She silently vowed not to shed another tear till the culprit had been brought to justice.

She glanced at N, who was sitting bolt upright and looking composed, playing the part of the bereaved family member to the hilt. He actually wasn't dressed too badly, she realized. The cargo pants and hoodie were regular clothes and didn't seem too casual. It also helped that he was clean-shaven. Now that Nga-Yee thought about it, it was only at their first meeting that he'd looked like a homeless bum. Every time she'd seen him since, there hadn't been a hint of stubble on his face. Perhaps his outfit was why Miss Yuen had lowered her guard—someone in a suit asking this many questions might have provoked suspicion. Looking at him now, no one would have thought he was a detective.

Perhaps this was more social engineering, Nga-Yee thought.

Miss Yuen soon returned with a stack of dog-eared papers. "This is all her homework for this year, ten pages in all." She placed the essays in front of them. Nga-Yee felt a wash of sadness at the familiar handwriting, but she refused to let herself be distracted as she reached out to look through them. The topics were the usual: "Planning for the Year in Springtime," "My Dream Job," "Tea House Observations," and so on. There were a few more difficult subjects, such as "An army can change its general, but a man can't change his ideals. —*The Analects*. Discuss."

"Siu-Man's grades weren't too good, were they," N said, glancing through the stack. Her handwriting wasn't bad, but every essay had been given a grade of around 60.

"She was average—not too good and not too bad," said Miss Yuen, smiling. "Most students aren't able to produce good writing yet. Siu-Man was better at science, and no one can be the best at everything."

Miss Yuen was selling it well, but the comments she'd left on the assignments told a different story: "Quite smooth, but you haven't said very much and didn't address the main point."

"Your argument is unclear. Please write with more attention." The essay on "My Dream Job" had the lowest score, and Miss Yuen had written, "You're going around in circles. Just say what you think."

"Siu-Man wasn't great at writing," said Miss Yuen, noticing that Nga-Yee was going through the essays in detail. "Her vocabulary was all right, but she lacked substance. Probably she hadn't experienced enough of life. If only—no, I'm sorry, I shouldn't have said that."

"It's all right. Thank you for giving these to us, Miss Yuen." Nga-Yee felt as if she were seeing an unfamiliar version of her sister in these pages, and it might help her mourn. Now that she thought of it, once Siu-Man started secondary school, she'd stopped asking for help with her schoolwork, and that's why Nga-Yee had had no idea about her grades.

"Did Siu-Man behave herself in class?" N asked.

"She was a little playful in year one—I taught her Chinese that year—but she gradually learned to behave." Miss Yuen turned to Nga-Yee. "In the second half of year two she grew quite introverted, probably because—because of your mother's illness."

Nga-Yee felt a burst of sadness.

"Did she have friends in class?" N asked, still playing the part of a close family friend. "She did mention one or two names, but I can't remember . . ."

"Well, she did spend a lot of time with Lily and Kwok-Tai at one point, though they seemed to drift apart later."

"This is Lily Shu and Chiu Kwok-Tai? Now you mention it, I do remember. They came to visit once, I think, though I haven't met them."

It took everything Nga-Yee had to sit quietly through N's blatant lies, but she told herself that he must have a plan.

"Yes, that's them. I don't know what happened, probably some kind of love triangle. Young people these days grow up so soon." Miss Yuen sighed.

"Love triangle?" The words were like needles stabbing into Nga-Yee. She'd thought of her sister as a little girl, nowhere near ready to start dating, but she had no way of knowing whether this was true. Less and less certain that she knew her sister at all, she thought of the picture kidkit727 sent, and the accusation in the post that Siu-Man had stolen someone's boyfriend.

"Apart from them, was there anyone else? Any other schoolmates?" N asked.

"Mmm, not that I can think of. She seemed to get on fine with people. If you're asking whether she was bullied, I'm pretty sure she wasn't."

"No, no, nothing that serious. I didn't mean to imply that."

"After what happened to her on the MTR last year, there were some rumors going around the class. The boys especially came up with all sorts of embellishments. Then the school sent them all for counseling, and the children understood that their behavior was hurting the victim a second time, so they stopped. When that post appeared, I didn't notice any unusual reactions among the students, maybe because we'd already counseled them."

"Could we meet some of her classmates, Miss Yuen? Just for a chat. Lily and Kwok-Tai were at Siu-Man's funeral, and we'd like to thank them."

"Um . . ." Miss Yuen hesitated a moment. "All right. The exams are over, so they're spending their morning making up lessons and checking their answers with each other. The afternoon is self-study and extracurriculars. It's almost lunchtime now; I'll bring you to their classroom."

"Thank you," said N, thrusting the plastic bag of textbooks at Nga-Yee. Apparently carrying these would be her task, while he took the essays and condolence book.

Miss Yuen led them out of the meeting room, but as soon as they got to the corridor, N pulled her aside and whispered into her ear. By the time Nga-Yee noticed this, Miss Yuen was nodding and saying she had to go take care of something in the staff room.

"What was so urgent?" Nga-Yee asked curiously. The two of them were now alone in the corridor.

"I didn't want her to get in our way, so I got rid of her."

"What did you say?"

"I said you were sick."

"What?"

"I told her you had chronic insomnia after what happened to your sister, and the doctor said that speaking to her friends might help you get past some of your psychological blocks," N said, back to his regular monotone. "I said that if she was there, the kids might be inhibited, and that wouldn't help your rehabilitation. So she told me where the classroom is. We can go in as soon as the bell rings."

Nga-Yee bit back her annoyance at this fake illness—again, she had to trust that he was doing this for a reason. "Miss Yuen seems nice," she said instead.

"Nice, my ass." He glanced back at the staff room behind them.

"Huh?"

"Never mind that for now." He shoved Nga-Yee toward the stairs at the end of the corridor.

They went down the stairs and crossed the empty quad. N flipped through the notebook of condolence messages, remarking as he read, "What a bastard that teacher was. Terrible."

"What are you talking about?" Nga-Yee was at a loss. Miss Yuen had clearly answered their questions with care and attention, then went above and beyond by giving them Siu-Man's homework and letting them speak to her classmates.

"I'm talking about that creature who doesn't deserve to be called a teacher. Maybe let's go with 'admin stooge.'" N sounded venomous.

"How has she offended you?" Having formed a good impression of Miss Yuen, Nga-Yee couldn't help feeling a bit defensive at N's invective.

"You're so easily fooled. Someone says nice things, and you assume they're kind," N sneered. "Miss Yuen appears friendly, but all she thinks about is herself. Anytime a sensitive issue came up, she dissociated herself as quickly as she could and insisted the school was following some bullshit protocol. That's just word salad, straight out of some Education Bureau directive. She must have memorized those documents and recited the same story to other parents. Just like this notebook. Maybe two or three people actually wrote something sincere. The rest put down fake sentimental crap. If the students' hearts aren't in it, why force them to pretend? But Miss Yuen didn't care, she just went through her 'standard protocols' like a robot. You didn't hear what she said to me when I asked if we could meet Siu-Man's classmates alone. The first thing she said was, 'That's against the rules.' She didn't care why I was asking, or if it would hurt the kids. It's not them or their feelings she cares about, it's whether their parents will complain."

"But—but Miss Yuen came to the funeral! Why would she do that if she doesn't care about her students?"

"What did she say to you at the funeral?"

"I don't really remember. Probably just expressed sympathy—"

"Did she apologize?" N asked, looking directly into her eyes.

"I don't . . . I don't think so. But she hasn't done anything wrong."

"Her students are individuals, but as a teacher, shouldn't she have noticed unusual behavior? Shouldn't she feel guilty about her negligence? Even if she couldn't have prevented your sister's suicide, she should still say sorry. I don't mean kowtow to you or make a full confession, but anyone with even a bit of empathy should feel some guilt at this happening under their charge. To her, everything that went wrong was someone else's fault. She would never speak from the heart. She sees herself as a cog in the machine, and her job is to get rid of trouble before it reaches her bosses. We're inundated with people like that who don't want to rock the boat. They're the reason this country is rotting from the inside."

N sounded like an anarchist, but Nga-Yee found it hard to disagree.

"At any rate, we know she isn't kidkit727," said N, suddenly changing his tone.

"Why?"

"She'd never risk getting herself—and the school—into so much trouble. If she really had some grudge against your sister, she wouldn't resort to smears on the internet. As far as she's concerned, these students are like raw material in a factory, to be poured into molds and emerge as identical mannequins, any individuality burned away. From there, they'll get delivered into the machine we call society and become unremarkable cogs just like her."

Nga-Yee didn't know what to think. N's viewpoint seemed extreme, but she'd never considered the situation from this angle. Ever since she was a child, she'd absorbed the idea that you have to study and work hard to be a useful member of society. That had been her goal, but after the sudden deaths of her mother and sister, she was starting to wonder what the point of being useful was.

"Why did you ask for Siu-Man's homework?" she asked, trying to shake this mood.

N ignored her, flicking through the condolence book. "Do you know, even if these are completely made up and not one word is true, the writers have still revealed something of their personalities. Of course you need to know what you're looking for; otherwise you could search for a hundred years and not pick out the right details."

Nga-Yee had no idea if he was making fun of her. She stayed silent, not playing his game.

"It's about time. We should wait by the classroom. You can say hello, but I'll ask the questions." N shut the condolence book, marking his place with Siu-Man's assignments.

He led the way to the school's east wing, striding up staircases and along corridors without a moment's hesitation. Nga-Yee was surprised by how familiar he seemed with this place. She almost asked if he'd been here before, then realized he'd probably looked up the blueprints online.

Kwok-Tai and Lily were in Siu-Man's class, 3B, on the fourth floor. Students poured out as soon as the lunch bell rang, many of them staring curiously at Nga-Yee and N. When the pair they'd been waiting for stepped out, they noticed Nga-Yee right away, and were already bowing in greeting, looking a little shocked, before she could call their names.

"Chiu Kwok-Tai and Lily Shu, right? I'm—"

"You're Siu-Man's big sister," Kwok-Tai interrupted.

"Yes, and this is my friend Mr. Ong."

"We came by to pick up Siu-Man's textbooks," said N, "and thought we might as well talk to her friends while we were here. When we asked Miss Yuen who Siu-Man was closest to, she mentioned you two right away. And you were at the funeral, weren't you? Thank you for that." Kwok-Tai and Lily nodded blankly at his speech, but Nga-Yee thought she'd seen something change in their eyes when N mentioned Siu-Man's name.

"Don't mention it," said Lily. Although she wore a brash expression, her voice was almost a whisper.

"Are you going for lunch? Why not eat with us?" N was wearing his friendly face again. "Siu-Man left us so suddenly, we'd love to hear a bit more about her life at school."

Lily looked hesitantly at Kwok-Tai, who nodded. "All right, but it's just the school cafeteria."

"That's perfect. I'm sure Nga-Yee would like to see where Siu-Man had her lunches."

Nga-Yee didn't know if he was being sincere, but she felt a wave of emotion nonetheless. Sitting where her sister once sat, eating the same food—it might fill a little of the gap in her heart.

The cafeteria was on the ground floor of the west wing, near the main entrance. It would normally have been more crowded, but this close to the end of the semester many students had chosen to have a leisurely meal off campus.

There weren't many options—despite the name, it was more like a snack bar than a cafeteria. Even the plates and cutlery were disposable. Nga-Yee wasn't hungry, so she got a sandwich, while N ordered a full pork chop meal. The kids both opted for soup noodles. They chose a corner seat by the window, through which they could see, past the basketball court and trees, the twenty-odd stories of the Cityview hotel on Waterloo Road. As Kwok-Tai and Lily slurped at their noodles, Nga-Yee couldn't help staring at the table in front of them, where they'd placed their phones. These had to be turned off during class, so naturally everyone took advantage of the lunch break to catch up on what they'd missed. Nga-Yee's sandwich might as well have been made of wax; seeing Lily's iPhone had killed what appetite she had. All she could think of now was whether this plain-looking girl in front of her was the culprit.

"Did you two get on well with Siu-Man?" N asked breezily, slicing into his pork chop.

"Um, I guess so—" said Kwok-Tai. Distracted as she was, even Nga-Yee could sense the awkwardness of his answer.

"You brought her home once when she wasn't feeling well, didn't you?" she interrupted.

She'd only intended to bridge the gap between them a little, to help N with his questioning. Instead, the second the words left her mouth, both Lily's and Kwok-Tai's faces changed, like wild animals who'd sensed a predator approaching. At the same moment, N viciously kicked her on the shin under cover of the table, though when she turned to look at him, his expression hadn't altered one bit.

"Siu-Man liked One Direction, didn't she?" said N, still casual, as if he hadn't noticed how uncomfortable the kids were getting. Nga-Yee had no idea what One Direction was, but the words had a magical effect on Lily—she immediately grew more relaxed.

"Yes, we all did, I mean do . . . I discovered them first; then I introduced them to Siu-Man and she became a fan too."

"That song of theirs, 'What Makes You Beautiful,' was really popular. Even an old man like me has heard of it." That clued Nga-Yee in: One Direction must be some sort of band.

"Yes, and 'One Thing'!" Lily's eyes were shining. She clearly didn't meet many adults who shared her taste.

"Some people say their label bought their chart success, but I think that's going too far. The band came in third in X-Factor, after all—they must have some talent." N was starting to sound like a music critic. "Honestly, it's a bit naive to think that money alone could buy the whole world's attention."

Lily kept nodding. Apparently she agreed with everything he said.

"Which one's your favorite?" N asked.

"Liam," Lily replied shyly.

"Plenty of people like Liam." N took another bite of his pork chop. "I've got a British friend whose daughter is mad for Zayn. When he left the band, she cried for two days straight."

Lily suddenly looked downcast.

"Oh, I'm sorry. I shouldn't have mentioned Zayn leaving the band—that was sad."

"No, no." Lily shook her head as her eyes reddened. "It's because Siu-Man . . . We once promised each other that if One Direction ever came to Hong Kong, we'd go and see them. But by the time their concert happened, we weren't speaking to each other . . . and Siu-Man, she—"

Kwok-Tai handed her a Kleenex, and she dried her tears.

"I'm sure Siu-Man didn't blame you for that," said N.

"I was the one to blame! Everything that happened was my fault."

Lily was sobbing agitatedly. Were they about to hear a confession? A group of girls at the next table stole glances at them, pretending not to notice what was going on.

"I was the one who killed—"

"Don't talk nonsense," Kwok-Tai interrupted. "Ms. Au, what Lily means to say is that Siu-Man had no one to turn to because they'd drifted apart. She regrets that every single day."

Nga-Yee didn't know how to respond. Was Kwok-Tai telling the truth? Was that the only reason for Lily's tears? Or had their feud gone further than she was letting on, and her regret was actually for causing Siu-Man's death?

"Are you in a band, Kwok-Tai?" N asked abruptly. Nga-Yee stared at him, confused by the change of subject. Why wasn't he trying to find out more about Lily and Siu-Man's friendship?

"Oh—um—yes," stuttered Kwok-Tai, apparently also taken aback.

"I noticed the calluses on your left hand," said N, pointing. "Guitar?"

"Guitar and bass. I've only been playing for a couple of years, though. I'm not very good yet."

"I used to play the guitar. Not for many years, though. I've forgotten all my chords now," said N.

Nga-Yee remembered the electric guitar in his apartment and wondered if this might actually be true.

"What did you play? Folk? Rock and roll?" Kwok-Tai asked.

"No. J-rock. When I was your age, the scene was all about the Tokyo bands: X Japan, Seikima-II, Boøwy."

"My band is into J-rock too! We do covers of flumpool and ONE OK ROCK."

"I've seen those names online, but that's about it. I guess I'm old."

For the next ten minutes N and Kwok-Tai discussed rock music and bands. Lily made the occasional remark, while Nga-Yee had to listen in silence. She had no idea what they were talking about, but presumably N had his reasons for leading the conversation down this track.

"Your generation is much luckier than ours," said N, swallowing the last of the pork and wiping his mouth. "Back in the day, an effects pedal alone could cost a few hundred dollars, or even a couple of thousand if you went for a good one. Now all you need is a computer, or even a smartphone, and an adapter. With the right software, you can make it sound like anything you want."

"You mean an adapter like the iRig? The guy who teaches me guitar mentioned it a while back, but we're all newbies in my band. No one knows anything about software or anything." Kwok-Tai shook his head. "Anyway, don't you need a MacBook for that to work? Those are too expensive. If I had that kind of money, I'd rather spend it on a Squier or Telecaster."

"A Squier? Knockoffs might be cheaper, but they'll need repairs every few years. Telecasters are still manufactured at the original Fender plant—they're much better quality."

"Fenders cost far too much! Even if I had the cash, if my parents ever found out I'd spent that much, they'd lose it." Kwok-Tai smiled grimly.

N grinned sympathetically. He looked like he was about to say something, but then stopped himself, looking a bit crestfallen.

"Oh dear," he said slowly, looking thoughtful. "If Siu-Man were still with us, I'd wouldn't have come to this school and talked with you about guitars. Perhaps our meeting today was arranged by Siu-Man, wherever she is now."

Kwok-Tai and Lily started looking gloomy too.

"What did Siu-Man normally have for lunch?" N asked.

"Egg and tomato sandwich, just like Ms. Au's eating now," said Kwok-Tai.

Nga-Yee couldn't conceal her shock. She couldn't believe she'd just happened to pick the same lunch as her sister. She'd chosen this because she wasn't hungry, and because it was the cheapest item on the menu. Was N right? Had Siu-Man arranged all this from beyond the grave?

"That's not a very large sandwich. Was it enough for her?" N said.

"I guess so. We sometimes went for tea after class," said Kwok-Tai.

"Siu-Man had a good appetite at home too. You're growing kids, nothing wrong with eating a little more. Of course, make sure you have a balanced diet, don't be picky like me."

N's tone was light as he scraped around the pea pods on his plate, trying to hide them under the pork chop bone. The teenagers burst out laughing as Nga-Yee realized how clever he'd been. By starting with innocuous topics such as music, he'd lured the kids into thinking they shared a common language. Only then had he brought up Siu-Man. Even better, he spoke about her like someone talking to a new acquaintance about a mutual friend who'd moved overseas—there was nothing tragic in his voice. It was much easier for Kwok-Tai and Lily to be drawn into conversation, regardless of whether Lily was the one responsible for Siu-Man's death.

Nga-Yee kept her face blank. N was like a boxer, hopping in circles around Kwok-Tai as he idly chatted about the various things young people were interested in. Now and then he'd dart closer and land a couple of incisive blows by casually mentioning Siu-Man's name. Nga-Yee could tell that the teens were still reluctant to talk about her sister, but they'd let down their defenses a little. Now N was babbling on about Facebook's recent real-names-only policy, and the news about a famous internet singer getting arrested for stealing. Just as Nga-Yee least expected it, he let loose with an uppercut.

"The internet really has quite a reach. Whenever anything happens, everyone's heard about it within a few hours." N frowned.

"Just like that post accusing Siu-Man on Popcorn. That went viral in almost no time."

Kwok-Tai and Lily glanced at each other, then turned back to N and nodded slightly.

"Our teachers wouldn't let us talk about it, so things have been quite calm at school—on the surface," said Kwok-Tai.

"But your classmates must have talked about it among themselves," said N.

"Well . . . everything in that post was a lie. Siu-Man would never—"

"We know," said N, nodding in agreement. "But those were serious accusations. Do you know if Siu-Man had offended anyone at school so badly that they'd want to smear her name like that?"

"It must have been the Countess," Lily said suddenly.

"Countess?" N repeated.

"There's a girl in our year called Miranda Lai who's a complete queen bee. She has a whole tribe of courtiers fluttering around her all the time," Kwok-Tai explained. "They're basically our ruling class, so they set the tone, especially among the other girls. If the Countess and her followers decide they need to deal with someone, no one else dares to defend that person, otherwise you might find yourself becoming the next target."

"So there's bullying in your class," said N.

"Not really . . ." Kwok-Tai shook his head. "I've never seen them hurting anyone physically, and they don't throw away your textbooks or anything like that. Mostly they just isolate their victims and say nasty things now and then. That's not really bullying, is it? I'm sure there are far worse people in our year."

"But last year, the Countess suggested Disneyland for our class outing," Lily said. "All the girls except Siu-Man voted with her, and in the end Disneyland lost by just one vote, so we went to Ma On Shan Country Park instead." Lily looked unhappy. "The Countess loves stirring up trouble. I bet she was still pissed off with Siu-Man, so at the first opportunity, she came up with some nonsense—"

"You can't say that without evidence," Kwok-Tai interrupted. "Those girls didn't usually give Siu-Man a hard time. Besides, the Countess saw Siu-Man off—I don't think she can be that bad."

"Wait. Saw her off?" Nga-Yee was startled. "You mean she was at Siu-Man's funeral?"

Kwok-Tai and Lily looked puzzled. "Wasn't she?" Kwok-Tai said. "As we left the funeral parlor that day, we saw her standing outside by herself."

"Did you say anything to her?" N asked.

Kwok-Tai shook his head. "We're not close. Besides, Lily's never liked her. Normally they just pretend not to see each other."

"Was she in her school uniform?" asked Nga-Yee.

"Yes. That's why we noticed her."

"The only people there from your school were you two and Violet To," said Nga-Yee, scanning her memory in case she'd forgotten someone.

"Violet To? Not the Countess?" said Lily. "Did she have short or long hair?"

"Long. She was about this tall." Nga-Yee indicated. "And she wore square-framed glasses."

"That's Violet," murmured Lily.

"What's wrong, Kwok-Tai?" N asked. Nga-Yee glanced at the boy, who was frowning.

"It's nothing. I didn't know Siu-Man and Violet were friends, that's all." There seemed to be more to the story, but he didn't elaborate.

"I see. Well, I'm sure Siu-Man would have felt grateful for any of her schoolmates who came to say goodbye. But I'm really curious about this class outing." N skillfully changed the subject back to something inconsequential. "You mean kids these days have the option to visit Disneyland? I thought these school trips would only be to youth camps in the countryside. Healthy body and mind, that sort of thing. Um, I don't mean that Disneyland is *un*healthy for body and mind, of course."

Anyone around them would have thought this was a friendly conversation, nothing out of the ordinary except for the presence of two adults, though of course they could have been Kwok-Tai and Lily's teachers. Lily's mention of Disneyland sparked a buried memory in Nga-Yee: one day, her father saw on the TV news that construction had started on Hong Kong Disneyland, and he said he would bring the family there. Sadly, he died before the park was completed. Nga-Yee remembered her mother saying the tickets would surely be expensive, and her dad cheerily replying, "We'll just have to save up for it." Nga-Yee wasn't particularly keen on amusement parks, but it was gratifying to see her father so enthusiastic.

Would Siu-Man have remembered this moment? She'd been only three years old.

"You must have a class to get to. Lunchtime is almost over," said N, glancing at the clock. Most of the other students had left.

"We finished our exams last week, so our afternoons are mostly free now," said Kwok-Tai. "We can stay a little longer—"

"No, we can't," said Lily, shaking her head. "You've got band practice, and I have volleyball."

"So you're an athlete," said N as Lily smiled shyly. "We won't take up any more of your time, then. Thanks for talking to us—we're very grateful." He dipped his head in a little bow.

"It's our pleasure. We're glad we got to meet Siu-Man's family. It helps a little," said Kwok-Tai.

N pulled out a ballpoint pen and scribbled a string of digits on a napkin. "This is my phone number." He handed it to Kwok-Tai. "I enjoyed our chat. If you have any problems you want to talk about, feel free to call me. Hopefully we'll also find out a bit more about Siu-Man that way. She may be gone, but she lives on in our hearts."

"Sure." Kwok-Tai took the napkin. "Are you two leaving now?"

N looked around. "We might stay a little longer and have a stroll."

Kwok-Tai and Lily politely said goodbye and walked off. Now the cafeteria was empty, apart from N, Nga-Yee, and a school attendant eating his lunch at another table.

"What are we doing next, N?" asked Nga-Yee. She turned to him, startled to find him glaring disapprovingly at her, like a grumpy old man.

"Miss Au," he said icily, his brow furrowed. "I told you to let me do the talking. If you keep jumping in and interrupting the investigation, I'll quit right away."

"What did I do? You mean when I spoke up?" Nga-Yee's shin was still throbbing from the kick. "I happened to remember that they'd brought Siu-Man home, and I wanted you to—"

"I told you, amateurs shouldn't interfere." Even without raising his voice, N sounded threatening. "Kids of fourteen or fifteen are sensitive things. They get startled as easily as small animals. A moron like you with absolutely no psychological awareness should just shut up. You detonated a bomb as soon as you sat down—it took me a huge effort to salvage the situation, otherwise they'd have treated me like the enemy. But I managed to prize out only a few clues, and we never got to the heart of the matter."

"What's that?"

"The thing you opened your big fat mouth about."

"Them bringing Siu-Man home? How is that the heart of the matter?"

"This is why I hate know-nothing idiots who think they have all the answers." N reached into his pocket for Siu-Man's little red phone and pressed a few keys, then waved it in front of Nga-Yee. "I guess you'd like to know where this picture came from?"

Nga-Yee gasped. It was the kidkit727 photo of Siu-Man being groped by the teenage boy.

"When digital photography first became popular, the Japan Electronic Industry Development Association created a format known as the exchangeable image file format, or EXIF. This allowed a whole range of metadata to be stored along with the image itself." He started tapping at the phone again. "Phones today use the EXIF format for storing photos, so they'll capture information such as the brand and model number of the camera, shutter speed, light sensitivity, aperture size . . ." He placed the phone in front of Nga-Yee again. "As well as the date and time it was taken."

In a box on the screen were a few lines of text, including "2013/12/24, 22:13:55."

It took Nga-Yee a couple of seconds to realize why this date was important: the day Kwok-Tai and Lily brought Siu-Man home was indeed Christmas Eve of the year before.

"So—that means, the same—the same day—"

"And you mentioned that as soon as we sat down, so there was no way for me to go back to it." N glared at her. "People are irrational. They judge something's importance not by the facts, but by their instincts. As soon as those two decided we were on the same wavelength, they were willing to talk about all sorts of things completely unselfconsciously. But even after I spent an hour getting them to feel comfortable with us, if I'd mentioned Christmas Eve, they'd have shut down right away—because of that first impression you left on them while we were still strangers. So now you understand how you ruined everything?"

"How—how could I have known? You didn't tell me any of this," Nga-Yee retorted. She recalled how, when she'd recognized Lily and Kwok-Tai from the Facebook photo, N had asked more than once about Christmas Eve. Obviously he'd already known.

"Of course not. You'd have given the game away! If I'd told you that kidkid727's photo was taken on the same date as Lily and Kwok-Tai's only visit to your place, would you have sat there calmly with a smile on your face, playing the part of the bereaved sister for a whole hour?"

Nga-Yee had nothing to say to that. N was clearly correct, and his instructions to let him lead the conversation had been very clear.

"I'm . . . I'm sorry," she managed to utter, after a pause. She hated N's attitude but was self-aware enough to see that she was to blame here.

"Whatever." At least N was willing to move on, even if he hadn't exactly accepted Nga-Yee's apology. "Just trust me, Miss Au. You hired me to investigate this case, so you'll have to go along with my methods. That's the only way to get the answers you're looking for."

"I understand." Nga-Yee nodded. "So it looks like Kwok-Tai and Lily were at that party too. If Siu-Man really was an escort or took drugs, they'd have known about it."

"Escort? Does that photo look like she was a hooker?"

"Doesn't it? You mean to say that nasty-looking guy with the red hair was her boyfriend? When kidkit727 said she stole someone's boyfriend—that's him?"

N's brow crinkled, and he looked her in the eye. "Are you ready for some bad news, Miss Au?"

She forced herself to nod. After all, she'd promised herself to accept whatever the truth was.

N went back to the photo and zoomed in on one portion. "See that?"

Nga-Yee bent over the screen. N had enlarged a section of the bar table, which was littered with random objects: beer bottles, glasses, instant coffee, peanuts, a dice cup, cigarettes, and a lighter.

"You're trying to tell me that Siu-Man smoked?"

"No, this." He pointed at the sachet of instant coffee. "Even if you did want a cup of coffee in a nightclub, wouldn't you order it? Don't you find it odd that someone would have brought their own?"

"Oh! So that was drugs? Ecstasy?"

"Half right. If it was ecstasy or acid, they could have kept the pills in a candy box. Only one drug needs to be disguised as instant coffee: Rohypnol."

This was a thunderbolt. Nga-Yee gaped.

"It's quite a common trick," said N, unflustered. "Scumbags like that take women out and get them drunk, but most women know to stop before they're unconscious. These animals then say coffee will sober them up, and they produce a packet of instant. It doesn't look like it's been tampered with, so the girls have no way of knowing it was actually cut open and sealed again after the stuff was poured in. If you looked closely, you might be able to tell it was smaller than a regular coffee packet, but with the dim lighting in a bar, most people wouldn't notice."

"So when they took that picture of Siu-Man—"

"She'd been roofied."

"Then she . . ." Nga-Yee couldn't bear to finish her sentence.

"Might have been assaulted as well."

Nga-Yee couldn't breathe. She'd thought the most painful thing she could hear was that her sister had been selling her body or hooked on drugs, but the reality was even more painful. She couldn't do or say anything; it was as if she were plunging into an abyss, a bottomless pit of darkness and sorrow.

"I said 'might,' Miss Au."

N's words were like the strand of spider silk Buddha lowered into hell, pulling Nga-Yee back from utter desolation.

"Might?"

"You said Kwok-Tai and Lily brought your sister home at eleven that night. When a thug has his way with an unconscious girl, he usually isn't done with her that quickly."

Nga-Yee breathed a sigh of relief, and understood why N had
been so angry earlier. If she hadn't jumped in, N might have gotten the truth from Kwok-Tai and Lily about what happened to
Siu-Man before they'd brought her home. N could have tackled
it from this angle and, following the vine to the melon, found
out kidkit727's identity that way.

"Is there any way we can get another chance to ask Kwok-Tai
and Lily what happened?" she asked frantically.

"Once a chance is gone, there's no way to get it back. We'll
have to wait for the next opportunity." N put Siu-Man's phone
back on the table. "You already know some of the details, I
might as well tell you the rest," he said. "The karaoke bar in
the picture is in King Wah Centre on Shantung Street in Mong
Kok. I've asked someone who knows the neighborhood to dig
up Red Hair's identity."

"You located the place by its decor?"

"No. Smartphones don't just attach EXIF data when they take
pictures, they also have GPS coordinates. There's only one karaoke bar in King Wah Centre, so it had to be this place. That was
a year and a half ago, though, and the bar's gone out of business
since. Even if we could track down the former employees, they
wouldn't necessarily remember anything about the incident. In
other words, Kwok-Tai and Lily were our best means of finding
out the truth about that night."

A wave of defeat swept over Nga-Yee.

"So Siu-Man liked that band, One Direction?" she asked.

"One Direction isn't a band, it's a group of teen idols. Didn't
she have any posters up at home?"

"No."

"Mmm." N went back to Siu-Man's phone and pulled up an
album cover showing five handsome men. "The only music your
sister had on her phone was One Direction. She and Lily would
share news about them on Facebook. I knew this subject would

make these two lower their guard. Same with Kwok-Tai—even before I saw the calluses on his fingers, I knew from Twitter that he played guitar. You made me give you all that data about your sister's classmates. Didn't you notice any of this?"

Nga-Yee was stunned. She'd spent at least two days poring over these kids' social media pages, but hadn't paid any attention to their interests or daily life. She'd only been searching for posts and pictures involving her sister.

"Oh yes—were there any text messages on the phone?" asked Nga-Yee. "Did Siu-Man chat with any of her classmates?" She'd suddenly thought that even if her sister didn't appear anywhere on social media, she might have had private conversations.

"Nothing." N jabbed at the screen. "Not even advertisements from her provider. It looked like your sister was in the habit of erasing her in-box. She'd installed Line, but didn't have a single contact. Again, she might have used it, then wiped it afterward. It's possible that after what happened, she was so afraid of stirring up more trouble that she deleted all her contacts and messages."

"Line?"

"It's a sort of instant messaging program—like SMSes," said N, looking at her as if to say, "Oh right, I forgot you're from the last century."

"Ah!" Seeing the lens on the back of Siu-Man's phone made her think of something else. "She must have had photos on her phone. Were there any clues there?"

"Only a few. I looked at the metadata, and it's the same story as her text messages and Line: your sister deleted most of them. Of the ones remaining, only one of them has any schoolmates in it."

N opened Siu-Man's photo album and showed her: Siu-Man and Lily, both in uniform, standing in a school corridor. From the angle, it looked like Lily had been holding the phone. Their faces were close to the lens, and both were grinning. Lily's hair was longer in the picture than now.

"This was taken in June the year before, when they were still in year one," said N.

Tears sprang to Nga-Yee's eyes. How long had it been since she'd seen Siu-Man smile?

"So that means . . . Lily probably isn't kidkit727?" Nga-Yee looked up. "She was so close to Siu-Man, and cried so much at her funeral. She looked close to tears just now too. I don't think she could be the culprit, could she?"

N shrugged. "Maybe she's a very accomplished actress."

Nga-Yee found this hard to swallow. "An actress? She's only fourteen or fifteen, a child."

"Don't underestimate youngsters today, especially in this sick society. From a young age, kids must learn how to survive in a jungle of deceitful adults. In order to get their children into elite schools, parents make their five-year-olds sit through interviews pretending to be perfectly polite snot-noses. Then they get back home and they can go back to being monsters, little emperors ordering their servants around."

"That's a bit extreme—"

"It's the truth," N snapped. "Like Kwok-Tai said just now, the school forbade the students to say anything about your sister. That's sheer hypocrisy. So you stop them talking about it—does that mean it didn't happen? You think you can just weed out the source of the disturbance, plug everyone's ears and cover their eyes, and go back to playing happy families? What kind of foundation are they laying? With the staff behaving like this, there's no way the kids won't learn from them."

Nga-Yee had nothing to say.

"All in all, until we find conclusive evidence, don't trust a single person." N stuffed Siu-Man's phone back into his pocket.

"Where would we find this evidence?"

"No idea, but I do know who we should talk to next."

"Who?"

"The Countess."

"Because Lily and Kwok-Tai saw her on the day of the funeral?"

"No, because of this." He reached into another pocket and pulled out a white smartphone. How many of these did he have on him? This was a small one, no larger than a business card, but almost half an inch thick. N tapped the screen and held it up to Nga-Yee. It was a Facebook photo: a pretty girl in a white dress, her hair in a bob and her features so delicate she could have been a doll, holding up her phone for a mirror selfie in what looked like her bedroom: everything around her was pink. Just as Nga-Yee was about to ask N if this was the Countess, she realized that the picture looked familiar.

"I've seen that before—Oh!"

She'd seen it yesterday. In Miranda Lai's hand was an iPhone.

"She was one of the eighteen iPhone owners," said N.

Nga-Yee had to marvel at N's memory: he'd clearly dredged up this fact the instant Kwok-Tai mentioned Miranda's name.

"So—So she's our lead suspect. Lily said she had a grudge against Siu-Man. And she must have come to snoop on the day of the funeral, but didn't dare to show herself—"

"There you go again. Remember what I said to you?"

Nga-Yee froze. N's rebuke as he'd looked at the eighteen names sounded in her ears: *The worst thing you can do is go in with preconceived ideas. It's fine to have a hypothesis, but you have to remember it may not be true. You should actually work hard to disprove your hypothesis, rather than looking for evidence to prop it up.*

"Got it. The Countess might be the culprit, or she might not. But where is she now? Miss Yuen said everyone's working on their extracurriculars."

"The fourth-floor rehearsal room, right above us." N pointed at the ceiling. "The Countess is in the Drama Society. They'll be getting ready for the combined schools performance a month from now."

"How do you know?"

"Unlike a certain person whose head is stuffed with straw, I don't find it hard to remember basic information about eighteen students." N never let slip a chance to have a dig at her. "I knew we were going into the lion's den today, so I made sure to have everything I needed to know at my fingertips. I'll need every trick I have to get these little devils to tell the truth. I'm not like this person who wastes her time worrying what people will think of her because of her colleague's outfit."

Nga-Yee wanted to argue—after all, she wasn't a professional, of course she wouldn't be as good at ferreting out information as N—but she swallowed the words. This wasn't the time for an argument.

N led the way to the rehearsal room. As they walked down an L-shaped corridor toward the stairs, they passed a number of students who glanced at the two strangers, then lost interest when they noticed the visitor passes dangling from their necks. Nga-Yee guessed that plenty of parents, reporters, or government officials must show up here.

"How much pocket money did your sister get?" N asked as they started up the stairs.

"Why do you need to know that?"

"Never you mind, just answer the question."

"Three hundred a week."

"Including food and travel?"

"Yes. And she ate breakfast at home." Nga-Yee had wanted her little sister to learn thrift, so when she started secondary school, she and her mother had discussed her allowance. By their calculation, travel would cost fifteen dollars a day with a student card, and the remaining two hundred-plus was enough for her lunches and snacks. If she wanted weekend spending money, she'd have to save up during the week. Nga-Yee didn't know if Siu-Man had ever asked their mother for more, but since their mother passed away, Siu-Man hadn't taken a single cent extra from her.

They reached the fourth floor. The rehearsal room door was open, revealing a dozen or so students in a space the size of three regular classrooms. There were about thirty rows of chairs, though the front ones had been pushed aside to clear the space. The kids were clustered there: three boys in the center, the others standing or sitting to one side, watching the trio.

"'Three thousand ducats, for three months. Let me see the rate.'"

"'Well, Shylock, shall we be beholding to you?'"

The name confused Nga-Yee for a moment, and she thought they were talking about Sherlock Holmes. A few lines later, she recognized it: *The Merchant of Venice*. She'd read it a few times, but this seemed a little different—probably abridged.

"Cut! You're being too choppy," called out a girl—apparently the director. "Don't just say the lines, be more natural! Five minutes break, everyone, then we'll run it again."

N seized the opportunity to rap on the door, and a plump boy walked over. "Can I help you?"

"Sorry to interrupt. We're looking for Miranda Lai." N's friendly face was back.

The boy turned and hollered, "Countess!" As he wandered away, a girl came toward them. Even in her school uniform and not wearing makeup, she was unmistakably the person from the selfie.

"Hello there," said N politely, taking a step closer. "You're Miranda from three B, aren't you?"

"What if I am?"

The Countess might look sweet, but nothing in her words or gestures suggested any respect for N and Nga-Yee—she probably addressed her acolytes the same way. Princess syndrome, Nga-Yee thought.

"Could we have a word? This is Au Siu-Man's sister," N murmured, quietly enough that no one else could have heard.

The Countess looked alarmed and took half a step back. As far as Nga-Yee was concerned, that slight movement was a clear sign of guilt.

"What's this about?" She seemed wary of N, and her tone remained hostile.

"Um . . ." N nodded at the room, where several students were clearly eavesdropping. It seemed that strangers coming to see the Countess was quite an event.

The girl led them to the far corner of the room, where a table stood littered with props, costumes, and scripts. Nga-Yee noticed quite a few copies of *Merchant* with ENOCH SECONDARY DRAMA SOCIETY stamped on their covers. The Countess glared at N impatiently, waiting for him to speak.

"Sorry to bother you." N put the condolence book down on the table to free his hands and got out his wallet, from which he extracted a couple of bills. "Siu-Man borrowed two hundred from you, didn't she? We only found out after she passed that she'd been asking her classmates for loans. She didn't get much pocket money, after all. And even though she's gone, we'd still like to honor her debt."

"Huh? She did no such thing."

"Really? We found a notebook among her things with a record of who she owed. Some water got spilled on it and blurred some of the words, but I made out your name."

"I never lent her money."

"Your name is Miranda Lai?"

"Yes, but I never lent Au Siu-Man a cent."

N clutched his wallet, looking perplexed. "Do any of your classmates' names start with M?"

"Um . . . yes, there's Mindy Chang."

"Oh, maybe it's her, then. Was she close to Siu-Man?"

"I don't know." The Countess seemed in a hurry to end this conversation.

"We'll try Mindy, then. Siu-Man talked about you all the time, that's why we were so certain."

"She talked about me?" The Countess was genuinely confused. Her eyes drifted from N to Nga-Yee and back.

"Yes, she said there was a Drama Society girl in her class who was surely going to be a big star someday. Siu-Man could be socially awkward, and not everyone understood her . . . Oh, she did mention that she'd made you look bad, so I told her to apologize to you."

"Apologize?"

"Didn't she? She voted against Disneyland for the school outing when everyone wanted to go, and I think she said you were the one who suggested Disneyland in the first place. She actually would have liked that, but her big sister here is such a stingy—I mean, such a thrifty person, she'd never have paid for it. That's the only reason Siu-Man said no."

It took everything Nga-Yee had not to defend herself, but she forced herself to nod in agreement.

"Why didn't she just say so? I could have lent her the money for the admission fee and whatnot." The Countess's voice went up a little, and her brow furrowed.

"She'd already borrowed from quite a few classmates by then. She probably already owed so much, she didn't dare mention it."

The Countess had a complicated expression on her face, part resentment and part remorse. Nga-Yee couldn't tell if she was regretting not having gone to Disneyland or upset about causing Siu-Man's death over such a trivial matter.

"Well, if she didn't say it, then I will," said N. "Sorry." His face was utterly sincere. "And that incident she got involved in must have caused all of you quite a bit of trouble. Sorry for that too."

"Oh that—That was fine, actually," said the Countess, apparently unsure how to handle an adult bowing and scraping to her.

"Siu-Man must have offended someone at school pretty badly to make them want to smear her that way," said N. "You were in her class, Miranda. Can you think of anyone who'd do that?"

The Countess's face sank, and she crossed her arms. "I don't know."

"You never discussed it with your classmates?"

"Our teachers told us not to. If anyone was blabbing away to reporters or other strangers, I didn't know about it."

The Countess was clearly saying as little as she could, which made Nga-Yee even more suspicious. She waited for N to prod her into revealing even more, but his next words took her completely by surprise.

"Never mind, then. I don't want to take up any more of your rehearsal. Sorry to disturb you."

He nodded goodbye. Nga-Yee had no idea what was going on, but she'd agreed not to interfere, so she stood there and smiled at the Countess, who gave them a polite little bow that Nga-Yee thought looked completely fake.

"Oh, one more thing." N turned abruptly after a couple of steps. "You were at Siu-Man's funeral, weren't you?"

A tiny tremor went through the Countess, and she stared at N for a couple of seconds before mumbling, "No. You must have the wrong person."

"Ah, sorry about that. Bye now."

They left the rehearsal room and walked down the open-air corridor to the other end of the fourth floor. N stopped by the stone balustrade and pulled out the white smartphone, as if he were checking for messages. Four stories below them was a volleyball court, on which a group of girls in athletic gear were in the middle of a game.

"Did she do it?" asked Nga-Yee, having checked to make sure no one was around.

"No idea." He shrugged and slipped the phone back into his pocket.

"No idea? Then why did you let her go so quickly? You should have asked more questions!"

"No use." He crossed his arms, imitating the Countess's pose. "That girl's so guarded, we wouldn't have got past her defenses no matter what. And there were so many witnesses around, pestering her would probably have made things worse."

"What, then?"

"We'll have a chat with her another time, that's all."

"If she's being so careful, she might not even be willing to speak to us again."

"I promise you she will." N waved an object that looked like the condolence book, but Nga-Yee realized it was a *Merchant of Venice* script. In one corner were the words "Miranda Lai."

"You stole her script?"

"Nonsense. I'd put my things on the table, then I, uh, accidentally picked this up along with your sister's condolence book. I'm going to very thoughtfully come back here another day, and I'll insist on returning it to her in person." So even as Miranda was leading them to the corner, N had spotted her script on the table and planned this little trick. He must have carried out the switch when he was fumbling with his wallet. It was a slim booklet, only twenty or thirty pages, and easily picked up.

"Huh, she's playing Portia," N said, flicking through. "Seems quite serious. Look, she's made lots of notes next to all her speeches. I guess that means she'll be eager to get this back."

This sounded a little like extortion to Nga-Yee, but given the circumstances, it was probably the best thing to do—because she was now certain that the Countess was kidkit727.

"She actually shivered when you said Siu-Man's name, didn't she? When you threw that last question at her as we were walking away, even I could tell she had something to hide."

"You're right, but that can't be considered definitive evidence."

"That's not enough?"

"All right, you tell me why and I'll defend her. We'll see how conclusive your evidence actually is." N shut the script, stacked it with the other books, and looked up at her.

"She tried not to answer our questions and was hostile."

"Any fourteen-year-old is going to be a bit grumpy when a couple of adults they've never seen before come snooping around asking this and that."

"When you mentioned Siu-Man apologizing to her, she got quite agitated. Surely that's guilt?"

"There are other things she might be guilty of."

"When you asked who would have smeared Siu-Man's name, she ducked the question. That means she's the culprit."

"The school told the kids not to talk to anyone about this. Of course she wanted to keep her mouth shut. She doesn't know us. What if we told her teacher what she'd said? She'd be in big trouble. Enoch seems to enforce their rules quite strictly."

"Okay, fine, that all sounds plausible. But the biggest piece of evidence is that she lied about coming to the funeral parlor!" Nga-Yee flung this down as if it were her ace in the hole.

"How do you know it's not Kwok-Tai and Lily who're lying?"

Nga-Yee stared at him. After he'd explained about the karaoke lounge photo, she'd crossed Lily off her list of suspects. Surely no one who'd helped Siu-Man out of a bad situation could be so evil.

"You still think she's an accomplished actress?"

"We don't know," said N. "But she might be misleading us on purpose, so we can't trust what she says. Think about it. If you'd caused the death of a former friend, and that friend's family came by to ask questions, wouldn't you push the blame onto someone else as hard as you could? All the better if that person had already clashed with Siu-Man. Doesn't that make sense?"

"Well . . ." Nga-Yee couldn't refute this.

"That's just a supposition, of course. I can't prove or disprove that Lily or the Countess are kidkit727. All I'm saying is that it's too early to draw any conclusions."

Nga-Yee thought about it and nodded. She'd jumped the gun. Ever since stepping on campus, she felt a strange pressure growing inside her.

Was it too much for her to bear, being in the same space as the culprit?

"Let's go," said N. "We need to have one last chat today."

"Who's that?"

"Violet To, the other girl at the funeral. When you mentioned her name just now, Kwok-Tai seemed a little jumpy. Maybe something happened between her and your sister, and she might know more than she's letting on."

"I suppose you looked into her too? Where is she now? Which club?"

"Same as you."

"Huh?"

"She's a librarian."

The Enoch library was on the fifth floor of the west wing, right above the rehearsal room, and it took up half the floor. As they walked past the chemistry labs that made up the other half, Nga-Yee glanced at the long workbenches with their sinks and Bunsen burners, thinking back to her own school days. Their library had also been next to the labs.

As they walked into the library, Nga-Yee felt some of the tension drain from her. Here were wooden shelves with the marks of time on them, books neatly lined on the shelves and more on the trolley waiting to be shelved, all reassuringly familiar.

Perhaps because most of the students were busy with their various clubs, the library looked deserted, no one sitting at the tables or computer terminals. The only people around were a scrawny boy flipping through *Newton Science Magazine* and a long-haired girl behind the counter, reading a novel. Nga-Yee recognized her: Violet To.

"Hello there." N nodded to Violet in greeting. She looked up and seemed startled to see two adults walking in, but when she spotted their visitor tags, she turned as nonchalant as everyone else.

"Can I help you?" she asked politely. Her wispy voice, thick glasses, and slight hunchback made Nga-Yee suspect that she'd chosen the library because she wasn't particularly athletic. Reinforcing this impression was the blue sweater she wore, even though the air-conditioning wasn't particularly cold. Of course, Nga-Yee recalled, some of the more developed girls might cover up to avoid male attention. During her own adolescence Nga-Yee had too been busy helping her mother run the household and taking care of her little sister to worry what boys thought of her.

"Violet To? From three B? We're Au Siu-Man's family. This is her big sister."

The girl seemed shaken, and it took her a few seconds to stammer, "Hel—Hello."

"We had to pick up some of Siu-Man's things today and thought we'd take the opportunity to thank you for coming to the funeral."

"It's okay." Violet looked wary. "How did you know my name?"

"Not many of Siu-Man's schoolmates came. We described you to a couple of people, and they told us who you were right away." N made this sound perfectly plausible. "Were you close to Siu-Man? She didn't tell us much about school."

Nga-Yee wondered why he was taking such a different approach with her than he had with the Countess. He'd made Miranda believe that Siu-Man mentioned her all the time, and now he was doing the opposite with Violet. She turned it over in her mind: they'd known about Siu-Man's quarrel with the Countess, so it made sense to use that as an opening gambit. By contrast, they had no idea what Violet's relationship was with Siu-Man.

"Not very close." Violet shook her head. "She came to the library after class to do her homework, so we saw quite a lot of each other, but we hardly ever spoke. Still, when she passed away, I thought I should at least say goodbye."

"Thank you for the thought," said N, smiling warmly. "What was she like normally? Did she get on well with her classmates?"

"Um, okay, I guess. She didn't seem too badly affected by the—incident, but we may have avoided her a little because we didn't know how to talk about it. Then the—um—the next thing happened, and our teachers became even stricter about not letting us discuss it. After that, people stayed away from Siu-Man more."

"Did she still come to the library often?"

"I'm not sure, I'm not here every day . . . But whenever I was here, I did see her." Violet pointed at one of the long tables. "That was her regular seat."

For a moment Nga-Yee imagined Siu-Man slumped over the table, scribbling in her homework book with a ballpoint pen. Her posture had always been bad, and she would often sit with her nose practically pressed against the page. Nga-Yee had tried her best to correct this bad habit, but as soon as Siu-Man was distracted, she would fall back into it.

All kinds of memories tugged at Nga-Yee, and she could feel her heart churn. She was starting to realize how many moments she'd started to forget.

"Excuse me, could I get my phone?"

N and Nga-Yee turned to see the *Newton* magazine boy standing behind them.

"Sure." Violet took his student ID, scanned the bar code, and reached under the counter to hand him a phone. He thanked her and walked off, already swiping at the screen as he walked out the door.

"Students have to leave their phones behind the counter?" asked N.

"No. We provide a charging service." She pointed at a wooden rack behind the counter, with phone-size slots in it and a tangle of cables beside it. Most of these plugged into a gray power bank with a dozen USB ports, with one black charger standing on its own. "They installed one of these in every classroom for our tablets and phones. Later on, we got them in the library and club rooms as well."

"Oh, that's a good idea." N studied the wooden rack, apparently admiring it. "And it's linked to the student IDs so everyone gets the right phone back?"

"Yes. We're fully computerized here."

"You must know this program well, as the librarian," said N.

"It's much easier now than it used to be. We don't have to bother with stamped cards and so on. I heard that one time, a librarian set the stamp wrong, so all the books we lent out that day had the wrong due date. Now everyone just gets an email as soon as the book is borrowed, and when the book is due, they'll get a text message to remind them."

"That's convenient *and* environmentally friendly. But there must still be morons who don't understand technology and think stamped cards is simpler." N glanced mockingly at Nga-Yee. She bit her tongue, though she wanted to protest that she understood these systems just fine—it wasn't very different from what she did at her own library. It was only the internet, which seemed to change every single day, that confused her.

"Violet, do you know if there's anything Siu-Man wanted?" N got the conversation back on track. "We don't know if there was anything troubling her at school, and while we're here, we could help fulfill her final wishes."

Violet spent a few seconds thinking, but finally shook her head. "I don't know. I'm sorry. We really weren't that close."

"That's all right, don't worry about it," said N. "Siu-Man left very suddenly and was tormented by rumors beforehand, so we thought there might be something we could do for her now."

Violet said nothing, just nodded.

"Apparently your teachers said you weren't allowed to talk about these rumors, but I'm sure everyone did it secretly . . . Oh, did anyone in school particularly dislike Siu-Man?"

Violet looked at him blankly, nonplussed.

"I keep thinking she must have made an enemy, if someone wanted to blacken her name like that. All those lies—" N sighed. "If she really did offend someone, we'd need to find this person and thaw their heart. Only then will Siu-Man be able to rest in peace."

"Well . . ."

"Yes? You've thought of someone?"

"I can't be certain, but I think Lily Shu had some beef with her." Her voice shrank to a whisper—it seemed she wasn't happy speaking ill of her classmates. "They used to be good friends, the sort who hung out all the time, but then they suddenly stopped speaking."

"So you think Lily was the one spreading these rumors?"

"I don't know for sure, but I've seen a lot of friends turned enemies, and they do the most horrific things. These days, with the internet, it's so easy to twist the truth."

It was a shock to hear Lily's name, though of course N had warned Nga-Yee that she and Kwok-Tai might be the liars. Right away, her warm feelings and trust for Lily evaporated.

"You have a point," said N, looking sad. "She spent a lot of time in the library. Did you ever see her chatting with other classmates? Maybe I could speak to them too."

"She was always alone," said Violet. "Other people stay to do their homework here, but not many, and everyone keeps to themselves. The library's quiet after hours—people mostly come here to read magazines or to charge their phones once the classrooms are locked."

Nga-Yee understood how she felt. She was passionate about reading too, but most young people would rather read internet garbage than crack open a book. Some American institute did a study showing that the average person read fifty thousand words online each day—practically a whole novel.

"Could we have a look around the library? I'd like to see what Siu-Man's daily life was like."

"Of course."

N thanked Violet, then led Nga-Yee away from the counter as the girl went back to her book. Nga-Yee made a beeline for Siu-Man's usual seat and touched the table in front of it, as if she were standing by her sister's side. A buried memory surfaced: Nga-Yee at the folding table in their house, helping her eight-year-old sister with her homework.

A ringtone sliced through the silence, bringing Nga-Yee back to reality. She looked up to see N across the room, scrabbling for his phone.

"Sorry," he called to Violet before hurrying out the door. Nga-Yee wondered if she should follow, but he waved for her to stay. She'd never have expected N to pay attention to library rules, but then her eye landed on Violet and she realized he was still inhabiting the role of a nice guy related to Siu-Man—for social engineering purposes.

Now that she'd been roused, Nga-Yee didn't allow herself to sink back into her memories. She wasn't here to commemorate Siu-Man, but to find out the truth. She sat in Siu-Man's usual chair and looked all around. She'd vaguely expected to notice some kind of clue, but this seemed like a perfectly ordinary school library. The shelf closest to her had history and geography books, then language and literature below that, all arranged according to the Chinese library classification system. On the wall above the computers to her left was a poster for a "Secondary School Top Readers" competition, a list of magazine subscriptions, and news about recently acquired books. The only notice unrelated to the library was from the school admin, reminding students to exercise caution online, safeguard their passwords, and so on. Ultimately, though, it seemed unlikely that many students paid attention to these bits of paper, whether they were about "New Books" or "Web Safety."

Nga-Yee felt a sudden stab of loneliness. She thought about the hubbub as the volleyball team practiced, and the commotion in the rehearsal room. The stillness of the library made it feel removed from the world. Her solitude slowly froze over, squeezing the life from her body. Was it the library or the light streaming through the windows that made her feel this way? Or was it that she couldn't help thinking about Siu-Man?

Her sister had once sat right here, trying to escape everyone's notice, head bent over her books.

"Had enough? It's time to go."

She turned to see N behind her. She hadn't noticed him coming back in. She stood and said a silent goodbye to the spot.

"Thanks for your help, Violet. We're going," N called out. The girl put down her novel and nodded. Nga-Yee noticed the title—Kanae Minato's *Confessions*—and wondered if it was suitable for a fourteen-year-old.

"Do you think Violet was right, that Lily and Siu-Man were enemies? Could Lily be the culprit?" Nga-Yee asked as soon as they got to the staircase, where no one would hear them.

"You really are easily swayed, Miss Au," said N. "Violet told us your sister had a falling-out with a good friend. That doesn't make her friend a killer."

"Did you find any clues in there?"

"Yes, but not enough to draw conclusions, so there's no point telling you. What do you think?"

"About Violet To? I like her, to be honest—she's an introvert who enjoys reading. And I'm a librarian too, so we have that in common—"

"I'm not talking about the To girl." N stopped walking and turned to face her. "You met your sister's classmates today and heard how they felt about her. You walked through the same spaces that Siu-Man once did, sat where she sat, and saw what she saw. What do you think the difference is between the real Siu-Man and the one in your head?"

Nga-Yee didn't understand the question. "Siu-Man is Siu-Man, that's all."

"Forget it. Pretend I never asked." N pursed his lips, making it clear he didn't think it was worth explaining anything to her. He turned and stomped away. Nga-Yee had no idea what she'd said to get the cold shoulder. She could only silently curse this arrogant bastard.

"Do we need to meet anyone else? What about the other iPhone owners on the list?"

"No need. We're leaving now."

"The investigation's over?"

"It's continuing, but let's talk about it when we've gotten away from here."

"We should at least say goodbye to Miss Yuen—"

"No point. You want to tell her we're leaving? That's not going to make her happy, and she won't appreciate your good manners. Worst-case scenario, she might start wondering why we're still here and what we've been doing."

"Miss Yuen wouldn't—"

"Fine. You speak to that woman. I'm going home. Up to you whether you come with me."

Nga-Yee had to give in and follow him. The investigation was much more important to her than whether Miss Yuen thought her rude.

They returned their badges at the gate, then walked down Waterloo toward Nathan Road. N led the way. As Nga-Yee trotted behind him, she wanted to ask what their next step was, but she kept her mouth shut.

"Let's grab a coffee there." They were on Nathan Road, almost at the MTR station on Pitt Street, when N pointed at a sign up ahead: PISCES CAFÉ. This turned out to be on the second floor of a skyscraper. Rent was expensive in Yau Ma Tei and Mong Kok, and the only way an independent café could survive was to give up a street-level entrance. A sandwich board on the ground floor listed the opening hours, with an arrow telling them where to go. The coffee shop's logo was two fish in a green circle, suspiciously like the Starbucks mermaid, though it seemed unlikely that anyone would mistake this place for the global chain.

They went up the stairs. Inside, the furniture and color scheme were also Starbucks rip-offs, down to the self-service counter.

"Medium iced latte," said N to the barista. He didn't ask Nga-Yee what she wanted, but by this time she hadn't expected it. She glanced at the menu and blanched at the prices: coffees started at thirty dollars, and even the cheapest item, a cup of tea, would cost her twenty. She was still living on the eight-hundred-dollar loan from Wendy, but she wanted to find out more from N, so had no choice but to stump up twenty dollars for a cup of tea that couldn't have cost more than two to brew.

It was still before three o'clock, so the coffee shop was mostly empty. N brought his iced latte to a corner table, and Nga-Yee followed with her hot beverage.

"Okay, now can you tell me if we're done for the day?" she asked urgently.

N chewed on his straw and took a sip of latte, then pulled the white phone from his pocket. As he tapped at it, he said, "I didn't tell you before, but there's another reason we were at the school."

"What's that?"

"To make sure that kidkit727 is one of your sister's schoolmates."

"Hadn't you already deduced that?"

"That was just a deduction. I'm talking about evidence now." He looked up. "Conclusive evidence. Remember what I said before, about the emails kidkit727 sent from MTR stations?"

"Yes, those things—what do you call them?—IP addresses."

"And I told you an IP address is like your queue number at the bank or hospital. You have to get one each time you go in. Remember?"

Nga-Yee nodded.

"So when you get online using Wi-Fi, another string of numbers gets recorded by the provider. To go on with the bank analogy, that's like having to produce your ID to prove you're who you say you are, and only then will they give you a queue number—or IP address."

"ID?"

"Yes, a number that's unique to you." N pointed at the phone in his hand, then at the public telephone by the counter. "Every device with Wi-Fi capability has a media access control address, or MAC for short, assigned by the manufacturer. To put it simply, there are ten million smartphones in use in Hong Kong, which means there are ten million MAC addresses. Like human fingerprints, no two can be identical."

"What does that mean?"

"When I was looking up the IP addresses kidkit727 used to get online, I also found out the iPhone's MAC address: 3E06B2A252F3." N rattled off the numbers and letters without blinking.

"3E—"

"3E06B2A252F3. In theory, all we have to do is find an iPhone with this MAC address, and we've found kidkit727."

Nga-Yee almost jumped to her feet. "Then let's go back to the school right away and look up the MAC addresses of all eighteen iPhone users!"

"Already done."

"And?"

"First, let me give you a lesson about wireless technology. Do you know what Wi-Fi is?"

"It lets a tablet or phone get online without being plugged in," said Nga-Yee. After N told her that Siu-Man had been sent those emails over Wi-Fi, she'd found a book in the library with a simple explanation of this technology. Unlike most people, she still preferred getting her information from books.

"When you press the button telling your phone or tablet to connect to the Wi-Fi, what happens?"

Nga-Yee stared at him. The book had only talked about how to use it.

"I knew you'd have no idea. But to be honest, most smartphone users don't know either. All they need to do is pick out the right network from a list and click on it." N gestured at a sign behind the counter. "Can you read what that says?"

Nga-Yee turned her head. FREE WI-FI, read the sign, and below it, ID: PISCESFREEWIFI.

N placed Siu-Man's phone on the table and pulled up a list: CSL, Y5Zone, Alan_Xiaomi, and so on. Next to "PiscesFreeWiFi" it said "Already connected."

"These others are nearby networks. Think of them as overhead cables that all connect to fiber-optic lines underground. Your phone connects to the network, which connects to the fiber-optic line beneath the ground. With me so far?"

Nga-Yee nodded.

"This is the bit most people don't notice. Why do you think all these names appear? CSL, Y5Zone, and so on?"

"The phone gets them from somewhere? Like a radio picks up certain stations?"

"Half right. The networks send out their own names and other data, and when your phone is within range, they'll connect. The part you got wrong is that your phone is also sending out signals all the time, and even if you aren't online, it still exchanges data with nearby networks."

"Huh? Doesn't that only happen when you tell it to connect?"

"No. The machines already exchange quite a bit of information before you get to that point. And even if it's already connected to a network, it still sends out a signal from time to time, to see what else is out there. That's known as a probe request. It's like saying, 'Hi, I'm a cell phone, are there any networks I can talk to?' When the networks hear this, they send out a probe response: 'Hi, I'm PiscesFreeWiFi, I'm available.' And that's why its name appears on your phone."

"Okay, I get it now. But why do I need to know all this?"

N put the little white phone on the table next to Siu-Man's red one. "While we were at the school, I set my phone to be a hot spot the whole time, so it made a record of all the probe requests around it. Oh, I forgot to say: one of the pieces of information collected by a probe request is the device's MAC address."

Nga-Yee looked at the rows of text on the white phone's screen. One of them had been highlighted: "3E:06:B2:A2:52:F3."

"We walked right past kidkit727's cell phone earlier today," said N simply.

"Was it Lil—Lily?" Nga-Yee stuttered. She thought about the iPhone on the cafeteria table.

"Going by the time log, the MAC address was picked up starting when we met Lily at her classroom. But that doesn't mean it was her. It could have been someone else around there, or even someone upstairs or downstairs—Wi-Fi signals can pass through walls and ceilings."

Nga-Yee realized what N was hinting at. All three iPhone-owning suspects had been within range the whole time: the Countess in the fourth-floor rehearsal room, Violet To in the fifth-floor library. Perhaps they'd been in the cafeteria too, even if Nga-Yee hadn't noticed them. And with volleyball practice taking place on the ground floor, Lily's phone would have been in the vicinity.

"So our suspects are Lily, Violet, and the Countess."

"Not necessarily, but I first picked up the signal in the classroom, so we need to focus on your sister's classmates."

"Why not necessarily?"

"Two reasons." N took a mouthful of his latte. "First, we can't eliminate the possibility that kidkit727 just happened to be somewhere else in the west wing. It doesn't make sense to restrict ourselves to the suspects we've already spoken to."

Nga-Yee nodded, though she still thought it was probably one of those three.

"Second, not to pour cold water on this idea"—N smiled grimly—"MAC addresses aren't like fingerprints. They can be changed."

"Oh?"

"As long as you have the right software, you can alter your MAC address. Given the way the iPhone 5S is set up to be compatible with iOS 8, you could make your phone send out a random fake MAC address to probe requests and use the real one only when it's actually connecting to Wi-Fi. Apple says they enable this to protect their customers' privacy, but many of their rivals think it's just another way of giving them a monopoly over data."

"So today was a waste of time," said Nga-Yee.

"No, no, no," said N, flashing a smile at her. "Just picking up 3E06B2A252F3 at the school takes us a big step ahead. Even if a new iPhone was sending out a decoy MAC address, the chances of randomly generating this particular one are one in 280 trillion. In other words, impossible."

"But you just said it could also be changed deliberately."

"Yes. Remember, our main enemy is the Rat, who's hiding behind Little Seven as he helps her with his tech knowledge. He could be trying to lead the investigation in the wrong direction by showing Little Seven how to use a fake MAC address when she sent those messages to your sister, the same way she made use of the MTR station Wi-Fi. These programs are easy to use. With the right guidance, even you could learn how in five minutes."

"So I was right?" asked Nga-Yee, puzzled.

"You still don't understand. We're facing two possibilities now: if the Rat didn't help Little Seven disguise her MAC address, then we can identify Little Seven from her phone."

"And if he did?"

"Then Little Seven is trying to frame whoever has the 3E06B2A252F3 phone—otherwise why not just use a random number?"

Nga-Yee understood. "So, no matter what, we have to track down the owner of that 3E-whatever phone. Either that's our culprit, or it's someone our culprit wants to set up."

"You're not wrong, though there is another method I want to try."

"What's that?"

"How many times have I told you, Miss Au, don't ask about my methods. I guarantee you'll be happy with the results, and that's all you need to know."

Nga-Yee pouted, taking a mouthful of her now-cold tea.

N stroked his chin for a few seconds. "Let's broaden your horizons a little. Watch this."

Nga-Yee looked where he was pointing. A couple of tables away, a woman of about twenty was surfing the net. She was facing away from them, and Nga-Yee could see the screen of her tablet over her shoulder.

"Watch what?"

N gently pushed the white phone, and a small keyboard popped out one side of it. So that's why it was so thick. N's thumbs flew across the keys.

"Dog, cat, or rabbit?" he said, still jabbing away.

"What?"

"Choose one. Dog, cat, or rabbit."

"Rabbit, I guess."

"Look at her screen."

The woman clicked on a link on her news site, and Nga-Yee almost spat out her tea.

Filling the screen was a picture of a white rabbit, with the headline DISCOVERED IN ENGLAND: KILLER RABBIT GUARDING THE HOLY GRAIL.

The woman seemed surprised. She flicked her finger across the screen and returned to the previous page. When she clicked on the link again, the rabbit no longer appeared.

Nga-Yee turned back to N, who was grinning smugly. He showed her what was on the white phone's screen: the same rabbit.

"You hacked into her tablet?"

"Of course."

"Just like that?"

"That's all there is to it."

"Is that really possible?" Nga-Yee thought of what she'd seen in movies: hackers with all sorts of equipment physically breaking into server rooms and messing around with cables.

"Free public Wi-Fi is full of vulnerable spots. More important, people don't have any sense of self-preservation these days. You're actually better off because you know you're ignorant. Most people think they can use technology, but their devices are much more powerful than they imagine."

"What's wrong with Wi-Fi?" What N just did still looked like a magic trick to her.

"Guess how I did that?"

"You're controlling her tablet!"

"Nope." N pointed at the PiscesFreeWiFi sign on the counter. "I'm controlling the Wi-Fi network she's connected to."

"Huh?"

"This is known as a man-in-the-middle attack, or MITM for short. Hacking techniques are actually simple. Just a sort of third-rate magic trick. But because there's a layer of science over the top, people think it's complex." N glanced over at the woman with the laptop. "I got my phone to pretend to be PiscesFreeWiFi. My signal was stronger than the shop's router, so her tablet jumped to my network. At the same time, I connected to the real PiscesFreeWiFi, turning myself into an invisible go-between. Do you know what your computer does when you surf to a web page?"

Nga-Yee shook her head.

"To put it as simply as I can, when you type in an address, your computer sends out a request to the remote server, which sends the right words and images to your computer. And it's the Wi-Fi network that makes the connection between them. It's like when you're at the library and someone wants to borrow a Harry Potter book. They ask for it at the counter, and you get it from the shelf for them. You're the Wi-Fi in that scenario."

This analogy made sense to Nga-Yee—after all, that's what she did all day long.

"What I've just done is to put on a librarian badge and set up a fake counter by the entrance. Customers think I'm the real thing, so they ask me for the Harry Potter book. I take off my badge, go to the real counter, and ask you for the book. You give it to me, and I pass it on. Neither you nor the borrower would notice that anything was wrong."

"But you've found out that this person wanted a Harry Potter book."

"Yes. It's a complete infringement of the customer's privacy. And if I wanted to make trouble, I could take a Harry Potter dust jacket and put it on a copy of *The 120 Days of Sodom . . .*"

Nga-Yee knew where this was going. When the woman with the tablet clicked on the link earlier, N had intercepted the request and sent her something about killer rabbits instead. In this example, if the borrower had never read any of the other books in the series, they might end up believing the Harry Potter novels were set not in Hogwarts School, but amid the perversions of Château de Silling. What's more, she realized, if the fake news had been something less obviously ridiculous than a killer rabbit, the woman would never have noticed, but simply taken it as the truth.

"Oh!" Nga-Yee exclaimed. Lowering her voice, she went on. "If she'd been doing online banking, you could have gotten her log-in and password or tricked her into transferring money to you."

"There'd be a few more steps if it were a bank—you'd need a fake home page to bypass verification—but you're basically right. Give me ten minutes, and I could find out that woman's name, address, job, relationship status, recent worries, bra size, and so on. Give me an hour, and I'd find a way to shape her mind or change her behavior. That's why I said not knowing anything about computers can be a plus. At least you don't need to worry that people will discover your fetishes by seeing what specialized sex toys you buy online."

Nga-Yee felt a chill go down her spine. She'd known there were issues with privacy online, but had still assumed that what happened to Siu-Man was out of the ordinary. Now N was showing her how people might think they were unobserved, not understanding that the walls around them were made of glass and any number of eyes could watch their most intimate moments.

Watching N sip his iced latte without any sign of concern gave Nga-Yee goose bumps. How many of her own secrets had he uncovered? She didn't visit many websites, and still he'd known the exact amount of money she had in her bank account, as well as her work schedule and god knows what else. As far as he was concerned, she was an open book.

The only crumb of comfort was that this terrifying man was on her side.

N abruptly reached out to grab Siu-Man's phone, along with the white hacker one, both of which vanished back into his pocket. Nga-Yee didn't know what he was up to, but now his expression was changing too, back to the warm smile he'd used at the school.

"Remember, don't butt in."

With that, N half stood and waved at someone just entering the coffee shop. Nga-Yee turned and was startled to see Kwok-Tai striding toward them.

"Hello, Mr. Ong, Ms. Au," he said politely, putting his bag down. "I'll go get a coffee."

N nodded. While Kwok-Tai was at the counter, Nga-Yee hurriedly leaned over to N and hissed, "What's he doing here? How come he's acting like we have an appointment?"

"Remember when I said we'll have to wait for the next opportunity?" N grinned. "I left the door open to make up for your blunder, though I didn't expect it to be this soon."

Nga-Yee recalled him giving Kwok-Tai and Lily his phone number in the cafeteria.

"Ah! So when your phone rang in the library, that was him?"

"He said he'd meet us here. Apparently he has more to tell us about your sister."

How annoying that N hadn't bothered telling her, Nga-Yee thought. If she'd lost her temper earlier and gone off, he would have met Kwok-Tai on his own and she'd never have found out.

"Don't butt in," said N, shutting her up as Kwok-Tai slid into his seat, clutching an iced coffee.

"Not eating anything?" N asked. "When I was your age, I was always so hungry after school, I could have eaten a horse."

"No, I don't—don't feel hungry," said Kwok-Tai, forcing a smile.

He took a sip of his coffee and looked down, clearly wanting to speak, but not knowing how to start. After a long while he turned to Nga-Yee and asked, "Siu-Man . . . Did she ever mention me?"

Before Nga-Yee could figure out how to answer that, N had jumped in. "No."

"I guess she still hadn't forgiven me." Sorrow was written across Kwok-Tai's face.

"Did something happen between the two of you?"

"We, um, dated for a short while," said Kwok-Tai. "Broke up after a couple of weeks."

Nga-Yee couldn't believe her ears. Her sister, dating? So Miss Yuen was right—Siu-Man had relationship issues. Yet Nga-Yee had never noticed any signs that she was seeing someone. Worse, did this mean that kidkit727's accusation was true? Had she stolen someone else's boyfriend? And did that mean the other things—selling herself, taking drugs—had also happened?

"How did it start?" N asked.

"Lily and I were classmates in primary school, and we lived near each other, so we were always playmates." Kwok-Tai's voice was level, but his features were etched with pain. "Siu-Man was Lily's classmate in year one. In fact, their desks were next to each other, and after a while they became close friends. So I saw a lot of Siu-Man too. The three of us got together in this coffee shop every Friday after class, just to hang out and drink tea. Sometimes we'd go strolling around Mong Kok afterward. That was a fun time. We saw quite a lot of each other during the summer vacation as well. Then I . . . I started falling for Siu-Man."

Nga-Yee tried hard to remember, but she had no idea what Siu-Man had gotten up to the previous summer. She worked at the Central Library, so summer was her busiest time. Not only were students free, working folk borrowed more books too, and the elderly came by to enjoy the free air-conditioning. She and her coworkers all had their breaks cut short. She really couldn't say whether Siu-Man had gone out a lot then; she'd been too tired to say much to her sister and mother when she got home. In fact, she was now startled to discover, her memory of this time was an almost complete blank. Each day she went through the ritual of getting out of bed, going to work, returning home in time for dinner with her family, reading a few pages of a novel, then sleep. A monotonous, repetitive life, doing nothing but turning her time into money. Her sole aim was to increase her bank balance to support her family; nothing else mattered.

"In year two, Lily got on the volleyball team and had to practice after school, so it was just me and Siu-Man hanging out. I think it was November when I told her that I had feelings for her. She was surprised, but the next day she agreed to go out with me," Kwok-Tai went on. "I was the happiest guy in the world until she ghosted me a week later. I thought I must have said or done something wrong, but she wouldn't tell me anything. Two weeks later, she finally got in touch to say we should break up because we were too different. I couldn't understand. When I tried to change her mind, she got really scary."

"Scary how?"

"I felt as if she hated me from the bottom of her heart. I'd never seen her face like that. Finally I couldn't stand it, so I just shouted at her for messing around with my feelings. And that was that."

"She never forgave you because of this?"

"No, no." Kwok-Tai shook his head in misery. "That was nothing. Just me being stupid. Afterward, Siu-Man also stopped talking to Lily. I was so lost, but Lily kept trying to cheer me up . . . and so I started dating her."

Nga-Yee had been thinking what a dependable boyfriend a guy like Kwok-Tai would have been, but after hearing this, she had to revise her opinion. How could he have gotten together with another girl so soon after breaking up with her sister? Then again, perhaps it was Nga-Yee herself who was behind the times—for all she knew, teenagers these days were all into these fast-food romances, and Kwok-Tai was a good guy for only dating them one at a time.

"Are you and Lily still together?" asked N.

"Yes, though there was a rough patch. That's when I found out what was really going on." Kwok-Tai sighed. "Last May, something seemed off with Siu-Man. I asked our teacher, and found out that her mother had just died. It felt like the right time to put aside the past. I'd promised Lily I wouldn't fall for her again, but at a time like this, she'd need her friends' support. I told Lily we should make amends, but she refused. I thought she was still upset that Siu-Man had hurt me. I didn't know the half of it."

"Something happened between Siu-Man and Lily?" N ventured.

"You guessed it. I was a real idiot." Kwok-Tai grimaced. "I kept asking Lily, until finally she had to tell me: Siu-Man had told Lily she'd agreed to go out with me. I had no idea, but Lily had liked me since we were kids. She went wild—lashed out and accused Siu-Man of stealing her true love. She told her she wouldn't be friends with someone like that. Siu-Man broke up with me not long afterward. That's the real reason those two stopped speaking. When I found out, I didn't know what to do. In the end, I decided to stay with Lily and let them go on ignoring each other."

This might seem like three kids playing house, but Nga-Yee understood how hard it must have been. Fourteen-year-olds get worked up over the slightest thing, and it wouldn't take much to rip apart their fragile friendships. Lily must have wanted to come clean over lunch, but Kwok-Tai had stopped her, probably out of fear that she'd get yelled at. Instead, he'd arranged to meet N in private.

"When Siu-Man died so suddenly, you must have felt a lot of regret," said N. There was no blame in his voice.

Kwok-Tai nodded. His eyes had reddened.

"When neither of you brought it up today, I guessed Siu-Man never even told you we were dating. That just made me sadder. Shout at me if you like, but please don't blame Lily. It was my fault—I should have seen what was going on with them. And we didn't reach out to her when she needed us most. That was— that was my fault too."

A tear rolled down his cheek, and he started to sob. Nga-Yee didn't know what to do until N nudged her and pointed at her handbag, and she reached into it and handed him a Kleenex. He looked so woeful that Nga-Yee was seized with an urge to tell him it really wasn't his fault, that the person responsible for Siu-Man's death was someone named kidkit727.

Kwok-Tai dried his tears, and the three of them were silent for a while. Nga-Yee was holding her tongue because N had ordered her to. His silence was probably more strategic: allowing Kwok-Tai to recover, so the interrogation could continue.

"Kwok-Tai," said N a moment before the lack of conversation started feeling weird, "you said Lily made you promise not to care for Siu-Man *again*. Does that mean you tried to do something else for her after you'd started dating Lily?"

The boy froze for a second, then nodded. "Yes. It was a dangerous situation, so I couldn't care too much about what Lily thought."

"Are you talking about what happened at the karaoke lounge on Christmas Eve?"

"You know about that?" Kwok-Tai stared at him. "Did Siu-Man tell you? I thought she wouldn't say anything, especially since she probably didn't even know what was going on."

"She didn't. I happened to find out some details, and guessed the rest. We aren't sure what actually happened to her, though."

Kwok-Tai glanced at N and then Nga-Yee. After hesitating a long while, he bit his lip and said, "You already know we were dating, so I guess it can't hurt to tell you the rest."

Nga-Yee swallowed.

"It was December twenty-fourth, the year before last. I'd thought I would be spending the holidays with Siu-Man, but ended up with Lily instead." Kwok-Tai spoke very slowly, as if reluctant to return to that awkward triangle. "I hated myself. Even when I was on a date with Lily, I'd still be thinking about Siu-Man. I felt like scum. That evening, Lily and I were out shopping. We'd planned to have dinner at a Japanese restaurant, but on our way there, we bumped into an older schoolmate from my band. He mentioned Siu-Man."

"He knew her too?"

"Not really, but Lily and Siu-Man sometimes came to watch band practice, so he knew we were good friends . . . Of course he had no idea about all the trouble. He told us as he was walking past Langham Place earlier, he passed a large group of people including Siu-Man. A couple of those guys were notorious for being in bands just to score with women—they were terrible musicians. Rumor was that they would persuade young girls to be escorts—"

Those last two words reminded Nga-Yee of the accusation.

"Did Siu-Man know them?" asked N.

"I don't know." Kwok-Tai frowned, clearly suffering. "I'd never have believed Siu-Man would ever hang out with them, and yet . . . I felt uneasy all the way through dinner, so I called Siu-Man while Lily was in the bathroom. She only answered the second time, and I couldn't get any sense out of her—she was slurring her words. I could tell from the background noise that she was in a karaoke place."

"Was Lily there when your bandmate told you about what he saw?"

"Yes, she heard everything."

"Didn't it bother her?"

"This wasn't long after they fell out, so we never talked about Siu-Man. When my bandmate mentioned her, it was a bit awkward, so we continued with our evening as if nothing had happened. But I could tell she was worried too—she didn't even finish her favorite uni sushi."

"So after you spoke to Siu-Man on the phone, you told Lily the two of you had to go get her?"

Kwok-Tai nodded. "She sounded so strange. I thought Lily would say no, but she agreed. All she said was, 'But this is the last time you see her.' We quickly paid the bill and hurried over to the karaoke bar at King Wah Centre."

N raised an eyebrow. "How did you know that's where the she was?"

"When Siu-Man called, the song in the background was the new Andy Hui hit. I knew only one karaoke chain had the rights to that, and their only Mong Kok branch was in King Wah Centre."

N's mouth turned up appreciatively. "Did you find her there?"

"No—much worse." Kwok-Tai sighed. "We got there around ten thirty and saw Siu-Man on the street outside. She was being carried along by two men, heading toward Sai Yeung Choi Street. I ran over to stop them, and those two bastards had the nerve to warn me not to make trouble. So I shouted that she was underage, and when passersby turned to look at us, they abandoned Siu-Man and ran away."

"What state was she in?"

"Dazed, like she'd been drugged." Kwok-Tai sounded like he was still angry.

"Thank goodness you were there. If you'd been a minute later, god knows where they'd have brought her," said N approvingly. "Then you and Lily brought Siu-Man home?"

"Yes. We sat in McDonald's for a while so she could sober up, then got a taxi to Wun Wah House. She was a bit more clearheaded in the car, and she muttered something it took me a while to make out: 'Don't tell my mom.' That's why I made up that story about Siu-Man feeling ill at a party."

Finally knowing the truth swamped Nga-Yee with conflicting emotions: gratitude that Kwok-Tai was there to rescue her, worry at the thought of the horrors she might have suffered in the bar. And, she abruptly realized, her mother might have figured out the whole thing. She'd taken care of Siu-Man all night long, and someone who'd lived as much life as Chau Yee-Chin wasn't easily fooled.

"Does anyone know about this apart from you and Lily?" Now N had got to the heart of the matter. Nga-Yee pricked up her ears and waited anxiously for the answer. If Kwok-Tai said no, then Lily became a much stronger suspect.

"Uh—that was actually unfortunate." Kwok-Tai looked nervously at N. "No one was supposed to find out, but I started hearing rumors that a girl from our school had been assaulted on Christmas Eve. The older kids were talking about it a lot. No one named the girl, so our teachers didn't do anything about it, just got the principal to say something about watching our words and behavior—the usual. I asked my bandmate, and apparently one of those thugs had a cousin in our school. All the gossip was coming from him."

Nga-Yee's heart sank, but N nodded a little, as if he'd been expecting this answer.

"Mr. Ong, Ms. Au, when you thanked Lily and me today for coming to the funeral, I felt so guilty. We let her down so badly, and we owe her so much." Kwok-Tai grimaced. "We didn't comfort her when she lost her mother. We weren't with her when she got groped on the MTR. We didn't stand up for her when she got slammed on the internet. We only thought about ourselves. It was too awkward, too much had happened between us. And now we've lost our chance to make up. We weren't fit to be her friends. You shouldn't thank us."

"Kwok-Tai, it's in the past. Don't give yourself a hard time," Nga-Yee blurted out, breaking her vow of silence. She couldn't help it, the boy looked like he was about to burst into tears. "Thank you for your courage, telling us all this today. I'm sure Siu-Man wouldn't blame you if she could hear. Please take care of yourself, and of Lily. That would please Siu-Man too."

"But—" He was such a ball of tension, he hadn't taken in a single one of Nga-Yee's clichés.

"If you really think you let Siu-Man down, then you'll have to live with that guilt forever."

N's words startled Nga-Yee, and Kwok-Tai gaped, wondering why kindly Mr. Ong had suddenly turned so harsh.

"Human beings are such forgetful, selfish creatures." N's voice was calm, and his expression hadn't changed, but Nga-Yee could tell he'd dropped the mask. "Asking for forgiveness is just another self-interested thing to do. You receive absolution, and you can move on. But in the end, it's just hypocrisy. If you think Siu-Man wouldn't have forgiven you, you can bear that guilt for the rest of your life. Every single moment, you'll have to live with the knowledge that you treated a good friend terribly and there's no way to make up for it, not ever. But remember, you have a duty to use your life well. Only by listening to your innermost self and making the right choice can you whittle away at your pain and redeem yourself. This guilt will become your very flesh, and also the proof that you're a good person."

Kwok-Tai's frown faded, and he nodded vigorously. "I understand, Mr. Ong. Thank you."

"As long as you understand." N smiled, easygoing again. He sipped his latte. Nga-Yee had always thought he was full of nonsense, but what he'd just said—well, she wasn't sure if it was sense or nonsense, but it was undeniably more powerful than what she'd come up with.

"Oh yes." N put down his cup. "One more thing. Do you know Violet To?"

"Sure, she's in my class." Kwok-Tai's face sank, as if N had stabbed him.

"When we mentioned her name in the cafeteria, you looked like you wanted to say something," said N lightly. "I thought it was odd, that's all."

"Mr. Ong, when you asked who would have hated Siu-Man enough to smear her name, Lily said the Countess, but I think it's Violet you should have your eye on. The Countess and her handmaidens are big talkers, but if you're looking for the sort of busybody who'd go behind someone's back, Violet's at the top of that list."

"What happened between her and Siu-Man?" N asked.

"Nothing. But she has a history."

"What did she do?"

"It started in year one." Kwok-Tai looked a little mollified. "I was in one B, while Siu-Man and Lily were both in one A. Violet was the student aide. There was a girl in one A called Laura who was very popular—she was so nice, and her grades were good. Quite a few of the guys in my class had crushes on her, but she turned them all down. There was a rumor that she was dating an upperclassman, possibly someone on the basketball team or the debate captain."

Dating in year one! Nga-Yee marveled at how quickly young people were growing up.

"Then . . . It was sometime in our second semester, maybe around May. A teacher caught Laura in an, uh, intimate situation on the rooftop, with an older student. This became a big incident, and Laura was forced to 'voluntarily withdraw from school.' The other student was just waiting to graduate after finals, so there was nothing they could do."

"Didn't they make a police report?" said N. "Even if she consented, a thirteen-year-old is still considered a child. That's assault."

"No, because the school didn't want a scandal. Anyway it wasn't assault. From what I heard, it was just a bit of kissing."

"What's so scandalous about a bit of kissing?" N asked, puzzled.

"The other student was a girl," said Kwok-Tai. "We're a mission school, and in some ways it's still very conservative."

"What did Violet To have to do with this?" asked N.

"She was the one who told the teacher," said Kwok-Tai angrily. "I had to hand in some homework in the teacher's room, and while I was there I saw Violet talking to the discipline master in one corner. They looked very serious, and I heard him ask her, 'Did you see this with your own eyes?' 'Yes.' 'On the rooftop?' 'That's right.' I didn't know what they were talking about at the time, but when it all came out the next day, it was obvious what had happened. Apparently the discipline master interrogated Laura as if she were a criminal and called her some terrible names. We were all disgusted. Don't they know it's the twenty-first century? Some countries even have same-sex marriage these days! Isn't this an abuse of human rights? But it wasn't just the teacher we were angry with—we hated Violet To even more."

"So that's why you think Violet is more likely to have destroyed someone's reputation than the Countess—she'd already done it once?" said N.

"Exactly."

"But she hadn't fought with Siu-Man, had she? At least the Countess had a reason to be upset with her, after the Disneyland incident."

"Laura hadn't done anything to Violet," said Kwok-Tai. "I saw on TV that there's a sort of person who thinks they're standing up for justice and righteousness, but actually they're just moral extremists who want to get rid of everything they consider sinful. She probably thought Laura deserved a death sentence for kissing another girl. She must have somehow found out that the girl in the Christmas Eve scandal was Siu-Man, and she got a one-sided version of the story that made her think Siu-Man was hanging out with gangsters or something. That's why she started the rumors."

"What happened to Laura? Have you heard anything from her?"

"I think she ended up transferring to a school in Australia. Her parents are quite wealthy, so they sent her out of the country to keep her away from the older girl."

Nga-Yee hadn't expected such a dramatic story, but then she hadn't imagined that the bookish Violet To would turn into such a moral crusader. When Kwok-Tai mentioned "far worse people" than the Countess, he must have had Violet in mind.

"That's why I was so surprised when you said Violet was at Siu-Man's funeral," Kwok-Tai went on. "She doesn't normally care about anyone else, so why would she show up? Crocodile tears?"

"Lily says it's the Countess, you say it's Violet. But those are both guesses, right?" said N.

"Well, yes . . ."

"Thank you for telling us so much." N smiled. "Never mind why Violet and the Countess showed up. It was still just the handful of you who came to say goodbye to Siu-Man. That must be a kind of fate. Siu-Man might have left us, but she'll always live on in our hearts."

Nga-Yee nodded in agreement, even though she knew N was getting at something else. Siu-Man probably lived on in kidkit727's eart as well—but as an object of hatred.

Kwok-Tai said goodbye around 4:15. Volleyball practice ended at half past, and he had to head back to the school to meet Lily.

"I'm afraid her imagination will run wild," he said as he went. It was clear he was referring to their meeting earlier that day.

As Nga-Yee watched Kwok-Tai leave the coffee shop, her brain was a whirl of confusion. At the school, she'd been certain at several moments that one person or another must be kidkit727, but now she had no idea: everyone seemed suspect. Countess Miranda Lai acted guilty and was hostile to N and Nga-Yee; Lily could be the culprit, because hate is the flip side of love, and losing a good friend—especially over a boy—could make someone do terrible things; then there was Violet To. Might this mild-mannered librarian have a secret, terrifying side? And of course it could be someone else altogether—only circumstantial evidence had made them narrow the field of suspects to three.

"How much longer do you want to stay? We're done for today. I'm going home," said N, looking unconcerned, standing up.

"That's it? Shouldn't we keep investigating?"

"My dear Miss Au, it's a good thing you don't run a company. Your employees would surely be worked to death." N did a little stretch. "You only paid me eighty grand. That doesn't entitle you to all my time."

"But you haven't come up with any answers—"

"You want answers? I'm ninety percent certain that one of the people we spoke to today is the one we're looking for. Don't ask why. Until I get my hands on conclusive evidence, I'm not going to show my cards."

Nga-Yee had no idea whether he was serious or if this was just something to fob her off.

"But—"

"I have to leave now, otherwise Barbara might die."

"Who's Barbara?"

"My sacred lily—I forgot to water her this morning. I'll be back in touch if there's any progress." N walked out of the coffee shop without a second look. Was he looking for an excuse to flee? She remembered the evergreen plant in his window, which definitely hadn't looked fragile enough to die from missing a single day's watering. More crucially, N didn't seem like the sort of person who would name a houseplant Barbara.

It was only when Nga-Yee got home that she realized N had gone off with everything they got from the school, including

Siu-Man's textbooks and homework, plus the condolence book and the script he stole from the Countess. She didn't mind, because all that stuff had only been an excuse to get onto the premises. She sat down at her computer and opened a browser window to look up Lily, the Countess, and Violet once more. With luck and a closer look at their social media pages, she might be able to find more clues.

Lily's Facebook page was mostly posts about One Direction—Nga-Yee had ignored these in her previous investigation—and food pictures, quite a few of Japanese cuisine, probably from dates with Kwok-Tai. Nga-Yee had never understood the point of photographing your dinner, but everyone around her seemed to be doing it. The Countess had filled her Facebook with selfies, as if she were a celebrity, and every one of her pictures had hundreds more likes than Lily's; the captions below each image were peppered with cutesy emojis, although Nga-Yee had trouble imagining the surly girl they'd met actually speaking like this in real life. Violet only had a book blog. Nga-Yee had skipped this the first time around because it didn't seem to contain any personal information; now she went through it, but all she learned was that Violet enjoyed reading Haruki Murakami, Eileen Chang, Carlos Ruiz Zafón, and Gillian Flynn. These short reviews didn't seem to contain any information connected to Siu-Man.

Although N had said he'd be in touch if there was any progress, Nga-Yee started getting antsy after a couple of days. She was distracted at work, her head filled with thoughts about Lily and the others. She chewed over N's words, wondering if he was trying to mislead her when he'd said the culprit was someone they'd spoken to that day: that wouldn't be only the three girls, but also Miss Yuen and Kwok-Tai, not to mention the attendant in the cafeteria, the student actors, the magazine-reading boy in the library, or maybe even the woman whose tablet N hacked in the café. Could any of them be kidkit727? Nga-Yee grew more and more confused and longed for N to put her out of her misery, but there was not a peep from him. She had an early shift on Wednesday, and when she got out of work, she boarded the tram without even thinking about it, heading to N's flat.

By the time she got to Central, she'd had second thoughts.

Losing Siu-Man might have thrown her off-kilter, but despite her constant unease, Nga-Yee was rational down to her bones. She understood that some things can't be rushed, and she couldn't forget how she almost ruined the investigation by not following N's orders in the cafeteria. Maybe she ought to trust N and let him get on with it.

As she wrestled with her thoughts, the tram reached Sai Ying Pun. Reason won out in the end, and she got off at Whitty Street instead of going on to Second.

I've come all the way here, I might as well have dinner, she thought, recalling the delicious wonton noodles at Loi's—one of the few tasty meals she'd had recently, now that she was on such a tight budget. She looked in her wallet to make sure she had enough to get through the next week, then went across the road to the restaurant.

Nga-Yee chose a counter seat. There were no other customers, and the owner had been watching the news on a tiny TV screen. "Hi. A small bowl of wonton noodles, please."

"Sure, small wonton noodles coming up." He went over to the stove to start cooking, then turned back to add, "Don't you need to get something for N too?"

Nga-Yee groaned inwardly, then thought that she could take the opportunity to correct the earlier misunderstanding.

"No. Just me today. I'm not really friends with N, we were just working together on something."

"Working together, are you?" He swirled the noodles in the boiling water for less than twenty seconds before plunging them into a cold bath, then back into the heat. "I see. Lucky for you he's willing to take your case."

Nga-Yee stared at him. "N told you about me?" she asked. Weren't detectives supposed to keep their clients secret?

"No, but I'd guess nine out of ten people 'working together' with N are actually his clients." The proprietor smiled at her. He drained the noodles and starting cooking the wontons.

Nga-Yee cursed herself for her stupidity. Asking that question had just confirmed his guess. Still, now that they were talking openly, she might as well see what she could find out.

"Do you know what N does for a living?"

"More or less. He helps people solve their problems."

"You said I was lucky. Is that because he doesn't take many cases?"

The proprietor paused for a moment to stare at her, then chuckled as he went back to preparing her broth. "Miss, you don't seem to understand how good N is. He's a real maverick."

"A maverick?"

"Neither cops nor criminals dare to get on his bad side."

"Is N—a triad leader?" Nga-Yee asked nervously. She knew hackers had to do some shady things, but actually being involved with the criminal underworld would be a whole different matter.

"No, no." The man grinned. "He's even more powerful than that. He's not in any triad, yet all the gang bosses respect and fear him. If he gets in their way, they just have to chalk it up to bad luck. I heard that he had dealings with a police officer in the Western District, and the cop had to bow and scrape too."

Nga-Yee thought back to when those gangsters tried to kidnap them. When they got out, the proprietor had said, "Those idiots don't know what they're getting into." So this is what he'd meant.

"See this?" The man pushed his hair back to reveal a half-inch scar. "A few years ago, some gangsters came to make trouble. They insisted that their boss had a bellyache from eating my wontons. I thought they were after protection money, the usual, but before I could even ask how much, they'd already gotten to work. They overturned the chairs and tables and smashed up my counter. I've been in business more than twenty years, and of course I've seen these sorts of shenanigans before. I could have put up with it if this was just a one-off, but those bastards turned up again the next week. When they did it a third time, I couldn't stand it anymore and tried to stop them. I ended up in the hospital getting six stitches."

"Did you make a police report?" Nga-Yee wasn't sure why he'd brought this up, but she went with the flow.

"Yes, but it didn't do any good. I got this injury falling over in the confusion. Those gangsters were smart—they smashed up my stuff, but never attacked me. The police could only treat this as a case of criminal damage, which meant it was a lower priority for them." He turned to scoop some wontons into the pot. "The strange thing was, they stopped coming after that, as if their boss had suddenly stopped being angry or they'd discovered their consciences. It was only half a year later that I found out the real reason."

"And that was . . . N?"

"Yes." The man nodded. "He never said a word, but I have friends who keep one ear to the ground, and they told me the triad leader was out of the picture—someone from outside the gang had got rid of him. Of course, it turned out that the stomach ache was just an excuse. A businessman had hired them to harass me so I'd give up my shop. If this space was vacant, they could buy up the whole building, tear it down, and build a luxury condo. That would make billions."

"How did you know this outsider was N?"

"N had asked me about the gangsters: Did they have any identifying marks, what did they say as they were smashing up the joint? I thought he was just curious. When I asked him about it afterward, he didn't deny it. All he said was, 'If Loi's were to close down, that would be a real loss for the neighborhood.'"

Nga-Yee wondered if he was hero-worshipping N just a little too much, but then she recalled N's uncanny ability to find clues in seemingly irrelevant details, and the way he'd terrified those gangsters right in front of her.

"Plenty of people in and out of the underworld want N's help, but he's picky with his cases. If he doesn't want to do something, no amount of money will persuade him. But then sometimes a case just happens to catch his interest, the old busybody. Have you read Jin Yong's *Demi-Gods and Semi-Devils*? N is like that floor-sweeping Shaolin monk who never interferes with the kung fu world, but as soon as he steps in, not even Murong Fu or Xiao Feng can stop him."

Even though Nga-Yee *had* read *Demi-Gods and Semi-Devils*, she found it hard to connect any of the characters in this martial arts novel to N. The proprietor seemed to be quite a fan, and he went on at great length to discuss the differences between the various TV adaptations. Nga-Yee smiled and nodded till he put a delicious-smelling bowl in front of her: plump wontons and delightfully chewy noodles, all in an aromatic fish broth. After she'd gobbled it down, he poured her a cup of hot tea, making this one of the best meals ever.

She paid up as soon as she finished her tea. Although the shop was still relatively empty, it was tiny enough that she didn't want to take up space for any longer than necessary.

As the owner was handing Nga-Yee her change, another customer walked in. "Large wonton noodles, reduced noodles, extra scallions, soup on the side, fried greens, no oyster sauce."

Nga-Yee's head whipped around. It wasn't N, but someone more surprising.

"Oh! Miss Au?"

Standing in the doorway was a man of about fifty with a head of gray hair: Wendy's uncle.

"Mr. Mok?"

"What a coincidence." He came and sat next to her. "Or are you here to visit N? Not such a coincidence, then."

"Nope, that's not why I'm here." It was true, she told herself: from the moment she'd decided to come to Loi's for noodles, she was no longer in Sai Ying Pun to see N.

"But you know about this place through N? He brought me here a few years ago, and I've been hooked ever since. Stop by for a bowl every time I'm in the neighborhood." He beamed. "Plenty of noodle restaurants these days scrimp—you're lucky to get six wontons in a bowl. But this place gives you four in a small portion, eight in a large. It's really a taste of old Hong Kong."

"Did you have work in the Western District today?" asked Nga-Yee, avoiding words like "investigate" because she wasn't sure what detectives were allowed to talk about in public.

"Yes. It was for your case."

"Mine?"

"N asked me to check up on some details, and I came to give him my findings." Detective Mok unwrapped some disposable chopsticks. "He said I'd palmed you off on him, so I had to provide some 'after-sale service.' Strange fellow. Calls himself a computer expert but makes me deliver everything in person. Apparently sending documents by email isn't safe."

"What did he ask you to investigate?" Nga-Yee asked anxiously.

"The red-haired teenager, the one in the photo with your sister . . ."

Nga-Yee jumped to her feet, said a quick goodbye to Mr. Mok and the store owner, and hurried up Second Street to number 151.

Tak-tak-tak-tak-tak-tak-tak-tak-tak. Having dashed up six flights, she kept her finger on the doorbell, though this dull racket didn't do enough to express her frenzy. A moment later the white wooden door opened to reveal N's grumpy face.

"Miss Au, didn't I tell you I'd call when—"

"I just ran into Detective Mok."

N's brow furrowed. With a sigh, he opened the door to let her in.

"What did he tell you?" he said as he walked over to his desk.

"You said you'd find someone familiar with Mong Kok to check up on the red-haired guy." Without waiting to be asked, she sat down across from him. "And that was Detective Mok."

"Yes."

"What did he find out?"

"Didn't he tell you?"

"As soon as he said what he was doing, I ran straight here," gabbled Nga-Yee. "Even if he told me the guy's name, I wouldn't know if he had anything to do with Siu-Man or kidkit727. You're the only one who can put the pieces together."

N rested one foot on the opposite knee and clasped his hands behind his head. "Your reasoning is correct, but that's a dead end. This guy has nothing to do with kidkit727."

"How do you know?"

"He was sent to the detention center on Lantau Island last March and hasn't been released yet."

Nga-Yee blinked. There were four of these facilities in Hong Kong, for offenders age fourteen to twenty-one.

"This fucker's called Kayden Cheung. He was arrested for burglary and assault last year, about a month after the karaoke incident. Remember Kwok-Tai mentioned those two scumbags who join bands just to pick up girls? He's one of them. His cousin's at your sister's school and has been raising hell since Kayden was sent up."

"What's his name? Was he in Siu-Man's class?"

"The cousin's called Jason, and he was a year above your sister—until he transferred out last year." N shrugged. "It seems Enoch has a habit of forcing unsavory characters to 'voluntarily' leave."

"So this Jason—"

"I'm in the middle of an investigation, Miss Au, so please stop asking." N slumped forward, cradling his face in his hands. "Honestly, you're the most aggravating client I've ever had."

Nga-Yee had more questions, but seeing how pissed off he looked, she gave up.

"Go home. I'll call you if anything comes up."

Nga-Yee stood dejectedly and headed for the door. She couldn't help noticing that in just a few days N's apartment had returned to its previous squalor, with trash and plastic bags littering every cranny of the living room. She glanced into the kitchen; the teapot and cup she'd used the other day were on the counter, exactly where she'd left them. She bet the tea leaves were still in there, steeping away.

"N, why didn't you—"

She'd been about to lecture him on his slovenliness—he hadn't even offered Detective Mok a cup of tea!—when a realization stopped her in his tracks.

"Detective Mok came to tell you about Kayden Cheung and Jason?" she asked, standing in the doorway.

"That's what I said."

"You're lying."

Her interjection put a wary look on his face.

"Me? Lying?"

"Yes. Detective Mok told me you asked him to check up on 'some' details. If it was just Kayden he was looking into, he'd have said 'a person' or something like that."

"I'm not responsible for Detective Mok's choice of words."

"That's not the main thing." She strode back over to the desk and rested both hands on it. "He also said you made him come here because it wasn't safe to send documents by email. If he was just looking into the red-haired guy, there'd be no need to come to Sai Ying Pun when all he found out was his name and that he was locked up—a phone call would do for that. He brought you a document—that means a physical object. What was he looking into? What document?"

N glared at her, and she met his gaze steadily. After a few seconds he sighed and reached into a drawer for a USB stick.

"You really are the absolutely most annoying client in the world." He stuck the USB into his computer.

"What's that?"

"Listen."

N clicked the mouse a few times, and voices came from the speaker:

"Thanks very much for letting me know, Mr. Mok. As soon as you told me, I fired Victor. I've made careful enquiries about the information he leaked, and I'm sure it won't lead to any legal difficulties."

"That's fine, Mr. Tong. I wasn't planning to push the issue of legal responsibility, I just wanted a bit more information. If my client wanted to take things further, I wouldn't have come to see you today."

"That makes things much simpler, then. Victor's just graduated high school. He's still so immature, he didn't know any better, that's why he made such a serious mistake. Young people these days are so lazy. They just sit around at work playing with their phones. It's a nightmare."

"How did Victor meet the girl?"

"Our team goes to community halls in various districts to give free legal talks. People often come up to us afterward asking for advice, and I get the interns or assistants to deal with them. That's how Victor started talking to her. He's never had any luck with women, so when she came up and started chatting, he completely forgot his professionalism. Now I think of it, she

*must have targeted him deliberately, to pump him for
information."*

"How much did Victor tell her?"

"Most of it was already public, such as what Shiu Tak-
Ping said the first time he was questioned. The rest was
stuff we were keeping back to use in his defense, such
as his relationship with his wife, suspicious points that
worked in his favor, and so forth. I'm sure none of this
infringed anyone's privacy, including my client."

"You don't need to keep reminding me, Mr. Tong.
Besides, you've already fired Victor, so you've dealt with
the matter."

"Right, right."

"How many times did Victor see the girl?"

"Three, maybe four times. She told him she wanted to
study law, that older students said she should get practi-
cal experience with a live case, to give her more to talk
about during her interview."

"And he believed her?"

"He's a bit of an idiot. Didn't even stop to wonder if
she was tipping off a journalist or something. We dodged
a bullet when we fired him. Oh yes, Mr. Mok, who is
your client? I hope it's not a newspaper looking to settle
old scores?"

"Like you, Mr. Tong, I have a duty to maintain my
client's confidentiality. But don't worry, I can guarantee
anything you're telling me will remain secret."

"That's all right, then."

"Did Victor mention the girl's name?"

"Um . . . what was it—oh yes, it was quite an unusual
surname: Shu. Her name was Lily Shu."

Monday, June 22, 2015

> We're in trouble. Au Siu-Man's sister and her boyfriend just came to the school. They asked a whole bunch of questions. 16:25 ✓

> Maybe they know what I did? 16:31 ✓

sorry was in a meeting 17:14

what did they ask? 17:15

> Mainly about when Siu-Man was still alive, at school . . . 17:17 ✓

> They definitely know what we did! 17:17 ✓

> What if they've already called the police? 17:18 ✓

> I'm so scared. 17:18 ✓

or maybe they just wanted to say hi to the teachers 17:41

there's no way in hell they know who you are 17:42

stop thinking about it you just make yourself crazy 17:43

> All right . . . 17:50 ✓

> Are you free tonight? I'd like to see you. 17:55 ✓

difficult tonight and tomorrow, work stuff 18:02

big client 18:03

will message you later 18:03

CHAPTER SIX

1.

Sze Chung-Nam stood at the corner of Shanghai Street and Langham Place in Mong Kok, stunned and elated, and also a little anxious. From time to time he looked around, scanning the crowd.

It was 6:45 p.m. on Thursday, June 25, five days after Chung-Nam had "bumped into" Szeto Wai at the Cultural Centre. Ever since exchanging numbers with the chairman of SIQ, Chung-Nam had kept an eye on his phone, terrified of missing a call. Yet there'd been not so much as a text. For the first two days, he'd kept a lid on his anxiety—Szeto was probably busy. By the fourth day, he'd been frantic. Even Ma-Chai could tell that something was up. He thought about making a call himself—after all, Szeto had said he'd like to meet again to hear more insider gossip about GT—but Szeto was practically superhuman, and Chung-Nam didn't feel he could bother him like that.

Just as he was hesitating about what to do, Szeto Wai had phoned him at work. When Chung-Nam saw the number flash up on his phone, he pretended to need the bathroom, and he hurried out of the office, away from watchful eyes, before answering.

"Chung-Nam? Szeto Wai here." As before, he spoke Cantonese with a slight accent.

"Mr. Szeto! Hello!"

"We mentioned having dinner. Are you free tonight?"

Chung-Nam glanced at his watch. It was 4:30 in the afternoon.

"Yes, sure! I'm free!" He actually had somewhere to be, but this was more important than any other appointment.

"Great, see you at seven! Hangzhou food in Tsim Sha Tsui okay?"

"Hangzhou's great, but I might be late. I don't get off work till six thirty. It's hard to get a taxi at rush hour, and the MTR's so crowded you have to let two or three trains go by before you can squeeze on."

"You don't drive?"

"I don't have a car. It's too expensive in Hong Kong." Six-tenths of Chung-Nam's salary went on rent alone. If he bought a car, his parking space would probably eat up the other forty percent.

"Then why don't I pick you up near your office? Six forty-five at the side entrance of Langham Place Hotel on Shanghai Street. Okay?"

"Oh no, please don't bother—"

"I'm on my way to a meeting at the InnoCentre in Kowloon Tong right now, so this will be on my way. It's no trouble at all. See you at six forty-five."

Westerners are always so decisive. Szeto Wai hung up without giving Chung-Nam a chance to refuse.

Chung-Nam thought it was great that Szeto Wai was so down-to-earth, but he hadn't turned down the lift out of politeness. It was self-interest. It was easy to hide his identity online, but in real life there was no way to use a different name or wear a mask. If any of his coworkers saw him meeting in secret with a potential investor, he might end up joining the ranks of the unemployed.

To minimize the risk of being spotted, Chung-Nam didn't leave the office till 6:40, then had to dash from their location at the corner of Shantung and Canton to Langham Place. Ma-Chai,

Hao, and Thomas were all working overtime, so he only had to stay clear of Mr. Lee and Joanne, who'd both left work around six. They'd left separately, but Chung-Nam suspected that was just to throw everyone off the scent, and they were actually meeting up later. That probably meant that they'd gone far away rather than sticking around Mong Kok where someone might see them. Even so, Chung-Nam found himself unable to relax. He kept turning to look down the street in either direction.

Naturally, his excitement far outstripped his anxiety.

When he was still a kid, Chung-Nam's parents had taken him to a fortune-teller, who said that the boy was destined to be more than just a regular fish in the pond. He was going to achieve great things. And so, despite enduring more than his share of eye rolls, he firmly believed in his own superiority. He had been at the top of his class, and even more, he was proud that his extraordinary brain was good at detecting hidden layers of meaning. Szeto Wai's attitude toward him was different from his attitude toward Mr. Lee. He couldn't say different in what way exactly, but he intuited that Szeto Wai was trying to win him over.

This made no sense. What could this international talent with a personal worth of billions see in a lowly director of technology?

Just as he was contemplating this, a sleek black car pulled up.

The window opened, and Szeto Wai stuck his head out. "I hope I haven't kept you waiting?"

Chung-Nam quickly recovered, but he couldn't help gasping at the sight of this car. Although he'd had a license for years, he didn't own a vehicle—it was a dream of his, as it was for many Hong Kong men. The standard markers of success for someone like him would be a fancy house, a brand-name car, fine wine, and a beautiful woman. He kept up with all the auto websites and never missed an episode of *Top Gear*. When Szeto offered him a lift, he'd imagined someone of this stature would have rented a Porsche or an Audi. Yet this surpassed his expectations—not even a tasteful Rolls-Royce or a flashy Ferrari, but something even more suited to Szeto Wai's role as a tech genius: a Tesla Model S.

"You look surprised," Szeto Wai said, chuckling as he opened the door. Chung-Nam hastily nodded his thanks and got in. The first thing he noticed wasn't the famous Model S dashboard, which was basically a tablet computer, but that their driver was Doris, the Eurasian woman from the other day.

"Something wrong?" Szeto asked as they shook hands.

"No, no. It's just my first time in a Tesla." Chung-Nam was trying hard not to act like a kid in a candy store, staring hungrily at everything around him.

"This model's pretty snazzy—same horsepower as a sports car, plus four-wheel drive. Shame Hong Kong traffic is so bad, or I could floor it." Szeto smiled. "You a gearhead?"

"Yes. I can't afford to own one, but I love checking out the car mags and so on."

"I see."

For the next fifteen minutes or so, Szeto Wai talked cars—he had an opinion about everything from the history of auto manufacturing to which models were most cost-effective. The USA really was a nation of car nuts.

"It's a shame Hong Kong's so crowded. There's not enough space for everyone to have cars, like in the States," said Chung-Nam.

"Life without cars is a snore," said Szeto, looking smug to be American. "Cars tell you a lot about their owners, just as you can judge a person's taste from his clothes."

"Hong Kongers show our personalities through our phones." Chung-Nam laughed. "We can't afford cars, so we change our phones like mad. They're as seasonal as clothes, for us."

"You have a point. I heard there are seven million people in Hong Kong, but over seventeen million phones. That's more than two per person! You guys probably change models about as often as real auto freaks in the States do their cars." He thought about it for a moment. "No, you're probably much crazier, actually."

"Ha! It's much cheaper to get a new phone."

"True." Szeto turned to look at the passing scenery. "Well, as long as there's consumerism, the world's economy can keep functioning, and investors like me can go on creating wealth."

Chung-Nam followed his gaze out into Tsim Sha Tsui, to the luxury-brand shops lining Canton Road and their well-heeled customers. This neighborhood was Hong Kong in a nutshell: a place that valued money over humanity. Whether you'd accumulated your wealth by honest hard work or by screwing over other people, riches were what commanded respect. Even if you didn't agree with this power structure, in order to survive in this society, you had to abide by it. He remembered Hao saying, *This city's about survival of the fittest, fleece or get fleeced.*

The car turned onto Peking Road and stopped opposite iSQUARE shopping mall to let Chung-Nam and Szeto Wai out. Doris then turned onto Hankow Road.

"Isn't she joining us for dinner?" Chung-Nam asked, a little confused.

"This isn't official business, so Doris doesn't need to stick around." Szeto grinned. "Or did you mean you'd rather be on a date with her?"

"No, no, of course not."

"Nothing wrong if you did." Szeto laughed brightly. "Doris is an attractive woman. What straight man wouldn't be interested?"

"Mr. Szeto, are you—with her—" Chung-Nam stammered, uncertain how to ask this tactfully.

"No, she's just my assistant," said Szeto, unruffled. "Don't the Chinese have a saying—rabbits don't eat grass by their burrows? She's good at her job, and I definitely don't want to affect our working relationship or make her less efficient. Besides, I know plenty of hotter women who *don't* work for me."

Chung-Nam couldn't help thinking of Mr. Lee and Joanne. Clearly Mr. Lee would never achieve the heights of a Szeto Wai.

They walked into iSQUARE and headed for the elevator. When Mr. Szeto pressed 31, Chung-Nam gaped. This mall had all sorts of shops, plus an IMAX cinema, but everything above the twentieth floor was fine dining; the higher the floor, the more expensive the restaurant. These places could cost one or two thousand Hong Kong dollars for a single meal, not something a wage slave like Chung-Nam could afford.

"My treat tonight—don't argue," said Mr. Szeto blandly, as if he'd read Chung-Nam's mind.

"Oh, ah, thank—thank you." Chung-Nam thought of putting up some token resistance, but his wallet wasn't up to the task, and he couldn't risk Mr. Szeto's suddenly agreeing to let him pay. Better to simply accept. Who knew what exquisite foods awaited him?

The lift doors opened, and they were greeted with a wall of pale yellow rock formations, a very fancy Chinese restaurant entrance that combined Asian and Western styles. The name TIN DING HIN was carved into the stone. Standing behind a counter was a hostess in her twenties. Her tight purple uniform showed off her model-like body, and her features were even more outstanding—it wasn't hard to see why she'd been chosen to be the first face customers saw on entering.

"Good evening, Mr. Szeto. This way, please."

With great deference, the hostess led the two men inside. Chung-Nam had never been anywhere this classy, but he guessed that Mr. Szeto must be an honored guest.

When he saw their table, Chung-Nam knew he was right.

They were in a private room with floor-to-ceiling windows looking over the eastern side of Victoria Harbour. There was enough space for a dozen people, but right now there was only a small square table set for two. Their server was also in purple, and just as stunning.

Chung-Nam silently rejoiced that he'd worn a suit and tie—his normal outfit of shirtsleeves would be far too casual. Mr. Lee had kept up the exhortations to dress suitably and appear professional, probably worried about a surprise visit from Mr. Szeto.

Mr. Szeto gestured for Chung-Nam to sit, and he took the chair farther from the door.

"The lighting here is just right," said Mr. Szeto. "It's bright enough, but we can still enjoy the nighttime view. That took skillful design."

The last rays of the setting sun had coated the skyscrapers on both sides of Victoria Harbour with a sheen of red. Neon lights in all sorts of colors were coming on, setting the stage for the evening. Chung-Nam had read that during the Edo period in Japan, shoguns would look out over cities from their towers as thousands of households slowly lit up. Perhaps this setting was a contemporary version of that ritual, allowing the wealthy to feel as if they ruled over all they surveyed.

The hostess left, and the server offered a menu to Mr. Szeto, but he refused it, turning instead to Chung-Nam. "Is there anything you don't eat? Seafood, for instance?"

"No." He shook his head

"That's good." He turned back to the server. "Two imperial set meals, please."

She nodded and politely withdrew. As soon as she stepped out, another long-haired server entered, this one in a black suit and tie.

"What would you like to drink tonight, Mr. Szeto?" she asked, handing him the wine list.

"Mmm . . ." He put on his glasses and looked. "The Buccella Cabernet Sauvignon 2012, please."

"Very well." She smiled and left them.

Mr. Szeto looked as though he'd just thought of something. "Do you drink red wine, Chung-Nam?"

"Yes, of course—though I don't know much about it, and I haven't tried it with Chinese food."

"I thought wedding banquets here usually served wine with the meal. Anyway, I recommend this one—it's every bit as good as anything from Europe."

"From Europe? So this isn't French?" Chung-Nam had thought a billionaire would surely be drinking a French Bordeaux.

"No, it's American, from Napa Valley. That's in California, same as Silicon Valley. When Satoshi and I set up Isotope, we had quite a few staff retreats to Napa. It was only a couple of hours by car. Have you been to California?"

"No. Nor anywhere else in North America. To be honest, the farthest I've ever gone is Japan."

"You should go, if you ever get the chance."

Mr. Szeto was in the middle of describing various Californian tourist attractions when the sommelier returned with a dark-colored bottle on which the year 2012 appeared in an artistic font on a white oval, with a red seal above it. The whole thing had an austere feel to it.

"Buccella Cabernet Sauvignon 2012."

The sommelier held the bottle up for Mr. Szeto to inspect, and when he nodded, she placed it on a side table, pulled out an opener, and carefully removed the cork. A tiny amount went into Mr. Szeto's glass. He held the ruby liquid up to the light, sniffed it, sipped a little, and nodded.

The sommelier filled Chung-Nam's glass halfway, then topped up Mr. Szeto's.

Chung-Nam had never seen red wine handled properly—normally he bought a bottle at the supermarket, brought it home, and gulped it down. Luckily, this was a Chinese meal—he thought. There probably weren't as many rituals involved. If they were at a French restaurant, he'd be embarrassing himself left and right.

"Go on, try it. I've always thought this goes well with Hang-zhou cuisine. California wine is more acidic than European, and its unique jamlike taste doesn't clamor for attention, so it won't get in the way of the food."

Chung-Nam took a sip. He had no idea what French wine tasted like, so it was not as if he could make a comparison, but he could tell how rich and delicious it was.

As Mr. Szeto held forth about red wine, the purple-clad waitress came in again with a silver tray and started serving their dinner.

"Hangzhou Dragon Well shrimp."

Chung-Nam's only experience of Chinese food was family-style platters. This looked more like a French dinner: tiny dishes containing expertly peeled prawns appetizingly surrounded by a vegetable garnish.

This was followed by course after course of exquisite food: honey-glazed ham, fried stuffed bean curd rolls, West Lake vinegar fish, Dongpo pork belly, and other Hangzhou delights, along with premium seafood that didn't have much to do with Hangzhou: abalone, sea cucumber, fish maw, complemented by such Western ingredients as black truffle or asparagus in a perfect example of fusion cuisine. Portions were small, the variety endless. It reminded Chung-Nam of Japanese kaiseki, though the order of courses and plating was more like a European meal.

Szeto Wai kept up a stream of bright chatter through the meal, but only around three topics: food, cars, and travel. Chung-Nam wanted very much to know what he'd meant a few days ago when he'd said, *You seem like a smart person*, but he restrained himself from mentioning GT Net or SIQ Ventures. Bringing up anything work-related would seem desperate. He'd have to wait for Mr. Szeto to broach the subject, then trim his sails according to the wind.

Finally Mr. Szeto brought up their encounter at the Cultural Centre, but from a completely unexpected angle. "Chung-Nam," he said, nibbling at his bird's nest dessert and sipping some red wine, "you don't actually have a good friend who likes classical music, do you?"

"Huh?" Chung-Nam thought he must have misheard.

"You came to the Cultural Centre on your own last Saturday, and you weren't there to hear the concert." Mr. Szeto gestured with his wineglass for emphasis, his tone level.

Chung-Nam's heart was thudding so wildly he wondered if Mr. Szeto could hear it from across the table. Trying to calm himself, he was about to protest that their encounter *had* been a complete coincidence, but just before opening his mouth, he had a vague sense that this wasn't the correct answer.

"Uh . . . yes, I came there to see you."

"Very good." Szeto Wai smiled. "That was the right call—you know when to lie and when to tell the truth. The industry is full of bluffing and trickery. That's never bothered me, but when you know I've seen through you, and you insist on keeping up the pretense? That becomes an insult."

Chung-Nam felt a huge weight lifted off him.

"Another question." Szeto Wai put down his glass. "This idea of packaging G-dollars and information trading like financial products—that was just some nonsense you made up on the spur of the moment, right? Your company has no such plans?"

Chung-Nam nodded.

"Do you watch football, Chung-Nam? Soccer, not American."

Why the sudden change of topic? "Not particularly, but I do keep an eye on the UEFA League."

"And here I was thinking that nine out of every ten Hong Kongers were soccer-mad." Mr. Szeto grinned. "Then you don't know the difference between a first-class forward and a regular one?"

Chung-Nam shook his head, not understanding where this was going.

"It's in the ability to take opportunities as they arise. For instance, let's say Team A has a forward who gets one goal every ten attempts, while Team B's forward has a one-in-five rate. Now say there's a match where each team creates seven opportunities. Team A might manage to get a goalless draw, whereas Team B has a shot at a one-zero win. This is a bit oversimplified, but my point is that a first-rate talent can quickly see the lay of the land, identify where the advantage lies, and make the most of the opportunity. Any forward might get lucky during a particular match and score five or six goals, but a true talent is consistent across an entire league, able to seize every opening. And that's who an intelligent coach would choose for his first team."

Szeto Wai paused briefly, then lightly jabbed a finger in Chung-Nam's direction. "In the whole of your company, you're the only one with this ability."

"You're—You're too kind."

"When I picked holes in your business plan and said it might never be profitable, your boss Kenneth couldn't string a sentence together to defend himself. He clearly can't think on his feet and has no flexibility at all. Your coworkers were all far too deferential in that very Chinese way—they didn't dare step forward without the boss giving them leave. The usual mind-set: do nothing and make no mistakes. You were the only one who took action—you understood that I was a big fish and you mustn't let me get away, even if you had to invent a project out of thin air. You even went on about some 'proprietary information' to further pique my interest."

Szeto Wai was never interested in GT Net, Chung-Nam realized. He was just giving them a hard time to see what they were made of.

"You sounded so confident, I almost fell for it," Mr. Szeto went on. "If Kenneth's every thought hadn't been written on his face, I would have thought that these 'intelligence stocks' actually existed. Ridiculous. Let's be honest—GT's whole plan is deeply stupid. Gossip will never be a real commodity. You can manufacture infinite amounts of it, but good luck trying to trade that on the open market!"

Chung-Nam almost confessed that Mr. Lee was making him and Hao work day and night to make this ridiculous plan a reality that would be presented to Szeto Wai in half a month. He knew perfectly well that the idea of trading gossip was sheer fantasy, and his chances of producing a coherent report were not great. For the last few days, he and Hao had been stressing out about how to salvage a project that became more obviously lousy the further they got.

"Even though it's a crazy scheme, I'd still rate your performance that day more than ninety out of a hundred," said Szeto Wai. "So I carried out a second test, and you didn't disappoint me. You passed."

"A second test?"

"Why do you think I started talking about classical music in front of you and said I'd be at the concert on Saturday?"

So this was part of a plan the whole time—and to think Chung-Nam had been smugly congratulating himself on snaring Szeto Wai.

"This meal is my way of congratulating you." Szeto Wai raised his glass. "When I meet a talent who combines decisiveness, action, and confidence, I always treat them to a good dinner and fine wine. Quite a few of these individuals have become important partners of SIQ."

Screaming and cheering inside, Chung-Nam felt as if he'd won the lottery. Even though Szeto Wai hadn't actually promised him anything, he reckoned he'd successfully gotten this tech titan's attention.

"Don't get too excited, though," Szeto Wai went on without waiting for a reply. "I peg the value of this gift to performance. This Buccella cost only two hundred American dollars—that's about fifteen hundred Hong Kong dollars. I once opened a thousand-dollar bottle for another young person. If you'd come up with a workable idea rather than this nonsense about futures and options, we'd be sitting on the hundredth floor of ICC."

Indeed, the ICC—or International Commerce Centre, to give it its full name—was the tallest building in Hong Kong. The top eighteen of its 118 floors housed a six-star hotel and a number of exclusive restaurants, all of which cost the earth.

Chung-Nam felt a twinge of regret that he hadn't come up with a better idea, but that passed in a flash. The main thing was to seize the opportunity presenting itself to him right now. Never mind dinner at ICC, he had bigger dreams. Maybe one day he'd buy the Burj Khalifa!

"Mr. Szeto, how did you know I wasn't at the Cultural Centre to hear the concert?"

"You haven't said a single thing about music this evening. If you were going to keep up the lie, you should at least have mentioned it during dinner." Szeto Wai chuckled. "Anything else you want to know? Ask away!"

"Why did SIQ set its sights on our company? If you really think GT Net will never be profitable, then SIQ has no reason to invest in us. No matter how good my performance is, that doesn't change."

"Have you heard of Metcalfe's law?"

"It's something to do with the internet, isn't it?"

"Very good. Metcalfe's law states that the effect of a telecommunications network is proportional to the square of its users. That means a network with fifty clients is worth twenty-five times as much as one with ten—not five times. This explains why big tech firms are always buying up smaller companies with a similar model. If a firm with fifty clients buys up one with ten, they've only increased their customer base by twenty percent, but their value has gone up fifty percent."

"What does that have to do with GT Net?"

"Haven't you worked it out?" Szeto Wai smiled meaningfully.

In a flash of inspiration, Chung-Nam saw the answer. "SIQ's invested in a similar firm in the States?"

"Right." Szeto Wai looked directly into Chung-Nam's eyes. "I won't give away too many details, but the model your company has for buying and selling information is very like one of our major investments. We think it's going to develop into the next Tumblr or Snapchat, so we're getting ahead of the curve and buying up similar companies around the world."

"You mean the way Groupon bought up uBuyiBuy?"

"Yes, just like that."

In 2010 two young Hong Kongers had spotted the vast potential in China's web shopping craze, and had set up a retail website called uBuyiBuy. Six months later, they were bought out by Groupon, which was just expanding into Asia at the time, and they did the same thing in Taiwan and Singapore.

"Any other questions?"

"Um . . . Is SIQ planning to open a branch in Hong Kong?"

Szeto Wai hesitated. "Why would you think that?"

"Because we rode here in a Tesla," Chung-Nam replied. "You said you were in Hong Kong on vacation, Mr. Szeto, so I would expect you to have rented a car. Electric cars aren't popular here, and none of the local car rental places would offer a Tesla. If you'd borrowed it from a friend, that would have come up in conversation—but you talked about the car as if it were your own. You live in America, but you have your own car in Hong Kong. The only explanation that makes sense is that SIQ is opening a branch here very soon, and this Model S is actually a company car. For all I know, you were at the InnoCentre today making connections with local businesses on behalf of SIQ."

"Looks like I made a mistake." Szeto Wai tapped the wine bottle. "I should have ordered a five-hundred-dollar one."

Chung-Nam silently cheered to receive this roundabout compliment.

"SIQ is preparing to move into China. We'll set up an office in Hong Kong first, as our Asia HQ," said Szeto Wai, no longer evasive. "There are a number of new companies on the Mainland set up by very young people who have just as much talent as anyone in the West. China's economic growth has slowed in the last few years, which is a great opportunity for SIQ to invest and scoop up all these new tech companies that have so much potential. That's not why I'm in Hong Kong, though. Kyle's the one with his hand on the wheel right now. I just speak with clients or headhunt now and then."

Before coming to dinner, Chung-Nam had looked up everything he could find about SIQ, so he knew Szeto Wai was telling the truth. There'd been quite a few interviews and press conferences on YouTube, but the person speaking was always fifty-something mustachioed Kyle Quincy.

"If SIQ's moving into China, does that mean you're going to take center stage and lead the company in Asia?" asked Chung-Nam. "I guess Mr. Quincy would have more influence in the West, but being Asian, you'll probably find it easier to connect with people here."

"You're right, though I'm not planning to put myself in the spotlight." Szeto Wai shrugged. "I'm very happy with my life as it is. I go from country to country, enjoying good food and wine, and never have to worry about my investments. At most, I do a bit of thinking and come up with new ideas for the company. I don't want to be on the front line. Kyle's already started looking for someone to head up the Asian branch."

"What about Mr. Satoshi?" Two out of SIQ's three leaders were Asian, after all, and Chung-Nam thought it would be silly of them not to use this advantage.

"Ha!" Szeto Wai let out a bark of laughter. "God knows where Satoshi is right now, or what he's doing."

"Huh? Isn't Mr. Satoshi one of SIQ's directors?"

"He has a title, that's all. He hasn't shown up for any board meetings for years now, and he doesn't seem interested in what happens to the firm. The guy's a genius, but he doesn't have a business brain. That's just how he is—he'd rather hide away and tinker. I haven't seen him for several years—don't even know how to get in touch with him. When the board needs to speak to him, though, he always emails us first. It's as if he's keeping a close watch on things. Sometimes I wonder whether he's hacked into our system and is surveilling us that way."

"Is he that good?"

"If he wasn't that good, how would Isotope have gotten so many patents?"

"Patents are one thing, but hacking into your system is another level."

"Have you heard of a man named Kevin Mitnick?"

Chung-Nam shook his head.

"Kevin Mitnick runs a computer security firm in America. He helps businesses test their systems, looking for vulnerable points where a hacker might get in. He's very well known in the tech world." Szeto Wai drew his index finger through the air, as if turning time back. "But before 2000, Mitnick was one of the world's most feared hackers. The most wanted cybercriminal in the States. He made his way into many business and government networks around the world and stole a significant amount of confidential data."

"Ha, he sounds like Mr. Satoshi—Oh."

"You said it, not me." Szeto Wai shot him a look.

Chung-Nam didn't press the issue. He knew there were some things that shouldn't be said too openly. According to what he'd read online, Satoshi Inoue had been involved in the creation of several cybersecurity agreements. It wouldn't be surprising if he had knowledge and experience of how to break into a network.

"Enough about that guy," said Szeto Wai. "Any other questions?"

Chung-Nam was about to brag that he hacked a bit himself, but he stopped: Was this a third test? It took him a second to find the right question.

"According to what you said, we're almost certainly going to get funds from you. Right?"

"Right."

"So tell me—what can I do for you?"

Szeto Wai smiled with satisfaction; Chung-Nam had correctly deduced that the investment was a foregone conclusion—after all, ten or twenty million Hong Kong dollars was nothing to SIQ—in which case, the request for a report was just a cover.

"After SIQ invests in your company, of course Kenneth will go on being the manager," said Szeto Wai. It was all Chung-Nam could do not to laugh out loud at the thought of his boss being described as a "manager." "But we have no idea if he'll actually be able to develop the way the parent company would like. I need someone who knows how to observe and adapt, who can keep us up to date, let us know if things are going well."

Chung-Nam smiled. "So you want me to be an informant?"

"That doesn't sound good. Let's call you an inside man." Szeto Wai grinned back.

"I'm yours to command." Chung-Nam stood and held out his right hand; Szeto Wai stood too, and they shook on it.

After that, they went on drinking wine and talking about food and cars. Chung-Nam's brain was in a completely different place than it was an hour ago. The opportunity he'd been waiting for had finally arrived, and his plan would soon be realized.

"I should be heading back," said Szeto Wai, glancing at his watch. It was about nine thirty. "I thought of taking you to a bar next, but I have an early meeting tomorrow, so we should call it a night."

Chung-Nam was a little disappointed, but he told himself there was no hurry—he had an entry ticket to SIQ now. "Do you have time for another meal before you head back to America?" he asked.

"I'll be in touch—I've got your number." Szeto Wai waved his BlackBerry.

There was a knock at the door, which had remained shut since the last course was served. Chung-Nam thought this was probably something they did at high-class restaurants when their most honored guests had private business to discuss.

"Oh, hello Doris."

Indeed, it wasn't a waitress or a sommelier, but Szeto Wai's assistant. She didn't say anything, just stood in the doorway waiting for his instructions.

"Where do you live, Chung-Nam?"

"Diamond Hill."

"Ah, I was going to offer you a lift if you were anywhere on Hong Kong Island." Szeto Wai stroked his chin. "The apartment I'm renting is in Wan Chai."

"Don't worry about it, I can get the MTR. Tsim Sha Tsui station's just downstairs."

"That's all right, then."

As the trio walked out, the purple-clad waitresses and the sommelier in her suit lined up to say a formal goodbye. Chung-Nam wondered why they hadn't had to pay the bill; then he realized that Doris must have taken care of it.

After saying goodbye, Chung-Nam almost skipped through the ticket barrier and onto the train. Even though it was long past rush hour and there were plenty of empty seats, he chose to stand in his usual spot by the doors. He got his phone from his briefcase, turned it back on, and quickly answered the messages that had come in during dinner. How could he take advantage of Szeto Wai's remaining time in Hong Kong to cement their bond?

This evening had been almost perfect. Nothing was going to spoil his good mood.

He was wrong.

As his eyes drifted idly down the aisle, someone caught his attention: a man sitting near the middle of the car. Something wasn't right. When he took a second look, his puzzlement turned to unease.

He'd seen this man before.

Three hours earlier, as he was waiting for Mr. Szeto on Shanghai Street, he'd kept looking around uneasily, worried about being seen by his coworkers or boss. This man had been standing across the road, outside an egg waffle stand, reading a newspaper and looking like he was waiting for a friend. He'd been ten yards from Chung-Nam the whole time, the same distance as now.

Could that be a coincidence?

At Mong Kok, Chung-Nam had to change to the Kwun Tong line. He got off the train, looking nervously behind him the whole way. Sure enough, the man was on this other platform too.

Was he being followed?

Chung-Nam didn't want to make any sudden movements in case he tipped off his tail. But who would want to follow him? Had Mr. Lee discovered his secret dealings with SIQ? Or was this industrial espionage? Perhaps anyone who met with Szeto Wai got snooped on like this.

Chung-Nam suddenly thought of another possibility: The police?

He reached into his pocket and touched the phone he'd just put away.

But no, the police would have gone straight to his home. Even if his evil deeds came to light, the police were hardly going to put a plainclothes officer on his tail. It's not as if he were the mastermind of a criminal gang or anything like that.

A lot of people got on the train, and Chung-Nam lost sight of the man. He scanned the platform when he got off at Diamond Hill, but the man wasn't there. He looked around uneasily all the way home—still no sign.

Had he been worrying over nothing?

He got back to the small apartment where he lived alone, and sank into thought.

But then he shook his head and tried to dismiss the whole thing. This evening would be a milestone in his career, and he ought to savor it.

Ping! A new message.

He loosened his tie, settled into his comfortable office chair, and awakened his sleeping computer. He closed the pop-up window reminding him about a system update and opened the Popcorn chat he looked at every day after work. At the same time, he glanced at his phone.

"Could we make it tomorrow at seven?"

Seeing her message, Chung-Nam couldn't help flashing back to the man on the train. It felt as if he were a spirit lurking in some corner of Chung-Nam's apartment, watching his every move.

2.

"The train to North Point is arriving. Please let passengers exit first."

The platform announcement brought Nga-Yee back to the present. She was at Yau Tong station, waiting to change trains. Ever since hearing Detective Mok's words at N's place, her mind wouldn't stop going back to his revelation.

Lily Shu was kidkit727.

Right at the beginning, N had said the post that started everything had the feel of a lawyer defending a client in court, and that he'd follow up on that. Nga-Yee hadn't expected that he would deputize Detective Mok for this task. She was surprised to learn that Lily had pumped the lawyer's assistant for information. And the culprit hadn't merely attacked Siu-Man, but had deliberately waited till after Shiu Tak-Ping's case was resolved to take her down, gathering material to smear her on the internet.

The most surprising thing, though, was N's response.

"All right, you've heard the recording. Now will you leave?"

That was all he said. As if Martin Tong's words had no relevance to him.

"Leave? Doesn't this recording tell us who the culprit is? Why didn't you tell me the investigation was over? Were you waiting for me to get my wages so you could extort more from me?"

"This still isn't conclusive evidence."

Nga-Yee almost exploded at the way N seemed determined to draw this out. Lily Shu had an iPhone, just like the culprit; she'd fought with Siu-Man over a boy, which meant she had a grudge; she was one of the few people who knew what happened in the karaoke bar on Christmas Eve; and the lawyer Mr. Tong had confirmed that she had information about the Shiu Tak-Ping case that the general public didn't. No matter how you sliced it, Lily was clearly kidkit727. They had witnesses, material evidence, and a motive. How was this not conclusive? The only explanation she could think of was that N was trying to save face: he'd been circling their suspects with his high-tech methods, only to have Detective Mok get there first with old-fashioned legwork.

She'd argued with N for a few more minutes, but he wouldn't budge. The most she managed to extract from him was a promise to bring her along the next time he questioned Lily. She was filled with rage all the way home, and she couldn't sleep at all that night.

For days now, she'd been thinking about Lily, Kwok-Tai, and Siu-Man. How deep was Lily's hatred? Even though Siu-Man had stopped speaking to the other two, pulling out of their love triangle, Lily still felt the need to intimidate her by the strongest means possible. When Nga-Yee thought back to the other day, a shiver went through her. If Lily's tears meant that she regretted going too far and causing Siu-Man to kill herself, at least there was still a shred of humanity left in her. But what if she'd realized that Kwok-Tai was going to reveal their romantic entanglement, and had put on a guilty act to deflect suspicion? If those were crocodile tears, this girl was truly terrifying.

On Sunday morning Nga-Yee had just arrived at the library to start her shift when her cell phone, which had been silent for days, started ringing.

"Tomorrow, twelve thirty p.m., Enoch school gates."

There was no number on the display, but Nga-Yee recognized N's voice. When he barked these orders peremptorily at her, she couldn't stop herself from snapping back, "What the hell? So I'm supposed to be at your beck and call? Aren't you going to even ask if I'm free?"

"It's your day off tomorrow, of course you're free. If you don't feel like coming, that's fine too. I'll work better without someone dragging at my feet."

Nga-Yee's face flushed red and white with anger.

"Fine, I'll be there," she said coldly, then couldn't resist adding, "What excuse did you use this time? Or are we going to ambush them at the gates?"

"We're returning a book."

"You mean we're giving the Countess back her script?"

"No." N's voice moved away from the receiver, as if he'd turned aside to look at something. "The stack of books Miss Yuen gave us included a school library book. I guess your sister had it in her locker, and Miss Yuen didn't notice. I've phoned Miss Yuen to arrange a meeting; then I got in touch with Kwok-Tai and made some excuse to have lunch with them again."

"Siu-Man borrowed a book from the library? What was it?"

"*Anna Karenina*, Volume One."

This was a surprise. Siu-Man had always thought that even light reading was too much effort, and she never picked up a novel unless she had to read it for class. Nga-Yee couldn't imagine her sister having any interest in Tolstoy *or* Russian literature.

The next day at half past noon Nga-Yee went to her sister's school once again. Unlike the previous week, the weather was bright, yet her spirits were darker than ever. She didn't know how she was going to behave when she saw Lily.

Should she show her cards, ask Lily why she wanted to hurt Siu-Man? Or would it be better to keep a poker face and just observe, prodding her to see if she was truly regretful? Nga-Yee's heart was full of doubt and confusion. She loathed the demon who'd forced her sister into suicide, yet when she thought of the two girls' radiant smiles in that photograph, she couldn't bear the idea of doing anything to her sister's former best friend.

She waited ten minutes, but there was still no sign of N. Lunchtime had arrived; boys and girls in uniform were walking out of the gate in small groups. Just as she was about to call N, her phone pinged and she saw that she had a new text message:

"Busy. Will come later. You go in first. Arranged to meet Kwok-Tai in library."

Nga-Yee frowned, but all she could do was haplessly follow N's instructions. She walked in and saw the security guard they'd seen the week before, eating his lunch out of a thermos. She said hi.

"Oh hello, it's Miss Au, isn't it? Miss Yuen said you can give me the library book." He was about sixty and a little plump. Beaming, he added, "Miss Yuen can't meet you—something came up that she needs to take care of."

"What kind of thing?" asked Nga-Yee, a little taken aback.

"The year-end exam results are supposed to be out tomorrow, and then it's summer vacation. Something went wrong with the computers, and all the marks are gone. The teachers have to record and check the results manually by tomorrow. Starting this morning, the staff room was in a complete panic. I heard that the IT consultants they hired couldn't get the data back."

"Oh dear." If only N were here, Nga-Yee thought—he might know of a solution.

"The book, Miss Au?"

Nga-Yee hesitated. If she said that N had the book and he wasn't here yet, would the attendant stop her from entering the school grounds? But N had arranged to meet Kwok-Tai and Lily in the library. What if they got tired of waiting and left?

All of a sudden it came to her—*social engineering*.

"I'd rather bring it to the library myself, if that's all right," said Nga-Yee, patting her bag as if the book were in there. "I don't want to trouble you. With the computers down and all the teachers busy, I'm sure you have a lot of extra work today."

"I do indeed." The attendant smiled ruefully. "I usually alternate lunch breaks with my coworkers, but they've all been called away by the principal and department heads to pitch in. I can't leave my post. Do you know where the library is?"

"Fifth floor, right?"

"Yup. I'll leave you to it, then."

"The last time I was here, I came with a Mr. Ong—do you remember him? He's in the public restroom nearby—upset stomach. When he arrives, could you tell him where to find me?"

"No problem. There've been a lot of upset tummies recently. It's so hot, and restaurants can be careless with the way they handle their food—"

Nga-Yee didn't wait for him to finish, but turned and headed for the stairs. That was not a bad bit of social engineering, if she did say so herself. Of course, leaving N literally in the shit was maybe not the most elegant way to finish things.

"Hang on! Miss Au!"

Her heart thumped. Had she given herself away? She turned to see the attendant holding out a plastic badge.

"You forgot your visitor's pass," he called out, still smiling.

She thanked him and pulled the lanyard around her neck as she hurried up the stairs, trying hard to stay out of his line of vision. She wasn't cut out to be a liar.

At the fifth floor, she found the library more occupied than on her previous visit, though that was still only four or five people.

These older students weren't here for the books, but clustered around the computer tables, printing batches of what looked like club notices. Violet To was behind the checkout desk again, though this time she wasn't reading a novel, but watching the group around the printer. When she noticed Nga-Yee standing in the doorway, her first reaction was surprise, but she recovered and nodded in greeting.

"Hello there," said Nga-Yee. Kwok-Tai and Lily didn't seem to be there yet, so she thought she might as well talk to Violet. "Isn't it your lunchtime?"

"We have our lunch break in shifts," said Violet a little awkwardly. "I have to be on duty for half an hour, and someone will take over later."

Violet had been in the library after lunch the week before— probably the roster changed a lot, thought Nga-Yee.

"What brings you to school today?" asked Violet.

"Siu-Man had a library book she forgot to return." Half the truth would have to do for now. Nga-Yee could hardly say, "I'm here to expose the true face of Lily Shu."

"I don't remember her borrowing anything—I guess I wasn't on duty then," said Violet. She looked at Nga-Yee for a few awkward seconds before Nga-Yee realized that she was waiting for the book.

"Um, I don't have it with me." She smiled in embarrassment. "Mr. Ong is coming with it. You know, the man you met last week . . ."

"Oh." Violet nodded and turned her attention back to the students at the computer table. Was she worried that they would damage the printer?

"Hey, I got your text. What the hell?"

Nga-Yee spun around, startled to see Miranda Lai. Her two handmaidens were behind her, and although they didn't look too different from the other girls, their elaborate hairstyles and overaccessorized phones made it clear they weren't wallflowers.

"Yes?" said Violet.

"I got a text saying I owe you people money." The Countess kept talking to Violet, having apparently decided to blank Nga-Yee.

Violet tapped at her keyboard and studied the screen. "Right, you did some printing that you haven't paid for. That's HK$135. It's almost the end of the school year, so you should really pay this by today—"

"I don't owe anything!" The Countess took an aggressive stance. "I've never exceeded my allowance! We get fifty dollars a day free, right?"

"That's only for black-and-white. The records show that you printed in color. That's three dollars per sheet, and you printed forty-five pages." Violet spoke slowly, completely calm. "Maybe you pressed the wrong button and printed in color by accident?"

"I'm not that stupid!" spat the Countess. "This isn't a new printer—I've been using it forever. It must be your mistake."

"Yeah, Vile-let," sneered one of the handmaidens. "Don't think everyone's as dumb as you."

"If you won't pay, I'll have to report it to the teacher in charge," Violet grumbled.

"Oh yes, you snitch, you love tattling, don't you? Go on then!" This was the other handmaiden.

"It's just a hundred-plus. Obviously I can afford it," sneered the Countess. "But I'm not going to pay if I don't have to!"

"Up to you, but rules are rules," said Violet placidly. "If you don't pay, I have to tell the teacher, and he'll tell your parents."

"Oh, now you're threatening me?"

Nga-Yee backed away. As the only adult in the room, she wondered if she ought to intervene, but the visitor's badge diminished her authority. If she tried, the Countess and her handmaidens would probably turn their sarcasm on her.

She'd retreated as far as the long table, where the students standing by the printer had noticed the commotion, when Kwok-Tai and Lily walked in.

"Hello, Miss Au. How are you?" said Kwok-Tai politely. Lily bobbed her head in greeting.

Nga-Yee froze. She'd have loved to slap Lily hard, grab her by the collar, and demand to know how she could be so vicious, yet she couldn't bring herself to say or do anything. Perhaps Lily was already tormented by guilt, and—forcing the culprit to suffer this burden for the rest of her life, rather than beating her to a pulp now, would be the greater punishment—

"Where's Mr. Ong?" asked Kwok-Tai, interrupting her thought.

"He's—He's on his way." Nga-Yee forced herself to keep her voice level.

"Okay." Kwok-Tai had noticed the quarrel between Violet and the Countess. "What's going on over there?" he asked.

"Some misunderstanding over fees for the laser printer," said Nga-Yee. Trying to distract herself from Lily's presence, she went on. "Don't you pay cash when you use the printer?"

"Normally. But if there's no one on duty in the library or computer room, we put it on our tab and pay later."

"How can you tell who owes how much?"

"We have online accounts, the same ones we use for the school chatboard—"

An almighty bang stopped everyone dead: Kwok-Tai and Nga-Yee's conversation, Violet and Miranda's quarrel, the other students' covert observation of it. Standing in the doorway, dressed in his usual hoodie and panting hard, was N. The crash was the library door swinging open violently.

"N? What's wrong?" asked Nga-Yee. She'd never seen him so flustered.

"Call—call Miss Yuen. Tell her to come here now," gasped N to Violet, not even glancing at Nga-Yee. Violet clearly had no idea what was going on, but did as she was told.

N charged over to where Nga-Yee was standing, pulled out a chair, and slumped into it. Nga-Yee opened her mouth but he waved her away before she could speak, still breathing hard.

Less than a minute later Miss Yuen hurried in.

"Mr. Ong! Miss Au! What's happening?"

N's breathing calmed a little as he walked over to the counter, where he set down a book: *Anna Karenina*, Volume One. Nga-Yee recognized the green cover—this was a Taiwanese edition from the eighties, now out of print.

"So stupid of me—I can't believe I didn't notice this before," N babbled. "On the way here, I happened to look inside, and found—"

He flipped open the book. About a hundred pages in were two miniature sheets of pale yellow notepaper. He unfolded them and spread them out on the counter:

Dear Stranger,

By the time you see these lines, I might no longer be here.

Recently, I've been thinking about death every day.

These slips of paper, palm-size with a border of cartoon animals, brought tears to Nga-Yee's eyes, and she had to stop reading. "That's Siu-Man's handwriting," she said, her voice choked.

Miss Yuen looked stunned, and the students were now openly staring.

"Siu-Man did leave a suicide note—but we didn't know where to look for it," said N. He set the two sheets of paper side by side. The paper was ruled, thirteen short lines on each. Nga-Yee continued reading.

I'm so tired. So very tired.
I have this nightmare every night: I'm in a
wilderness, then dark things start chasing after me.
I run and scream for help, but no one comes to my
rescue.
I know for certain that no one is coming to rescue
me.
The dark things rip me to shreds. As they rip off my
limbs they laugh and laugh.
Such horrifying laughter.
The most horrifying thing is that I'm laughing too.
My heart

is rotten too.
Every day, I can feel thousands of eyes full of
hatred boring into me.
They all want me dead.
I have nowhere to run.
On my way to school and back, I think if the MTR
platforms had no barriers, I would step in front of a
train.
An end to everything.
Maybe it's better if I die. I'm dragging
everyone down.
Every day in class, I look at her.
She doesn't show it, but I know she hates me.
And I know what she's done in secret.
She calls me boyfriend-thief, drug fiend, whore.
Although

"And then?" Nga-Yee flipped the notepaper over, but the other sides were blank. Like a madwoman, she began flipping frantically through *Anna Karenina*.

"That's it. Just these two pages," said N, looking somber. "When I realized this was only part of the letter, I thought of something—if we're lucky."

Nga-Yee and the others watched, uncomprehending, as he dashed over to the bookshelves. They only came up to his shoulder, and Nga-Yee could see that he was going quickly through the titles. Finally he grabbed one and came back to the counter.

Anna Karenina, Volume Two.

N put the book down and began flicking through it. Nga-Yee realized what he'd meant about being "lucky" when he came to page 126: an identical folded sheet of pale yellow paper nestled there. Trying to keep her hand from shaking, Nga-Yee reached for it.

"Luckily no one tossed it out," N murmured.

The letter's contents didn't help their confusion.

> already.
> I didn't write her name as an accusation.
> After all you don't know me, and I don't know you.
> I just wanted a stranger to hear everything I've
> suffered as proof that I once existed in this world.
> By the time you read these lines, I might not any
> more.

"That doesn't line up, does it?" said Kwok-Tai.

"It looks like there's a page missing," said Miss Yuen.

N riffled the pages with his thumb three times, but nothing fell out.

"Is there a Volume Three?" he asked Violet.

"No—" she started to reply, but Nga-Yee got there first. "This edition only has two parts."

"Then—" N lowered his head in thought, then abruptly turned to Violet. "Quick, check Siu-Man's borrowing record."

"Her record?" Miss Yuen repeated.

"She borrowed the first volume to hide the pages in. I don't think she'd have checked out that one book and inserted the rest of the letter just anywhere in the library. Much more likely that she took out a stack, divided the letter among them, and brought them back—accidentally leaving one in her locker. The rest of the note is probably in another book or books."

Kwok-Tai frowned. "Why would she do that?"

"No idea." N shook his head. "Maybe she wanted to make sure we wouldn't see the letter before she killed herself, so she left it in this roundabout way. Dividing it among several books made it more likely to be discovered. Not many students read books these days, after all. If she'd put it in a single volume, it could have stayed there undiscovered for years, until long after she'd been forgotten."

Nga-Yee felt a stab of pain. How could Siu-Man have said all these things to an imaginary stranger, but not to her own sister?

"She must have felt very confused as she wrote these words," N went on. "On one hand, she didn't want other people to know how she was feeling, but she desperately needed to unburden herself. And so she chose to share her thoughts with someone she didn't know, who might or might not exist—"

"Found it," Violet interrupted. She read off the screen, "*Anna Karenina*, Volumes One and Two. Nothing else."

"Nothing else?" chorused N and Nga-Yee.

"No." Violet clicked a couple of times. "She borrowed these after school on April 30 and returned Volume Two on the morning of May 4. I guess in the break after third period."

Siu-Man had died on May 5. Sorrow welled up in Nga-Yee. So Siu-Man had already been suicidal, even before that final assault from kidkit727.

"She'd never borrowed any other books?" asked N.

Violet shook her head. "The borrowing record only shows these two."

"I don't remember her ever mentioning library books," said Kwok-Tai.

"Oh!" Nga-Yee exclaimed. "Could it be among her other books? Maybe those textbooks—"

"Good idea. We should go look. Miss Yuen, could you keep an eye out in case the rest of the note ended up in her locker or somewhere else in the school?"

"Of course. I'll carry out a thorough search."

Clutching the three pages tightly, Nga-Yee bowed in thanks. She felt pulled a hundred different ways, with no idea what she should do next.

"Let's meet another day," said N to Kwok-Tai as he pushed open the library door. The boy nodded.

Nga-Yee and N returned their visitor passes, then hurried along Waterloo Road toward Yau Ma Tei station. Nga-Yee was so dazed she'd forgotten about confronting Lily. Nothing was more important now than finding the rest of her sister's last words.

And even in this partial letter, it was clear that Siu-Man knew who was smearing her, and that this person hated her.

She had known what Lily was doing to her. An agonizing thought.

"Hey! This way!"

Nga-Yee turned to see N standing by the side entrance of the Cityview hotel, pointing at the automatic doors to the lobby.

"Aren't we going to your place to look for the missing pages?" asked Nga-Yee.

"Stop asking questions, just come with me." N strode into the hotel, and Nga-Yee could only run after him.

They hurried through the foyer and into the elevator. N pressed the button for the sixth floor. When the doors opened, he led Nga-Yee down the corridor to room 603. Ignoring the DO NOT DISTURB sign hanging from the handle, he produced a keycard and swiped it so the red light turned green and there was a faint click.

Nga-Yee felt as if she'd stepped out of reality. It was a fairly standard four-star hotel room. On the bed were two laptops with multicolored cables running from them, and on the desk, by the complimentary fruit basket, were several black boxes about the size of take-out cartons, two screens, and a keyboard with a touch pad. More cables of various thicknesses ran haphazardly across the floor, several of them plugged into the forty-two-inch wall-mounted TV. Three tripods stood by the window, the ones on either side fitted with video cameras (one long lens and one short), and in the middle was a circular receiver, like a satellite dish. A dark-skinned, severe-looking man was sitting at the desk. He had earphones on and was staring intently at the screens, breaking focus only momentarily to wave in their direction when N and Nga-Yee entered.

Nga-Yee felt as if she'd tumbled into a Tom Clancy novel.

"Any movement?" asked N, walking over to the window.

"Not yet."

"I'll take it from here—you can go."

The man removed his earphones, grabbed a black rucksack from near his feet, and walked toward the door. He nodded at Nga-Yee as he passed her, but didn't say anything, as if her presence was no surprise.

"Who was that?" asked Nga-Yee as soon as he was gone.

"He's called Ducky. I guess you could say he's part of my support team." N was in the chair, staring at the screens as Ducky had been a moment ago.

"Ducky?"

"He used to have an electronics stall in Sham Shui Po on Apliu Street—Apliu as in duck house. Hence the nickname." N didn't take his eye off the screens. "He's now the owner of several computer components shops."

"And what are you up to here?"

"Do you have to ask? Surveillance, obviously."

"But what are you—oh!" Nga-Yee suddenly realized what was on the screen: the Enoch library. She darted over to the window, and sure enough, the cameras were aimed at the school. They were several hundred yards from the west wing, too far for Nga-Yee to make out details, but these cameras were powerful enough to produce a sharp image of what was going on inside.

"Don't touch those tripods," N called out. Nga-Yee had barely brushed one of the cameras, but even that was enough to make the screen image wobble.

"What's going on? Who are you watching?" All this spy equipment was making her uneasy.

"You hired me to find kidkit727, so of course that's who," said N simply.

"Isn't that Lily Shu? We have all the evidence we need, so what's all this for?"

"Haven't I already said, what we have isn't conclusive?" N glanced at Nga-Yee, then beckoned her over. "Let me show you what conclusive evidence looks like."

"What?"

"Can you see what's going on here?"

Nga-Yee looked at the screen. Through the library window, she could see rows of shelves, and beyond them the entrance. Miss Yuen, Kwok-Tai, Lily, the Countess, and her handmaidens were all still there, as were those busybodies around the laser printer and Violet behind the counter. Miss Yuen was talking to Lily and Kwok-Tai while the Countess and her lackeys were continuing their quarrel with Violet. It had been only four or five minutes since Nga-Yee and N left the library, and nothing seemed to have changed.

"Do you know what the Zhiwen Press edition of *Crime and Punishment* looks like?" N asked.

"Of course. It's the one with a bronze statue of Dostoyevsky on the cover."

"There are two copies of *Crime and Punishment* in the Enoch library: a new translation brought out last year by Summer Publishing, and the 1985 Zhiwen edition." N paused for a moment. "In a while, someone's going to walk over to the bookshelf, ignore the new version, and pick up the old one. That person is kidkit727."

Nga-Yee still didn't understand, but N had already put on the earphones, signaling that the conversation was over. All Nga-Yee could do was wait and see what the big mystery was. On the screen, Miss Yuen was walking out of the library. The Countess seemed to lose the argument with Violet; she dug a couple of banknotes out of her purse and flung them on the counter, then stomped off with her handmaidens. The older students left too, one of them clutching a stack of printed papers. Kwok-Tai and Lily sat at the table; Lily dabbing at her tears, Kwok-Tai comforting her. They left a minute later, she leaning against him. Violet To was now alone in the library.

What Nga-Yee saw next astounded her.

Violet left the counter and went over to a bookcase by the window, where she grabbed a book from the fourth shelf. Even though the resolution on the screen wasn't very high, Nga-Yee recognized the man with the enormous beard on the cover: Russian literary titan Fyodor Dostoyevsky.

That wasn't all.

Violet quickly flicked through the pages of *Crime and Punishment* and retrieved a folded, pale yellow sheet. She slipped this into her pocket, replaced the book, and hurried back behind the counter.

"She's the person you're looking for, Miss Au," said N, removing his earphones and looking at the dumbstruck Nga-Yee.

"Then . . . that's the missing page from Nga-Yee's suicide note?" Nga-Yee asked, stepping back toward the door, as if she were about to run across the road to rip the pages from Violet's hands.

"You need to calm down." N stood, grabbed another chair, and pressed Nga-Yee's shoulders to force her down into it. "The letter is a fake."

"Fake? But that's Siu-Man's handwriting—"

"I copied it."

Nga-Yee stared at him in disbelief. "Why would you do something so cruel?" she screamed, her face bright red. "Siu-Man departed without a word, and you let me believe she'd left something behind—"

"That was the only way to find kidkit727," said N, his face expressionless. "I've never lost sight of what you hired me to do, Miss Au: find the person who wrote that blog post. You were the one who forgot our goal as soon as you set eyes on that note. You have to understand that this was the only way I could find conclusive evidence."

"The only way?"

"Everything you said before about eyewitnesses and proof was circumstantial," N explained, unhurried. "None of that told us kidkit727's real identity. This person posted on Popcorn without leaving any traces, then sent your sister those messages from the MTR, also untraceably. Even if I managed to get hold of kidkit727's phone and hacked into her mailbox, I still might not find the post or those emails. And even if I could prove that the messages came from a particular smartphone, I'd have no way of showing that the person using it was kidkit727 herself. Look at it this way: if I hacked into someone's phone, used it to send threatening messages, and managed to get out without leaving any evidence, then you'd wrongly accuse the owner of the phone. I always knew the data alone wouldn't help us find our culprit."

"Then why did we gather all that evidence?"

"To narrow the list of suspects. When we'd got it down to a few, it was time for the second step: making a trap for the culprit to fall into. She herself proved that she's kidkit727. The reason we went to the school last week was to study the terrain and look for the best place to set a snare. Didn't I tell you how reconnaissance works?"

Nga-Yee remembered him using that word after the triad gangsters kidnapped them.

"So you thought up the fake suicide note last week?"

"I thought of it the day I accepted your case, but I only decided to deploy it last week. Your sister didn't leave a note, so that was an excellent way to psychologically interfere with the culprit."

"But how did you manage to copy Siu-Man's—"

Before she could finish her sentence, N reached into his bag and produced a sheaf of papers: Siu-Man's homework.

"With all these samples, I just had to spend a few days practicing to produce something roughly like it. The handwriting only had to be similar enough to convince you. I needed you to say this was real in front of all of our suspects. If Siu-Man's own sister verified it, none of them would question it."

Nga-Yee understood: she'd been N's pawn. Although she understood his motives, it was hard not to be upset at being tricked yet again.

"*Anna Karenina* and *Crime and Punishment*?"

"That was me, too, of course."

"You broke into the school beforehand to plant the notes?"

"No. All this happened right in front of you," N said nonchalantly. "Last week, I didn't just steal the Countess's script—I also took one other book away with me."

"Huh?"

"I'd been thinking about which book to pick when Kwok-Tai phoned. I had to make a snap decision, so I stuffed *Anna Karenina* Volume One into my jacket as I ran out. That's quite a common shoplifting tactic."

"Siu-Man never borrowed it?"

"No."

"I did think it was odd. She never read novels, let alone Tolstoy."

"After I'd forged the suicide note, I phoned you and said we were going back to the school," N went on. "I told you the book was among the stack Miss Yuen gave us; then I told her we'd found it at your home. That way, both of you were fooled. Volume One was the line, Volume Two was the bait, and as for *Crime and Punishment*, it was the fishhook—"

"Ah! So you planted the second and third sheets of paper just now!"

"Exactly. You couldn't see what I was doing, because the bookcase was in the way—a few seconds was all it took.

"When I deduced that the killer had to be someone your sister knew, I decided the fake suicide note would be the best way to make the culprit reveal herself. If she thought the note revealed kidkit727's actual name, she'd do whatever it took to get rid of that evidence.

"Of course, kidkit727 had no way of knowing whether the letter had her name or someone else's, but she wasn't going to take the risk, not after having gone to such lengths to keep her identity secret." N's eyes were still fixed to the screen, watching Violet.

"So whoever went to the translated literature shelf must be the culprit?" said Nga-Yee. "But what if Violet was just curious or she was helping us search?"

"How do you think I knew kidkit727 would go to the right book?" N glanced at Nga-Yee. "Violet gave herself away even before we left the library."

"How?"

"Didn't you wonder how there could be a borrowing record for *Anna Karenina*, when I stole it?"

Nga-Yee gaped. "You—you hacked into the school system!"

"Right." N smiled. "Enoch's borrowing record is online only; they've got rid of stamped cards, which made my life a lot easier. All I had to do was press a few keys to change the status of each book. Look, this is your sister's page now."

He tapped on the keyboard and shoved a laptop closer to Nga-Yee. The table on the screen was titled "Name: Au Siu-Man/ Class: 3B/ Student ID: A120527." Then three lines:

889.0143/ *Anna Karenina*, Volume One/ Summer Press/ 4.30.15/ OVERDUE

889.0144/ *Anna Karenina*, Volume Two/ Summer Press/ 4.30.15~ 5.4.15/ Returned

889.0257/*Crime and Punishment*/ Zhiwen Press/ 4.30.15~5.4.15/ Returned

"That's what Violet To saw on the screen, but she told us that Siu-Man only borrowed *Anna Karenina*. In that moment, she proved she was kidkit727." N jabbed at the screen.

Nga-Yee couldn't breathe. Violet had seemed so unflustered and helpful, but she'd been lying through her teeth the whole time, treating them like idiots. Nga-Yee didn't understand how a human being could be so wicked, let alone a fifteen-year-old girl capable of deceiving two strangers without turning a hair.

Ping. A new notification popped up on the screen showing Siu-Man's borrowing record.

"Oh, interesting!" N exclaimed.

The browser window had turned red, and in a corner were the words "Editor Mode." As Nga-Yee watched, one line of text was highlighted, then vanished from the screen.

"889.0257/*Crime and Puni . . .*" has been deleted.

Nga-Yee quickly turned back to the surveillance screen, where Violet was still at the counter, working on her computer.

"This screen mirrors the library computer. Whatever you see here is happening in real time."

"She's destroying the records." Nga-Yee had been hoping this was all some kind of misunderstanding—if nothing else, as a fellow librarian, she'd felt close to Violet. But everything she'd just seen made it clear that this apparently quiet, bookish girl was her sister's killer.

"Ha, that's clever of her. Now there's no way anyone could know," said N drily.

"But . . . but the culprit was supposed to be Lily . . ." Nga-Yee was having trouble accepting the truth, having spent the last few days convinced that Lily had tormented her sister out of jealousy.

"You still don't believe me? Your brain really is more stubborn than a donkey," N grumbled. "I went to the trouble of arranging for all the suspects to be present. Isn't that enough for you? If Lily were kidkit727, her reaction would be first shock and then pretending to be calm while working out her next step—not sitting in a corner and bursting into tears."

"You arranged for all the suspects to what?"

"Why do you think I asked to meet Lily and Kwok-Tai at the library when Violet was on shift? And how do you think the Countess showed up at that precise moment?"

"Hang on. I understand that you made up some excuse to lure Lily and Kwok-Tai there, but it was just a coincidence that the Countess—"

"I don't rely on luck or coincidence in my work," N snapped. "The Countess didn't owe the library a cent. I hacked into the system and sent her that alert."

"Wait—So that means you were late on purpose?" Of course he was, she realized—arriving with the book when everyone was present would create maximum impact.

"Correct. I got here first thing this morning and started the surveillance with Ducky, to make sure every step went according to plan. If a student had happened to borrow *Anna Karenina* Volume Two or *Crime and Punishment*, I'd have altered your sister's record again. Though the summer vacation starts in a couple of days and all books need to be returned tomorrow, I didn't think anyone was going to check out a thick Russian classic right now." N smirked. "Oh, and to make sure we could get to the library, I did something bad—the teachers are still suffering from it."

Nga-Yee stared at him. "You hacked into the school server and deleted the exam results?"

"Naturally. If I hadn't, Miss Yuen would have been waiting at the gates to take the book from us. What excuse could we have used to get up to the library? I had to do something to make sure she'd be otherwise occupied. And you didn't disappoint me—your acting was a little stiff, but you managed to bluff your way past that attendant. I didn't have to use my backup plan."

"Wait, you knew that I was—oh!"

N had pressed another key. Siu-Man's borrowing record vanished from the screen, replaced by another image: the school gates.

"There's a camera in the car parked across the road, and a listening device in one of the planters by the gate. I heard everything the two of you said." N tapped his earphones. "When you made it into the school, I went downstairs to wait. Ducky continued watching the screen, and when everyone was assembled, he gave me the signal and I charged up five flights of stairs to act out the next scene."

Nga-Yee still had some doubts.

"If Violet is kidkit727, how did she get hold of the Christmas Eve photo? How did she know what happened to Siu-Man that night?"

"Kidkit727 doesn't actually know what happened in the karaoke lounge. The post only vaguely mentions drinking and 'unsavory characters,' and the email to your sister only had the photo, with no text. I think the picture is all she had, and she made up a story to fit it. As long as she sounded like she knew what was going on, and other people believed her, that would be enough."

"But the photo—"

"I would guess Jason sent it to her."

Jason was the cousin of the red-haired guy—the one Detective Mok said was at Enoch too.

"Violet knows Jason?"

"Unclear, but that doesn't matter." N tapped the screen. "If she wanted, she could easily steal data from any number of her schoolmates. Remember the phone charging station at the library?"

"You mean she waited for Jason to plug in his phone, then quietly downloaded the photo?"

"Something like that." N pulled out Siu-Man's phone and turned it to show Nga-Yee the charging port. "This can also be used to download data. Once it's plugged into a USB port, some basic tech knowledge is all you need to retrieve whatever you need. That's known as juice jacking."

"Violet knows how to do that?"

"No idea, but the Rat certainly does," said N, reminding Nga-Yee of his theory that kidkit727 was actually two people. "Actually, I don't think she was looking for this picture in particular. I bet she collected quite a few of her schoolmates' secrets through the charging station, whether for her own amusement or some other reason, and it was only later that she realized this photo was of your sister. Kwok-Tai told us that quite a few of the older students gossiped about what happened, and I'm sure Jason shared this with his buddies. All it took was for one of them to charge his phone, and Violet would have the picture too. You should be grateful there wasn't anything more salacious in the image, or it might have gone viral. There've been quite a few cases in America—photos of a sexual assault spreading through a school."

"But this is just guesswork?"

"Sure. I can't prove that's how Violet got hold of the photo, but I'm a hundred percent certain that someone used the library's charging station to steal data."

"Why?"

"Because I'm a hacker." N pulled a black device from his pocket and placed it on the table. "The library didn't just have a gray power bank, there was also this charger that siphons data. Most people can't tell the difference between the two, but there's only a few models in Hong Kong that do this, so it's not difficult to spot them."

Nga-Yee vaguely remembered that the first time they were in the library, she'd noticed a single charger standing separate from the rest of the power bank and thought it odd at the time.

"But how can you explain Detective Mok's recording? Martin Tong's assistant identified Lily as the one who tried to find out more about the case."

"It was someone calling herself Lily Shu—that doesn't mean it actually was Lily," said N, sounding impatient. "Kidkit727 has shown that she'll go to great lengths to cover her tracks. Do you think she'd use her real name? It's not important whether it was Violet or someone else impersonating Lily. Like I said, the only thing that mattered was getting kidkit727 to reveal herself. Everything else is at most evidence to confirm our hypothesis."

Nga-Yee still wasn't convinced. "What about the Countess? Kwok-Tai and Lily said she was snooping around on the day of the funeral. That means she felt guilty. Or do you think Kwok-Tai was lying too?"

"Some people have sharp tongues, but their hearts are as soft as tofu. The Countess may seem haughty, but she's actually a compassionate person." N pulled out the condolence book and flipped it open. "Have a look at this."

Nga-Yee looked at the page. It was one she'd seen before: "Siu-Man, I'm sorry. Please forgive my cowardice. Since you left, I can't stop wondering if it's our fault. I'm so, so sorry. May you rest in peace. I hope your family can recover from their grief."

It wasn't signed, but Nga-Yee guessed what N was getting at.

"This was written by the Countess?" she said dubiously.

"See for yourself." He handed over the stolen *Merchant of Venice* script. Nga-Yee was confused for a moment, until she realized that the acting notes and amendments were in the same handwriting as the condolence page.

"Well—" It was still hard to believe that the arrogant Miranda Lai could have come up with these humble words, but even an amateur could see at once that the writing matched.

"Are you going to say she was faking it?" N asked. "I can't prove it, of course, but I actually think it's the other way around: what she wrote in the book is much closer to her true self than her everyday behavior. The entry wasn't signed, so there was no need to pretend. That makes her appearance outside the funeral parlor easy to explain: she really did want to say goodbye to your sister. But maybe she was afraid of spoiling her image, or maybe she saw Kwok-Tai and Lily and in the end didn't go in."

"Why is she normally so rude, then?"

"Weren't you ever in high school, Miss Au? Don't you re-member how important it was that your peers thought of you a certain way? Very few kids these days are able to ignore the way others look at them. If everyone agreed that two plus two equals five, would you go against the crowd? Disagreeing too loudly could mean being ostracized. If the Countess's friends sensed any weakness in her, she'd be back to being a commoner in no time at all. Every one of them is wearing a mask of one kind or another, forcing herself into the shape of her ideal person. Grown-ups ought to tell them to have more confidence and be themselves, but in our sick society, education is about creating batch after batch of robots who'll defer to authority and conform to the mainstream."

Nga-Yee had no answer to this—another thing she'd missed because her earlier life had been such a scramble. Now that she considered it, N's theory about the Countess made sense. Kwok-Tai had mentioned seeing her alone, without her handmaidens. That's when we are most ourselves, when there is no one around and we let down our defenses.

"But—but the Countess must have known someone might recognize her writing—"

"It's a loose-leaf book. Everyone wrote on a separate sheet of paper and handed it to the teacher, so none of her classmates would have seen it. Besides, most people don't go around analyzing whether some words in a condolence book are sincere."

Nga-Yee was stumped. "I . . . I didn't think of using this script to prove the Countess's feelings . . ." she stammered.

"I didn't think of it either." N shrugged. "It was just supposed to be a prop for what we did next, but then Violet To revealed her guilt, and the backup plans became unnecessary."

Nga-Yee felt a flicker of unease; something still didn't make sense to her.

"Only Violet To could have fallen into the trap you set today. She was the only one who could have changed the borrowing record, for example. When did you start suspecting her?"

"When I met her at the library last week, I thought there was an eighty or ninety percent chance she was the person you were looking for."

"What? But that's before we heard from Kwok-Tai about Siu-Man and Lily's feud or the karaoke lounge incident!"

"Yes. I wanted to get more information from Kwok-Tai so we could definitively eliminate Lily as a suspect."

"But why Violet? This was before Kwok-Tai told us about that girl she forced into quitting school—what was her name, Laura?"

"You were with me the whole time, but you didn't notice that Violet was the only person to say something strange."

"What?"

"I asked all the kids and Miss Yuen roughly the same question that day. Do you remember?"

"You mean who Siu-Man had offended to make them smear her like that?"

"Correct. And do you remember how they answered?"

"Miss Yuen said there was no bullying in the class, Lily said it was the Countess, the Countess said she had no idea, Violet said it was Lily, and Kwok-Tai told us about the incident with Violet. You suspected Violet because she pointed the finger at Lily? But we didn't know about Detective Mok's recording yet."

"You're missing the point. It doesn't matter whose name they mentioned, just how they understood my question."

Nga-Yee stared at him.

"Lily said the Countess was a blabbermouth and probably gossiped about it; the Countess said the school had told them not to discuss it, so she didn't know who'd been talking to outsiders about it; Kwok-Tai said Violet was prejudiced against Siu-Man and might have spread rumors about her; and Miss Yuen just went straight to talking about bullying." N paused for a moment. "Violet was the only one who talked about friends turning on each other, and how these days anyone can just go online and post what they like."

"What's wrong with that?"

"When we went around the school asking who smeared Siu-Man, who were we looking for?"

"Kidkit727, of course!"

"But as far as your sister's schoolmates were concerned, the person smearing Siu-Man was someone else."

"Someone else?"

"According to Shiu Tak-Ping's nephew, all the information about your sister's boyfriend-stealing habits and unsavory friends came from one of her classmates."

"But Shiu Tak-Ping doesn't have a nephew . . . Oh!"

Now she understood. From where the kids were standing, the person Nga-Yee was searching for was the classmate *mentioned* in the post—"according to a classmate." None of them should have known that the actual *author* of the post was in their midst.

"All of them mentioned talking to strangers, reporters, and so on. Only Violet spoke about posting online, as if she knew there was no nephew. That moved her to the top of my suspect list." N tapped at Violet's image on the screen. "And her unwitting confession just now proved I was right."

N's explanation was like peeling an onion, revealing additional layers of purpose to their two visits to the school. Finally Nga-Yee was ready to accept that Violet To was kidkit727. Her heart filled with hatred for Violet and sorrow for Siu-Man, but even more with a sense of powerlessness. They'd found the culprit, but so what? How would it change anything?

"I've found the person you hired me to find, Miss Au. If you don't have any further questions, the case is closed," said N.

"But . . . what should I do? Can I question her? Should I expose her to the world or scream at her in public?"

"That's entirely up to you."

Nga-Yee stared dejectedly at the screen, where Violet was sitting woodenly at the counter, as if staring at her face long enough would make something happen.

Unexpectedly, that worked.

A short-haired girl walked into the library and nodded in greeting at Violet. She said something as she walked over to the counter and took over the chair that Violet now vacated. Violet emerged from behind the counter and left unhurriedly.

"I guess she's taking over the shift after her lunch break—oh!" N gasped.

"What?"

"She turned right." N strode over to the window. "Both the cafeteria and the school gates are to the left."

Nga-Yee kept her eyes fixed on the screen, but Violet was soon out of frame. N grabbed the video camera fitted with a long lens and opened the viewfinder. Glancing at it, he shifted the camera, using his arm to keep it level. The image on the screen tracked to the right too. N's hands were very steady, she noticed. Soon Violet appeared again. She glanced up and down the corridor, then pulled open a door next to the library: the science lab. She stuck her head in first, making sure the room was empty, then went in. Although the angle was awkward, N's camera could still pick up Violet clearly, standing at the first bench by the blackboard.

What's she doing in there? Nga-Yee wondered. There was no one else around—presumably the lab assistant was at lunch too.

What Violet did next filled Nga-Yee with rage.

The girl picked up a box from the bench and pulled from her pocket the folded, pale yellow fake suicide note. She hesitated for a second, then seemed to steel herself and open the box: matches. Violet lit one, then held a corner of the note up to it until the paper was swallowed by the flame. When most of it was ash, she dropped the remnant onto the table—which was just below the frame—presumably into a fireproof dish.

"Pretty good. That's how you dispose of the evidence." N sounded half mocking, half admiring.

Nga-Yee didn't hear what he said. Her insides were being pulled through a wringer, her heart sliced thinly. She'd caught sight of Violet's face.

The girl had a faint smile on her lips.

That smile was all it took to snap Nga-Yee's rationality clean in two.

She jumped to her feet, grabbed the knife from the fruit bowl, and headed for the door.

N turned and saw her, vaulted across the bed, and grabbed her by the arm.

"Let go of me! I'm going over there to slaughter that bitch!" Nga-Yee struggled. "She's smiling! Not a speck of regret! Didn't even bother reading the note, just burned it! If Siu-Man really did write that, it would be gone. No one would ever know her last words. That harpy doesn't deserve to be in this world! As if it's not enough that she killed Siu-Man, now she wants to scrape away every last trace of her, like she never existed."

Nga-Yee's hysterical rant broke down into sobs, and she kept trying to break free of N's grip.

"Drop the knife! Go ahead and kill her if you want, but not with a weapon from this room," N roared ferociously. "The police will trace it here. Murder anyone you like, but don't get me involved."

Nga-Yee froze for a second. She tossed the blade onto the bed and tried to rush from the room, but N didn't release her.

"I dropped the knife! Why are you still holding me? I'm going to get revenge for Siu-Man."

N's expression had gone back to its usual placidity. "Do you really want revenge?"

"Let go of me!"

"I asked you a question. Do you really want revenge?"

"Yes! I want that monster ripped limb from limb."

"Calm down, let's talk about this."

"Talk about what? Are you going to say I should go to the police? Let her face the law or whatever—"

"No. The law won't be able to deal with Violet To," said N coldly. "Although incitement to suicide is a crime in Hong Kong, it won't apply in a case like this. We'd need evidence of means to get a conviction—if she'd supplied or suggested the method, for example. Violet tormented your sister with those messages, but never actually threatened her or suggested suicide."

"That's why killing her is the only way to get justice!"

"You've never asked why I'm called N."

This unexpected change of subject threw Nga-Yee, and she actually calmed down a little.

"Why should I care what you're called? You could be N or M or Q . . ."

"It's short for my web handle, which is *Nemesis*. Detective work is just something I do to pass the time. My true vocation is helping other people get revenge." He let go of her arm. "It's not cheap, but I guarantee satisfaction."

"Are you serious?"

"Remember the first time you came to see me, and we got abducted?"

"How could I forget?"

"Want to know what I did to provoke them?"

Nga-Yee looked suspiciously into his eyes, wondering what he was up to, then nodded anyway.

"One of my clients was cheated out of ten million dollars, and hired me to get revenge. I was to extort over twenty million dollars from the swindler—the original sum, plus interest. My client came to me because there was no legal way to get the money back. And you know what happened next."

"Twenty million?" Nga-Yee gaped at the number.

"Twenty million is nothing—I've dealt with much bigger sums." N grinned. "It may be hard for the average law-abiding citizen to understand, but these revenge cases are more common than you'd expect. An eye for an eye. Especially in this society, where there might be a thin veneer of civilization on the surface, but the law of the jungle is in our blood. Survival of the fittest. I normally deal with businessmen working in, um, gray areas, but I can take on a smaller case like yours."

"I'm not after money."

"I know. I've done this sort of dirty work too."

N's expression pinged something in Nga-Yee's memory. She'd seen him looking like this once before, at the moment he'd turned the tables on those gangsters in the van. She'd thought he was bluffing, but for all she knew, he really had been prepared to hurt the driver's child or put brain-eating parasites in that other guy's drinking water. Having seen the lengths he'd gone to investigating Violet To, he didn't seem like someone who'd use empty threats.

"How much are your fees?" she asked.

"For you, five hundred thousand dollars."

"I don't have that kind of money, as you well know," she said icily.

"Revenge cases work differently from investigations. I won't take a cent from you up front. When it's done, I'll come up with a payment plan that suits you."

"Can you promise that Violet To will get what's coming to her?"

"Violet To and her accomplice will get their retribution."

Nga-Yee sucked in a breath. She'd been so focused on getting revenge on kidkit727, she'd forgotten all about the Rat. She wondered what N's personally tailored payment plan would consist of—probably something like selling her organs. Yet the demon of vengeance had its claws so deep in her, she would happily have sacrificed anything.

"All right, it's a deal."

N smiled. Something in his face stirred another memory in Nga-Yee, this time from a book. She couldn't remember the exact words, but it was something about flames dancing in someone's eyes so you felt your very soul being sucked into them. This was from a description of Rasputin, as he'd wreaked havoc with the tsar's family who both loved and hated him.

Maybe I've sold my soul to a devil like Rasputin, she thought.

Even so, she didn't regret her decision.

Monday, June 29, 2015

Siu-Man's family came again. Today they found her suicide note.

15:32 ✓

I was scared to death.

15:32 ✓

suicide note?

15:54

Yes, but I got rid of the most important page.

15:55 ✓

what did it say?

15:56

I don't know, I burned it.

15:57 ✓

I didn't dare read it.

15:57 ✓

all right, well done

15:58

Can you come out tonight?

16:12 ✓

Dad's in Beijing for the next ten days, so I don't need to sneak out.

16:14 ✓

Never mind if you're doing overtime again.

16:16 ✓

should be okay

16:25

seven at the usual place

16:26

CHAPTER SEVEN

1.

"Nam, what's this 'repeat bonus'?" said Hao, pointing at a line on the laptop screen.

Sze Chung-Nam and Hao were in GT Technology's tiny conference room, coming up with the report for Szeto Wai. Mr. Lee had gotten in touch with Mr. Szeto's assistant to arrange another visit the following week, and now they had to hustle to get this done.

"When customers sign up for a regular purchase of G-dollars, the system gives them a little extra each month, but the additional dollars are available only after three months," Chung-Nam answered without looking up. He was bent over a calculator, checking the figures in his model.

"What's the point? I thought only insurance companies did stuff like that."

"Never you mind. We need to add in a few more points to make the report look better."

"This is a bit of a stretch," said Hao drily. "Szeto Wai isn't some rube. He's going to see through this right away. If he asks for details, don't you dare push the question on to me."

"All right, all right."

For more than a week now, Chung-Nam and Hao had been preparing the materials for this second visit and having constant strategy meetings. Hao wasn't familiar with the finance world, and Chung-Nam didn't know much about it either, so they had no choice but to blunder through, trying to make "gossip commodities" and "G-dollar futures" sound real. Chung-Nam hit on the idea of dividing news items into tiers and allowing their users to sign up for a preview of related articles for a small amount of G-dollars. They could then sell this right to other users for a price they would negotiate between themselves. At a glance, it did start to look like trading shares, though Chung-Nam had to wonder if this would work in practice. Hao pushed for the simpler idea of allowing users to choose between different subscriptions, to be paid for with G-dollars. For a small amount, they could purchase information from a particular source. Chung-Nam thought this sounded like following a YouTube account, but for a fee. Mr. Lee barely participated in the discussion. In their meetings every couple of days, he approved whatever Chung-Nam suggested, and always finished with the same words: "Just do whatever it takes to make SIQ invest in us."

Chung-Nam also considered restricting the quantity of G-dollars to increase the value of the futures and options, but G-dollars were an artificial commodity intended to make users part with actual cash in exchange for gossip, and keeping circulation down would only make users lose interest, so that wasn't worth it. Whatever schemes they came up with were incompatible with GT's core business model, and had to be abandoned.

Since his private dinner with Szeto Wai, his ideas had gone through a 180-degree turn.

Even if SIQ did end up investing in GT, this report would only be a fig leaf. All Chung-Nam had to do was drag this out sufficiently—he knew he had nothing to worry about. At this point, the real purpose of the report was to fool Mr. Lee, who appeared to believe that nonsense phrases like "repeat bonus" were enough to persuade Szeto Wai. Chung-Nam knew just how shallow Mr. Lee's knowledge was, and how much confidence he had despite that. If he and Hao could make this ridiculous proposal sound convincing enough, Mr. Lee wouldn't say anything, even if he did have his doubts, for fear of exposing his ignorance.

Everything was within Chung-Nam's grasp. In the last few days he'd grown sloppy working on this report with Hao, trying only to cram as much stuff into it as possible. Another voice was telling him that he had to push his advantage and make use of this opportunity to fulfill his ambition.

He'd taken advantage of the previous day's public holiday—the anniversary of Hong Kong becoming a Special Administrative Region of China—to phone Szeto Wai and ask for another meeting.

"Hello," said a voice after a couple of rings. Chung-Nam recognized it: Doris.

"I'm—I'm Sze Chung-Nam from GT Technology. Is Mr. Szeto in?" He kept his voice calm.

"Mr. Szeto isn't available right now. May I take a message?"

"Sure." Ching-Nam swallowed. "I have some matters pertaining to GT Technology I'd like to discuss with Mr. Szeto. It would be great if we could meet in person."

"All right, I'll let him know."

"Uh . . . Okay, thank you." He didn't know what else he could say to such a brief response.

He hadn't been prepared for anyone but Mr. Szeto to answer the phone—he'd had all his lines ready and the next steps planned. Instead, he was reduced to waiting passively for the other man to return his call.

A whole day passed, and Mr. Szeto still hadn't called. Chung-Nam cursed Doris—he was certain she'd forgotten to pass on the message. He decided to phone again after work, but right after lunch, when he and Hao were back in the conference room working on the text and slides for the proposal, he heard the ringtone he'd been waiting for.

"I should take this," he said to Hao, and hurried from the conference room to the passageway outside the office.

"Hello, Chung-Nam speaking."

"Hi. Sorry about yesterday. Doris has such terrible handwriting, I thought it was a different Charles who'd called." Szeto Wai chuckled. "She tells me you want to meet. What's up?"

"Um, it's not convenient to talk right now." Chung-Nam kept his voice low, turning back to glance at the office door, terrified that Hao or one of his other coworkers was eavesdropping.

"Sure. Are you free tonight? Want to come out for a drink?"

"All right. I'm free whenever."

"Let's say nine o'clock—I have dinner plans," said Szeto Wai. "I'll pick you up in Mong Kok?"

"No, no, I don't want to trouble you. Tell me the place and I'll find my own way there." Once again, Chung-Nam was anxious about being spotted by someone from work.

"This is a members only bar that I'm bringing you to, you won't be able to get in on your own—" Mr. Szeto hesitated, then said with exaggerated seriousness, "Also, there's something I want to show you. It's best if we meet in Mong Kok first."

Chung-Nam found this odd, but in order not to be left standing on a street corner again looking anxiously for his boss or coworkers, he hastily said, "Actually, now that I think of it, I have an errand to run after work. I'll be at Quarry Bay on the eastern side of Hong Kong Island—why don't we meet there?"

"Okay. Let's say nine o'clock at Taikoo Place?" This was a well-known business district in Quarry Bay. IBM had its Hong Kong offices there.

"Great, thank you!"

Chung-Nam picked this location purely to reduce the chances of running into his coworkers. No one in his office lived on Hong

Kong Island, and even if they had dinner plans there, they were much more likely to be hanging out in Causeway Bay or Central.

Trying not to look too smug, Chung-Nam went back to the conference room, where Hao was still bashing away at the computer, entering words and numbers he didn't understand.

"Girlfriend?" he said out of the blue.

It took Chung-Nam a few seconds to realize he was referring to the phone call.

"Ha, you know I'm single." He smiled to cover his anxiety, putting on a nonchalant air.

"Oh—wasn't that your girlfriend on the line? Even if she wasn't your girlfriend . . . but I guess not, she didn't really look the type," Hao said, not looking up from the keyboard.

"Just an old classmate asking me out to dinner next week," said Chung-Nam, reaching for the first excuse he could think of.

"I didn't mean the phone call." Hao glanced up at him, smiling sleazily. "That girl looked really young. She can't have been cheap."

"What are you talking about?"

"A few days ago I was at Festival Walk for a movie. Afterward, at the food court, I saw you on a date with a teenage girl." Hao cocked an eyebrow. "PTGF?"

Chung-Nam froze. He hadn't realized he'd been seen.

"Don't talk nonsense," he said, frowning. "That was my little sister."

PTGF stood for part-time girlfriend, another way of saying "escort."

"You have a little sister? How come you've never mentioned her?"

"Oh please." Chung-Nam lightened his tone. "If you and Ma-Chai knew I had such a cute little sister, you'd pester me to death asking for an introduction."

"No way. I'm not a pedo. I don't like them so young. Anyway, your sister isn't that good-looking."

"Enough of your nonsense." Chung-Nam sat down next to Hao. "Have you turned the projected user numbers into a trend line?"

"Here it is. But I don't think these numbers look too good."

Hao went on explaining the problems, but Chung-Nam didn't take in a single word. He couldn't believe Hao had seen him the other night. Not that it mattered what Hao saw or didn't see, but it bothered him that he hadn't realized he was being observed. He thought again of the suspicious man he'd noticed on the MTR after his dinner with Szeto Wai.

"I'm going—I have something urgent to take care of," he said at seven, leaving Hao buried in documents.

"Hey, at this rate, we'll never get this done by next week."

"I'll do some more on the weekend."

"Fine, but don't expect any weekend overtime from me—I already have plans." Hao grinned. "Even a hanged man needs to catch his breath."

Chung-Nam flashed him the okay sign, then trotted out of the office with his briefcase.

From the busy streets of Mong Kok he caught the MTR to Quarry Bay. Not that it was a bay these days—the boatyards had been replaced with a fancy apartment complex, Taikoo Shing, while Taikoo Place stood where sugar processing plants once had. Only the occasional street name such as Shipyard Lane remained as a reminder of the past. There were a lot of restaurants around Taikoo Place, catering to the many office workers, while low-cost food stalls in the alleyways served longtime residents. Chung-Nam had planned to have dinner at an American-style place on Tong Chong Street called The Press, but a quick glance at the menu by the door showed appetizers alone going for over a hundred dollars. His pockets weren't deep enough for this; instead, he ducked into the next street, where a rather run-down noodle establishment was able to satisfy his pangs.

After some dumplings and noodles—which were unexpectedly delicious—Chung-Nam waited in the restaurant until the appointed time. He kept running through various scenarios, hoping this encounter would go as smoothly as the last one. There weren't many customers, and the servers sat around staring at the TV, ignoring the distracted anonymous office worker lurking in a corner.

At 8:50 Chung-Nam was shaken out of his reverie by his phone ringing.

"I'm at Quarry Bay, on King's Road," came Szeto Wai's voice. "Where are you?"

"Hoi Kwong Street."

Szeto Wai repeated the street name and was answered by a beep—probably his GPS finding the location. "I'll meet you at the corner of Hoi Kwong and Tong Chong."

Chung-Nam hastily paid the bill and hurried out of the shop, expecting to see the black Tesla Model S. But no—as he approached the junction, there was Szeto Wai, standing by a dazzling red sports car.

Chung-Nam shook his hand, unable to take his eyes off the vehicle. "Mr. Szeto, is this . . ."

"I told you I had something to show you," Szeto Wai crowed. "Recognize the make?"

"Of course! It's a Corvette C7." Chung-Nam was so overwhelmed he forgot to let go of Mr. Szeto's hand. This was the latest model, its horsepower and sleek lines every bit as impressive as a Porsche or a Ferrari. There were hardly any of these in Hong Kong.

"I borrowed it from a friend. Let's go for a spin!" Mr. Szeto looked as thrilled as a kid with a new toy.

Chung-Nam got in the passenger seat, even more excited than he'd been over the Tesla. The seats alone, with their magnesium alloy frame and twin-flag Corvette logo, made this car a cut above.

Compared with European models, Chevrolets had a sort of wild energy that matched the mood of dominance Chung-Nam was after.

"It's Doris's day off, so I thought we'd take the two-seater," said Szeto Wai, getting in on the driver's side. "Besides, I'm sure you understand—if I let Doris drive, I'd feel embarrassed sitting next to her."

"Mmm, true, it would be weird to see a woman drive a Corvette." As far as Chung-Nam was concerned, this was an extremely masculine vehicle.

"That's not a problem. I just worry I'd look like a beta male."

Szeto Wai seemed to be opening up to him—a good sign. That meant he was starting to see Chung-Nam as a friend. Szeto had dressed casual again: a grayish-white shirt, no tie, deep blue lightweight jacket, khakis, and dark brown shoes. The whole ensemble made him look several years younger than his actual age. These clothes looked informal, but closer examination would reveal exceptional craftsmanship that, along with the Jaeger-LeCoultre watch on his left wrist, indicated he was exceptionally wealthy.

As Szeto Wai buckled his seat belt, Chung-Nam noticed something. "Hey this Corvette is a right-hand drive!"

"Of course, left-hand drives can't be registered in Hong Kong." Szeto's lip twitched. "Unless you're a diplomat or someone, uh, powerful from China."

"But I remember reading that Chevrolet doesn't even make right-hand drive C7s."

"It doesn't matter if you have money." Szeto Wai grinned. "Actually, I acted as an intermediary in the States to get my friend this car. Connected him to people in America, bought spare parts from a dealership, had the left-hand drive changed to right. After that, all he had to do was to arrange shipping to Hong Kong and pay the import taxes, get it licensed and registered, and he could legally drive it here."

"That can't be cheap. Surely the modification, shipping, and registration taxes added up to more than the cost of the car."

"Oh yes, for sure," said Szeto Wai drily, nudging his glasses up his nose. "But it's still not that much—about six hundred thousand for the car, plus another million for everything else. A four-hundred-square-foot apartment in Hong Kong costs five or six mil these days, so what's one million?"

Chung-Nam quickly ran through the numbers—he was right.

"My friend's a businessman. As far as he's concerned, this C7 is just a toy. Only something like a Pagani Zonda is a real car." Szeto Wai stepped on the gas. The engine roared, shaking away the last of Chung-Nam's worries.

They zoomed down King's Road, past Taikoo Shing, and onto Island Eastern Corridor, then through the tunnel of Eastern Harbour Crossing. The lights of Victoria Harbour greeted them when they rose into the open again. The lights of Kai Tak Cruise Terminal and Kwun Tong gleamed like precious jewels. The sea was dark, but if you looked closely, you could make out ships and boats of all sizes moving slowly across the surface. There wasn't much traffic, and Szeto Wai was able to floor the pedal. As the scenery flashed past, Chung-Nam felt the acceleration pressing his back into the seat.

"Zero to sixty in less than four seconds," Szeto Wai bragged. "A shame the limit's forty. If you want to really enjoy the C7's speed, you have to let rip on North Lantau Highway, where you can go up to seventy. Of course, not even American highways let the Corvette reach its full potential—their limit is eighty-five at most."

"What's the Corvette's max speed?"

"One-eighty." Szeto Wai grinned. "You'd need a private race course to reach that. Or just go to Australia, their highways have no speed limit. I once got up to a hundred and twenty there."

"I'd like to try that at least once in my life."

"You'll get your chance. Shame this isn't my car, otherwise I'd let you take a turn at the wheel."

It was Thursday night, so traffic was smooth. In just a few minutes they'd reached Admiralty and turned off the highway.

"There isn't much traffic—let's take the scenic route."

Before Chung-Nam could work out what he meant, Szeto Wai had turned the car onto Queen's Road Central. In less than a minute Chung-Nam understood what they were doing here. A flame-red sports car gliding between these shop fronts dripping with European luxury goods, attracting the envious stares of flashily dressed young things on their way to the pleasure palaces of Lan Kwai Fong, made him feel for a second as if they were in Paris or Manhattan.

So this is what rich people do for kicks, he thought.

The car cruised onto Hollywood Road in Sheung Wan, then turned back to Central. Chung-Nam had assumed their destination was Lan Kwai Fong, but Szeto Wai parked next to The Centrium on Wyndham Street, some distance from the bars Chung-Nam had in mind.

"We're here," Szeto Wai said, removing the key from the ignition. "You can leave your briefcase in the car."

"It's okay, I'll bring it with me."

They went into the building, where a bearlike foreign man in a black suit stood by the elevator. When Szeto Wai called out a greeting, the man's stern features relaxed into a smile. He took the car key from Szeto, politely summoned the elevator, and ushered Szeto and Chung-Nam in.

"That was Egor," said Szeto after the doors had shut. "He's not just the valet, but also this private nightclub's bouncer. Whether you get to enter depends entirely on his mood."

"Isn't this a members only club?"

"Anyone who gets past Egor is a member. Of course, there are different criteria for men and women."

Chung-Nam guessed what he was getting at: Egor probably judged male patrons according to their status in society, and a sad sack like Chung-Nam would never have been let in on his own. Women, on the other hand, needed only to be sufficiently attractive to encourage the men to buy more drinks.

The elevator was clearly for the bar's patrons—there was only one button other than the ground floor. The doors opened onto a wood-paneled room filled with mellow jazz and soft lighting. Behind the long bar by the entrance, two bartenders mixed drinks. Farther in were a dozen or so tables: low ones surrounded by armchairs, high ones with backless stools. At the far end was a floor-to-ceiling window with a balcony beyond it, through which the neon lights and endless streams of pedestrians below were visible. There were less than twenty customers, mostly clustered around the tables in small groups, though a couple were sitting at the bar.

A waitress in a waistcoat led them to a corner table and took their drink order.

"I'm driving, so I'll just have a Jack and Coke," said Szeto promptly.

"Me too." Chung-Nam had never tasted a Jack and Coke, but this seemed like the safest choice. He had no idea if asking for a martini would seem too flashy, or if ordering beer was vulgar.

"Nice place," said Chung-Nam, looking around. He'd only ever been in crowded, noisy bars that blared rock music or had DJs mixing electronic beats. This place was classy and sparsely attended, which made for a relaxing atmosphere, perfect for business talk or catching up with friends. Even striking up a conversation with other bar patrons didn't feel awkward here.

"If we'd stayed out later last week, I'd have brought you here," said Szeto Wai.

"Do you come here often?"

"Not really, only when I need to."

"When you need to?"

"I mean—"

Szeto was interrupted by the waitress, who arrived bearing two collins glasses. She placed coasters in front of them and then served their drinks.

"Do we pay at the end?" Chung-Nam had pulled out his wallet, determined to pay for at least one round, but she hadn't left a bill.

"They'll just put it on my tab," said Szeto, smiling and gesturing for him to put away his wallet. "Let's drink to our working together."

Chung-Nam clinked glasses with him and took a sip.

Szeto came straight to the point. "All right . . . you said you had something you wanted to discuss?"

Chung-Nam set down his glass. "My coworker Hao—our 'customer experience designer'—has been putting together a new proposal, which we'll present to you next week."

"Fine. Are there any problems? After all, even if the report's not quite up to scratch, I'm still going to invest in your firm."

"The problem is that Kenneth isn't playing any part in this." Chung-Nam almost stuttered, still not being used to calling Mr. Lee by his English name.

"Oh?"

"He didn't give us any vision at all, just said to come up with some ideas like last time, to make you interested in putting money into the company." Chung-Nam frowned. "I think that's a serious problem. Kenneth set up GT to disrupt chatboards and give those old farts at Popcorn a run for their money. Whether or not he succeeded, at least that showed some spirit. But now there's nothing in his eyes except dollar signs."

"Really?"

"I think the company's lost its sense of direction." Chung-Nam sighed. "GT might have a small staff, but work used to be allocated fairly. Kenneth's the boss, so he focused on fund-raising. Ma-Chai and I were in charge of the tech side, while Hao was more customer-facing. But ever since Kenneth took part in that VC project, he's been throwing money willy-nilly at developing GT itself, even though that's the wrong way around."

"You have a point."

"Right now, the company has a chance of getting funds from SIQ. Kenneth should be overseeing this new strategy himself rather than tossing it to his subordinates."

"Why do you think Kenneth is behaving like this? Is it just that he doesn't understand the plan you proposed, or something else?"

"Well . . ." Chung-Nam hesitated for a few seconds. "He's dating Joanne."

"His secretary?"

Chung-Nam nodded. "Nothing wrong with an office romance, unless it gets in the way of work. Kenneth's meant to be our leader, but he's too infatuated to do his job."

"In that case . . ." Szeto Wai picked up his glass and sat looking lost in thought.

Chung-Nam sneaked a glance at his expression, trying to work out if his words had the desired effect. He'd told only the partial truth: Mr. Lee had indeed played no part in devising the proposal, but that was because he had no idea what "options" were, so he was happy to leave that to his subordinates while Chung-Nam and Ma-Chai focused on getting the video streaming and cell phone apps done. Mr. Lee and Joanne were very careful to be discreet in the office, and it was Mr. Lee's incompetence that affected his work, not their affair.

"It's disappointing," Szeto Wai said.

Chung-Nam cheered to himself. It had worked. Then Szeto's next words plunged him from paradise into hell.

"Chung-Nam, you've disappointed me."

Chung-Nam stared blankly at Szeto, uncertain how to respond.

"I asked you to be my eyes and ears so you could tell me what was happening behind the scenes, not so you could tattle on your coworkers," said Szeto Wai evenly. "Don't you think it's rash of you to tell me this before SIQ's made our investment? What would you do if you were me? Would you shout at Kenneth for not showing strong leadership, or would you just drop the whole thing?"

Szeto's tone was mild, but Chung-Nam could tell he was furious. He might have gone too far, but having led with this move, he had no choice but to put more chips on the table and keep on gambling.

"Please look at this before you say anything more." Chung-Nam reached into his briefcase and pulled out six or seven sheets of paper, which he placed before Szeto Wai.

"What are these? Did you steal confidential documents from your own firm?" Szeto said icily. "This is getting worse and worse."

"No. I wrote these in my spare time." Chung-Nam kept a lid on his unease and pressed on. "Ever since I met you last week, I've spent some time going over SIQ's investment records and anything related I could find online—official financial reports as well as blog rumors."

Szeto Wai looked a little puzzled, but allowed Chung-Nam to continue.

"In the last year, SIQ has invested in only eight internet services. This is the one closest to GT." He pointed at a line in one of the English-language documents. "A website called Chewover. It's about the same as we are in terms of design and chat capability, but it can host images, clips, and audio independently. Scores are given out based on clicks and ratings, and highly ranked users have special privileges, or even cash rewards. Just like YouTubers get revenue from ads. I reckon SIQ wants to buy GT to merge us with this American site first."

"First?"

"Of course." He pointed at another part of the document. "At the same time SIQ was investing in Chewover, you also took up an unremarkable company called ZelebWatch, which operates a news site of the same name, mainly aggregating gossip on American celebrities and public figures. In the beginning it was just a content farm for showbiz magazines, but later it put together an editorial team who doubled as paparazzi and auctioned off photos and videos invading celebs' privacy. That made it more like a tabloid paper."

Chung-Nam looked up and stared at Szeto Wai. "SIQ is going to merge Chewover and ZelebWatch."

"How did you come to that conclusion?"

"Because you're letting SIQ's investment in GT go forward. If these two websites combined, they'd more or less duplicate everything GT does."

"And this document of yours explains that?"

"No. This is GT's forecast and development analysis—a five-year projection for the hypothetical situation I just mentioned."

Szeto Wai's expression softened just for a second. "I believe that GT Net will become a new form of entertainment media and disrupt the current model as we know it," Chung-Nam said. "The USP is volatile pricing of posts according to popularity. If we can make G-dollars exchangeable with real money, that effectively turns all our users into showbiz reporters. YouTube is a good example of what happens when you break a monopoly—anyone with a computer or even just a smartphone can be a YouTuber."

Szeto Wai flipped through the document as he listened.

"If we think of computer terminals as entertainment centers, the future of GT Net is easy to imagine," Chung-Nam went on rapidly, aware this might be his only chance to perform. "YouTube succeeded by turning everyone into directors. We have to turn them into paparazzi, editors, copy editors, printers, delivery people, and newspaper vendors. With technology, all those jobs can be done by regular people. The phones we carry around are just as good as old-school professional cameras. Online posts don't need to be laid out or printed. And with online payment, readers can pay content providers directly. GT Net will allow amateurs to be reporters, photographers, and editors. Gossip magazines will decline and vanish. That's step one."

"Is there a step two?"

"Yes." Chung-Nam nodded. "Step two involves new methods of collaboration. Some YouTube channels work together, making guest appearances in each other's videos, or even shooting coproductions. GT Net can do the same. Well-known users—maybe we should call them editors in chief—will attract people who want to work with them. Like ZelebWatch, we'll make it possible to provide regular users with news, pictures, and video. All we'll have to do is make it easy for them to communicate and disseminate their content, and we're sure to dominate the market, which should make our website very profitable."

"That's an interesting point of view," said Szeto, his eyes still on the document. "But what does any of this have to do with Kenneth?"

Chung-Nam swallowed, gathered his courage, and spoke the words he'd held in for the last two weeks.

"I believe I'd make a more suitable CEO of GT Net than Kenneth Lee."

Szeto Wai looked up, shock written across his face. He studied Chung-Nam carefully, as if they were meeting for the first time.

Chung-Nam worked hard not to let any fear show on his face. Even at university he'd already had dreams of running a successful business. As a shortcut, he'd taken a job at a small company, hoping the day would come when he'd find an investor with enough foresight to take a risk on him. The first time he met Szeto Wai, though, Wai said something that inspired Chung-Nam to change his goal.

Szeto Wai had happened to mention that the Hong Kong Philharmonic's conductor was Dutch, the principal guest conductor was from Shanghai, and the principal violinist was Chinese Canadian.

Why find investors to help set up my own business when I can just steal one instead? was the thought that flashed through his mind.

Much easier to snatch an existing firm than set one up from scratch. It didn't matter who'd set up the orchestra, van Zweden was in charge now. He decided how it was run and what its future was. The Hong Kong Philharmonic was the manifestation of this man's spirit.

If Chung-Nam could just get rid of Kenneth Lee, GT Net would be his for the taking.

Having had this idea, Chung-Nam put everything he had into realizing this goal. Knowing that Szeto Wai would be in Hong Kong for only a month, he'd made sure to bump into him at the Cultural Centre, badgering him into conversation, all to ensure his future position.

"Once SIQ invests in GT and becomes the majority shareholder, you'll hold all the power." Chung-Nam's heart was racing, but he spoke confidently. "Including the power to change the leadership."

Szeto Wai was silent, his arms folded in front of him and his brow furrowed. Chung-Nam could tell he wasn't upset, but struggling to choose between two alternatives.

"You're much bolder than I'd expected, Chung-Nam," he said after a long while. "That's not a bad thing. I've always believed that one only achieves great things by being sufficiently ruthless. Playing it safe means missing opportunities. But you know, Brutus died a terrible death in the end, and it was Octavius who took power."

"Kenneth Lee is no Caesar. At the very most, he's a provincial governor somewhere in the Roman Empire."

Szeto Wai chuckled at that, thawing the atmosphere a little.

"There have been changes of leadership in previous SIQ investments, but very few, and only many years after we first put money in," said Szeto Wai. "And actually, most venture capitalists won't use this power. We'd rather cut our losses and pull out than get involved in HR matters. If an investor were seen to be abusing his power, not only would that damage the company, it would hurt the VC's reputation too. After all, there's no way to guarantee that the person we choose will improve performance. True, after SIQ gets involved, Kenneth will gain a considerable sum of money from the sale of his shares. Still, he'd feel betrayed if we removed him right away, and that would affect your co-workers too. If he set up another firm and poached some of his former staff, that would hurt us even more. A VC isn't investing in the business itself, but in the talent and creativity within each business."

"What if I can hold on to all our staff?"

"Really? Even the secretary?"

"Joanne is only Kenneth's assistant. She doesn't bring any value to running the company—any college graduate could replace her," said Chung-Nam earnestly. "The people who really keep GT running are myself, Ma-Chai, Hao, and Thomas. If I were steering the ship, most of the problems you brought up earlier would be easily resolved. It's not like I'm parachuting in—by promoting someone from within the existing staff, you'll show that you reward talent, which should increase everyone's sense of belonging to the company. So how about it, Mr. Szeto? If I can promise you that the other three will stay put, will you consider my proposal?"

Szeto Wai didn't answer, he just picked up the document and started reading attentively, stroking his chin from time to time as if seriously considering it. Chung-Nam waited on pins and needles for the decision of the future chairman of the board. The two of them sat in complete silence for fifteen minutes. Chung-Nam was so worked up that a quarter of an hour seemed to last more than a day. Without realizing it, he'd finished his drink, but didn't feel he could order another.

Finally Szeto Wai nudged his glasses up his nose and put down the document.

"You said you and your coworkers are preparing the report for next week?"

Chung-Nam nodded.

"What's it about?"

Chung-Nam went through the plans and ideas he'd shoved into the report, including transferable access and pay-to-read options, as well as the "repeat bonus" that even he found ridiculous. Szeto Wai listened with a grin, as if Chung-Nam were telling a big joke.

"All right," said Szeto Wai, cutting him off. "That's enough. It's unbelievable that Kenneth didn't object to any of this—I can't imagine how he even came up with the idea of GT Net in the first place. Fine, I'll accept your proposal . . ."

It was like getting his exam results and seeing that he'd come in first. Chung-Nam's heart exploded with joy, and it was all he could do not to stand up and cheer. He sensed that Szeto Wai still had more to say, so he stayed quiet and let him finish.

". . . provided you submit to a test."

"A test?"

"Your analysis of the situation isn't bad, but this is just a first draft." He jabbed a finger at the document. "I need you to write me a full report, not just about GT Net's technology and prospects, but also a financial statement, breakdown of its holdings, market intelligence, business plans, and so on. I'll forward it to SIQ's finance department for them to look through. I also want a formal statement explaining the contents of the report."

Chung-Nam didn't have access to the financial information, but he was pretty sure that if he told Mr. Lee he needed it for the report on "G-Dollars as Financial Instruments," it would be handed over with no questions asked.

"No problem. And could I ask when my proposal will be put into action?"

"Next week, when I visit your office."

Chung-Nam gaped. "You—you want me to confront Mr. Lee with it?"

"No." Szeto Wai took a sip of his drink. "I want you to take advantage of the moment to show off your abilities. As you said, Kenneth doesn't have the first idea about these G-dollar options you pulled out of thin air, so he'll almost certainly let you handle the presentation. Seize the moment and give me the new report. Though I should warn you, I'm not going to go easy on you. If I'm not happy with what you say, I'll let you know right away. On the other hand, if I approve, I'll make it clear that it was your revised report that secured my investment. After that, you'll be able to use that as an excuse to take Kenneth down, and that should make the takeover go more smoothly."

Chung-Nam hadn't got as far as this in his plan, but now that he thought about it, this probably was the most effective tactic to damage Mr. Lee's authority and win the support of his coworkers. After all, if Mr. Lee kept saying "Do whatever it takes to make SIQ invest," and Chung-Nam did just that with a report he'd secretly prepared on his own time, it would highlight his boss's incompetence.

That said, Chung-Nam had no way of knowing whether his report would convince Mr. Szeto. If it went badly, he might find himself in a tricky position: losing the support of his peers without gaining Mr. Szeto's recognition. Mr. Lee might even realize what he'd been plotting, in which case he might find himself at the receiving end of a termination letter.

"I'm not forcing you," said Szeto Wai, smiling. "And you don't have to give me an answer. I'll just turn up at your office next week and see which version of the report I hear."

"Okay—" Chung-Nam's stomach was churning. Success was within his reach, but in order to get what he wanted, he'd have to take an enormous risk. If he abandoned his plan and obediently presented the nonsense about "G-dollar futures," the company would get a huge cash infusion, and his own salary and job description would surely rise too. No downside there. Yet he understood that if he wanted to eliminate Mr. Lee, this would be the most direct, most effective method. If he believed in his plan, he'd have to seize the moment and do everything he could to improve his odds.

"You haven't said what you think of my first draft, Mr. Szeto, nor whether I was right about Chewover and ZelebWatch. You could at least tell me whether I'm on the right track. That's only fair."

"So now you're bargaining with me?" Szeto Wai scolded, though his expression stayed friendly. "Obviously I can't say anything about Chewover or ZelebWatch, because of the NDAs, but the first two steps you named do indeed fit with my future plans for GT Net. In fact, there's also a step three."

"Step three?"

"Remember the Boston Marathon bombing a couple of years ago? You know which media organization had the fastest response, with the most information?"

"CNN?"

"No. It was BuzzFeed."

This was a surprise. "BuzzFeed isn't a mainstream news source, is it?"

"Certainly not back then." Szeto Wai shrugged. "But the fact is, they won this round. While traditional outlets like the *New York Post* were still wrongly reporting that twelve were dead, BuzzFeed had the right number on its website, plus photos from the scene and quotes from the Boston PD. Regular newspapers send reporters out to gather information, but BuzzFeed used the internet: Twitter, Facebook, YouTube, and so on were its sources. They verified each picture and piece of information as it came into their New York office until they'd pieced together the truth. A *New York Times* reporter tweeted that he actually got his updates from BuzzFeed."

Chung-Nam hadn't known any of this, but then he wasn't American and didn't pay much attention to foreign news.

"After this, BuzzFeed was no longer seen as a frivolous website, but a new media outfit that shouldn't be underestimated. Even the president's chief of staff understood this point. Since March, BuzzFeed has been allocated a space at White House briefings, at the same level as Reuters, AFP, CBS, and so on." Szeto Wai paused for a moment. "There's another website behind BuzzFeed's success."

"What's that?"

"Reddit."

Chung-Nam gaped. As GT's director of technology, he'd heard of Reddit, of course, but hadn't done much more than surfing through a few posts.

"Less than fifteen minutes after the bombing, the 'News' subreddit already had a thread," said Szeto Wai. "People at the scene posted reports and pictures, and even people who weren't there reposted news from other sources. Someone linked to the marathoners' finishing times, so others could check if their friends and relatives were safe. Some of the photographs were disturbing—survivors with severed limbs being carried away, and so forth—but that was the reality, much more than the sanitized images we see on TV. There's no way to prove this, but plenty of people suspect that the BuzzFeed editors must have used this thread to get hold of firsthand accounts."

"So step three is . . ." Chung-Nam was starting to guess what he was getting at.

"Yes. I believe this is the next wave in the news revolution." Szeto Wai smiled crookedly. "GT Net won't just be an aggregator of gossip or entertainment news, but of *all* news. Long ago, in order to satisfy the public demand for information, papers would put out an evening edition or a special issue if something big blew up. With the arrival of TV, people had a more direct source of news, and the papers evolved to be more a vehicle for deeper analysis and commentary. Evening editions and special issues disappeared. The internet disrupted this model once again. Like you said, regular people have replaced professionals, and we're entering an era when the entire population are reporters. The public can now get unfiltered, unsorted data and see for themselves what's really going on, diminishing the authority of the press and the media. Do you know who the Boston Marathon bombers were?"

"Wasn't it a pair of brothers who'd immigrated to the States?"

"Correct. But do you know who found them?"

Chung-Nam shook his head.

"The first person to identify the suspects, from photos of the scene, was a Reddit user."

Chung-Nam took a moment to process this. "People online found the culprits?"

"The Feds won't admit this, of course." Szeto Wai grinned. "But even before they started circulating any pictures, quite a few people on Reddit had already pointed out that the two men with backpacks, one in a white cap and one in black, were likely suspects. They came to pretty much the same conclusions as the police, and probably had an easier time—everyone online is very happy to talk and exchange information, batting ideas around until they reach a logical conclusion. The FBI, on the other hand, only has finite resources to carry out their investigation."

Chung-Nam hadn't thought things like this happened outside of movies or novels.

"These days, people have forgotten what the function of news is," Szeto Wai went on. "News is a mechanism by which people can understand what's happening in their society, and something that satisfies our human curiosity about the world. Most important, it's a weapon that allows us to live without fear. Journalists report on political scandals not to provide fodder for watercooler gossip, but to inform us that our rights are being infringed, that our shared wealth is being stolen by some selfish bastards. Murder suspects are named to remind us to be alert and to show that justice is being done. The internet has woken up a desensitized generation, reminding them to pay attention to their rights, their duties, and their surroundings. No longer will they allow information to be stuffed down their gullets like ducks being fattened. Instead, they use their own eyes and ears to decide what's true and what's false."

Szeto Wai shook his glass so the melting ice tinkled. "I believe you now understand why I think GT Net is worth investing in. When the entire population has been turned into reporters and their firsthand accounts can be found on your website, people will naturally be willing to pay for access. For any VC, this is the most ideal, effective type of investment, with the highest returns."

Chung-Nam realized that he'd been looking at this far too narrowly. He'd thought GT Net wasn't commercially viable, but he'd failed to spot its enormous potential. He had always regarded himself as the smartest guy in the room and looked down on everyone around him. He'd been unpopular all through secondary school and university, but he put this down to people being jealous of his talent. He graduated with excellent results, which he threw in their faces. In front of Szeto Wai, though, he realized that all this was a lie. A good degree was just so much scrap paper, and he seemed worldly only because his co-workers were so pathetic. Like many office drones, he'd been full of dreams that he'd reach untold heights and achieve great things. Most people overestimate their abilities. Their dreams run through their fingers, and after twenty or thirty years they're left lamenting that they've achieved nothing, that the world has not bent itself to their will.

In this moment, Chung-Nam felt a wave of inadequacy. This man before him was extraordinary—not because of his fancy clothes or posh watch or expensive car, but because he was unquestionably the real deal, someone with an impeccable eye and a nimble brain. Chung-Nam had ingratiated himself with Szeto Wai because he wanted access to power; now he was starting to realize that there was a lot he could learn.

He might as well take this opportunity to find out all he could about future tech trends. "What impact do you think the cloud will have on the internet, Mr. Szeto?"

Szeto Wai didn't hold back, but answered all his questions. They moved on to big data, wearable technology, and the great firewall of China. Most of their conversation had nothing to do with GT Net—Chung-Nam wanted to expand his horizons as much as possible.

"Excuse me—I need the restroom," Chung-Nam said. After more than an hour, he could no longer contain himself.

"Over there." Szeto Wai pointed at a corner by the bar.

The bathroom was empty. Chung-Nam quickly peed, then washed his face at the sink. The person in the mirror looked reborn. He hadn't got what he wanted, but he knew this game of chess was almost over. Szeto Wai had come up with quite a few—really, quite a few dozen—ideas for how to turn GT Net into the dominant web service of their era. Chung-Nam lacked Szeto's vision, nor did he have a partner with a mind as sharp as Satoshi Inoue's. There was no way he'd ever build anything as accomplished as Isotope or SIQ, but he believed he could be a more than capable lieutenant, and that he'd triumph under Szeto Wai's leadership.

He broke into a broad grin. His reflection smiled too, humoring him.

On his way back from the bathroom, Chung-Nam saw that there were many more customers than when they'd arrived—he'd been too absorbed in their conversation to notice. There were now only two or three empty chairs in the place, and every table was occupied. On the balcony, several foreign-looking guests chatted away happily as they smoked cigars. As he passed one of the tall tables, a young woman happened to meet his eye. She looked away after less than a second, but she left a deep impression on him—reminding him of a particular Japanese starlet, with willow-leaf brows, almond eyes, and oval face, not to mention the faint curve of her scarlet lips. The resemblance was uncanny, apart from her hair, which was straight where the starlet's was wavy. Her sleeveless black dress came down to her knees, yet even without showing too much skin, she emanated a fierce sensuality that was at odds with her doll-like face. Next to her was a short-haired woman in her early twenties with equally striking features, though neither the plunging neckline of her pink minidress nor her fashionable Korean cosmetics could make up for the gulf between her and her companion.

Chung-Nam got back to his seat just in time to see the waitress setting down two fresh glasses of Jack and Coke. "I saw your glass was empty, so I ordered you another," said Szeto Wai.

"Thanks," said Chung-Nam, smiling, his mind still on the woman. Without meaning to, he turned around and glanced behind him.

"Someone you know?" asked Szeto Wai.

"Oh, no, no. I just thought she looked like a Japanese actress." Chung-Nam tried to pull himself together and stop making a fool of himself in front of Mr. Szeto.

"Which one—black or pink?"

"Black."

"Ah." Szeto Wai smirked, guessing what was on Chung-Nam's mind. "So that's your type."

"Uh . . . I suppose." Chung-Nam took a sip of his drink to cover his embarrassment. He wasn't sure if this turn in the conversation would be another danger zone.

"Go say hi."

Chung-Nam almost choked—he hadn't expected this. Could it be another test?

"Relax, Chung-Nam." Mr. Szeto chuckled. "Let's not make this all about work. We're at a bar—you ought to take it easy. Let your hair down, have a bit of fun."

"Just go over and talk to her? I'll get shot down," said Chung-Nam. Striking out was no big deal, but having it happen in front of Szeto Wai would be a disaster.

"Out of every ten women who come to a bar, nine want to be chatted up." Szeto Wai leered. "Especially the ones at the bar or the high tables—that's a signal that they're willing to be approached, because a man can just saunter over, stand next to them, and start talking. I reckon those two are ours for the taking."

"I'm not you, Mr. Szeto. Women aren't interested in me like that." Chung-Nam had tried to pick girls up in bars, but the attempts always ended so badly, he'd finally given it up.

"Nonsense," said Szeto Wai sharply. "This has nothing to do with looks or wealth or status. If you don't have confidence in yourself, obviously you're going to fail."

"Fine, I guess I'll buy them a drink—"

"Oh my god, you're hopeless." Szeto Wai grabbed his hand before he could summon the waitress. "You know what you're saying when you buy a woman a drink? You're telling her, 'I have no luck with women, so I'm buying five minutes of your time with this beverage.'"

"I thought that was the most normal way to start a conversation in a bar."

"Forget it. Come with me." Looking amused, Szeto Wai grabbed his glass and stood up. Chung-Nam was startled, but then he did the same without a second thought.

"Pardon me." Szeto Wai had arrived at the two women's table and was ignoring their skeptical looks. "I'm from New York and don't know Hong Kong very well. My colleague here insists he's seen the two of you in a magazine, but I don't believe it's that easy to bump into celebrities in a city of seven million people. Help us settle a bet: Are you models or film stars?"

"Of course not!" The women burst into giggles. "Your colleague is too kind."

"See, Charles? You owe me dinner," Szeto Wai called out. "Ladies, could you recommend a restaurant? The more expensive the better—that guy's paying. If I don't name a place, he'll probably take me to some hole in the wall and tell me it's a cult favorite."

And just like that, the conversation flowed. The women reeled off French and Japanese restaurants in Central. Chung-Nam watched as Szeto Wai casually placed his glass on the table, and as they talked, he naturally slid into the empty seat by the short-haired woman. This was blowing Chung-Nam's mind. He'd always thought that picking up girls in nightclubs was all about being suave and plying them with drinks, yet Szeto Wai's understated method was clearly much more successful.

"I'm Wade, by the way, and that's my friend Charles over there," said Szeto Wai about five minutes later. He probably didn't use that English name very much, Chung-Nam thought.

"I'm Talya with a Y," said the short-haired woman. She pointed at the beauty in black next to her. "And this is Zoe."

"That's a coincidence—one of my coworkers in the States is named Talya. Her dad's British, but her mom's from a famous Jewish family, so I always assumed it was a Jewish name . . ." Szeto Wai paused, sizing up Talya. "You're not from a famous family, by any chance?"

"No way!" Talya giggled. Even Zoe was smiling now. "What do you do in the States, Wade?"

"Something to do with the internet," he said vaguely. "Charles too, though he's based in Hong Kong. He's a great director of technology."

The women reacted to that. A moment ago, they'd only had eyes for the debonair, witty Szeto Wai. Chung-Nam hadn't managed to insert himself into the conversation, and he might as well have been invisible. Now, though, they were looking at him with interest.

"Only at a small firm," said Chung-Nam, forcing a smile. He wasn't sure if Szeto Wai was being mischievous by emphasizing his fake job title, or if this was a tactic he used: offering someone else up as a distraction to keep his own status hidden. After all, if he said, "I'm a multibillionaire entrepreneur," that would probably scare off some women while attracting gold diggers.

Over the next hour, Chung-Nam felt a sort of satisfaction he'd never before had with a woman. The conversation was frivolous—which nightclubs and restaurants they liked, gossip about this or that celebrity, random American jokes that Szeto Wai tossed out—but it was the women's reactions that pleased him. He was aware that he had nothing interesting to say, yet they stared at him with fascination, smiling along with him, eyes gleaming with admiration. If he were alone, Chung-Nam thought, they'd probably have lapsed into awkward silence after ten minutes, but Szeto Wai was a master of repartee. Soon the atmosphere had warmed up so much, they could have been mistaken for old friends having a get-together.

"I know a psychological test that's quite accurate, want to try it?"

Every time things quieted down, Szeto Wai came up with something to draw the women back in. He focused his attention on Talya, leaving the field wide open for Chung-Nam to flirt with Zoe.

"Blue? That means you're probably not too popular," said Szeto Wai to Zoe. The test had consisted of choosing colors.

"There are different shades of blue," said Chung-Nam, defending her. "I bet you were thinking of light blue, so pale it's almost white." Talya had chosen white earlier, and Szeto Wai said it meant she was good in social situations.

Zoe laughed, but Chung-Nam felt he was having trouble connecting with her. As they chatted, he liked her more and more. Apart from her looks being exactly to his taste, she was easygoing and well-mannered. He started to feel a rare stirring of true emotion. Should he work harder to win her over?

"I'm getting another," said Talya, draining her glass. She raised an arm, but it was after eleven now, and there were more customers keeping the servers busy.

"I'll go to the bar," said Zoe, jumping to her feet. Chung-Nam noticed that her glass was empty too.

There was a crowd at the counter. Having trouble attracting anyone's attention, Zoe squeezed her way to the front. Just as Chung-Nam was hesitating over whether he should help, Szeto Wai was already striding over and having a word with the bartender. A short while later they came back with two glasses of honeydew-green margaritas.

Chung-Nam kicked himself for his hesitation. Szeto Wai and Zoe took each other's seats when they came back—Szeto Wai had been between Chung-Nam and Talya before, but now he had one woman to either side and was giving Zoe more of his attention. She'd clearly made an impression on him at the bar. As for Talya, now that she was next to Chung-Nam, she kept trying to whisper in his ear.

"So you're a director of technology. Have you ever met Steve Jobs or Bill Gates?"

The tenor of the evening had changed. On the surface, the conversation seemed as warm as before, but Zoe was now shooting meaningful looks at Szeto Wai and bestowing her tinkling laugh on him. Meanwhile, Talya was leaning closer and closer to Chung-Nam, making sure he had a good view of her cleavage. He stayed friendly, but it was turning him off.

"I should head home," said Zoe at around 12:50.

"It's still early," said Chung-Nam, hoping to buy more time so he could win her back.

"Zoe lives quite far away. It'll be after two by the time she gets home," Talya interjected.

"Where?" asked Szeto Wai.

"Yuen Long."

"I'll drive you home."

"Thanks." Zoe agreed without even thinking about it. Her face was flushed. Watching, Chung-Nam understood that he'd missed his chance. He had only himself to blame.

Szeto Wai stood and gestured at the waitress, who nodded and spoke a few words into her mouthpiece. This probably wasn't for the bill, Chung-Nam thought—Szeto Wai's tab would go straight onto his credit card—but for Egor to bring his car around.

Talya and Zoe headed for the elevator. Chung-Nam started to follow, but Szeto called him back.

"You forgot your briefcase."

Indeed, it was still at the table they'd been sitting at earlier. He hurried back for it.

"Thanks."

"Pissed off?" said Szeto Wai unexpectedly.

"What?"

"I took the one you wanted."

"It's fine, Mr. Szeto. If you like Zoe better, of course I'd—"

"I'm not particularly into her." Szeto Wai shrugged. "I just wanted to make you understand that ambition alone isn't enough. You have to use the right methods to achieve your goals."

Chung-Nam froze. He couldn't find anything to say.

"Why do you think I ignored Zoe to start with and made up some nonsense about her being unpopular? I was negging her to get past her defenses. You can use the same tactics in the business world. If you want to replace Kenneth as CEO, you'll have to understand all these theories. Striking out tonight is nothing—all you miss out on is a fuck. But mess up in business, and you could be saying goodbye to the career it took you all these years to build."

"Un-understood." So this had been another of Szeto Wai's tests, and Chung-Nam had failed. He knew how manipulation worked, he just hadn't dared pull the trigger at the critical moment, and he wasn't sure that his methods would have been effective with Zoe anyway.

"Don't get too stressed out," said Szeto Wai lightly. "Talya's pretty hot too. Just make do with her for tonight."

"Make do?"

"Bag her up and take her home. She's into you. Haven't you realized?"

"They're not like that, are they?"

"Didn't I tell you they were ours for the taking?" Szeto Wai smirked. "I don't care what you do, but I guarantee that Zoe isn't making it home tonight."

All the way down in the elevator, Chung-Nam's heart was churning. He'd known Zoe for only three hours, but he still didn't believe she was the sort of girl who'd jump into bed with a man she'd just met. To talk about her in the same breath as any woman he'd ever met would be an insult.

When they got to the street, he knew he was wrong.

"This is your car?" Zoe asked. Zoe and Talya were slack-jawed at the sight of the Corvette. They walked over like kids who'd just spotted some candy. Zoe's expression told Chung-Nam that his goddess was no more than a vulgar creature who'd happily prostrate herself before money and power, handing over her body for a little piece of it.

Well, this was reality, after all, Chung-Nam thought bitterly, smiling grimly at his earlier naïveté.

Szeto Wai took the keys from Egor and said to Chung-Nam, "Hey, remember when you asked if I was a regular here?"

Chung-Nam thought back to their interrupted conversation. Szeto Wai had said he came here "when he needed to."

"This is what I meant by needing to." Szeto Wai glanced at Zoe, who was peering through the windshield, trying to make out the car's interior.

Chung-Nam could only watch helplessly as he opened the door and ushered Zoe into the passenger seat.

"Sorry I can't offer you a lift, it's a two-seater," said Szeto through the window. "See you next week, Charles."

The flame-red car zoomed off, leaving Chung-Nam writhing. He swore to himself that he'd strike it big and leave a trail of women in his wake, rather than remain the sort of loser who kept getting dumped on like this.

"Should we go somewhere else?" asked Talya. She was flushed, her footsteps unsteady. Although she spoke without slurring, it was clear she was far gone. After the margarita, she'd had a Long Island iced tea and a negroni.

Well, she was serving herself up on a plate. Talya might not be his type, but he needed to reclaim some ground. He would take Mr. Szeto's suggestion and "make do" with her.

"I have alcohol at home. Why don't we carry on there?" he said.

"Fine, where's your car?"

"I . . . didn't drive."

"Oh." Talya frowned for a second, then smiled again. "It's okay, we'll get a cab. Taxi!"

She waved wildly even though there wasn't a single cab on the road. Chung-Nam started to wonder if she was even drunker than he'd thought.

"Hey, Charles, what kind of car do you drive?"

"I told you, I don't drive."

"I know you didn't drive today. I'm asking about normally."

"I don't own a car."

"No car?" Her face was a picture of shock. "Your American colleague Wade has a fancy sports car. You must have a Porsche or two?"

"American colleague? We don't work for the same firm. We're more like—business partners." Chung-Nam had thought of lying, but he was in a bad mood, and allowed the alcohol to tell the truth.

"You're not the tech director of a multinational firm?"

Now he understood. When Szeto Wai called him a "colleague," Talya must have assumed that meant he was working in the Hong Kong branch of an American company.

"No, it's a Hong Kong firm."

"Oh my god, I thought you were just being modest when you called it a small firm." She looked disbelieving. She raised her voice. "How many people work there? How many of them work under you?"

"Six."

"You only have six subordinates!" she shrieked. "You're just a department manager?"

"No. There are six people in the whole company. Only one of them works under me."

Talya was looking at him as if he were a con man.

"Bastard! Good thing I wasn't born yesterday, or you'd have tricked me into bed," Talya screeched, pointing at him, ignoring the stares of passersby.

"Fucking whore, I'm not interested in a dried-out hag like you." If she was going to scream at him in public, he would give as good as he got.

"Beggar. Piss on the ground and have a good look at your reflection. No one would want you unless you had money."

"I wouldn't touch you if you paid me."

The quarrel lasted barely half a minute. A taxi passed by, and Talya hailed it, tossing a couple more swear words Chung-Nam's way as she clambered in.

"Damn it." Chung-Nam walked through Lam Kwai Fong toward Queen's Road Central. All around him were drunkards, playboys, and sexy women, their smiles holding all sorts of meanings. He was the only one scowling.

When I've made it big, that female will be offering herself up to me like a bitch in heat, he thought. When he got to the MTR station on Theatre Lane, he discovered that misfortunes come in pairs: the last train had left, and the employees were just pulling down the metal shutters.

He sat down heavily at the steps by the entrance, wishing he had some way to let out all the anger inside him.

Then he gradually calmed down, reaching into his briefcase and pulling out the document he'd shown Szeto Wai earlier. This was the most important thing. Getting rejected by a woman and shouted at in public were trivial next to this.

As he put the document away again, he caught sight of his phone and pulled it out.

Not a single message. He quickly typed out a few words and sent them off. It was past one in the morning, but he thought the recipient would still be awake.

Stuffing the phone into his pocket, he walked over to Pedder Street to wait for a taxi. An empty one showed up before too long, and he hailed it.

"Lung Poon Street in Diamond Hill," he said as he got in. The driver nodded somberly and started the meter.

As they moved off, Ching-Nam took out his phone and glanced at the screen. The message he'd just sent had been read, but there was no reply. The phone remained silent all the way into the underwater tunnel. This was a little strange. He'd given strict instructions that his messages were to be responded to right away.

As he waited, he suddenly remembered Hao's words that afternoon, implying that he was "a pedo."

For no reason at all, he was beginning to feel a glimmer of unease.

2.

Violet To opened her eyes to the silent white ceiling. She turned to glance at the alarm clock. Short hand between eight and nine.

A gentle breeze ruffled the pale blue curtain, allowing in darts of soft dawn light that spilled over her calves.

So quiet, she thought.

Now that summer vacation had started, she hadn't bothered setting the alarm, allowing herself to wake up naturally. She was usually up before it went off, anyway, disturbed by the pigeons that congregated on the aircon ledge outside. Today they seemed to have read her mind and had left off their cooing so she could sleep in peace.

Sleep in peace. It had been a long time since she'd done that.

For the last two months her nerves had been wound tight. She'd never expected Au Siu-Man to kill herself.

On May 5, she sent off the final anonymous message. When there was no reply after a long time, she assumed she'd won. Siu-Man must have deleted all the messages, she thought, burying her head in the sand. But there was no avoiding the truth. She'd wanted to make Siu-Man realize that actions have consequences, and the powers that be use mortals as their weapons to teach the guilty a lesson.

How could she have known that by that point, Siu-Man was no longer in this world?

When she'd read the news of Siu-Man's suicide online, her mind had gone blank. She thought it must be someone of the same name, or some mistake. Then she looked at the brief report more carefully, again and again, and realized what she'd done. Siu-Man had killed herself as a result of Violet's messages. Even if she hadn't pushed her out the window with her own hands, she still had to bear the guilt.

I'm a murderer.

Two warring voices started tussling for control inside her.

It's not your responsibility. You didn't hold a gun to her head and force her to jump.

Stop lying to yourself. You wrote her a message telling her to die, and she did.

Violet kept trying to absolve herself of Au Siu-Man's death, but the voice known as reason gradually overcame the other. Over and over, it made the same accusation in her ear: *You're a murderer.*

When she came back to her senses, she was leaning over the toilet bowl, vomiting.

She'd never known life could weigh so heavily on a person.

That day, just like this one, her father had gone on a business trip up north, leaving her alone in their large home. They lived on Broadcast Drive in Kowloon City, one of the few fancy residential neighborhoods in Kowloon. Starting at the intersection of Junction and Chuk Yuen Roads, the half-mile-long Broadcast Drive started and ended at the same point, like an ouroboros, carving out a heart-shaped zone on Beacon Hill. All of Hong Kong's radio and TV stations used to be here—the two roads that ran through it were named Marconi and Fessenden, after the radio pioneers—but they had moved away one after another. Now all that remained were Radio Television Hong Kong (RTHK) and Commercial Radio Hong Kong, as well as many exorbitantly priced condos. The To family lived in a ten-story building where there were two apartments per floor, more than a thousand square feet for the two of them. The living room opened out onto an east-facing balcony, and the master bedroom had its own bathroom. This was a life most office workers in Hong Kong could only dream of.

When Siu-Man died, though, Violet felt suffocated by the place. She turned on all the lights, the TV, and the radio, but that couldn't change the fact that she was all alone at home, consumed by anxiety, with no one she could talk to. They used to have a Filipino housekeeper named Rosalie, who'd been with them for so many years that Violet treated her as family. Then, last May, her father fired Rosalie and started using contract cleaners instead, isolating Violet even more.

That evening, Violet had taken a deep breath and, with trembling fingers, sent a text to the only person she trusted: her brother.

The female is dead!!!

Click. Violet's reminiscences were interrupted by the door opening and closing. Every morning at nine, their housekeeper, Miss Wong, would come and clean up. She returned at six in the evening to make dinner for Violet and her father. When Violet wasn't at school, she'd also make her a simple lunch. They got breakfast on their own: Violet had bread, while her dad left early and went to a diner.

There'd been a time when breakfast looked very different in the To household.

Breakfast time used to be the moment Violet most looked forward to. Rosalie would be busily cooking in the kitchen as her father drank coffee and watched the TV news while her mom complained about Rosalie's fried eggs. It wasn't a moment of great family unity or anything like that, just a chance for Violet and her parents to sit around the same table. Much of the time, Violet's dad was away on trips or working overtime, and her mom was often out. Then, six years ago, her mom had left a note stating simply that she was leaving her silent husband, and she never returned home again.

Violet's father was an engineer and had been working for the same large construction firm since college. He'd risen to join management, and now earned a respectable salary. He'd bought the Broadcast Drive place when the housing market was at its lowest, reaping the profits when it rose again. He had been close to fifty when he married. Violet suspected that her mother had been after his money and had cut him loose when she realized that wealth couldn't make up for the sheer monotony of being married to a workaholic who never spoke. Instead, she sought an unrealistic happiness in the arms of other men.

The weirdest thing was, Violet's father didn't react to his wife's departure.

He didn't even seem upset, just continued going to work with the same regularity as before. Nothing in his life changed. Perhaps his wife and children were completely unimportant to him. Violet's aunt, who'd died a few years earlier, once told Violet that her father had had no interest in marriage, but simply gave in to her mother's desire.

As a result, Violet's feelings for this man were fairly complicated. On one hand, she didn't have any kind of family warmth; her father seemed more like a roommate than anything else. Still, she was grateful to him for providing for all her needs. She had much more than many others in material terms, yet much less emotionally.

Whenever she saw a father with his child or a happy family, she couldn't help fantasizing what a different person she'd be if she were part of a normal family.

After washing up, she wandered into the kitchen for a glass of water. "Good morning," said Miss Wong, who was cleaning the extractor fan.

"Morning."

"Want some fresh-baked buns?" she asked, pointing at a plastic bag on the table.

"No need—there's still some left over from yesterday." Violet got a walnut bun from the fridge and warmed it in the microwave.

The housekeeper smiled approvingly at this sign of frugality. Violet wasn't being particularly virtuous, though—she just didn't want to spend a cent more of her father's money than she had to. She was trying to be as unlike her mother as possible.

As she grew up, Violet dreaded the way her appearance was changing. When she looked in the mirror, she could see herself growing more like her mother with each passing day. Violet's mother had been a beauty, and even in her thirties she was always being chatted up by men who thought she was a college student. When she smiled, enchanting dimples appeared on her cheeks. Violet inherited these dimples, along with a pair of dewy eyes. She wouldn't let herself admit it, but she was becoming a beauty too. Thinking of how her faithless mother had brought nothing but misery to her husband and children, Violet started to hate the way she looked. She wore square-framed glasses, which didn't suit her, and kept a lid on her emotions, so she hardly ever smiled.

"A girl your age ought to dress up a bit. No sin in being beautiful," her brother once said to her.

He was the only spiritual support in her life.

She returned to her bedroom with a glass of water and the walnut bun. She often hid in here—the enormous living room made her feel lonelier. Her bedroom was more spacious than many low-income households' entire apartments. Apart from the bed, wardrobe, and desk, there was a chaise longue and a low table where she could relax as she enjoyed her beloved novels. She placed the glass on her desk and returned a book to the shelf—a Japanese detective novel she'd pulled out yesterday. Though she'd read it many times, she wanted to look at the ending one more time, thanks to a new comment on her reading blog.

Dear Blogmistress, I just read this book and I'm shook. Went online for reviews and found ur blog. U r a brilliant writer! U said everything I felt. So sad abt the 2 main characters, I cried at the end. But I don't understand why the guy had to kill himself. If he was the girl's secret lover or something I cld still understand, but I don't think they were? Why would he sacrifice his life like

that? Redemption? But he didn't do anything wrong! Pls
enlighten me, Blogmistress! Thank u!!
~posted by Franny, 6/30/2015 20:13

This was in response to her post about a novel by Keigo Hi-
gashino. Violet wasn't that fond of his work, but this book was
one of her favorites. She'd taken more time than usual with this
review, which went up last spring, and this was the first comment
after more than a year. Violet's blog didn't get a lot of traffic—
after all, most Hong Kongers were not readers. According to the
analytics, quite a few of her readers were actually from Taiwan.
From her IP address, this Franny was Taiwanese too.

Ever since seeing this comment yesterday, Violet had been
pondering how she should reply. She wanted to tell Franny that
what lay between the two main characters wasn't romantic love,
that they'd ascended to a different plane. This was hard to explain. There were certain things Violet was meticulous about, and
she never allowed herself to dash off a slipshod answer. Seeing
as someone had actually responded to her, she wanted to make
this a proper exchange.

As she chewed on her bun and let her eyes run across her
bookshelf, she was a little surprised at how peaceful she felt—
almost as if she'd spent the last few days shedding a layer of
skin and had left all the pain and trouble behind her. Her soul
had been renewed. Perhaps this was time healing all wounds,
perhaps it was because summer vacation meant she no longer had
to see Au Siu-Man's empty seat in their classroom, or perhaps
the blog comment had simply distracted her. The main reason
for her serenity, though, was that she'd burned the page from
Siu-Man's suicide note with her own hands.

The appearance of that note had thrown her mind into chaos.
She'd managed to stay calm in front of everyone, all the while
frantically thinking of how to deal with this new threat. She
was glad she'd been able to think on her feet, which was all

down to her brother's constant encouragement. She'd turned the situation to her advantage and avoided being exposed by the crucial page from Siu-Man's letter. True, she hadn't read it, but she thought there was a good chance that her name appeared in the note.

Violet had read somewhere that in the course of human civilizations developing, people often used external practices like ritual to bring about changes in their thinking—adjusting to shifting social hierarchies or receiving spiritual protection. Perhaps the action of burning the letter was the ritual she needed to feel absolved.

When she met her brother the other day, he'd praised her for finally setting herself free. She knew very well that Au Siu-Man had been a thorn in his side as well, he just hadn't shown it, because he needed to stay strong and be her only refuge.

"It's like I told you—you need to learn to be more selfish. Grow a thicker skin," he'd said to her. "We live in a cruel society, and anyone who shows weakness will be mercilessly attacked. That Au girl didn't die because of you. If we all jumped off a building when someone wrote a couple of things about us, there'd be thousands of suicides every day. She died because she wasn't strong enough. It was the only way she could escape the stress of this ridiculous society."

Even though this sounded like twisted logic, his words made Violet feel better.

As she picked up her glass of water, she almost splashed the report card she'd received the day before. Her results this semester weren't as good—she'd gone from thirteenth to seventeenth in the class—which was understandable, given that she hadn't been able to concentrate on her studies recently. Violet was no longer as obsessed with academic grades. She'd topped her class last year, and even though her parents never pushed her, she'd always forced herself to work hard, in the mistaken belief that if she could only do well enough at school, her parents might start caring about her. She was in elementary school when her mother walked out, and Violet told herself that if she came first in her class just once, her mother would come home. Even when she got old enough to realize this was a fantasy, she couldn't let go of the relentless drive. The pressure she put on herself was eating her from the inside. She could barely breathe.

In the end, it was her brother who changed her mind-set and allowed her to let go.

After her mind cleared, Violet was grateful that, unlike most of her classmates, she didn't need to account for herself to her parents. Her father was completely indifferent—he neither rewarded her for doing well nor scolded her for doing badly. He was two days into the current business trip and hadn't called home yet.

Ping. Just as Violet was thinking about her father, a notification flashed up on her phone:

Reminder from Enoch Secondary School Library. Your items &#65297, &#65299, &#65294, &#65302, &#65303 are due in three days. For more information or to renew, please visit http://www.enochss.edu.hk/lib/q?s=71926

This was baffling. The library was closed over the summer, and the system shouldn't be sending out any messages. Besides, she knew she had no books out. Even more confusing, the message looked exactly the same as any other notification, but it had nonsense strings of letters and numbers instead of book titles. Something must be wrong. She clicked on the link, which opened a browser window on her phone, but nothing loaded for a long time. After about twenty seconds she found herself on the Enoch School home page.

Could the IT company be carrying out maintenance? she wondered. She'd heard their exam results were almost delayed by computer issues, but the teachers managed to re-input all the data.

She clicked through to the library page and logged in to her account. Sure enough, her borrowing record was blank. Next, she went into the school chatboard to see if anyone else had been affected. There was a library thread, though not many people hung out there.

Topic: [borrowing] Anyone else get a weird notification?

That was the first topic she saw. It was from last night, and there were already four posts, all of which were people reporting that they'd had strange messages like the one she received. Violet stopped worrying. She decided to start her day by heading to the nearby Lok Fu Place mall to buy some new books. Before getting off her phone, she clicked on "return to menu" out of habit, which is how she saw the alarming words "what happened yesterday."

Even though this didn't give much away, she felt a tightness in her chest as she anxiously clicked to expand the conversation.

Group: Library
Posted by: WongKwongTak2 (Ham Tak)
Subject: [chat] What happened yesterday
Time: June 30, 2015 21:14:13

I heard there was a little incident in the library around noon yesterday.
Something to do with That Thing in Class 3B. Anyone have info?

That was all. Violet thought it must be a gossipy student who'd caught wind of what happened and put it out there to find out more. Posts like this were usually deleted pretty quickly by the moderators, but maybe the maintenance was holding up the process, or maybe no one had seen it yet, but it had stayed up long enough to get quite a conversation going.

—I thought we're not allowed to talk about That Thing?
—You again, Ham Tak! XD
—We have the right to know! The teachers can't keep us in the dark.
—Not scared of trouble? They can still give you summer detention~
—Yay freedom of speech! (please don't give me detention)
—Weird that the mods haven't taken this down.

The discussion groups were moderated by student aides, but the library teachers were in charge of this one, and grown-ups tended to be slower getting things done on the internet. Violet quickly skimmed these comments, and just as she started to think maybe she'd been overreacting, she came to a longer post at the bottom of the page.

Posted by: LamKamHon (Boss Hon)
Topic: Re. [chat] What happened yesterday
Time: July 1, 2015 01:00:48

I was there that day. The Chess Society was printing leaflets for our summer activities – we saw the whole thing. I'm not sure exactly what went down, but That Girl's family found her suicide note in the library. I caught a glimpse. Looked bad. Probably complaining about some other student. I don't want to speculate if she killed herself as an accusation.

I'm not going against orders, but since this is the truth (that I saw with my own eyes), there's nothing wrong

with me saying it, rather than letting rumors spread. If
Miss Yuen makes an announcement with more info, even
better.

    Anyway I bet this post gets deleted soon.

Violet inhaled sharply. She'd thought destroying the missing page would put an end to the matter, but now there was a complication. She knew the head of the Chess Society by sight, and he had indeed been there in the library. He was fairly well regarded in the school, having won quite a few chess tournaments, not to mention excellent exam results as well. His popularity meant the other students would tend to trust his version of events.

If too many other people believed him, she might be in trouble.

After all the trouble she'd gone through getting rid of the incriminating portion of Siu-Man's note, word was getting out anyway that the culprit might be someone from Siu-Man's class. Worry churned in her, and she felt as if she might throw up the bread she'd just eaten. She quickly opened Line, clicked on her brother's name, and tapped in:

Bad news, someone posted on the school chatboard about

But she didn't complete the sentence. Her thumb hovered over the screen as she wondered whether this was something she ought to be telling him. He'd mentioned that his company was dealing with a major client and he'd be in for a promotion and a raise if it went well. She hadn't paid a lot of attention—all she really took in was that he was going to be busy with work for a while. Maybe he shouldn't be worrying about her too.

It's not that big a deal, really, she thought. She knew he could enter the school chat and give himself admin privileges, so she wanted to ask him to delete these posts. But when she calmed down, she realized this situation was different. No need to go overboard. Siu-Man's accusation was just words on a page. Even if Violet's name had come to light, there was still no evidence linking her to the death. Thanks to what her brother had taught her, she knew there was no way to connect those emails to her. Lily Shu was surely much more of a suspect—there were at least five or six people in the class who knew why Lily and Siu-Man had drifted apart. Any normal person would assume that Siu-Man's suicide was caused by the love triangle. Who would suspect it was actually Violet pulling the strings?

This was like releasing a safety valve: once again she calmed down. She opened her laptop again and logged into her blog, ready to answer Franny's question. As she typed, she pondered whether she ought to visit the bookstore before or after lunch. Reading would help steady her nerves.

And so the first day of summer vacation passed peacefully for Violet.

She had no idea that the next day, this "complication" was due to blow up.

Posted by: ChuKaiLing (Ling Ling Chu)

Topic: Re. [chat] What happened yesterday

Time: July 2, 2015, 03:14:57

Someone posted on Popcorn about That Incident!
http://forum.hkpopcrn.com/view?article=9818234&
type=OA

The following morning, Violet turned on her computer and logged on to the school chatboard again to see if the mods had deleted the thread yet. Not only was it still there, but there was a reply that shocked her. Shaking a little, she clicked on the link and a new tab opened. In the top left corner was the familiar Popcorn logo.

POSTED BY superconan ON 07-01-2015, 23:44
Mastermind behind girl's (14) suicide?

I, SuperConan, Prince of Popcorn and Keyboard Warrior, have explosive news for you all. Today's bombshell is about that classic post from three months ago, "Fourteen-Year-Old Slut Sent My Uncle to Prison!!" that I'm sure had all us Popcorners cheering and munching popcorn—but what went on behind the scenes? The forgetful may wish to refresh their memories here:

http://forum.hkpopcrn.com/view?article=7399120m

It seems after this j'accuse made its appearance, a mob of public-spirited Popcorners naturally stood up for justice and came down like a ton of bricks on this fourteen-year-old ho who sent an innocent stationery-shop-owner to jail. They banded together to dig up her real name and address, plus her school photo, all to uphold righteousness and punish wrongdoing. Finally, the little monster jumped out of a window and ended her wretched life. Once again, Popcorners saved the day. Well done! Well done all of us!

Ha, I bet many of you have doubts, but you don't want to say them? Let me, SuperConan, one of the eight wonders of Popcorn, speak the truth you dare not.

You. Are. All. Murderers.

I, SuperConan, have taken part in countless flame wars, and god knows I have my haters, but I've never, ever kicked a person when they're down. The people screaming about justice are always complete bastards, never heroes. I'm not going to name names, but the Popcorn community should know who among you had a part in pushing this girl out of the window. Never mind if the shop owner was guilty or not. Even if he was wronged, does that really deserve a death sentence?

Anyway, never mind that. I didn't come here to guilt you guys, I came to drop truth bombs.

First, click on this: http://forum.hkpopcrn.com/user?id=66192614

That's the home page of the Popcorner who wrote "Fourteen-Year-Old Slut," Mr. kidkit727 (or Ms. kidkit727, I guess). As you can see, Mr. or Ms. K has posted exactly once, commented zero times, and logged in for the first time on April 10. Last log-in? Also April 10. Nothing wrong with that, maybe he or she created a burner account to defend this uncle. But to drop out of the discussion, never log on again, not help take down the little slut? That seems strange. Even using my SuperConan powers, I couldn't find anything on the whole wide web connected to kidkit727. No email, no Facebook, no Weibo. No one who wants to raise the Popcorn army would be this secretive. Fanning the flames would make more sense. Which just makes me think: could this be a case of catfishing?

So what I'm saying is, maybe you're not murderers. Maybe you're just morons and did a murderer's work for them.

I suppose you're going to say I'm talking nonsense?

Of course SuperConan can back up his words. Yesterday, I got a DM with the inside scoop. Remember this K guy or gal called the man in jail "Uncle"? Well, guess what. This dude had no brothers or sisters. So where did this nephew or niece come from? My info is reliable, but I'm sure you Popcorners have your own ways of verifying it.

If this K person isn't actually related to the man who went to prison, then how to explain this 1000+ word post? Defending a stranger? Or could there be some other motive at work?

Ha! My dear, clever Popcorners, how do you feel now? HOW DO YOU FEEL NOW?

As Violet read this bizarre post, she felt chills creeping down her spine. It seemed clear that SuperConan was an old hand at Popcorn—the internet was full of idiots like this who spent their days shooting their mouths off on all sorts of forums, as if they had no purpose in life apart from arguing with strangers on the internet. Although this post might look like pointless sarcasm, Violet understood very well who it was targeted at—particularly with that little detail about Shiu Tak-Ping not having a nephew.

When she and her brother had come up with the plan to incite an online mob against Siu-Man, one of the things they discussed was what identity to hide behind. Violet knew from having pumped Martin Tong's intern that Shiu Tak-Ping had no nephews or nieces, but her brother pointed out that this would be better than impersonating someone who actually existed.

"Think about it, Vi. If we post as his wife or some friend of his, the real person could step forward and the whole thing would fall apart," he'd said. "Besides, people need to identify with this poster. A family member would be more convincing than some old classmate or friend. Sure, we're taking a risk by inventing a nephew, but I bet the Shius won't reveal the truth, especially with Tak-Ping in prison. His wife and mother won't be stupid enough to give reporters something else to talk about."

"Why not?"

"It won't help Shiu Tak-Ping. He didn't even bother defending himself, just pleaded guilty. Reopening the case now wouldn't do the family any good."

"What if someone who knows the family casts doubt on the poster's identity and motives?"

"We're going to post this and disappear. Even if the journalists wanted to find us, they couldn't. And if Shiu Tak-Ping actually does speak up to say he doesn't know who this is, that just creates a Rashomon-type situation. There's no downside for us. At the very least, we've lit the flame. You remember our goal?"

"Yes. To eliminate Au Siu-Man."

His words seemed to make sense at the time. Now Violet realized that they'd missed one important point: everything would change after Siu-Man's death.

She went back to SuperConan's post. He mentioned someone DMing him—could this also be someone from the library? She hadn't thought Shiu Tak-Ping knew anyone at her school, but this went up just a couple of days after the suicide note came to light, which seemed like too much of a coincidence. Fighting to stay calm, she tried to think up possible scenarios. Could it be that this person knew all along that Shiu had no nephew, but let it go at the time, only to think of going public when the suicide note appeared—so he got in touch with SuperConan then?

No, that didn't seem quite right, though Violet couldn't say why.

She hesitated, then typed:

Check out Popcorn! Someone's stirring things up!! What should we do?
http://forum.hkpopcrn.com/view?article=9818234&type=OA

Although she hated to disturb her brother at work, he was the only one she could turn to.

After sending the message, she sat with her eyes glued to her phone, waiting for a response. She knew he could get busy, and she prayed he'd find a moment to read it soon. After a minute, it still didn't say "read." All she could do was turn back to the computer screen, which was still on the Popcorn site, though she looked back at her phone every ten seconds.

Five minutes later the "read" symbol finally appeared. She grabbed her phone and waited frantically for his reply. Her left hand was clenched tightly in a fist, and she hadn't even noticed that her nails were digging into her palm hard enough to draw blood. It took another agonizing five minutes for the message to appear:

> no need to worry, it's just some moron

Violet quickly typed back:

> But he knows there was no nephew!

She pressed send and settled in for another anxious wait, though this time it only took half a minute:

> really, don't worry
> no one ever believes this jerk
> check out the replies

SuperConan's post had only two replies. One told him to shut up with a number of colorful swear words—maybe this was one of the haters he mentioned—while the other was just a pained smile emoji, meaning that only an idiot would believe this nonsense. As a longtime user of Popcorn, her brother probably recognized the name. Most people certainly seemed to be ignoring SuperConan, but Violet didn't think they could let their guard down.

> Can I see you this evening?

They usually only met once a week, but this was serious. Better to be prepared and plan for the worst-case scenario.

> can't, sorry, have to work tonight
> busy lately, have to work this weekend too

His reply made Violet feel worthless. Her fear had made her weak. Not long ago, her brother had praised her for being calm, and now here she was again, as taut as a bow. She was tossing in a stormy sea, her arms wrapped around him as if he were a piece of driftwood. She quickly typed in a few words of agreement and ended the conversation so he could get back to his job. He was working hard to make something of himself, and not just for money.

"Before you graduate high school, Vi, I'll get you away from that house."

That was the promise he'd made to her.

"I can't give you a luxury apartment like that man, and there won't be a maid cleaning up after you, but I guarantee you'll have a happy life."

Violet couldn't remember how she'd replied, only how moved she'd been.

She was no longer alone in the world.

Even though she was still full of doubt, Violet did her best to persuade herself that this new complication would soon evaporate. There were hundreds of new Popcorn posts every day, and unpopular threads quickly fell off the home page in the standard economy of chatboards: the rich get richer and the poor get poorer. SuperConan might be a veteran poster, but the others didn't think much of him. If everyone continued ignoring this post, it would soon be buried.

Yet there was no way she could be certain this would happen.

Violet tried her best to forget about it and lose herself in a new Jeffery Deaver novel, which she'd very much been looking forward to. Even so, she found it hard to concentrate.

That evening at seven, Violet sat at the dining table. "Is something wrong with the food?" asked Miss Wong, who was getting ready to leave. Unlike most Hong Kong homes, this apartment was large enough for a dishwasher, so she didn't have to stick around to clean up.

"Huh? Oh, no, it's fine." Violet hadn't realized that she'd been staring at her plate. In front of her were fried pomfret, some broccoli and beef, and a cooling bowl of winter melon, sweet corn, and pork rib soup. This could have been a set meal for one at a restaurant.

"You haven't touched the fish, so I thought something must be wrong." Miss Wong laughed. "Normally you start with the fish."

"Everything's fine. I've just got a lot on my mind," said Violet, forcing a smile.

She'd been on pins and needles all evening. Every now and then she put down her book and headed back to the computer to see if there'd been any new replies under SuperConan's post. She breathed a sigh of relief every time she saw that it was off the home page, but occasionally someone would post "SuperConan's at it again" or something similar, bumping it back up. Her heart raced when this happened. She hadn't thought her anxiety would be obvious, but even Miss Wong had noticed.

Whooosh . . . whooooosh . . . The next morning, Violet was wakened by the sound of the vacuum cleaner coming from the living room. She glanced at the clock—it was already ten. She couldn't remember what time she'd fallen asleep, only that she'd tossed and turned for a long time after going to bed. Her sense of guilt came rushing back. What if another Popcorner sank his teeth into this case and refused to let it go? She knew how these things worked—internet bullying and the human-flesh search engine.

She grabbed her phone, hoping her brother had sent her a message on his way to work, but there wasn't anything, not even spam. After hesitating awhile, she gathered the courage to open her browser and click on the school discussion board, then the library tab. She calmed down a little after seeing the contents page—the post by Ham Tak had disappeared. The mods must have finally taken it down. In the same spirit of hope, she went into her bookmarks for the Popcorn page. How far back would

SuperConan's post have fallen—ten pages? What she saw instead was far worse than she could have expected.

POSTED BY zerocool ON 07-03-2015, 01:56
re: Mastermind behind girl's (14) suicide?

I've thought about this a long time before posting. Long post, sorry.

I'm a longtime Popcorner, but this is a throwaway account. Please don't try to find out who I am. I have my reasons.

My job is a bit unusual. My title is "Data Security Consultant." Sounds fancy, but that just means I'm a hacker. Don't misunderstand, I don't do anything against the law. People hire me to try to break into their systems, so I can tell them all their weak points. I'm a White Hat, in other words. Just like banks hire locksmiths to see if they can break into their vaults.

Normally it wouldn't be a big deal to say all this, but here's why I'm going incognito: because of work, I have to get into some . . . questionable parts of the net. I often use P2P sharing to download files, though unlike most people I'm not pirating films or music. All I care about is what kind of private data those websites transfer. For instance, telecom companies might leak client names, government departments might lose entire documents, and so on. I never used any of the data that I got in this way, but even admitting that I possessed it would be enough to land me in court.

Last month, while using PD—a type of P2P software—I got a damaged file from a hard disk. I won't say what kind of file (so you guys don't go looking), but I managed to

unfreeze it and found a heap of personal information, as
if someone accidentally installed a version of PD with, uh,
added ingredients, and had all their stuff stolen. There are
plenty of these altered programs—they basically create
a back door to your computer, so your files can be taken
without you noticing.

I noticed that these were all from personal computers,
so I ignored them—after all, I'm not interested in people's
secrets. (I get files like this once every few days anyway.)
But something about the OP's post reminded me of
something, so I went back through those files, and sure
enough, I found something shocking.

One of them was a text file, containing exactly the same
words as the post from April, the "Fourteen-Year-Old Slut"
one. I thought someone must have cut and pasted it from
Popcorn, but then I looked more closely.

The post appeared on April 10, but the file I had was
created on April 9. So maybe the Popcorn thing was a
repost? But I've searched the web, and April 10 on Popcorn
was the first appearance. In other words, this file might be
from the K person's hard drive.

OP mentioned K might have wanted to hurt the suicide
girl. I didn't know whether to go public with this, then I
thought someone's dead, so it's my responsibility to say
what I know. Hence the burner account. Don't bother
trying to track down my IP address—I'm a professional
Data Security Consultant, you'll never find me.

Violet was ready to faint—lucky she'd been reading this in
bed, or she would surely have collapsed. She quickly clicked on
the green Line icon to ask her brother:

Hav you ever used a file sharng thing called PD?

She sent it without even stopping to correct the typos—even a second's delay was too much. After two or three minutes, though, the message still hadn't been read.

This is important!

He'd once told her not to phone him at work, but to send Line messages instead. And so, no matter how urgent it was, she didn't want to call.

Five more minutes. Still no reply.

We're in trouble! This may

Just as she was typing in the third message, "read" lit up. She let out her breath, but the reply ramped up her anxiety even more:

what's up? sure, i've used PD

This confirmed that the Data Security Consultant hadn't been making things up. She deleted her draft and wrote a new message:

Go look at the Popcorn chat from yesterday!

Two minutes later, he wrote:

don't worry, it's nothing

She gawped. How could this be "nothing"?

Nothing?? They have your file!!

It took a long time for "read" to appear. Violet's stomach hurt, either from the anxiety or because she was still in bed way past breakfast time.

not necessarily mine
i trust my firewall
maybe someone's computer clock is a day slow
so the date registered wrong when they copied it

Violet hadn't considered this possibility. Even so, she felt uneasy. What if . . .

Were the files I sent you stored on the same hard drive? If those ever get out, we're in trouble!

She waited.

what files?

His nonchalant reply tipped her into rage:

The ones you made me steal from the school! The pictures, contacts, SMSes and all that from the other kids' phones! If anyone reveals your ID on Popcorn, you can just say the clock was a day slow or something. But if they find out we know each other, we're not going to get out of that!

Violet had never spoken to him like that, but she was even more anxious to keep him out of trouble than for herself. After Siu-Man died, Violet imagined the worst-case scenario: if those threatening messages were discovered and traced back to her, she would take responsibility rather than allow him to get dragged down.

In order to deal with Siu-Man, he'd helped Violet gather materials on quite a few of her fellow students. He gave her a little black box that looked like a charger, and as soon as a phone was plugged in, its contents could be siphoned, including photos, videos, contacts, text messages, and calendars. When no one was paying attention, Violet would fiddle with the chargers in the classrooms or the library, stealing more private data. This was all in order to prove a rumor against Siu-Man, one of the ways in which they planned to punish her.

The rumor had long been forgotten—that on Christmas Eve a girl from the school got herself screwed by a gangster.

Violet never said much at school, but she kept her ears open in the classrooms and corridors, gleaning stray bits of information from people's conversations. She was more or less certain that the girl in question was Siu-Man, but there was no proof—so her brother deployed this next-level strategy. She picked up quite a few secrets this way: who had a crush on whom, who was two-timing whom, who was particularly close to which teacher, and so on. She saw quite a few intimate photos and videos, some of them explicit enough to be used as blackmail material. Yet there was no sign of evidence for the Siu-Man rumor, just a picture of her being groped in a karaoke lounge, which was nothing compared with some of the other stuff Violet found.

With so much material to sift through, she'd sent everything to her brother so he could help. Now she was worried that these files would be what exposed her connection to him. Even if she insisted that she was the only guilty party, other people might not believe her, and he might end up in trouble too. She was still a minor, and even if she were convicted, her sentence would be light. Her brother was ten years older, though, and his treatment would be much harsher.

oh those files
don't worry

i think i put them in the other hard drive
stop scaring yourself
have a meeting now, chat later

This reply was just as unbothered as before, leaving Violet angry and frustrated. If there was one thing she didn't like about her brother, it was that he could be full of himself. Of course, in different circumstances, she admired that too—no matter how bad the situation, he'd remain confident in his ability to deal with it. All her subsequent messages went unread, and she had to accept that he was indeed busy.

There were more comments beneath the Data Security Consultant's post, but they were all pointless ones like "Hope you find the truth" or GIFs of munching popcorn. One was probably by an enemy of SuperConan: "Compared to that blabbermouth StuporConman, ZeroCool shows us a master at work."

"Don't . . . don't bother coming to cook dinner tonight," said Violet around noon, as Miss Wong put on her shoes before heading to her next house.

"Are you going out?" she asked.

"Yes," lied Violet, nodding. "I'm in my school book club. We'll be out all day, and I won't be back till after dinner."

"Oh, okay. I'd already bought you a lamb chop."

"Take it with you. Give it to your kid."

"I can't do that. If Mr. To finds out, he'll say I stole it."

"It will just go bad if you leave it in the fridge. That's a waste."

"That's true . . ." Although she sounded unwilling, her expression told a different story. "How many days will this book club go on for?"

"How about this—if I'm having dinner at home, I'll make sure to tell you the day before."

Miss Wong nodded. She got the lamb chop from the fridge and departed happily. Violet had no extracurriculars, she just didn't want to be home on her own, driving herself crazy with her thoughts. Better to be in the mall, surrounded by people, where she could distract herself. Her brother once told her that if she started to feel anxious, the best thing was to go out.

That afternoon, she took a bus to Festival Walk in Kowloon Tong. After dinner, she lingered in a coffee shop till eleven before heading home. Lok Fu Place was a little closer to her home, but the cafés and restaurants there closed much earlier. When she met her brother, though, it was usually at the Starbucks in Lok Fu—Festival Walk was much more crowded, especially on holidays; you could end up waiting up to half an hour for a table. They avoided it unless they needed something from there, such as cell phone spare parts or a visit to the Apple store.

Violet was actually much more rational than most people her age. In the library, for instance, she'd known immediately what she had to do to preserve her secret. And now she understood that constantly refreshing Popcorn and waiting for more bad news to arrive was a path to insanity. She knew perfectly well what the consequences would be if she allowed the stress to grow past her ability to tolerate it. She forced herself to relax and go to bed.

Yet this rationality wasn't able to save her from an assault on her senses.

Ding-ding-dong-dong-ding-ding-dong-dong-ding-ding-dong-dong . . .

Violet was pulled from her dreams by her cell phone ringing. She thought at first it was the alarm clock, but when she opened her eyes, the sky was still dark, and a glance at the clock told her it was only 3:30 in the morning. No number was displayed. Looking at the screen, with its "slide to answer," she was suddenly wide awake. Could something have happened to her brother? Most people might have thought of their parents first, but she cared much more about her brother than her distant father, who might as well have been a stranger.

She answered the call. "Hello?"

No sound.

"Hello?"

Abruptly, the caller hung up.

Wrong number, probably. Hugely relived, she was just about to go back to sleep when the phone rang again. Once again, no number was displayed.

"Hello?" she said, a little angry now.

Still no reply, but she could hear faint breathing.

"Who is it?" she yelled.

"Murderer."

And with that, the caller hung up. Violet sat frozen in bed. It was a woman's voice—or possibly a boy's—that had clearly said the word "murderer."

Just like that, logic fled from her brain. Somehow they'd got hold of her phone number. Someone knew what she'd done. She hastily went into her address book—never mind how late it was, she needed to ask her brother for help. Before she could click on his name, her "Wave" ringtone went off again, as if determined to slice right through the peaceful silence of the room.

"Who are you? What do you want? If you call again, I'll report you to the police!" she screamed.

"Fuck you! Ha ha."

A curse word, a couple of barks of laughter, then a click. Even in her panic, Violet noticed this was a different voice—a man this time.

Violet stared at her phone, cold sweat beading on the back of her neck. She couldn't stop trembling. The phone showed no mercy, but started ringing again. She didn't answer, pressing the key to terminate the demonic sound.

Ding-ding-dong-dong-ding . . .

No sooner had she rejected one call when the next came in. She didn't stop to think, just turned the phone off.

As the screen blinked out, Violet found herself staring into the gloom of her bedroom. Apart from the weak streetlight drifting in the window, everything was in darkness. She felt as if she were floating in a space full of wickedness. It wasn't cold, but she swaddled herself completely in her blanket, trying to stay calm. The wind outside and the ticking of her clock now sounded like wretched sobbing. No peace for her. She didn't sleep another wink till dawn.

Click. The front door, a reassuring sound. She'd managed to shut her eyes and drowse a little after the sun came up, until the cleaning lady woke her as she came in.

She glanced down to see her phone on the floor where she'd flung it the night before, and felt a chill in her heart. She reached out for it. Should she turn it on? In the end, rationality overcame fear, and she pressed the button. After all, she'd have to use it to ask her brother for help.

Unexpectedly, the phone stayed silent, though she had more than forty voice mails. She didn't dare listen to them—nor did she need to, since neither her brother nor her father would have left her a message between four and nine in the morning.

The situation was serious enough that she decided to phone her brother, even though it might disturb him at work. She needed to hear his voice. If she could hear him say just one sentence, she'd be able to calm down.

Ring . . . ring . . .

It rang more than twenty seconds, but there was no answer.

She looked at her alarm clock. It didn't seem likely that he'd been pulled into a meeting first thing in the morning, but when she thought about it, she had to admit it was possible. She had no support, then, and could only steel herself to open the Popcorn page to search for the cause of the disturbance last night. Her intuition told her that this ZeroCool must be behind it.

When she opened the thread, the first post she saw made everything go black before her eyes.

POSTED BY admin ON 07-04-2015, 07:59
re: Mastermind behind girl's (14) suicide?

Announcement: user AcidBurn has posted information
infringing an individual's personal privacy, breaking
Regulation 16. This account has been locked. If you wish
to file a complaint, please send a direct message to the
webmaster.

    *Popcorn Chatboard is a discussion platform and
cannot take responsibility for the text, images, video,
audio, or any other files posted here. Users assume legal
responsibility for their posts.

The words "personal privacy" made her scalp tingle. Going
back through the thread, she saw that a post time-stamped 3:15
a.m. had been deleted, leaving only the username AcidBurn.
Beneath that were all sorts of comments:

—wow nice work Mr. Z, that's ironclad evidence that this
  dude was the bad guy here
—ZeroCool and AcidBurn are both names from *Hackers*,
  right?
—There's even a phone number! Anyone called to check?
—I did, some female answered. Go for it, guys!
—looks like a dude's name?
—Maybe she has a friend. Something for me too!
—Sure I'll try I can't sleep anyway
—remember to enter 133 first so your number won't be
  displayed

These started at 3:20 and went on till just after five—about
twenty of them. Violet felt herself being enveloped by hatred,
even if the contents of these posts were more like playful children teasing someone. She could see the spite and cruelty hidden

behind the words. She was done for. This torture was no more than she deserved.

She wasn't sure at first what "ironclad evidence" was being referred to, until she saw a reply to AcidBurn's deleted post that stunned her:

POSTED BY kidkit727 ON 07-04-2015, 03:09
re: Mastermind behind girl's (14) suicide?

ZeroCool here. The password to this account was in the file I found. I'm 100% sure this bastard has something to do with it.

She'd never imagined that the kidkit727 account could be hacked. This should have been no big deal, given that she and her brother had set it up only to smear Siu-Man and never intended to log on again. But things were different now. ZeroCool finding the password here was proof that the file belonged to kidkit727.

"What's wrong? Aren't you feeling well?" asked Miss Wong as Violet walked into the kitchen. She knew what prompted the question—when she'd looked in the mirror a minute ago, her face was stark white.

"I slept badly." She forced a smile as she went to the fridge for her usual breakfast.

Back in her room, she noticed that her phone had lit up with a new message. Quickly putting down the plate and cup she was holding, she tapped on the screen.

what's up?

At this point, these words from her brother were all she had to hold up her battered soul.

Did you write down kidkit727's password anywhere?
Someone from Popcorn hacked in! Go look!

Violet asked urgently. She waited about ten minutes for a response:

i saw
don't panic, i never wrote down the password
i'll keep an eye on things
just deny everything if anyone asks
evidence like this isn't worth anything

Steady as ever. Was he really that confident, or was he bragging to puff up his courage?

Can we talk?

She typed tersely.

sorry, with my boss rn
v. busy today, meeting important client
will call later

This reply arrived after about five minutes. She was frustrated by his cold response, but her fear had turned to rage. All she wanted now was for him to understand how serious this was. She sent him a new message, but it never showed up as "read."

Violet felt as if she were about to collapse. She slapped herself hard across the face to steady her nerves. She had to be stronger, otherwise she'd hold her brother back. He always found time to respond no matter how busy he was, she told herself. The terseness of his replies today must mean he was dealing with something very important.

He'll definitely call later, she told herself—he said he would.

She sat in front of the computer all morning, monitoring developments on Popcorn. There were no more harassing phone calls, and no one posted any new messages. She considered logging on with a different ID to lecture the netizens on their behavior, but what if this caused a bigger backlash? Besides, she wasn't as tech-savvy as her brother and would probably leave tracks. He once told her that people get caught on the internet if they're too impatient and overplay their hand. Only by holding your nerve and keeping things low-key could you escape the notice of the law.

The reference to a "dude's name" in the replies told Violet it probably wasn't her name that had been exposed. Perhaps it was her brother's, or someone else altogether. She didn't understand why ZeroCool had her number. The only thing she could be sure of was that the backup file ZeroCool had was definitely her brother's—there was no way her original inflammatory post, her account number, and kidkit727's password could all be there by coincidence. Her brother had probably put her phone number first in the file record, leading ZeroCool to assume it was his.

"Are you okay?"

Violet jumped at the voice behind her. Miss Wong was standing at the bedroom door.

"I knocked a few times. I was afraid you'd fainted," she explained.

"No, I'm fine," said Violet, slamming the laptop shut before the housekeeper could see what was on the screen. She forced a smile. "I was really absorbed in this."

"I'm going home—I've finished the chores," said Miss Wong, her eyes shooting to the laptop as if she found Violet's behavior peculiar. "Shall I make you dinner?"

"No need. I'm going out later."

"All right. I've got tomorrow off, so I'll see you the day after. Are you sure you're okay?"

"I'm fine."

Violet hadn't planned to go out, nor did she feel like it. All she cared about was the chatboard activity, and waiting for her brother to call. She didn't want Miss Wong to notice how much time she was spending on Popcorn. This woman wasn't on her side.

Her father had secretly asked Miss Wong to spy on Violet, particularly if she did anything connected to her brother.

Violet also knew that the previous domestic helper, Rosalie, had been fired because Rosalie felt sorry for her.

It got to evening, and her brother still hasn't called. Not even a Line message. Each time she picked up her phone, she felt conflicted: hoping to see a text from him, but also terrified of the "42" on the screen. More than forty vicious voice mails pent up on her phone, waiting for her to unleash them.

She had no appetite, but decided to go get some dinner. Her brother once told her that it's even more important to make sure you eat well when you're in a bad mood, for hunger can affect your judgment. Her father didn't like her to eat instant ramen or snacks, so there was nothing in the house but rice, eggs, and raw vegetables. She didn't feel like cooking.

"Going out, Miss To?" said the security guard, smiling as she stepped out of the elevator. She nodded and went out without saying anything. The guard was another of her father's spies.

Broadcast Drive was a residential neighborhood, and there was nowhere to eat apart from the staff canteen at RTHK. Otherwise it was a ten-minute walk to Lok Fu Place, or along Junction Road to the area around Baptist University and Hospital. A day earlier Violet had wanted to be surrounded by people so she could be distracted from her thoughts. Now she was frightened of anyone looking at her. She turned down Junction Road.

There was a tiny park between Broadcast Drive and Junction Road. As a little girl, she'd often sat here with a library book in the shade of a tree while Rosalie chatted nearby with the other helpers. Passing by the park now, Violet gazed at the burgeoning grove of trees, thinking of the past.

"Murderer!"

Out of nowhere, a female voice cried out in her ear. She almost stopped breathing. Frantically looking around, she saw no one except a man in a maintenance worker's uniform about ten yards away, walking slowly down the slope of Broadcast Drive. She gaped, scanning her surroundings, but there was no one else around.

Could she have misheard? She shook her head, chest heaving. Calm down, she told herself. It must have come from an upstairs floor of a nearby building—probably someone's TV.

Now she felt even less like eating. She made her way to a Western restaurant by Franki Centre near Baptist Hospital, ordered a plate of spaghetti, and waited distractedly for the waiter to bring it.

"Murderer!"

The same female voice. Violet almost jumped to her feet. She was sure what she'd heard this time—the same tone and pitch as the harassing phone call she'd received the night before. She quickly looked around. At the next table was a guy who looked like a college student, silently spooning borscht into his mouth. About ten feet in front of her was a round table at which a couple sat whispering sweet nothings to each other, apparently unaware of anyone else in the room. Then there was the hostess at the front counter, but she was busy going through the menu for the benefit of an old man who was trying to order takeout, and she hadn't so much as glanced in Violet's direction.

Her spaghetti arrived, but her appetite was gone. She kept eyeing the student, then the female half of the couple, to see if either of them was watching her. Perhaps her name and address had somehow been revealed and she was being tormented in person—as if the phone calls weren't enough.

"Murderer!"

This third time, Violet finally realized something that plunged her deeper into chaos. No one had reacted—not the college student, nor the young couple, the server on his phone, the hostess, or the old guy getting the takeout box.

Violet was the only person in the restaurant who'd heard the voice.

She kept trying to think of explanations—could every one of these people be coconspirators and this was an elaborate prank? But no, she'd just decided to come to this restaurant. She didn't believe in ghosts, which left only one possibility, though she didn't want to accept it: this was a hallucination. She'd heard a sound that didn't exist.

In other words, she was going insane.

She leaped to her feet, tossed a hundred-dollar bill at the counter, ignored the startled cries of the hostess, and ran down the street as everyone in the restaurant watched. She didn't stop until she got home, where she turned on every light as well as the television, pushing the volume as high as it would go. Not even stopping to change, she jumped into bed, pulling the covers over her head. As if this were the only place she was safe.

From beneath the blankets, she thought about the string of nasty phone calls the day before, of SuperConan's and Zero-Cool's posts, of the hallucination just now. Her mind was spinning. She longed for her brother to call, but feared that the next time her phone rang, it would be more harassment.

Ding-dong!

Violet started trembling violently. Like a wild animal wary of predators, she stuck her head out from under the covers. It was the doorbell, not her phone. She hesitated a long time, wondering whether to answer. Could this be a hallucination too? But it kept ringing, *ding-dong, ding-dong*, as if in response to the people talking on TV. Finally, she steeled herself, tossed aside the blanket, and went to the vestibule.

She pressed her eye to the peephole and saw a familiar face: the night security guard.

"What's wrong?" she asked, opening the door without taking off the chain.

"Good evening, Miss To," he said, smiling. "Another resident complained that your TV is on too loud."

She glanced at the wall clock and realized it was already eleven. Grabbing the remote from the couch, she lowered the volume all the way down.

"Is that all right?"

"Sorry to have bothered you," said the guard, as polite as ever. "Is anything else the matter? Mr. To asked us to take good care of you while he's away."

"That's nice of you. I'm fine. I'm going to bed now."

"All right. Good night, then."

Violet shut and locked the door, then looked at the living room—it was blazing with light, yet she couldn't feel any warmth. The guard's words revolted her—she knew her father hadn't done this out of concern for her, a teenage girl home alone, but to prevent her from taking the opportunity to sneak her brother in here. Being disgusted with him was one of the few emotions her father permitted himself. When Rosalie allowed her brother in while her father was out last year, she'd been fired not long after that. Father hadn't said anything, but Violet understood what was going on. She could understand—as far as Father was concerned, her brother was just a random stranger. In a way, so was she.

Violet had no idea how many hours she slept that night. She seemed to hover between dreams and reality, thinking she heard her phone ring countless times—now with her brother's voice, now with that vicious woman screaming "Murderer!" Yet when she looked drowsily at her phone, the call register was empty. Or was that part of the dream too?

It was noon the next day by the time she fully awoke. Apart from the occasional burst of traffic noise from outside, it was silent in the bedroom, as if she were the only person left in the world. No more frustration or trouble—that was all someone else's. Yet when she caught sight of the phone on the bedside table, all the confusion in her burst out, as if she'd turned the key in a lock.

Why isn't my brother calling me? she wondered. There'd been too many strange events the day before for her brain to process. Even after a night's sleep, things didn't feel right. She turned on her phone, but there was nothing from him. He hadn't even read her last Line.

Full of unease, she turned on her computer and logged into Popcorn.

She was about to be greeted by the biggest shock yet.

POSTED BY crashoverride ON 07-05-2015, 02:28
re: Mastermind behind girl's (14) suicide?

Another burner ID, but this should be my last word. No more after this—back to my regular log-in and shitposting.

I decrypted the backup file and made a shocking discovery. In one folder was a bunch of photos—all of secondary school students—and chat records, the usual boring teenage crap. I looked closely at the uniforms—and it's the same school as that girl who killed herself!

I don't know how this dude got hold of all these kids' data or what he plans to do with it. All I care about is the invasion of their privacy. OP's (our pal SuperConan) point can't be ignored—things may be even worse than we thought. Like, criminal worse.

I've sent those files to the police along with an anonymous note explaining where they came from. I'm sure they'll want to investigate. Also gave them this guy's name and work address. If they want to find him for, uh, a little chat, it shouldn't be too difficult.

My last post got deleted for giving away personal
details, but I'm going to do it again now. I found a
picture of the dude in another file. I know some
Popcorners don't believe I'm telling the truth, so take
a look at this pic. You'll see it in the papers soon, when
he gets arrested.
    Attachment: 0000001.jpg

Below the post was a tiny little photograph: a man in a blue
shirt grinning at the camera in some coffee shop. Violet recognized it as the Starbucks at Lok Fu Place; she'd taken this
picture herself.

Seeing it now, she felt as if a swarm of ants were crawling
up her spine, along the back of her neck, onto her head, then
burrowing into her scalp. She phoned her brother again, but no
matter how many times she called or how long she let it ring,
he didn't answer.

At a loss, she went back to the post. There were several comments under the photo:

—*Sniff . . . Sniff . . .* I smell a conspiracy.
—could this guy have some weird thing going on with the
    dead girl? play for pay, maybe?
—Must be. Maybe they couldn't agree on a price so he
    pushed her until she jumped.
—Nah, that makes no sense. Can't get a hooker so you kill
    her?
—I think it's possible. The dead girl was definitely a hooker,
    so maybe this guy was a stalker and fell in love with her
    after just one time. Then he discovered she was only
    after his money, so he set off a bomb: pretending to
    defend the stationery shop guy, but actually exposing
    the girl's nasty part-time job to set an online mob on her.

> That's a classic one-two. Can't get the woman you love?
> Make her suffer.
> —well when you put it like that . . .

No, no, it was nothing like that. Violet could only defend her brother silently as they turned him into some kind of animal with their wild speculation. She thought once again about creating a new account to deny these accusations—but what if that just made things worse? Severe lack of sleep and the huge amount of pressure had taken away her judgment. She had no idea what to do.

Should she go look for her brother at his home?

Or at his workplace?

She felt as if she were trapped in a room, watching flames spread from a corner of the carpet. She couldn't make them stop, and she couldn't leave. This thread was now the hottest topic on the board—there was a new comment every few minutes, pushing it back up the home page.

After countless phone calls and text messages, she finally gave up. Her brother wasn't responding. Something was very wrong.

At four o'clock, a new Popcorn post finally gave her an answer:

POSTED BY star_curve ON 07-05-2015, 16:11
re: Mastermind behind girl's (14) suicide?

> Lookee here!
> http://news.appdaily.com.hk/20150705/realtime/
> j441nm8.htm
> [breaking news] *Police arrest man   Suspect stole*
> *student data*
> A twenty-five-year-old man has been arrested on
> suspicion of obtaining large amounts of secondary school
> students' data by criminal means, including cell phone

records. He was taken from his home this morning by police.

The police stated that they received an anonymous tip yesterday that this employee of a tech firm had infringed the privacy of many underage students. The internet security and IT crimes departments judged this case to be serious and expedited the suspect's arrest. They also seized two of his computers. The public is reminded that obtaining other people's private data is a serious offense, punishable by up to five years in prison.

Unconfirmed reports say the suspect is connected to the case of the schoolgirl who committed suicide at Kwun Tong District two months ago. The investigation is ongoing, and police have declined to confirm this information.

Her brother had been arrested. Violet's mind went blank at the thought. A strange ritual was now going on in the chatboard, with posts such as "So there is justice after all," "Serves him right," and "Five years isn't long enough."

Only one thought was going through Violet's mind: she should turn herself in.

If she surrendered, she might be able to take on some of her brother's guilt. After all, she was the one who'd come up with the idea. Everything he did was for her.

But was that the best thing to do? Her brain felt as if it were full of glue, and terror was eating her soul. It was exhausting just keeping her hands from trembling. As she hesitated, a new post gave her a moment of relief.

POSTED BY mrpet2009 ON 07-05-2015, 16:18
re: Mastermind behind girl's (14) suicide?

Don't be too sure. The way I see it, this guy will get out of it easily. He didn't post the stuff he had—ZeroCool went

and found it. In other words, even if the police find it on
his computer, he can say he downloaded it off the internet,
same as ZeroCool. It's really hard to prove stuff like this.
There was a case a while back—some guy got charged with
posting revenge porn, but he had a shared computer, and
they couldn't prove if it was him or his wife, so in the end
no one was found guilty.

She'd almost messed up. What was her brother always saying? Just stay calm and deny everything. So what if he'd been
arrested? He might not even be charged. They didn't go after him
for encouraging suicide or slander, just tech crimes. As long as
they didn't find out how he was connected to Enoch Secondary
School, there was a lot of space for him to maneuver.

As long as they didn't find the connection . . .

With a start, Violet realized that she was the key to the whole
thing. She started shaking again, and there was a stab of pain in
her throat, stomach acid rushing up her windpipe as she hadn't
eaten all day. Even so, she didn't care what was happening to
her body.

"As long as they don't find me, as long as they don't find
me . . ." she murmured like a chant. She didn't usually talk to
herself, but now couldn't help uttering her thoughts. She slumped
in a chair and wrapped her arms around herself, rocking back
and forth as she stared at the screen.

"We don't even have the same surname. They'll never find me."

Time ticked by, one second at a time. All she could do was sit
in front of the computer, looking out for new developments. She
waited to hear that he'd been bailed out. Would he come looking
for her? He must realize that she was the crucial element. That
means he'd stay far away from her, to make sure their connection
stayed secret.

By the time the sun set, Violet had been staring at the computer for almost seven hours. The ritual abuse on the chatboard

was still taking place as everyone enthusiastically debated whether her brother was guilty, what his motives could be, how he'd managed to get his hands on so much private data. What kind of illicit relationship had he had with Au Siu-Man? Most of this was pointless nonsense, but a few lines grabbed her attention.

—Do you think this guy was working alone?
—if he had an accomplice, they must be in hiding
—How useless do you think the police are? Hong Kong's so small—where would he hide?
—Hide in hell. Someone like that might as well be dead.

Dead?

Hey, Vi, never give up on life, no matter how hard it gets. Send your anger outward to other people instead! We live in a ridiculous society. All kinds of injustices happen around us every single day, big ones and small ones. If the universe is going to treat us like that, there's no reason to play fair. I don't care if the whole world hates me. Only the strong survive.

She remembered her brother saying that.

But it wasn't applicable at this moment.

Was her very existence a threat to him?

He'd suffered since he was a little boy. Now he was finally making something of himself, doing well at his career. If he became a criminal, his future would be over.

She thought of her reply to Franny.

. . . These two characters may not be lovers, but they're even closer than that. They're a single entity. We can't possibly judge them in earthly terms. I believe the author wanted to emphasize that these two are bound together. That's why the man doesn't regard it as a sacrifice when

he dies for the woman. As far as he's concerned, his life
and hers are the same thing . . .

At 9:26 a new reply came in—there were close to a hundred
posts on this thread now.

POSTED BY spacezzz ON 07-05-2015, 21:26
re: Mastermind behind girl's (14) suicide?

I know the man who was arrested. He's my coworker. I
never realized he was this sort of person. You can never
tell what's in someone's heart! I have insider info: he once
told me he has a little sister in secondary school. I've
seen them together. I remember her uniform—she's at the
same school as the girl who killed herself! There must be a
connection there.

Violet had stopped shaking.
She was no longer confused.

Sunday, July 5, 2015

We're in trouble! 12:48

Where are you? Someone reported you to the police!! 13:10

! 13:15

It's out of control! Go look! At Popcorn! 13:31

Are you there? 14:01

I'm so scared!! 14:42

Call me right away when you see this 15:13

Please 15:14

Brother 15:14

CHAPTER EIGHT

1.

"No problems here. Just keep an eye on Sze Chung-Nam," said N to Ducky on the phone as he stood beneath the streetlight. He hung up and went back to his vehicle, where Nga-Yee was sitting on her own, eyes fixed on the screen in front of her.

After confirming the identities of Little Seven and the Rat, N and Nga-Yee had been keeping a close watch on Violet To's movements. N's van had been parked near the To apartment for several days now. This was a white Ford Transit, a common enough model on the streets of Hong Kong that no one would pay too much attention. To remove even this small risk, N moved it to a different spot on Broadcast Drive every day, just in case an observant passerby or overzealous security guard might notice it. Right now he was at the junction of Broadcast and Fessenden Road.

This looked like a perfectly ordinary Ford Transit. Its exterior was a little grimy, its front bumper a little dented, and its windows covered, just like any other delivery vehicle. The interior, though, surprised Nga-Yee greatly when she first set eyes on it a few days earlier.

It was full of screens.

In the enclosed back of the van, the walls on either side had six computer screens of different sizes. Closer to the front was a metal rack, every shelf stuffed full of electronics—a riot of buttons, dials, and indicator panels. Every surface was covered with a spongelike substance, and a six-foot-long desk along one side held several laptops, keyboards, and mouses, as well as some items that looked a bit like remote controls. Empty Starbucks cups and snack packets littered the table. Cables snaked across the floor. Three chairs had been placed at the desk, beneath which were several cardboard boxes and, in one corner, a trash bag stuffed with paper cups and food cartons. This was about the same level of mess as at N's Second Street apartment, and a faint nasty smell permeated the space.

Nga-Yee had felt uncomfortable in this cramped space to start with, but several days in, she was used to it—particularly when she saw the results. She wouldn't mind being buried in rubbish like this, if she got what she wanted.

"What do you think? Will we get there tonight?" Nga-Yee asked as N came back into the van. Her eyes were fixed on Violet, who she'd never thought could be reduced to such a state in just a few days: hair disheveled, face withered, lips dry, eyes sunken, and empty of spirit.

"Yes. It will all be over tonight." N yawned and sat down next to Nga-Yee. His voice was unbelievably calm, as if this revenge plot meant nothing to him.

Yet they were planning the death of a young girl.

"How will you deal with Violet To?" That's what Nga-Yee had asked N that day they'd watched from the hotel room as Violet burned the fake suicide note in the lab.

"I suppose you want a life for a life?" he'd answered

N's answer had startled her. She'd thought he was just stalling so she wouldn't murder Violet with her bare hands, but now he seemed to be offering to carry out the killing for her.

"Are you—an assassin?" she stuttered.

"You don't have to kill someone yourself if you want them dead," said N, shaking his head. "For instance, if Violet To were to commit suicide, that would bring things full circle."

"Are you saying we should make her murder look like suicide?" Nga-Yee's voice shook. Her heart was full of revenge, but her mind couldn't cope with the idea of putting this desire into action.

"No. I said suicide. Actual suicide." N had looked straight into her eyes. "Wouldn't you rather see that? Violet taking her own life, just like your sister did?"

Nga-Yee swallowed. "How will you do that?"

"I don't know." N shrugged. "But I'll find a way."

"Oh sure, that sounds easy, forcing her to kill herself."

"You're wrong, Miss Au. I don't plan to force her. Coercing or compelling someone to commit suicide is no different from murder. Human beings are a higher species than other living things because we have free will, and we know we have free will. We're rational creatures: we understand that every effect has a cause, and that we must take responsibility for our own decisions. I won't force Violet to kill herself, but I will create the possibility of suicide, place it before her, and allow her to choose it. That's the most perfect revenge you could possibly get."

Nga-Yee had no idea what he was talking about, but she didn't care. If N could help her get revenge, he could use free will or anything he liked to make it happen.

From the moment she'd hired N to take vengeance for her, Nga-Yee had shed her victimhood. No longer was she vulnerable and easily hurt; now she wanted Violet to pay in blood for what she'd done. The three of them still formed a triangle, but its points had shifted: from client-detective-culprit, to revenger-assassin-quarry.

On Monday, after they watched Violet burn the note, they had followed her. That night she met a man in his twenties or maybe early thirties, medium-built, who looked like an office worker. There was no way to know who he was, but N had been immediately certain that this must be the Rat, Violet's techno-logical support.

"She's only just destroyed the note," he'd said. "Unless she's a criminal genius, her first instinct would be to go find her co-conspirator. She'd be afraid she'd slipped up somewhere and would want to know if there was anything else she needed to do to fix things."

Violet looked much more natural here than she had at the school, and her eyes were full of admiration. The Rat must be her lover, Nga-Yee thought. She felt a smoldering fury—Violet had no right to look so happy.

The following afternoon, she got a surprising phone call from N. After saying goodbye to Nga-Yee, he'd followed the man and found out how he knew Violet: he was her brother.

"Hang on. The surname you just said isn't To," said Nga-Yee. "Are they actually related?"

"It's a little complicated . . . I'll tell you more when I see you."

N sounded happier than normal. Perhaps he enjoyed revenge more than investigation.

Two days later, Nga-Yee was on her way to work on the bus when she got another phone call from N.

"Come to Broadcast Drive this afternoon. Meet me outside the Commercial Radio building."

"What?" N had told her that Violet lived nearby, but she didn't understand the point of her presence.

"I've done the reconnaissance. If you want to be part of this, come by this afternoon."

"Um, okay. I'll take the afternoon off." She'd been about to say she'd come after work, but she didn't know if turning down his request would mean getting cut off. "Are you sure you're okay with me being there?"

"This is serious business. You're such a moron, I can't have you running around loose—you might wreck the plan," N sneered. "This isn't like an investigation. If any of this gets out, it won't be easy to make it go away."

Nga-Yee's heart sank. She glanced at the other passengers on the bus, but no one seemed to be paying attention to her. She hadn't said anything incriminating, anyway. In fact, although N had said this wasn't murder, what they were doing went against every ethical and legal code, and they'd need to proceed very carefully. Even the phone she was speaking on was a burner N had given her three days earlier—the only safe way for them to get in touch.

At four that afternoon Nga-Yee arrived at the Commercial Radio building. There were never many people around on Broadcast Drive, and when she got off the bus, she didn't see N anywhere. Before she could call him, her phone started to ring.

"White van across the road," N's voice barked curtly. She looked up, and sure enough, there it was, parked in front of a private home, under a saga tree. She dashed across the road and knocked on the side door. N stuck his head out, pulling her in before she could say anything.

"Huh?"

It took her eyes a few seconds to adjust to the dark, and when that happened, she was confused by her surroundings. The strangest thing was that several of the screens had Violet on them, lounging on an easy chair, reading a book.

"This is real time," said N, gesturing for Nga-Yee to sit in one of the chairs. "She's in her room now. You can see everything she does on Screens 2 and 3. Those other three cameras are aimed at different parts of her bedroom."

"How are you doing this? Didn't you say she lived on the tenth floor?" There were only residential buildings here, so N couldn't have set up a surveillance point the way he did in the hotel.

"Drones," answered N, waving a gray device about the size of his palm with four rotors attached. "I sent a few up to perch on the window ledges and aircon units of the apartment across from hers. Once I adjusted the angle, I could see everything. If necessary, I could place one in her room and get an even closer shot. They do make a little noise, but that won't matter if she's fast asleep."

Nga-Yee thought back to the gangsters he'd threatened in the car. So that's how he got the picture of the golden-haired man—he'd never actually been inside his house.

"You sent one of those into her room?" said Nga-Yee, pointing at Screen 2, which was clearly showing details at close quarters —she could even read the titles of the books on the shelves.

"No. That's her laptop camera," said N. "And I can activate the ones on her phone too, front and back. She has so many windows, though, and she never draws her curtains, so the drones should be enough for now."

"Fine, you're watching her every move. What's the next step?"

"Like I said, we'll create the opportunity and put the choice in front of her."

He didn't need to say the word "suicide" for Nga-Yee to know what he meant.

"How will you do that?"

"The most satisfying way would be to turn her tactics back on herself. If she were to be tormented on the internet, for example . . ." N paused. "But that's not what I asked you here to talk about. Remember I said I'd tell you more about Violet's family?"

Nga-Yee nodded. She still felt a stab of pain every time she thought of Violet's face when she met her brother. She'd never be able to forgive these two bastards for taking her sister's life.

N pulled one of the laptops toward him and tapped on the keyboard. Several photographs appeared on the screen: some of an older man and more of the guy they'd seen meeting Violet.

"This is Violet's father," said N, pointing. He was in his fifties, stern-looking in a black suit. "He has a senior position in a construction firm—this is from his company website. He's on a business trip to the Mainland, which provides us with the perfect opportunity for revenge. He and Violet are the only people who live here, which means she'll be home alone till he comes back next week."

"What about Violet's mother?"

"She ditched them a few years ago."

Nga-Yee was a little surprised—did rich people abandon their families like that? But then she thought about it and decided that maybe only a rich person would be so selfish.

"And this is our Mr. Rat," said N, pointing at another photo. "He has a degree in computer studies from a technical college, and he works as a programmer at a small firm. He lives alone—"

As he reeled off Violet's brother's personal information, N kept clicking the mouse. More pictures appeared on the screen: the man leaving his apartment, going into the MTR, standing outside his office building.

"Wait," Nga-Yee interrupted. "That photo in the restaurant—there was a Dragon Boat Festival poster by the entrance. But that was two weeks ago! How could you have taken that in the last couple of days?"

"I didn't take that one," N answered glibly.

"Where did you get it?"

"I have my ways. This one is 'borrowed' from a detective agency."

"Detective agency?"

"Like I said, we're in luck." N grinned. "After you went home that day, I followed this guy and saw something interesting: someone was lurking in a black car, taking pictures of him with a long lens and checking what time he came home. I knew right away it was someone in the same line of work."

"Oh?" Nga-Yee gaped.

"Most detective agencies in Hong Kong have asked me to work with them at one time or another. I've seen that license plate more than once and could even tell you which agency he's with. Everyone I've ever done something for, I've put a back door in their computer system so I can go in and look at their reports. That's how I got all that info, plus the photo you just saw."

Nga-Yee recalled Detective Mok saying that all the detective agencies went to N when they encountered a problem they couldn't solve.

"Who's paying a detective to follow him?" Nga-Yee asked.

"Violet's father." N tapped the laptop screen.

"Why would he have his own son investigated?"

"Who said anything about a son?"

"Isn't he?" Nga-Yee was confused. "Then Violet isn't actually related to him? But you said on the phone . . . Oh! Do you mean he and Violet have different fathers?"

"No, same father, same mother. The thing is, Violet's current father isn't her biological dad. And To isn't her real surname."

Nga-Yee's face was a picture of puzzlement. She wanted to ask a question, but didn't know where to start.

"Violet's mother was a beautician. Back then, she was living with this shady guy, and had a son and daughter with him. They got together when she was seventeen. Then, at age thirty, she upped and left—probably realized she shouldn't waste her youth on a man like that. That's when she met Mr. To." N gestured at the photo again. "That was ten years ago. She brought her five-year-old daughter with her and had the child's name changed to her stepdad's. That was Violet."

"She loved her daughter more than her son, I suppose, and that's why she only brought her along when she remarried."

Nga-Yee wasn't sure if "remarried" was the right word—it didn't sound like she'd actually been married to the first guy.

"If she loved her daughter, she wouldn't have abandoned her the second time around. The way I see it, she had a very selfish reason for keeping Violet with her: it would be easier to win a man's sympathy with an adorable five-year-old in tow," N sneered. "The marriage wasn't even five years old before she got up to her old tricks and ran off with yet another man. Apparently this one was a stock market speculator—that is, a modern-day gambler. He may not have had more money or been able to give her a more stable life, but one thing she could be sure of: he wouldn't be boring."

"And Violet—"

"Stayed with her father. They're not related by blood, but he's her legal guardian."

This was a more complicated backstory than Nga-Yee had been expecting.

"So the father hired a detective to find his missing wife?"

"Years before she abandoned her daughter and second husband, she'd already left her son behind. You think he could find her whereabouts from this guy?" N chuckled. "Mr. To didn't even discover the boy's existence until his wife vanished. His stepdaughter was meeting her brother behind his back. They've gotten closer, and I don't think he's happy about that."

"You know all that from the detective agency?"

"No. I spoke to their previous domestic helper." N pulled up another photo, this one of a fiftyish Southeast Asian woman. "Her name's Rosalie, and she'd been employed by the To household for more than ten years. She was fired last year and now works for a family in Ho Man Tin. It was easy to track her down through her employment agency. I pretended to be a school social worker and said that Violet was experiencing some emotional problems, so I needed her help to answer some questions."

"Violet has been seeing her brother secretly?"

"Violet feels that her brother is the only person she can open up to, and Mr. To is just a stranger. But the brother seems to have been a bad influence on Violet. He came up with the plan of attack against your sister. A regular schoolgirl like Violet would never have thought of stealing personal data to turn the internet against Siu-Man."

Rage bubbled up in Nga-Yee—she'd never considered this. Little Seven was Siu-Man's classmate, and even if she'd decided out of a misplaced sense of justice or prejudice that Siu-Man was a bad seed who needed to be eliminated, she'd never have pushed her so far without the Rat's help. The Rat was an adult. Instead of correcting his sister, he became her coconspirator, using his tech know-how to help her. That was unforgivable.

Violet's family background was a surprise too. Nga-Yee thought back to the first Popcorn post, and how it sneered at Siu-Man for being brought up by a single parent—yet Violet was in the same boat. Nga-Yee could guess why the stepdad had hired a detective to tail the brother. In his place she'd have done the same: he knew the young man was a bad influence. Best to find out more about him. Perhaps there'd be a weak spot or a guilty secret to grab hold of, leverage to stop him from seeing Violet.

"The way Rosalie was talking," said N, leaning back, "she cared about Violet a lot. She watched her grow up, after all, and was sort of a mother to her. Maybe if she hadn't left and Violet had had another person to talk to, she wouldn't have gotten into this farcical situation."

"You've said a lot. Are you trying to tell me this wasn't Violet's fault?" Nga-Yee almost yelled.

"It's not my job to decide who's right or wrong. I'm just here to help you get revenge," said N simply. "I thought you'd like to know more about Violet's background. She's the enemy, isn't she, in this blood feud?"

Nga-Yee didn't know what to say. She couldn't have said when it began, but she'd stopped thinking of Violet as a human being, seeing her only as a target, a personification of guilt itself. She wanted Violet to be tortured, and she'd forgotten that there was any kind of reason behind this need for revenge.

So Violet didn't have a mother to love her—that's not an excuse for turning evil, thought Nga-Yee. She tamped down the pity rising up in her and hardened her heart till she was nothing but pure vengeance. Violet would have to pay in blood for what she'd done.

For the next hour Nga-Yee and N watched Violet in silence. When Nga-Yee finally asked what their next step would be, all N said was, "If you're bored, you can go home. Revenge isn't a Pot Noodle, it won't be done in three minutes."

Nga-Yee said nothing. What she didn't know was that behind his poker face, N was considering all kinds of strategies for turning their present knowledge into future action. He'd spent the last few days trying to come up with plots that Violet To and her brother wouldn't see through. It was much easier to uncover the truth than to predict what human beings would do, yet N preferred the latter. Setting a trap was far more thrilling and challenging than solving puzzles.

Beep!

Just as Nga-Yee was wondering what the point of this surveillance was, the laptop in front of N let out a sharp noise.

"Ah, he's here," N called out, opening the van door.

Nga-Yee steadied herself—this must be the next step. Who was here? She looked out and saw Ducky, the guy she'd seen at the hotel, a Starbucks cup in his hand. His expression didn't change when his eyes met hers.

"I'm counting on you tonight," said N to Ducky, and headed out of the van.

"What's going on?" asked Nga-Yee as N stood just outside the van door.

"Changing shift," said N. Ducky took his seat at the desk and started typing incomprehensible strings of text into the laptop. "I can't watch her twenty-four hours a day on my own, can I?"

"Should I—" Nga-Yee wasn't sure if she ought to stay or go, given that she didn't even know why she was watching Violet.

"I don't care if you want to stay all night, but I don't know what you're going to do about going to the toilet. We're just pissing into a bottle."

"Wait—" she called out, but N had shut the door. She tried to go after him, but it took her a while to figure out the door mechanism; by the time she opened it, there was no sign of him.

"Please shut the door, Miss Au," came Ducky's deep voice behind her. "We don't want to attract attention."

Nga-Yee could only do as he said. She retreated into the van's interior.

Although Nga-Yee didn't like N, they had at least spent enough time together that she knew how to deal with him. Ducky was practically a stranger, and it felt immensely awkward being stuck in such a small space with him.

"Miss Au," he said abruptly.

"Yes?"

"There's a public restroom where Broadcast Drive meets Junction Road."

"Oh. Thank you."

His eyes didn't leave the screens the whole time he spoke to her, but this brief exchange was enough to make her think better of him, even though his face remained as expressionless as a robot's.

Glancing at her watch, Nga-Yee was startled to realize that it was only half past six. Cooped up in the back of the van, it was easy to lose all sense of time. She sat down again and went back to staring at Violet on the screen. She thought of starting a conversation, but Ducky gave off a strong aura of not wanting to be disturbed.

"Who's that?" A woman had just walked into the To apartment.

"Cleaning lady. Cooks for Violet." Ducky clearly didn't believe in wasting words.

The woman went about her business in the kitchen. After a while she came back in to set two plates on the dining table, then went to call Violet. When she scooped out only one bowl of rice, Nga-Yee realized that all this food was just for Violet. Back when her mother and sister were still around, this amount—fried fish, mixed vegetables, soup—would have fed all three Aus. Her anger roared again. Violet lived without worries, her every need taken care of. Why had she felt the need to persecute Siu-Man? Nga-Yee had never cared much about inequality, but right now she hated all rich people.

Violet went to her room after dinner. She was at the computer for a while, then went back to her easy chair and her book. Nga-Yee kept watching her every move, but still had no idea what this surveillance was meant to achieve.

"Nothing's going to happen tonight," said Ducky abruptly, as if he'd read her mind.

"No?"

"You won't miss anything if you go home now. Come again tomorrow."

He might hardly say anything, but Ducky still seemed more like a normal person than N. At least he was more approachable. Nga-Yee didn't think he would lie to her, so she nodded and prepared to leave. She was getting hungry and, having just received her wages, would finally be able to eat her fill. Thinking of how she'd been surviving on instant noodles for the last few weeks even as guilty Violet To enjoyed her sumptuous meals, Nga-Yee felt a sense of injustice.

"Bye, then." Nga-Yee stood up to go. As she passed behind Ducky, she couldn't help noticing that his laptop screen was showing the Popcorn chatboard, and the thread header was rather unusual:

Mastermind behind girl's (14) suicide?

"Huh?" she couldn't help uttering out loud.

Ducky turned to look questioningly at her.

"Is this—You know what, never mind. I'm going."

She forced a smile and stepped out, then practically sprinted to Lok Fu station. After all this time, she had a pretty good sense of N's methods, and she knew he wasn't going to reveal his plans until they'd come to fruition. It seemed that the next step of this revenge plan, whatever it was, would involve Popcorn. Ducky was N's partner, so there was no point in asking him for more information. If she wanted to know what was going on, she'd have to find out herself. She forgot about her plan to eat a big meal and headed straight home, where she shoveled instant noodles into her mouth as she eagerly scanned Popcorn for the post she'd seen.

After a whole hour of searching, there was no sign of it.

She tried all the different chat rooms and scrolled back more than ten pages. It had been on the home page just a while ago, but she'd looked through more than a week's worth of posts with no success. Could she have been mistaken? Maybe it was a different website that looked like Popcorn. But she was new to the internet, and had no idea how to search for this.

Finally she gave up. She'd ask N after work the next day, and if he refused to answer, she'd badger him till he did.

Her boss had kindly let her leave the library early the day before, on the condition that she made up the time, which meant the next day she had to stay from the early shift right up to closing at nine p.m. As she walked out, she called N to let him know she was on her way to Broadcast Drive—only to learn there'd been a change of location.

"I'm at the Festival Walk parking lot, P2, Zone M."

"Festival Walk?"

"P2, Zone M."

He hung up. Nga-Yee stood there uncertainly, then decided that this must be an invitation to join him. If he didn't want her there, he wouldn't have mentioned his location.

It was about ten by the time she got to the mall. There were eight hundred parking spaces spread over three floors, almost all of them full, but she followed N's directions and managed to find the white Ford Transit. The side door slid open as she drew near, and peering at her from the gloomy interior was N.

"Why did you move the van?" she asked, climbing in.

He didn't answer, just nodded at Screen 2. The others were focused on the To apartment, as they had been the day before, but this one now showed a coffee shop. And there, reading a book in an armchair, was Violet To.

"She got to the mall this afternoon, visited the bookstore, had bibimbap at the food court, then came here to read."

"How are you filming this? You can't be using a drone in a crowded mall."

"Ducky's tailing her."

Nga-Yee looked closely. The camera must be on a table: there was an out-of-focus coffee cup to one side of the frame.

"Aren't you taking turns to keep watch?"

"Special circumstances." N sat back down, looking a bit annoyed. "When she went out this afternoon, she didn't take her usual walk to Lok Fu Place, but got the bus instead. There was no way of knowing whether she planned to take the MTR somewhere else, so I had to ditch the van, follow her onto the bus, and call Ducky to come grab the van. He met me here, and we swapped places."

"You were on the same bus as Violet? Didn't she recognize you?"

"I was in disguise. I have to hand it to her, though—I must admit I underestimated her. I'd thought a fifteen-year-old would want to hide at home after coming under so much pressure, but instead she's going out and trying to de-stress, and she's stayed out quite a long time. Not that I can't cope with this, but it's unexpected."

"Pressure? What kind of—" Nga-Yee faltered, recalling the laptop screen the day before. "Are you talking about the new Popcorn post?"

N raised an eyebrow and looked at her with a slight smile. "Ducky knows how to keep his mouth shut, so you must have seen this by accident?"

"Yes." No point denying it. "Something about a mastermind. And you talked about tormenting her on the internet. I put two and two together."

N picked up another laptop and set it down in front of her. "All right, sharp eyes, you might as well know the rest."

On the screen was a Popcorn page, with the header she remembered. She read what SuperConan had to say, and saw ZeroCool's revelation among the replies. Violet must have been thrown into a panic after reading these posts.

"Now Popcorn knows everything?" gasped Nga-Yee. "Are you the Conan person who started this whole thing by saying that Shiu Tak-Ping has no nephew? And I guess the one with that hard drive must be an associate of yours. It would be too much of a coincidence—that someone decides to reopen the case and someone else just happens to have some evidence handy."

"Wrong, Miss Au," said N. "I haven't revealed anything, and there isn't any associate. Every one of the people in this thread is me."

"All of them?"

"Yes. SuperConan is me, and ZeroCool is me. So are all the people kibitzing in the background, and the posts like 'save me a seat, just getting some popcorn.' All me."

"You hacked into Popcorn? But if you created so many fake posts under other people's names, won't the regulars think it's odd?"

N tapped a few keys, and another image flashed up on the screen. "Compare the two."

This new window also showed the Popcorn home page, but at a closer look, there was a small difference: in the second window, "[video] real footage of Hong Kong U student drunk out of her skull" came immediately after "I earn ten grand a month. How to buy a flat?" In the first window, "Mastermind behind girl's (14) suicide" came between them.

"It's . . . gone?"

"This thread never existed. It's fake."

"Wait, so that's all lies? No one knows about Shiu Tak-Ping not having a nephew, or all that security consultant stuff?"

"Correct." N nodded. "But Violet To thinks it's real."

Nga-Yee stared at him in bafflement.

"Do you remember what an MITM attack is?"

Nga-Yee recalled the killer rabbit on the woman's tablet in the coffee shop.

"So you hacked into Violet's home Wi-Fi and put the fake website on her computer."

"Yes."

So that's why I couldn't find it at home, Nga-Yee thought.

"But how did you do that? If you were pretending to be the service provider, your signal would need to be stronger than the original."

"I just took over her router." N pointed at one of the drones on the desk. "These things don't just take pictures, they can also intercept a Wi-Fi signal. While it was dark outside, I planted one of these on the aircon outside her window and carried out the remote attack from there. Wi-Fi routers have all sorts of vulnerabilities. Even with WPA2 authentication, if you use WPS for convenience, hackers have easy access anyway. A couple of hours tops, and I cracked it. Then it was just a matter of breaking into the router's protocol by brute force and pointing the DNS to my fake. Now I control everything on her home computer."

Nga-Yee could only stare at him blankly. N grimaced, giving up on his explanation. "Anyway, I'm now the middleman between Violet To and the actual internet. I control everything she sees and hears. And if she decides to post anything or send an email, I can change those too."

"But what for?" asked Nga-Yee. "If you're trying to stir up a hornet's nest against her, you don't need to bother faking posts."

"Several reasons. The main one is to keep other voices from interfering, so I can carry out your mission in the shortest possible time. You think it's so easy to create an online mob? Don't believe what politicians tell you. All sorts of things can go wrong when you try to manipulate public opinion—you need a long-term strategy. But one person's emotions? That's easy. You just need to control what information she receives, and you're in charge of her feelings."

Nga-Yee remembered him saying something similar about the woman in the coffee shop.

"But have you really cut her off completely? Won't she call her brother to ask for help when she sees those posts?"

"Won't happen."

"Why not?"

"MITM attacks don't just work on Wi-Fi." N turned and reached out to tap a lunchbox-size device on the metal rack. "This is an IMSI-catcher, more commonly known as a Stingray. It mimics a cell-phone tower and intercepts all signals within a certain area."

"You mean you're controlling her phone, just like you took over her Wi-Fi? Including what calls she can make or receive?"

"Not bad—this time you got it right away."

"This thing is available for sale? Isn't that dangerous? Doesn't that mean everyone in the world with a cell phone might get eavesdropped on?"

"It is available for sale, but ordinary people wouldn't be able to get hold of one easily. It's mostly used by governments, armies, the police . . ." N paused for a moment. "Oh, and of course hackers and criminals. This one isn't a commercial product, though. I made it myself."

"You mean Ducky made it?" Nga-Yee remembered him saying that Ducky owned a computer store.

"You're right, he supplied the parts. But the firmware actually came from my professor."

"Your professor?" Nga-Yee didn't know what firmware was, but this intrigued her more.

"The man who taught me how to be a hacker. His specialty is loopholes in signal security."

"Can this thing really pick up phone signals?" Nga-Yee eyed the box suspiciously. Surely modern technology shouldn't be so simple.

"How else would I have your phone number?"

"Huh?"

"That's how I knew whenever you came near my apartment."

Nga-Yee thought back to when she'd first tried to get N to take her case. He'd seemed to know all her movements, and even these last couple of days he'd opened the van door for her before she could knock.

"You hacked my phone?"

"I hack *all* the phones in my neighborhood," said N nonchalantly. "I've fitted an aerial to my roof and three others on nearby buildings, all connected to another Stingray. I know the phone numbers of every local resident, and if an unfamiliar number enters the zone for more than a minute, my computer automatically records it. I got your phone data the first time you came to see me, and after that I got an alert whenever you came within a hundred yards of my apartment. From the strength of the signal I even knew exactly where on the street you were standing."

"Exactly where? How's that possible?"

"Triangulation, like with satellites. If you want to know more, look it up while you're at work."

Nga-Yee only half believed him, but this certainly explained how he always seemed to know her whereabouts and how he'd been so ready for those gangsters who ambushed him.

"Okay, so you can prevent Violet from calling her brother, and vice versa. But won't they find it odd that they can't get in touch? Or are you able to fake their voices too?"

"I do have voice modifying technology, but even if it were able to completely replicate someone's voice, it would be hard to get the tone and vocabulary right. Anyone close enough to the person being imitated would know right away that something was wrong." N glanced at the screen, checking that Violet was still quietly reading in the coffee shop. "These days, though, people are used to communicating by instant message, and that gives us an opportunity."

N picked up a tablet computer and opened an app that resembled Line. Nga-Yee wasn't sure what she was looking at to start with, but after reading a few posts, it became clear.

"This is Violet To talking to her brother?"

"Correct. Except, I'm the brother." N grinned.

"You can do that?" Nga-Yee exclaimed. "How?"

"I guess I'll have to start at the beginning, otherwise you'll just keep asking why or how like a broken record," said N in a voice full of disdain. "The day after our second visit to the school I came to Broadcast Drive to walk the ground. I located the To apartment, and that night I sent drones to start the surveillance and infiltrate the Wi-Fi, as well as using the Stingray to grab all cell phone numbers in the neighborhood until I'd isolated Violet's. Then I was ready."

N took the tablet back, entered a string of commands, and placed it in front of her again.

"Two mornings ago, I used the Stingray to transmit this message to Violet's phone."

Reminder from Enoch Secondary School Library. Your items &#65297, &#65299, &#65294, &#65302, &#65303 are due in three days. For more information or to renew, please visit http://www.enochss.edu.hk/lib/q?s=71926

"What's that?"

"Enoch Library notification. Fake, of course. The point was for her to click on the link."

"What for?"

"I modified the Enoch page. As soon as Violet clicked on the link, her browser would connect to a server that downloaded fake software onto her phone."

"Fake software?"

"This is known as a Masque Attack—replacing actual programs with malware mimicking their appearance." N pointed at the Line page on the tablet. "This looks exactly like Line instant messenger, and it works the same when you use it. Most people wouldn't be able to tell the difference. When Violet logged on to this fake Line, I was able to get hold of every message she'd sent before, intercept any new ones, and impersonate whoever she was talking to."

"Just like man in the middle."

"Exactly." N's eyes twinkled. He seemed to find it hilarious that Nga-Yee was using tech lingo. "Everyone is so used to communicating by text that they've stopped wondering if the person behind the words is the one they think it is. That's why there are so many online scams."

"Didn't Violet find the library notice suspicious?"

"Before making the fake Popcorn thread, I used the same method to create fake messages on the school chatboard, to make it seem as if other students had got the same erroneous notification. I also stuck in a discussion about the ruckus in the library that day. Once Violet saw people talking about your sister, she naturally forgot all about that notification."

In order to make this fake thread—which would only be seen by Violet—more believable, N had gone through the Enoch School system to look up all the students who'd been using the printer in the library that day. He had actually been a little surprised that Violet hadn't got in touch with her brother right away after seeing this thread, but that also helped him understand a little more about the nature of their dependency, after which he adjusted his strategy.

"I knew Violet wouldn't ignore this eye-catching chat on the Library Board. She'd want to go through the whole conversation and see if anyone—such as the Countess—said anything more about the suicide note. That was the bait. The next day, I posted under a different student's name, with a link to the fake Popcorn chat I just showed you."

"Ah, so now she was on the hook," said Nga-Yee. "She thought her evil deeds had been exposed." Nga-Yee was starting to understand. "When she read SuperConan's post, then saw someone talking about finding more files on the hard drive today, and you stopped her asking her brother for help—"

Nga-Yee looked again at the screen. Violet might appear to be reading calmly, but her brows were faintly furrowed, and she was clearly trying hard to hide her unease.

"Hang on—" Nga-Yee said. "Violet's not at home now. Can't she get on to the real internet? If she goes onto Popcorn and finds the thread gone, won't the whole plan fall apart? Or what if her brother calls now? Does your Stingray reach as far as the coffee shop?"

"That's why Ducky's following her." N pointed at the screen. "He has a low-intensity Stingray in his rucksack, with a range of thirty feet. His laptop is mimicking a Wi-Fi server to continue the MITM attack. That ought to keep Violet isolated. Of course, if she goes rogue and decides to log on to one of the café's public terminals or call her brother from a public phone, we'd be in trouble. If that happens, Ducky will have to find some way to stop her. But I bet she won't do that, because she doesn't suspect there's anything wrong with her phone."

N seemed prepared for all contingencies. No wonder even Violet's unexpected visit to Festival Walk hadn't fazed him.

"Violet seems calm at the moment because her brother is on Line telling her not to worry. Of course, she's still pretty churned up inside," said N. "Her actual brother is completely in the dark. He's busy at work, probably not spending too much time worrying about what's going on with his little sister. So the basic setup is all in place, and we're ready for the next step."

"What's that?"

"If you want to be part of it, don't go home tonight." N smiled craftily.

Nga-Yee had no idea what he was planning, but it looked as if she wouldn't be sleeping in her own bed.

Not long after that, Violet started putting away her things. The wobbly camera followed her as she left the café and headed to the shuttle stop on Suffolk Road. From the angle, Ducky was standing ahead of her in line, with one passenger between them. There were quite a few other people there—probably also heading back to Broadcast Drive. Most people would think that tailing someone meant following them from behind, thought Nga-Yee, but it was a sign of N's and Ducky's superior skills that they were in front of Violet now. Nga-Yee could think of two advantages: first, it reduced the risk of getting left behind if the bus was crowded and Violet was the last passenger to squeeze on; and, more cunningly, no one would imagine that they were being followed by someone ahead of them. By anticipating Violet's actions, Ducky had managed to stay literally one step ahead of her.

"We should go." N stood and headed to the front of the van. Only now did Nga-Yee realize there was a narrow sliding door leading straight to the driver's seat.

"Stay back there and keep monitoring," he called, then slid the door shut.

The van juddered and started to move, but Nga-Yee didn't notice. Her eyes were fixed on Violet To. She and Ducky were at opposite ends of the bus. Fifteen minutes later they were back at Broadcast Drive. N found a parking lot and returned to the back. A few minutes after that, the shuttle arrived and Violet got off; Ducky did not.

"She's back within range of our Stingray," said N by way of explanation. Nga-Yee understood: the shuttle wasn't like a regular bus; all stops were by request to the driver. Violet would definitely notice if she asked to be let off and someone followed her.

Within five minutes, Violet was back in her apartment (and on their screens), and Ducky had rejoined them in the back of the van.

"Thanks for doing that," said N, taking the rucksack from Ducky.

"It's fine," said Ducky, as expressionless as ever. Tailing Violet was a better use of his skills, anyway—Chung-Nam had spent the last few days either at the office or poring over documents at home.

Nga-Yee couldn't quite work out N and Ducky's relationship. Ducky seemed to have a lot of respect for N, but that could have been the reliance of one partner on another. She thought again of Loi's face when he talked about N, and Detective Mok's reverence for him. As far as Nga-Yee was concerned, he was an annoying bastard who happened to be very good at what he did, and she had no idea how these other people had learned to trust him.

After Ducky left, N said to Nga-Yee, "Those seats tilt back. You can have a nap if you want."

"Nap? I thought we were starting the next step."

"It's still early." N pulled a snack bar from the plastic bag beneath the desk and bent over his laptop again.

Nga-Yee decided to follow his advice. It was dark in the van, and she was exhausted. Her eyes remained fixed on Violet, but their lids began to droop. She was hazily aware of someone shaking her by the left shoulder. Her eyes blinked open, and there was N, looking exactly as he had before she dropped off, in the chair to her left. Why had he woken her so soon? She glanced at her watch, surprised to see the small hand at three. She'd slept almost four hours.

"Awake?" asked N.

Nga-Yee rubbed her eyes and looked around. The screens still showed the To apartment, but everything was now tinted dull green. Camera 3 was on Violet's bedroom.

"Have . . . have we started?" Nga-Yee asked.

"Yes."

"What are we doing? Breaking in?"

"No, we're making phone calls."

"What?"

"Late-night nuisance calls."

Just like that, Nga-Yee was wide awake. "Nuisance calls?" she said. "You made me stay here all night for a childish prank?"

"It may be a prank, but there's nothing childish about it."

"How—"

"Don't ask." N put a microphone in front of her, then pressed a few keys on the laptop. On Screen 3, Violet jerked upright in bed and reached out to grab her phone.

"The night vision cameras can't go any brighter than that," said N. Now Nga-Yee understood the dull green tint.

"Hello?" Violet's voice came through the speaker. Nga-Yee turned and looked frantically at N, gesturing to ask what she should say.

"She won't hear you unless you press the mic button," said N, trying not to laugh. "Anyway the first call will be silent."

"Hello?" Again, Violet's voice from the speaker. N hit another key and ended the call.

"You do the next one," said N, hitting the key again as soon as Violet put down her phone.

"What if she recognizes my voice?" asked Nga-Yee.

"She won't. I've adjusted the mic to distort it."

"Hello?" came Violet's voice again, sounding a bit more annoyed.

"What should I say?" Nga-Yee's finger hovered over the mic button.

"Whatever you like, just don't use the word 'sister' or anything that might give away who you are. Keep it simple."

Nga-Yee pressed the button without having made up her mind. What did she want to say to Violet? She bit her lip and spat out, "Murderer!"

N hit the key to cut off the call, smiling at her as if in praise. On the screen, Violet looked frozen. Unexpectedly, Nga-Yee felt pleased with herself. All this time she'd wanted to accuse the person who'd caused her sister's death, and not only had she done that now, she'd left the culprit completely stunned. Two birds with one stone.

"Very good, though not exactly subtle. A bit crude, even." N pulled the microphone closer and hit the call key for the third time.

"Who are you? What do you want? If you call again, I'll report you to the police!" Her terror was plain to hear—it filled the van.

"Fuck you! Ha ha." Nga-Yee had never heard N sounding so thuggish. He hung up before Violet could say anything.

N tried a couple more times, but Violet rejected the calls, then turned off the phone.

"Ha! Game over," N crowed.

Nga-Yee couldn't help feeling a little angry at how lightly he was taking this.

"What's this meant to achieve?" she asked.

"Look at the state she's in."

Nga-Yee turned to the screen. Violet was huddled in a corner of her bed, her blanket clutched tight around herself. Nga-Yee hadn't expected her to be so terrified.

"When a normal person gets a nuisance call, at most they end up in a bad mood. You see what a guilty conscience does. A small tap, and the cracks show in her calm façade right away," said N. "These calls are just the fuse leading up to the next explosion."

"A fuse?"

N tapped away on the keyboard, then turned it to face Nga-Yee. The screen still showed the fake Popcorn thread, but there were some new comments:

—There's even a phone number! Anyone called to check?
—I did, some female answered. Go for it, guys!

"When Violet sees these, she'll think she knows where the harassing phone calls came from." N moved the page with his laptop touch pad. "It will appear that people on the internet have worked out that this kidkit727 who forced your sister to kill herself must have some unspeakable secret motive, and that her identity is about to be exposed."

One of the replies stood out from the others, under a name that came as an unpleasant blast of déjà vu for Nga-Yee.

POSTED BY kidkit727 ON 07-04-2015, 03:09
re: Mastermind behind girl's (14) suicide?

ZeroCool here. I found the password to this account in the file I found. I'm 100% sure this bastard has something to do with it.

"I guess—this one is fake too?" she said.
"Naturally."

"But what if Violet checks kidkit727's log-in record, or even tries to log in herself? She'd realize—"

"If I can fake a chatboard, then I can fake any page on that site, including the log-in." N was frowning—he couldn't stand Nga-Yee's stupid questions. "But even if I hadn't done any of that, Violet will never log in. She'd like nothing better right now than to cut herself off from kidkit727 forever. Why would she make more trouble for herself by logging in to the board if she didn't need to?"

Nga-Yee looked back at the screen. Violet was still curled up in her nest of blankets, shivering a little from time to time. N was right, thought Nga-Yee, this string of phone calls might well be more effective than she'd imagined.

"What now?" she asked.

"Violet will probably stay like this till dawn. I'll use that time to make up more fake replies to lead her farther up the garden path," said N, pulling a laptop over to himself.

"What should I do?"

"Enjoy Violet's suffering. Wasn't that what you wanted? That's what your sister went through every night as she was being smeared on the internet."

A chill went through Nga-Yee. Ever since she and Siu-Man stopped sleeping in bunk beds, she hadn't seen her sister asleep. For all she knew, Siu-Man had been huddled under her blanket every night too, feeling an invisible hand pushing her toward death.

Nga-Yee spent most of the next three hours staring at Violet on the screen, dozing off from time to time. She had no idea how N was able to do without a wink of sleep, but he just kept going. Perhaps he was used to living like this, completely untethered from a schedule.

At 6:20 a.m. Nga-Yee left Broadcast Drive to take the first MTR home, where she had a quick shower before heading to the library. N had said that the "climax" wouldn't arrive for another two or three days, so she decided not to waste any more leave. She would join N again after work.

Before she went, N had a question for her: "To make the whole thing convincing, I'm going to send harassing messages to Violet's phone," he said lazily. "How many do you want her to get?"

Nga-Yee had no interest in such a ridiculous question. "Forty-two," she said at random.

"Ha—the answer to Life, the Universe and Everything. Too bad it was mice in that, not rats, otherwise it would be even neater." N chuckled.

After work, Nga-Yee came back to Broadcast Drive. She'd had the early shift, so was there by five. N wore the same clothes as he'd worn the day before, but on the screen, Violet looked different. Nga-Yee was no psychiatrist, but even she could tell that the girl was on edge. Her features were haggard, and she seemed distracted. Right now she was sitting in front of her computer, staring anxiously at it, checking her phone from time to time, as if she expected a message. Each time, though, she looked disappointed.

"What's happened?" asked Nga-Yee.

N handed her the tablet with Violet's Line conversation.

"She tried calling her brother, but I diverted her to an unused number, so she thinks he's not picking up. This is from after that."

Nga-Yee glanced at it. Lots of messages about him being busy at work and his boss being around, but he'd call her later.

"In a way, I'm not lying—her brother really has been busy at work, and he's doing overtime almost every day. I guess that's how things are in Hong Kong tech firms: long hours, low wages, uncertain future. Maybe I'm doing him a favor by allowing him to focus on his job rather than spending time responding to his sister's messages," said N mockingly.

"I want to see the fake Popcorn posts," said Nga-Yee, as if it were an order. N found that a bit strange but handed over the laptop.

"You read most of the new comments this morning."

Nga-Yee ignored him and carefully read the whole thread. She'd had a thought at work that had given her doubts, and after reading all the comments, she was even more certain she was right.

"Are you lying to me again?" she asked.

"What would I be lying about?"

"You said you wanted Violet to suffer internet bullying, but these are all aimed at her brother." Nga-Yee had felt all along that something was wrong, and today she realized what it was.

N chuckled and shook his head. "So that's what you're worried about. What I said was, the best revenge would be to turn her tactics back on herself, so she could be bullied on the internet, for example. But the bullying isn't the main point, the outcome is."

"What outcome?"

"You want Violet to suffer. Isn't it secondary whether she's actually getting bullied or not?"

Nga-Yee had no answer to that.

"This will be much more effective than just bullying her. Every person has different vulnerabilities. You have to find their weak spots and hit them hard if you want to see results. Don't forget your ultimate goal."

Nga-Yee knew what he was referring to: Violet's suicide.

"See how she looks now?" N pointed at the screen. "Yesterday she could still pretend to be calm. Today she's abandoned her books and is only paying attention to her computer and phone. She's starting to panic. If we take things further tonight, we'll be within striking distance."

"Are we going to make more prank calls tonight?"

"No. Like I said, that was just a prelude. Wait around and you'll see what I mean." N laughed mysteriously.

A little before seven, Violet left the apartment.

"She's going out again?" said Nga-Yee anxiously. "Back to Festival Walk? Should we call Ducky?"

"No. She's probably only going to grab some dinner nearby. We can follow her in the van."

"How do you know?"

"She doesn't have a bag with her, and she's too casually dressed for the mall."

Sure enough, she didn't pause at the bus stop, but kept going toward Junction Road.

"Right . . . she crossed over, she's not going to Lok Fu Place, so she must be heading toward Baptist Hospital." N jumped up from his chair and opened the sliding door. "Probably Franki Centre. There aren't many restaurants there, so it shouldn't be too hard to guess where she's going."

N drove them over to Junction Road, found a place to park, and returned to the back.

"Time to fire the first shot."

"Shooting? You're not going to do anything dangerous, are you?" Once again, his words left Nga-Yee baffled.

"You really have no imagination. That was a metaphor." N held up a yellow box about the size of a smartphone. One side was covered in rows of black ovals in a beehive shape. Were they buttons? Nga-Yee couldn't tell.

N went to the far end of the desk, by the back of the van, and tugged at something on the wall. Nga-Yee hadn't noticed the window till he opened it. She went over, and they both looked out. Across the road, Violet was walking down the slope of Broadcast Drive and was almost at the entrance to a park.

"Stay out of my way—you can watch on the screen," said N, shoving her.

"But the screen—oh!" She'd been about to protest that the cameras were still pointing at the To apartment, but now Screen 2 had the window view. A few days earlier, after their second visit to the school, she remembered N saying that he was filming the school gate from his van—presumably there was a hidden camera on the outside of the vehicle.

"You'll see more results soon," said N, connecting that mini-phone of his to this strange box. He did something to his phone screen, and Nga-Yee saw Violet stiffen. The girl turned, then looked around anxiously.

"What happened? How did you attack her this time?"

N shut the window and turned to face Nga-Yee. He touched his phone screen again.

"Murderer!"

Nga-Yee reeled. It sounded as if the word were in her ear. It was the word she'd spoken the night before, but this didn't quite sound like her voice.

"Is this a speaker?" She pointed at the little box.

N didn't reply, just picked up the box and waved it front of her.

"Murder—"

This little gesture startled her. She could only hear the voice when it was pointing directly at her.

"What's this?"

"This little thing is called a directional speaker," N explained. "In simple terms, just like a flashlight can focus light in a single beam, this contains sound within a tight area. Only someone standing in line with the device can hear it. Ultrasound waves don't disperse in air, so they lock the sound in place. I won't go into too much detail. All you need to know is that Violet thinks she heard someone whisper 'murderer' in her ear."

Nga-Yee had had no idea that this technology even existed.

"One shot isn't enough." N put down the box and headed back into the driver's seat.

They followed Violet to Franki Centre, where she entered a restaurant called Lion Rock. N parked nearby on Kam Shing Road, then came back again and pulled a wrinkled gray jacket from a box beneath the desk. He put it on, followed by some brown trousers that didn't match.

"What are you doing?" asked Nga-Yee.

He ignored her, just kept changing. Next were a pair of tattered black shoes and a hat with a thatch of graying hair glued to it. He pulled a standing mirror from the box, studied himself critically, and stuffed a couple of cotton balls into his mouth to puff out his cheeks. Pale makeup whitened his eyebrows and stubble, and an old-fashioned pair of gold-rimmed glasses completed the look.

In an instant, N had aged twenty years and was now an old codger in his sixties. He squinted and furrowed his brows, the lines radiating from his eyes much deeper than usual. His upper lip was slightly raised, revealing his front teeth. His drooping jowls made it impossible to tell his real age.

"I'll just be a minute," he said, his voice deeper than usual, and opened the van door. As he got out, Nga-Yee recalled that he'd mentioned following Violet in disguise.

She turned her attention back to Screen 2, which now showed N walking into the restaurant, though the camera couldn't capture what went on inside. Just as she was wondering what to do, a flickering image on the laptop caught her attention. Looking closer, she realized that this old-fashioned wood-paneled room was the interior of Lion Rock. N must be wearing a GoPro.

"Table for one, sir?" came over the laptop speaker as a waiter appeared on the screen.

"No thanks, I'm just getting takeout."

As N spoke, the camera shifted to his left, where Violet was sitting in a corner.

"Of course. What would you like to order?"

"Oh my, do you have any sandwiches?"

"Certainly. We have quite a few types."

"So sorry, my eyes are bad, I can't read the menu—"

As N and the waiter talked, Violet's head jerked upright and she looked around nervously. Nga-Yee glanced at the desk and realized that the mini-phone and directional speaker were gone.

"I guess I'll have the corned beef."

"Very well, one corned beef. Twenty-eight dollars, please."

Nga-Yee barely took in what N was saying, so absorbed was she by watching Violet. Even though N's body camera wasn't very clear, it was obvious that the girl's expression had gone from anxiety to sheer terror. She stared at a nearby couple, then at a man at the next table, as if they were a horde of demons out to steal her soul. Nga-Yee realized now how diabolical this move was: once Violet understood that she was hearing voices no one else could, she might think she was going insane. The prank calls were just a bit of nonsense—as N said a prelude to the real mischief.

"Your corned beef, sir," said the speaker after ten minutes.

"Thank you. Could I have some napkins?"

In the background, a waiter set a plate of spaghetti in front of Violet. She didn't touch it, but continued glaring at the people around her. Then everything happened very fast: Violet jumped to her feet, trembling all over, her features pale and twisted. She hurried over to the counter, looking all around her, tossed down a banknote, and dashed out.

"Miss? Miss!"

Nga-Yee switched to the other screen, which showed Violet sprinting down the road. Soon she was out of view. At the same moment, N threw the door open and jumped in, dropped the plastic bag of food on the desk, slid into the driver's seat, and sped after her.

They parked near her apartment building and waited. Violet must be ready to collapse, thought Nga-Yee. She'd turned on every light in the flat and the television, and was in bed with her head under the covers.

"See? I wasn't lying. This really is the most effective way," said N, removing his disguise.

"Um, okay." Nga-Yee had no idea how to respond. Once again, he'd shown her something she could never have imagined—but she was damned if she was going to acknowledge that.

"This was an appetizer." N dabbed at his face with a wet wipe. "Tomorrow, the main course."

"Tomorrow?"

"Her reaction was more severe than I expected, so rather than let things drag out, we might as well take the final step. If you like, stick around and keep enjoying her suffering, but if I were you, I'd go get some sleep and be well rested for the finale." N opened the box from the restaurant and took a bite of his sandwich. "This came with fries—pretty good. Too bad there's no ketchup."

Having only caught a few hours' sleep in the van the night before, followed by a hard day's work at the library, Nga-Yee was exhausted. Only her sense that this was a crucial moment in her revenge allowed her, through sheer force of will, to keep watching Violet's punishment. Now N's words convinced her to go home and prepare for the final round.

She didn't sleep well that night. Perhaps out of overexcitement or unease, she woke several times. Violet's terrified face kept appearing in her mind, then morphed into Siu-Man's. Sorrow, rage, and fear surged over her until she was fully awake, by which time it was eight in the morning—almost time to leave for work.

"Are you okay, Nga-Yee?" asked Wendy during lunch. "You look tired. Do you feel unwell?"

"I'm fine, thanks for asking. I've had to deal with some personal stuff." Nga-Yee forced a smile. "Everything should be better tomorrow."

"I see." Wendy scratched her head. "As long as you're okay. You've been looking worse and worse each day—I was worried. You said something similar last month, and I thought you might have gotten into serious trouble. Sorry to be a busybody, but just tell me if there's anything I can do to help. Even if you need to borrow more money—"

"Um, thanks."

After this conversation, Nga-Yee found herself wondering: after this day, would everything really be over? If she succeeded in her revenge, would the thorn be pulled from her heart? Could she go back to living as peacefully as before?

She didn't dare keep thinking. At this point, it was too late to turn back.

2.

At seven o'clock that evening, Nga-Yee put aside her unease and made her way back to Broadcast Drive. N had parked the van thirty yards from the front entrance of Violet's building, beneath some large trees that partly shielded it from view. She walked up to the van, and once again the door slid open as she approached. N stuck his head out; he was talking on the phone, and gestured for her to sit in her usual spot while he stepped outside and shut the door behind him. Nga-Yee wondered who he was talking to—had something come up at the last minute?—but the thought vanished as soon as she caught sight of the screen on the wall.

She never expected Violet to be reduced to such a state.

Alone in the van, Nga-Yee watched this feeble, despondent girl. She kept jumping up to pace around the room, then sat down again to stare blankly at the computer screen. From time to time she picked up her phone, jabbed at it for a while, then flung it aside. As she perched in her chair, her body swayed from side to side, and she seemed distracted. Her eyes were vacant. Her shoulders were shaking, though it was impossible to say if this was due to rage or fear. Perhaps both. The only thing Nga-Yee could be sure of was that Violet had fallen into a state of extreme anxiety, and that spectral face made it clear that she'd slept very little, or maybe not at all.

The previous night's trick had been remarkably effective. Violet seemed to have fallen apart altogether. Nga-Yee thought she would feel joy at the girl's reduced state, but she found herself unable to take any pleasure in it. Nga-Yee's own sadness and grief were as powerful as ever, and all she could hear was a question from deep in her soul: Did you really think the fruit of vengeance would taste sweet?

No, I didn't think revenge would make me happy, I just wanted justice for Siu-Man.

Her thoughts were interrupted by N sliding open the van door.

"Did you say—it would all be over tonight?" asked Nga-Yee as he sat down.

"Yes, that's right," he said, yawning.

Clearly they were talking about Violet's suicide. Seeing her now, the personification of despair, Nga-Yee wouldn't have been surprised if she'd pulled out a knife and ended things right there.

"What did you do to her?" Something told Nga-Yee this couldn't have been caused only by the "voices" last night.

"Not much, just hit her weak spots hard."

N shoved his laptop over to face her. On the screen was the same Popcorn thread, but it was several times longer than the day before. Most eye-catchingly, a picture of Violet's brother appeared in the replies. Astounded, Nga-Yee read the text that went with it.

"This . . . this news is fake too, right?" she asked, staring at the headline: POLICE ARREST MAN: SUSPECT STOLE STUDENT DATA.

"Of course." N put a finger on the touch pad. "I can spoof news websites too. Even if Violet clicked on the link, she'd find it convincing."

"You just made up a crime? Will she believe that?"

"Hey, I made up the arrest, but the crime is real." N frowned. "Didn't I show you?"

"You mean that charger thing Violet used in the library that helped her steal Siu-Man's photo?"

"No, no, I mean this."

N pulled up a conversation she'd seen before on the tablet:

Were the files I sent you stored on the same
hard drive?
If those ever get out, we're in trouble!

                                                    what files?

The ones you made me steal from the school!
The pictures, contacts, SMSes and all that from
the other kids' phones! If anyone reveals your
ID on Popcorn, you can just say the clock was
a day slow or something. But if they find out we
know each other, we're not going to get out of
that!

"Violet hardly ever lets this sort of valuable information slip. Naturally I caught hold of it." N grinned craftily.

"You got the files?"

"No." He spread his hands. "But even if I had, it would be pointless. Knowing that she sent the stolen files to her brother was enough for me to invent a story. As ZeroCool, I made up some nonsense about student privacy and photos that can't be made public. Violet fell for it. Even if some details of my description didn't exactly match up with the files she stole, her judgment is weak at the moment. She'd probably think she missed something—not that I'm puffing myself up to look scary."

"How did you get that picture of her brother? This doesn't look like something from a detective agency's files." Nga-Yee looked at the laptop again.

"Like I told you, the fake Line app on Violet's phone. I have access to her past chats. She took this photo and sent a copy to her brother over Line. That's how I got it. At this point Violet's hardly going to believe that every single thing she's seen online has been a lie."

"Wait, that's her weak point?" Nga-Yee didn't quite understand. "Even if she was distraught at learning that her brother was arrested, would that really be enough to make her want to kill herself?"

"People end their lives under two circumstances." N was suddenly solemn. "First, and most commonly, because they're in more pain than they can bear. This could be physical—such as cancer—or mental, such as depression. The motive could be to escape this suffering, or as an accusation—so their death will create guilt in someone else. Strictly speaking, this is an irrational course of action."

"Is there such a thing as a rational suicide?"

"Yes—when it's a sacrifice to achieve a particular goal. Sure, it might not seem rational if you look at it objectively, but from the person's point of view it makes perfect sense. That's the second possibility." N looked at Nga-Yee. "If you and your sister were trapped in a fire, surrounded by smoke, and there was only one oxygen canister available, would you use it or give it to her?"

Nga-Yee's heart sank. If she'd known what was in store for Siu-Man, she would have done anything to take her sister's place, even if it meant plunging from the twenty-second floor herself.

"I said before that I'm not going to force Violet to commit suicide," N went on. "All I'm going to do is give her a rational choice, and she can decide. I don't want her to kill herself purely to escape her pain. She has to face the terror of death with clarity, completely understand the despair that causes someone to end their life, and fully grasp that this is her decision, made of her own free will, and not some half-formed, sloppy notion of putting an end to everything." He paused a moment. "I'm not a kind person, though. This is revenge, so naturally I'm going to skew the circumstances away from her."

He scrolled down on the laptop screen to a longer comment:

> Don't be too sure. The way I see it, this guy will get out
> of it easily. He didn't post the stuff he had—ZeroCool went
> and found it. In other words, even if the police find it on
> his computer, he can say he downloaded it off the internet,
> same as ZeroCool. It's really hard to prove something like
> this.

"I want Violet to believe that she's the main thing endangering her brother, and to form the idea that as long as the police don't find her, her brother might get away with it. There's no truth in that, but if she believes it, she'll act accordingly. And in a while she's going to see this message . . ."

N tapped on the keyboard, bringing up some text in a new window:

> I know the man who was arrested. He's my coworker. I
> never realized he was this sort of person. You can never
> tell what's in someone's heart! I have insider info: he once
> told me he has a little sister in secondary school. I've
> seen them together. I remember her uniform—she's at the
> same school as the girl who killed herself! There must be a
> connection there.

". . . so Violet will face a stark choice: her own existence versus her brother's safety. The more she loves and cares about him, the more easily she'll be swayed."

"Even if she thinks her brother might go to jail, infringing on someone's privacy isn't a major crime, is it? Surely that's not worth sacrificing your life—"

"If it goes to trial, the media spotlight will fall on him, and he'll be judged by the public. What Violet fears is that he'll be torn apart on the internet because of her, and he'll be seen as a pervert who destroyed someone else's life. Even the truth wouldn't get in the way of that—so she wouldn't consider turning herself in as a solution."

Nga-Yee was starting to wrap her head around this way of thinking. She knew how stressful it could be to become a talking point, and clearly Violet understood it too—having weaponized public opinion against Siu-Man.

"Over the last few days we've steadily applied more and more psychological pressure on her. Now she's liable to crack, believing that death can solve all her problems," said N crisply. "In this unstable mood, deprived of sleep, hearing 'Murderer!' shouted in your ear would make you lose touch with reality."

There was one thing Nga-Yee didn't know: It was N who'd left that comment about suicide on Violet's book blog.

After meeting Rosalie and learning about Violet's family background, the plan started to form in N's mind. That night, he commented on her blog as "Franny" in order to make Violet read the novel again and think about its protagonists' states of mind, so the idea of suicide as a rational choice would be implanted in her subconscious. He had no way of knowing whether this would work, but experience had shown him that going the extra mile never hurt. This was nothing like hypnosis or mind control, more the way an advertisement—a slogan or image—might subliminally influence a consumer's choice.

"Take a close look at the final day of Violet's life," said N, reclining his seat and tearing open a snack bar. "This is your revenge—you have a responsibility to watch it to the end."

For the next few hours Nga-Yee stared silently at the screen, observing the flame of life flickering in Violet. Hospitable for once, N offered her a snack bar, but she had no appetite. Her insides were flipping over and over. Much as she longed for her enemy to be punished, she also had a conscience, and she was uneasy at the taking of a human life. Humankind was capable of evil thoughts and poisonous words, but most people wouldn't be able to look directly at the results of this cruelty. Several times, Nga-Yee wanted to tell N that she was going home, that he should call her when it was done, but his words—that she had a responsibility to watch—kept her fixed to her chair. She was unable to tear her eyes away from Violet, unable to ask anything of the assassin sitting next to her.

A little after nine p.m. N posted the comment by an apparent coworker of her brother's. Violet's whole body language changed after reading it. She still looked stricken, but her eyes no longer roamed and her lips stopped trembling. Nga-Yee felt that she might abruptly open the window and take a flying leap to her death on the street ten stories below, but she remained where she was, eyes on her laptop, unmoving for more than an hour.

"How long is she going to be like this?" said Nga-Yee.

"That's heartless of you, Miss Au. Even a convict on death row is given time to say a last prayer, but you won't let her have these final moments." N smiled wickedly at her.

Nga-Yee hadn't meant anything like that—only that it was difficult to put up with this endless waiting, and she found herself on pins and needles. "I was just—"

N pushed the microphone over to her, cutting her off.

"If you can't wait, feel free to place the final straw on the camel's back."

"What?"

"Remember the directional speaker? I've fitted one on a drone, and it's facing Violet through the open window now. If she 'hallucinates' another voice urging her to sacrifice herself for her brother, she'll probably do it right away."

The black microphone before Nga-Yee seemed to emanate a deadly chill, and its red button beckoned her like a demon.

She had an impulse to hit the button and blurt out "Murderer!" or something equally venomous. Her arm twitched, but she couldn't make her finger do it. Was it her limb or her courage that had failed her? Or was it that heavy sense of responsibility?

"Hurry it up if you like. I have a lot of other work to get through to make sure you get your true revenge."

"True revenge?"

"Why do you think I'm dealing with Violet in such a convoluted way?" N smiled drily. "Think about it. Violet obviously isn't going to leave a suicide note. Tonight, after she dies, I'll retrieve all my drones, eliminate any traces that we were ever here, and restore her phone to its original condition. Her brother will have no way of knowing why his much-loved sister chose to kill herself. She was alive and well a few days ago, and just like that, she's gone. He had no idea that she was unhappy. For the rest of his life he'll be tormented by this, regret that he was so absorbed by his work that he neglected her. No matter how well he does in his career, he'll never get his sister's life back. Isn't that the truest revenge you could get for Siu-Man's death?"

It took Nga-Yee a moment to fully grasp what he was saying— so his guarantee of satisfaction hadn't been an empty promise. N understood her torment and everything underlying it. He wasn't just going to punish Violet; he would make her brother suffer everything Nga-Yee herself was going through. There was a darkness in him she hadn't sensed before, and she started to wonder if he was a person or a devil. What kind of Faustian bargain had she gotten herself into?

But no, he wasn't Mephistopheles, he was Nemesis. Like his namesake, N was the soul of revenge.

Nga-Yee looked again at the microphone. Should she do as vengeance personified told her? Give Violet To that final push?

"What should I say?" The same question she'd asked two days ago, finger on the button.

"Anything you like. Maybe your greatest hit, 'Murderer!' Or 'Are you brave enough to die?' 'Scum like you have no right to go on living.' 'Time to finish what you started last year.'"

Hearing N repeat lines from Violet's final messages to Siu-Man awakened the hatred in Nga-Yee once more. Then, in a lucid moment, she detected something amiss.

"What do you mean, 'started last year'? What did she start last year?"

"Nothing much." N pursed his lips. "She tried before, that's all. It's not hard to nudge someone into suicide when they've already attempted it. A little encouragement is usually enough."

Nga-Yee froze. "She's tried before?"

"Yes."

"How do you know?"

"From the scars on her wrists."

Nga-Yee's head swung back around, but the resolution on the screen was too low for her to tell.

"Don't bother," said N emotionlessly. "You won't be able to see. Long sleeves."

"So how do you know?"

"Long sleeves."

"You think that's the only reason people wear long sleeves—to cover scars?"

"Not now. I meant at the school."

Nga-Yee remembered the baggy sweater Violet had been wearing in the library.

"Wasn't that just to hide her figure? Many girls—"

"A sweater-vest would do for that. But a long-sleeved pullover in the summer?"

"You're just guessing!"

"You think I'd come up with such an elaborate plan without doing my homework?" said N, sounding exasperated. "The first time I saw Violet To, I was only ninety percent certain that she was covering up self-harm or attempted suicide. But that gave me enough to go on, and I was able to get confirmation from Rosalie. People open up more when you say you're a social worker."

"What did she tell you?"

"Sometime last May, someone rang the To household's doorbell frantically around midnight, then starting banging hard on the door. Mr. To was still out, leaving only Rosalie and Violet at home. Rosalie thought her employer must have forgotten his keys, but when she opened the door, it was Violet's brother, who'd never shown up at the apartment before. He pushed past without a word. When she followed him to the bathroom, Rosalie realized why he was acting so strangely: Violet was slicing her wrists open. There were already quite a few cuts along her arms, and blood was spattered everywhere."

"He came to stop her?"

"She'd sent him a text to say goodbye, probably thinking it wouldn't take long to die. But she'd underestimated how hard it would be, and he managed to get there in time." N shrugged. "But here's the punch line—Violet's father arrived home just then. He's supposed to be a mature adult, but he couldn't deal with the scene he was presented with: his stepdaughter's attempted suicide. On top of that, he finds out for the first time that his ex-wife had another kid and that Violet had been meeting him in secret all along. Worst of all, even the cleaning lady knew about it, while he'd been kept in the dark. Ha!"

"And then they sent Violet to the hospital?"

"No."

Nga-Yee gasped. "Why not?"

"Her wounds weren't very deep, and they managed to stop the bleeding. Mr. To stopped them from calling the police, and he chased Violet's brother out. He told the doormen to keep him away. Rosalie was fired a month later. Par for the course, I guess."

"But why not send his daughter to the hospital? She tried to kill herself!"

"Very simply, because they weren't actually father and daughter."

"So what? Just because they weren't related by blood, he didn't care about her?"

"No, you misunderstand. They weren't actually father and daughter, so if he called the police, she might be taken away from him."

Once again, Nga-Yee was caught off balance.

"According to Hong Kong law, parents and guardians have a duty of care over children under the age of sixteen, or they're guilty of negligence. Even if they aren't convicted in court, the authorities can still intervene to remove the children from their custody. And because Mr. To isn't biologically related to Violet and the mother is no longer there, if you were the judge, wouldn't you find yourself wondering about possible abuse? Don't forget, the brother was an adult. Violet could have been placed with him instead."

Now Nga-Yee understood why Violet's father had hired detectives—not to have strangers spying on his daughter, but to keep an eye on this man who was no blood relation to him, and to find out if he had the ability and intent—or the money—to break up his family.

"Why did Violet want to kill herself?" Nga-Yee was still having trouble accepting this. She'd made kidkit727 out to be a demon, and it was difficult to see her as a fragile being who'd once sought death.

"Family problems, academic pressure, depression . . . mainly that old cliché."

"What's that?"

"Being isolated at school and feeling lonely."

"She was bullied at school?"

"If you're thinking of being physically attacked or having her possessions destroyed, then no, she wasn't. But psychological harm and verbal abuse, yes." N curled his lip. "Frankly, beating people up is out of fashion these days—no kid would be stupid enough to do anything that leaves marks. Much easier to jeer, to gossip, to belittle. Even if a teacher catches you, you can talk your way out of it. Quite a few adults will think it was the victim who wasn't strong enough and should take some responsibility. What a snowflake."

"But why was Violet being ostracized?"

"You know why. Kwok-Tai said."

Nga-Yee had to stop and think. Kwok-Tai had said that Violet went to the teacher about that girl, Laura, and got her expelled for canoodling on school property.

"Kwok-Tai also mentioned that Laura was very popular. When someone like that gets forced to leave for 'grown-up reasons,' don't you think the other kids would turn on the tattler?"

"How do you know this happened to Violet? Are you just extrapolating from what Kwok-Tai told us?"

"When I was looking into your sister's friends, I got a good sense of the cliques within her class, so it wasn't hard to tell who was out on her own. Besides . . ." N opened a new window on the laptop. "Like I said before, the Enoch chatboard back end has all kinds of old stuff, including deleted threads." He placed the laptop in front of Nga-Yee:

Group: Class 2B
Posted by: 2B_Aide
Topic: The truth about Laura Lam's expulsion
Time: September 13, 2013, 16:45:31

Violet To's just been made student aide again, and I'm not going to stay silent anymore! Remember Laura Lam from 1A? She had to change schools this year. She didn't want to, she was forced, because she was seen kissing an older girl. And how did anyone find out? None other than the student aide of 1A, Violet To. She told the teacher, and Laura had to go.

Let's not get into whether you approve of lesbians
or not, just ask yourself if you want to be ruled over by
someone like this. Student aide? More like student snitch.
Should this bigot have so much power? With Violet To in
charge, we'll have to watch every step. For all you know,
the next person forced out of this school might be you.

Don't be fooled by this bitch's meek appearance. We all
know that silent dogs are deadlier than barking ones!

"Two years ago, this explosive post was up on the board for
three hours before the mods stepped in to delete it. That was
more than enough time for people to take screenshots and cir-
culate it. As a result, Violet stepped down as student aide, but
that wasn't enough to appease the mob. She became a pariah to
the entire school. After half a year of this, she slit her wrists."
N's tone was level, as if this were all trivial.

Nga-Yee remembered that one of the Countess's handmaidens
had called Violet a "snitch." Now she understood why.

"Well, she—she can't blame anyone else, can she?" For some
reason, Nga-Yee was feeling uneasy, and she found herself stut-
tering a little. "She's the bigot who insisted on getting involved
where she shouldn't have."

"She wasn't the tattler," said N calmly.

"What? What are you talking about?"

"Violet To didn't say anything to her teacher."

"But Kwok-Tai said—"

"Let's just say Enoch School is a hospitable environment for
hackers," said N, his tone changing. "Teaching records, extracurriculars, exam results, disciplinary notes—everything is digitized
and stored on the school server."

N hit a key and opened a densely packed text document.

"This is the report from the disciplinary teacher about Laura
Lam, for the principal, supervisor, and board to approve." N

scrolled down the page. "After the teacher heard about this, he asked Violet to confirm what happened, because the student who raised the alarm had named Violet as a fellow witness. What Kwok-Tai overheard wasn't Violet tattling, but the teacher asking her for more details."

Nga-Yee thought back to what Kwok-Tai had reported: *Did you see this with your own eyes? Yes. On the rooftop? That's right.* Yes, that fitted with this new version of events too.

"Even if she didn't start it, she still helped get Laura into trouble, so—"

"She was the student aide. When a teacher started asking her questions, didn't she have a duty to tell the truth? She couldn't have known what was in store for Laura. Wouldn't it have been wrong of her to lie?"

"But when her classmates started avoiding her, did she clarify what happened?."

"Like you said, her words ended up hurting Laura, so how could she defend herself? Besides, she'd have to say who the actual snitch was, which would make her guilty of snitching too."

"But who was it?"

"Lily Shu." N pointed at her name on the screen. "Quite a coincidence that she's on our radar too. If Kwok-Tai knew his girlfriend was the one responsible, there'd probably be trouble."

"All right, so Violet was bullied too. That makes it even more unforgivable that she led a mob against Siu-Man! What, she couldn't stand to see someone else doing well? She got hold of the idea that Siu-Man was a slut and had lied about Shiu Tak-Ping, so she became a vigilante and created a big stink?" All this shot out of Nga-Yee like a machine gun.

N shrugged. "I guess so."

Nga-Yee was expecting him to come up with more perverse logic, but he blandly agreed with her. Something was wrong.

"What are you not saying?" she asked.

"Mmm. Nothing."

"No, there's definitely something."

N stroked his chin in silence for a few seconds. "My guiding principle is never to say anything unless I can verify it. Do you really want to hear my speculations?"

"Tell me!"

"Violet may not have gone after your sister for any of the reasons you mentioned—like a misplaced sense of justice. It may be more rational than that."

"Sending an internet mob after a defenseless girl? How could that be rational?" Nga-Yee shouted.

"Her motivation could be the same as ours: revenge."

Nga-Yee followed N's gaze to the laptop beside her. Something like an electric shock surged through her brain. She knew what N was saying, but she couldn't accept it.

"You mean the person who posted on the chatboard two years ago, calling Violet a snitch—that was Siu-Man?"

N didn't reply right away, just moved the mouse to highlight the name of the poster. "This was written by '2B_Aide.' Which means the student aide at the time, Violet To. Obviously she wasn't denouncing herself, so someone must have broken into her account. Enoch students have to log in to their accounts all the time—to use the printer, for instance—so it wouldn't be too hard to see someone's password."

Nga-Yee recalled the poster in the school library telling students to be careful with their passwords.

"Remember I said the person in charge of the system was an idiot? He knew how to delete the post, but not how to get into the back end of the chatboard to find the real poster from their IP address."

"And the IP address was—"

"Pisces Café."

"But it wasn't just Siu-Man who used the Wi-Fi there, all the kids do."

"The IP address is not the only piece of data, remember? There's the user agent too."

N pressed another key to produce a string of letters:

```
Mozilla/5.0 (Linux; U; Android 4.0.4; zh-tw; SonyST2li
Build/ 11.0.A.0.16) AppleWebKit/534.30 (KHTML, like
Gecko) Version/ 4.0 Mobile Safari/534.30
```

"I showed you this before: a Sony Android ST2li." As before, N pulled Siu-Man's red smartphone from his pocket and waved it at Nga-Yee.

"But . . . but maybe one of her classmates has the same phone?"

"The user agent doesn't just make a note of the model, it records the serial numbers of the updates and the browser version too. Even an identical phone would have some differences here, and I haven't seen any of your sister's classmates matching these numbers." N leaned against the desk, turning a little toward Nga-Yee. "This was posted on September 13, 2013, a little before five in the afternoon. That was a Friday, the day your sister usually hung out at Pisces. Wouldn't it be too much of a coincidence that someone else was there with the exact same phone, browser, and so on, and happened to be posting about Violet just at that moment?"

"But Violet wouldn't have known—" Nga-Yee stopped, because she'd abruptly realized that Violet may not have had the tech knowledge to seek out things like user agents and IP addresses, but she was close to someone who *was* familiar with lots of hacking techniques.

"Looking at this objectively, kidkit727 does seem like someone who posted that Popcorn attack on your sister out of revenge, down to the word choices. Violet got called a 'bitch' on the school chatboard, so she said something similar about your sister in her smear. Because of their history, Violet was certain that your sister was distorting the truth once again and that Shiu Tak-Ping must be innocent. That's why she had no compunction asking her brother to help her stir up some trouble. I have no proof that the Rat hacked into the school system, so whether he discovered that your sister was the one who denounced Violet, I can only guess." N shrugged. "There's quite a bit of circumstantial evidence, but I can't say for certain that Violet did this to take revenge."

"I don't believe you! Siu-Man would never write a post like that."

"I didn't say she wrote it."

"What? You just said—"

"I said it was posted from her phone. Have you forgotten who was in the coffee shop with her?"

Nga-Yee thought back to the day they met Kwok-Tai at Pisces. He said that in year two, Lily's extracurriculars kept her away from their gatherings, so he and Siu-Man went to the coffee shop alone—and he hadn't liked Violet either. Nga-Yee saw where this was going.

"So it was Kwok-Tai."

"Yes. The text has the characteristics of Kwok-Tai's writing."

"What characteristics? Words like 'bigot'?" Nga-Yee remembered him calling Violet that.

"That too, but I was talking about his handwriting."

"What handwriting? This was all online."

"Do you think language loses its individual character online, Miss Au? Let me give you some examples: Violet is the bookish sort, so even the threatening emails she sent your sister were properly signed and addressed. Even her Line messages are in full sentences and properly punctuated. When she uses ellipses, it's always exactly the right number of dots, no more and no less. Her Chinese teacher must appreciate that. Her brother's the opposite—efficiency is everything. He often doesn't bother with periods, though he does put in commas—which many people don't. Some people leave a line after paragraphs, some indent. We can even work out what sort of keyboard someone uses by analyzing their typos. But people assume there's no such thing as digital handwriting, so they don't bother to disguise these elements, and that's how they give themselves away."

N brought up the post attacking Violet. "Look, every paragraph here starts with exactly three blank spaces. That's different from what your sister does in her messages, but it matches Kwok-Tai's Facebook statuses. Your sister tends to use short sentences and paragraphs. If she'd written this, it would have been split into ten more paragraphs."

"So Kwok-Tai wanted to harm Siu-Man by using her phone—"

"Don't be silly. Even if your sister didn't write this post, she must have known what was going on. She probably did it to help a friend—he probably made it sound like a funny joke to have her help him accuse Violet," said N, his deadpan voice mocking Nga-Yee for still finding excuses for her sister. "If Violet did this for revenge, she didn't have the wrong target—she just mistook the accomplice for the mastermind."

Nga-Yee's mind went blank. Should she keep trying to poke holes in N's hypothesis, or was it better to forget he'd said anything? Ever since Siu-Man's death, her hatred of kidkit727 had been the only thing propping her up. Finding the person responsible for her grief became her overriding mission. Every night, she tossed and turned, and by day she could barely force food down, all because Violet had taken away her only family member. Knowing who was responsible only intensified her fury into a desire for revenge.

And now a voice at the bottom of her heart was telling her she had no reason to hate this girl.

Everything Violet and her brother did, Siu-Man and Kwok-Tai had done before them. You could even say Violet's actions were the natural consequence of Siu-Man's. If Nga-Yee thought what she was doing to Violet was justified, how could she condemn Violet's treatment of Siu-Man? Nga-Yee felt caught in a horrific cycle that would pass this hatred on and on.

Yet she couldn't bear to give up.

She glanced at the screen. Violet was still sitting like a puppet in front of her computer, her face blank. Nga-Yee might have lost her grounds for hating Violet, but she still couldn't forgive her.

"How long have you known this?" she asked N, struggling out of her daze.

"I was already pretty sure when we started our revenge plot."

N's answer flooded her heart with bitterness, telling her once again that the man standing before her wasn't quite human.

"If you knew Violet had her reasons for what she did, why did you want to help me get revenge? Was it for the money? I thought the people who killed Siu-Man must be pure evil, but now I've become the thing I hated. How am I any different from them?"

"The difference is that Violet To was rescued last year, and your sister died."

The frostiness of this answer snapped the final string in Nga-Yee's heart.

N placed his hands on his knees and leaned forward. "You're confused now. But if I'd told you all this last week and you'd given up your plans for revenge, you'd have started to regret it when you realized you were all alone in the world while Violet and her brother were still alive and well. You'd have complained that fate wasn't fair to you, and started to feel how stupid you'd been for abandoning your plan. You might even have taken out your anger on me."

"I would never!"

"You would. But it's not just you—anyone in the world would feel the same way." N was looking directly at her, more serious than she'd ever seen him. "Human beings are never willing to admit that we're selfish creatures. We talk nonstop about morals and righteousness, but as soon as we're in danger of losing what

we have, we're back to survival of the fittest. That's human nature. Even worse, we love to find excuses—we aren't even brave
enough to own our selfish actions. Hypocrisy, in a word. Let me
ask you this: Why did you want revenge?"

"To get justice for Siu-Man, of course."

"What do you mean, for Siu-Man? The revenge was yours.
You were sad at having your family taken away from you, so you
went searching for someone to take your anger out on. That way,
you might find release. What does Siu-Man care about justice
now? It's a cunning strategy, putting words into the mouth of
someone who can no longer speak for herself."

"Stop talking like you know Siu-Man!" yelled Nga-Yee in a
fury. "I'm her sister. I know how much she suffered—and how
reluctantly she'd have given up her own life! What right do you
have to say any of this? You never even met Siu-Man!"

"True, I never met your sister—but that doesn't mean I don't
understand her." N picked up Siu-Man's phone, pressed a few
keys, and handed it to Nga-Yee.

"Don't try to tell me you can know a person from their phone,
that's—"

Her words faltered as she saw what was on the screen.

Dear Stranger, By the time you see these lines, I might no
longer be here.

"You . . . you put the fake suicide note on her phone?"

"The note you saw was a forgery, but I didn't say its contents
were fake," said N slowly. "I had to reshape it a little to achieve
the effect I wanted, but everything you read came from your
sister."

N took the phone back from Nga-Yee's shaking hand, scrolled
down, and gave it back.

"Start reading here."

June 14, 2014   23:11
Mom's been gone a whole month.
Every time I think of her, I feel a hole in my heart.
A hole that can never be filled.
When I come home from school, the house feels so cold.
I know this cold comes from the hole in my heart.

This was a recent Facebook post by "Yee Man." The profile picture was a white lily.

"This is . . . Siu-Man's . . . Facebook?" Nga-Yee stammered. "But the name—"

"Obviously that's not her real name. Keep reading and you'll see."

Nga-Yee frantically scrolled on.

June 19, 2014   23:44
I'm not as strong as my sister.
She's such a good person. I don't think anything could
leave a hole in her heart.
Mom always told me I should be more like my sister.
But I'm not her. I'm just pretending to be as strong as her.
I'll never be as good as her, not in my whole life.

This post was five days after the previous one. On this blue-and-white page, Nga-Yee read her sister's thoughts—thoughts she'd never known about. She was startled that Siu-Man would call her strong. In those days after her mother's death, all she'd done was copy how her mother had behaved in that early time of widowhood, when she'd had to force herself to carry on to keep the family going. She wished she could tell Siu-Man that their mother's death had bored a hole in her heart too, but she'd had to pretend it wasn't there.

July 2, 2014   23:51

The first thing I do when I get home every day is turn on
the TV.

I don't care what's on, I just want to pretend there are
other people at home.

I hate being home alone. That's why I stay back in the
school library.

I don't even like reading.

Sometimes my sister works late and doesn't get home till
after nine, but my school library closes at five.

Waiting for her to come home, I always think about the
past.

When my mom was at work, my sister stayed home. When
she started work, Mom stayed home.

Now no one's home.

No one talks, no one answers.

I have to turn on the TV to hear human voices.

Nga-Yee hadn't known any of this. She only remembered that
one day she'd come home to find Siu-Man in her room with the
TV on in the main room. Not knowing the reason, she'd scolded
Siu-Man for wasting electricity. Was that why she stopped doing
it—because of that tiny amount of electricity? Had Nga-Yee
unwittingly destroyed her small escape from loneliness?

The next few posts didn't say very much, so she skipped ahead
to find why Siu-Man was on Facebook in the first place.

October 3, 2014   22:51

Sometimes I think I'm stupid to be writing like this.

I haven't added any friends, so I'm the only one reading
these posts.

If no one sees this, then I'm basically talking to myself.

Only, that's not completely true.

I've heard that social media sites have mods who see everything.

If I wrote in my diary, no one would see it. Here, the mods might.

They don't know who I am, and I don't know who they are. We're strangers to each other.

If you're reading this, even though you can't respond, it still makes me happy.

Because then I'm a bit stronger than someone just talking to herself.

"This account—She didn't tell anyone about it?" Nga-Yee murmured.

"It seems not. The fake name was probably to keep anyone from finding it," said N. "It must have been like shouting into a hole in a tree, somewhere to release her feelings."

"Was she right? Would the mods read her posts?"

"The mods on any social media site can read whatever they want—they're responsible for keeping the site running, after all. If a user has a technical issue, they need to be able to get in there. Different sites have different policies, though, about what employees can do regarding user privacy. But Facebook has billions of users worldwide, four million in Hong Kong alone. That's hundreds of millions of posts every day. The chances of your sister's words being seen by some busybody mod are probably less than you getting hit by a meteor."

N paused for a moment, then went on. "Not that it mattered to your sister whether this stranger actually existed. She wasn't looking for a response, only someone to talk to. Sometimes people are able to say more to a stranger than to their own families."

Nga-Yee could never have imagined that Siu-Man would seek an outsider rather than talk to her own sister. She kept scrolling through these words that no one but N had ever read. When she got to a short entry from November, her heart sank.

November 13, 2014   01:12
I feel so dirty.

That was the first thing Siu-Man wrote after being molested on the train. Nga-Yee had never heard her say this. She'd tried so hard to comfort her sister. She'd told Siu-Man to lean on her, she'd cursed the pervert and said he should be thrown in jail, but she never once asked Siu-Man how she was feeling.

Nga-Yee had never tried listening to her sister.

December 5, 2014   23:33
My teacher asked me about that incident again today.
I didn't want to talk about it, but she forced me.
I don't dare have lunch in the cafeteria. Kids I don't know
point and stare at me.
I've had enough.
I miss you, Mom.

A lump was growing in Nga-Yee's throat. She knew how Siu-Man must have felt as she was writing this. She hadn't wanted to talk to her teacher out of shame at having to rehash the whole thing. The last line made her wince. Siu-Man could only have spilled her heart to their mother.

Why hadn't Siu-Man felt able to turn to her own sister for help? When had this gulf appeared between them?

February 16, 2015   23:55
Dear stranger,
I realized I have no one to talk to any more.
Today my sister told me I have to give evidence in court.
I know the man's lawyer is going to question and humiliate
me.
I want to throw up.
My sister says she'll support me.

She was smiling when she said this, but I know she was pretending.

I'm so useless.

All my life, I've held my family back. My sister, my mom.

I know my mom died because of me.

We had no money, so she held down two jobs to raise us.

She worked too hard and ruined her body. That's why she died.

If I'd never been born, my mom would still be alive.

It's all my fault.

"That's not right—not right at all! How could she think that?" Nga-Yee cried. She'd never imagined that her cheerful sister could have such dark thoughts, blaming herself for their mother's death.

"You watched your sister grow up, so you've always thought of her as an innocent child," said N. "But children eventually learn to think for themselves. Sometimes the answers they come up with are a bit extreme, but looking at this objectively, she does have a point."

"But—But Mom and I never thought that! We never complained—"

"Let's put it this way: if your sister had never been born, how much less would your household expenses have been? Would you have had more time for your studies? Could you have actually enjoyed your youth? Maybe your mom could have had one less job? And you might have finished school, maybe even gone to university?"

Nga-Yee had nothing to say to that. When had N done all this research into her background?

"Just keep reading."

February 26, 2015   17:13
Finally, it's over.

This short post from late February marked a brief period of calm. That was Shiu Tak-Ping's second day in court, when he'd changed his plea to guilty, so Siu-Man didn't need to give evidence.

But another storm was about to begin.

April 11, 2015   23:53
Why? Why? Why?
Why? Why? Why?
Why? Why? Why?
Why can't they leave me alone?
Is God punishing me?

Even without looking at the date, Nga-Yee would have guessed that this was after kidkit727's post appeared on Popcorn. She still deeply regretted how oblivious she'd been that weekend not to have noticed that Siu-Man was seriously struggling, leaving her to face this tsunami of internet criticism alone.

April 15, 2015   01:57
More and more people are talking about me at school.
The way they look at me is so frightening.
They all believe that guy's nephew.
Those terrible things he said about me.
I don't take drugs. I'm not a hooker.
But I know my classmates don't believe me.

At this point Siu-Man had been leaving more and more posts in her Facebook journal, always after eleven p.m. and sometimes in the small hours of the morning. Only now, two months after Siu-Man's death, was Nga-Yee finally seeing her sister's terror. Had she been lying awake all that time, suffering this unspeakable pressure alone? When Nga-Yee crept out of bed to read yet more vitriolic comments on the household computer, had

Siu-Man actually been lurking in the doorway, watching her helplessly from behind? She'd seemed so strong—was that just a charade for the benefit of her big sister? Had she blamed herself for creating yet more trouble?

Nga-Yee had no way to find out. All she knew was that despite her promise, she hadn't been a pillar for Siu-Man to lean on.

April 18, 2015   01:47
I overheard people talking about me in the bathroom.
Maybe they're right.
I'm cursed. I just drag others down.
I don't have the right to be friends with anyone.
I don't have the right to be happy.
I don't have the right to exist.

Those words, "the right," were like a lead pipe crashing down on Nga-Yee's soul. She wanted to hold her sister by the shoulders and tell her that she absolutely had the right, that no one could stop her from living happily, and even if she couldn't find any friends, Nga-Yee would always love and support her with all her heart.

April 25, 2015   02:37
Dear Stranger, By the time you see these lines, I might no longer be here.
Recently, I've been thinking about death every day.
I'm so tired. So very tired.
I have this nightmare every night: I'm in a wilderness,
then dark things start chasing after me.
I run and scream for help, but no one comes to rescue me.
I know for certain that no one is coming to rescue me.
The dark things rip me to shreds. As they rip off my limbs
they laugh and laugh.
Such horrifying laughter.

The most horrifying thing is that I'm laughing too. My heart is rotten too.

"This . . . this really was Siu-Man's suicide note," Nga-Yee sobbed, her right hand curling tightly around the phone. The counterfeit note had used Siu-Man's actual writing, word for word, from just ten days before her fatal leap on May 5. She hadn't committed suicide on a moment's impulse—this was already on her mind in April.

Nga-Yee hadn't noticed. She'd thought her sister was on an even keel.

April 27, 2015   02:22
I'm ready to collapse.
At the school, in the street, on public transport, I feel suffocated.
Every day, I can feel thousands of eyes full of hatred boring into me.
They all want me dead.
I have nowhere to run.
On my way to school and back, I think if the MTR platforms had no barriers,
I would step in front of a train. An end to everything.
Maybe it's better if I die. I'm dragging everyone down.

"Oh!" With this last line, Nga-Yee realized how wrong she'd been. After finding kidkit727's last messages to Siu-Man, she'd thought that was what pushed her sister into suicide. Looking at these entries, she finally understood her sister's state of mind.

It was true that kidkit727's words had been a catalyst, but not the ones Nga-Yee had thought—not *Are you brave enough to die?* or *have no right to go on living*. No, it was something from the second message:

You'll be a disgrace to your classmates.

That was what Siu-Man feared most: dragging other people down. She thought she'd held her mother and sister back, and perhaps her friends too—Kwok-Tai and Lily particularly. The brouhaha over her court case and the subsequent Popcorn post had roiled up the whole school. Siu-Man must have felt like an extra piece in a jigsaw, as if her existence were an unwanted blot on an otherwise perfect world.

It was also true that Nga-Yee had never once told her sister how much she meant to her.

April 29, 2015   02:41
Before I leave this world, I have to apologize to my best friend.
Or I should say my former best friend.
Every day in class, I look at her.
She doesn't show it, but I know she hates me.
She ought to hate me.
My carelessness hurt her deeply.
After that, we stopped speaking.
I have no right to be her best friend.
Maybe that's good. I won't hold her back any longer.

The next entry confirmed what Nga-Yee had been thinking: the person Siu-Man thought hated her was actually Lily. The other lines in the fake note were manipulated by N, but these were real.

May 1, 2015   03:11
When I'm no longer here, my classmates will be relieved.
They won't have to put on masks and play-act in front of me.
The teachers made them stop talking about it, so they do it in secret now, more than ever.

They think I took away their peace. Everyone's uneasy now.
Especially that girl. She must wish I would drop out.
I heard her telling her followers I should stop coming to school.
I've tried to catch her eye, but every time she looks away quickly.
She must hate me.
And I know what she's done in secret.
She calls me boyfriend-thief, drug-fiend, whore.
I know it's her, though I have no proof.
She told this nephew everything. Her or her followers.
They all have big mouths.
But who cares.
Soon, I'll give them what they want, and disappear.

"She's talking about—the Countess?" Nga-Yee muttered.

"The person she thinks spilled the beans to Shiu Tak-Ping's nephew? Probably," said N. "When the Countess said your sister shouldn't come to school, that may not have been malicious—she might have meant she shouldn't have to face all that nasty gossip. Sure, her handmaidens did go around spreading those rumors, but if the Countess herself wasn't as vicious as she liked to appear, this must have been hard for her too—to empathize with your sister but not be able to show it."

Nga-Yee scrolled down to find the final entry, written one day before Siu-Man killed herself.

May 4, 2015   03:49
Dear stranger, this may be the last time we speak.
I'm so tired. I can't keep pretending I'm fine.
Especially in front of my sister.
I know she's pretending too.

Why should the two of us keep faking it? Let's just end it
and rip off those masks.

When I'm gone, she can be happy again.

Mr. Stranger, my name is Au Siu-Man. I'm the girl who
caused all that fuss online.

If you don't know who I am, you can easily Google it.

I didn't write my name as an accusation. After all you don't
know me, and I don't know you.

I just wanted a stranger to hear everything I've suffered as
proof that I once existed in this world.

By the time you read these lines, I might not any more.

"How could I possibly be happy with you gone?" Nga-Yee
screamed at the phone in her hand, sobbing inconsolably. No
technology on earth could send this cry to Siu-Man as she sat
writing those words. Nga-Yee didn't care that N had copied
some of these lines into his fake suicide note, like a grotesque
collage, in order to mislead Violet, nor that a random mod may
have read these posts. All she wanted was to tell Siu-Man that
her suicide would only bring more pain to her sister.

She couldn't deny that she'd spent those weeks pretending
everything was fine, even as she'd worried nonstop about Siu-
Man. That time seemed like happiness compared with losing
her—at least she'd had someone to worry about.

"Did you know about this all along?" she growled at N,
trying to stay calm. By the time of their first visit to the school,
N had had Siu-Man's phone for two days; that was two weeks
ago. Even if he hadn't yet known who she was referring to, he'd
have read why she'd wanted to die.

"Yes."

"But you kept it from me?" Her voice was full of rage, ready
to explode.

"You didn't ask," said N callously. "People are always blindly
searching for answers, but it turns out they didn't ask the right

questions to start with. Miss Au, you hired me to find the person who posted on Popcorn attacking your sister. You never said I should also investigate Violet's motives or your sister's reasons for killing herself."

"But—but you knew—"

"I knew how important these would be to you, but I didn't say anything?" he interrupted. "Yes, but even if I 'knew' that you'd do anything to get your sister's last words, that was just my subjective view. You didn't ask about it, so why would I go out of my way to prove something that was none of my business? If you wanted the whole truth—well, that's not what you said when you came to me. Besides, your sister chose to write her thoughts on a secret Facebook page precisely so her family and friends wouldn't see it after she died. I was just respecting her wishes, and you're upset with me?"

Once again, his twisted logic silenced Nga-Yee.

"And besides," N went on, "I gave you plenty of hints about your sister's state of mind. Didn't I say you ought to have known more about her friends? Didn't I ask how the sister in your mind was different from the reality? If you'd asked me at the time, of course I'd have told you the truth. But you ignored it. And now you blame me for not speaking up sooner?"

Thinking back, Nga-Yee had to admit that N really had said those things to her. She was shocked, and also full of regret. She couldn't agree with everything he'd said, but she had definitely neglected something very important: both before and after Siu-Man's death, she hadn't truly cared about what her sister was feeling, nor tried to probe her innermost thoughts.

"I asked you how much pocket money your sister got," said N placidly. "That's when I knew that you might be close to your sister, but you had no idea what she was thinking."

"Huh?"

"You gave her three hundred a week. After subtracting MTR fare and lunch money, that's hardly enough for a secondary school student to live on these days. You know how much prices have gone up in the last few years. Twenty-odd dollars used to buy you a decent boxed lunch, but these days thirty isn't even enough for a plain bowl of noodles. You think your sister liked having sandwiches for lunch every day? She was just choosing the cheapest option. Where do you think she got the spare cash to have coffee with Kwok-Tai and Lily?"

"Siu-Man was never materialistic like that! She'd never starve herself just to afford a fancy phone or—"

"Who said fancy anything? I'm talking about ordinary social life. If her friends wanted to hang out, then even if money was tight, she'd have to save up enough to go along rather than pouring cold water on their plans. Isn't that what people do?"

"If she'd asked for more pocket money, I'd have given it to her!"

"Your sister wasn't just worried about keeping up with her friends, she also knew the family's finances were tight—that's why she didn't ask." There was a hint of mockery in his voice. "You know what your family went through—and you'd better believe your sister was aware of it too, even at her age. She saw how much you and your mother suffered—and that's why she was so insistent that she didn't want to hold anyone back. But you didn't see what she was going through. You thought everything was just fine."

"You're guessing."

"Yes, I'm guessing. Don't forget, you were the one who asked for my unverified hypothesis." N's expression was stern. "One Direction too—I bet your sister wasn't even into them. She just made herself listen to their music so she'd have something to talk about with Lily. You went through her stuff when you were looking for her phone—wouldn't a real fan have some CDs or music magazines? I knew there weren't any, because when I brought up One Direction with Lily, you had no idea what we were talking about. It wasn't such a stretch to deduce that your sister had worries about fitting in."

It was true, Nga-Yee realized.

"Miss Au." N sighed gently. "This may not be what you wanted to hear, but you and I are the same: we enjoy being alone. We love our isolation. Rather than waste time on point-less social interactions, we'd rather focus on the things we find important. You had no friends at school, because you wanted to take care of your family. Now you'd rather read books than spend time with your coworkers. We're fine going our own way and leaving the world behind. But you have to understand that your sister wasn't you. She felt peer pressure. She cared about fitting in with people her age, doing what they did, down to pretending to share their interests. That's probably why she agreed to date Kwok-Tai, though the way that turned out made things even worse."

"What are you talking about?" Nga-Yee stared at him. "Are you saying she didn't actually like Kwok-Tai, but agreed to go out with him?"

"Kids these days declare their love and start dating—but how often are both sides equally willing? One person probably just goes along with it if the other one doesn't totally disgust them. Everyone around them is dating, so they feel the need to do it too. And given your sister's situation, she might have thought this was her chance to turn her life around—"

"What do you mean, her situation?"

N stroked his chin and hesitated for a few seconds. "This is just conjecture, but I think your sister actually had a crush on someone else."

"Who?"

"She deleted all the pictures of her schoolmates from her phone except for one. She probably couldn't bear to get rid of that one."

Nga-Yee stared at him in shock. "Lil—Lily Shu? You're saying Siu-Man liked girls?"

"I'm not necessarily calling her a lesbian, but she certainly had feelings for Lily. Maybe she didn't know exactly what those feelings were. Don't you think it makes sense? That she'd pretend to like a certain band to get closer to someone? That she'd scrimp on her lunch to spend more time with someone she liked? She knew she couldn't actually be with Lily, and that's why when Kwok-Tai asked her out, she thought it might be a way of 'correcting' her 'unnatural' tendencies. Yet she ended up hurting the person she actually liked, and in the end she had no one at all."

Blood rushed to Nga-Yee's brain, and she grew dizzy. If Siu-Man had come out to her, she'd have accepted it once she got over the shock. What bothered her was that she hadn't known that this was worrying Siu-Man. How could she not have seen that Siu-Man needed her? Siu-Man must have seen something of herself in Laura Lam, and that's why she'd so eagerly teamed up with Kwok-Tai to take Violet down. Maybe Lily's casual homophobia was what told her she had no hope. And perhaps that's when Jason took advantage of Siu-Man's despair to lure her to the karaoke bar—and she'd been so desperate for someone to talk to that she'd agreed, only to land in even more trouble.

"I—I thought I was a good big sister. I gave up my studies so she could have a brighter future."

"There you go again." N frowned. "You did this for her, but did you ask what she wanted? Don't you think your noble gesture might have weighed on her, making her feel like she couldn't breathe? A lot of people do this, endlessly giving of themselves, but isn't that just their need for control? Have you ever stopped to think what family actually means to you?"

N took Siu-Man's phone from her and tapped it a few times. "Your sister kept only one classmate's picture. But she did have a picture of her with two other people."

When he handed the phone back, on the screen was a selfie. Siu-Man's face took up the left side of the screen, and on the right, just stepping out of the bathroom and drying her hair with a towel, was Nga-Yee. Standing nearby was their mother, making dinner. Nga-Yee and Mom were in mid-conversation and hadn't noticed Siu-Man sneaking a photo. This must have been when Siu-Man was in year one, not long after she got the phone. Siu-Man was grinning with satisfaction—not because she'd taken the picture without them noticing, but because she'd successfully captured a moment in the life of this family she loved, and the ordinary moment was now an image to be preserved.

Siu-Man treasured her family. Even this ordinary day, with the simple meal they were about to eat, was enough to fill her with joy.

Tears came to Nga-Yee's eyes, and she thought her heart would burst from guilt. This picture and those Facebook posts were making her think that Siu-Man's suicide could have come from the same impulse that made Nga-Yee give up her university place: a sacrifice. She'd always thought of her sister as carefree and cheerful, but now it seemed that was just a pose to make Nga-Yee and their mother happy. And now Nga-Yee knew why she'd been so dead set on ferreting out kidkit727—she still loathed the despicable person who'd launched this attack on her sister from the shadows, but there was someone she hated even more: herself.

The need to make a living had caused Nga-Yee to forget about something even more important. Earning money was a means to an end: to support the household and let her family live happily. But capitalist society lulls us into believing our wages are a goal in themselves, turning us into slaves of money. We forget that as crucial as money may be, there are even more important things that we can't afford to lose.

Siu-Man's such a sensitive child, she remembered their mother saying. And this sensitivity made her perceptive, allowing her to understand others more than they understood her. That meant she'd accumulated all kinds of fears. A moment floated into Nga-Yee's mind from long ago: they were in a moving vehicle after dark. Siu-Man, very young, next to her and stroking her cheek.

"Don't cry, Sis."

Bzzz.

A sudden electronic sound snapped Nga-Yee out of her memory.

N was frowning at another computer. He tapped a few keys.

"Not right now!" he spat, turning to the surveillance screens. Violet had walked out of range of her laptop camera. She was at the window, being captured by the drone—but because the light was behind her, they couldn't see her face.

"What's wrong?" asked Nga-Yee.

"Violet's brother is nearby—he probably realized something's up. Sharp of him." N pointed at the laptop screen. "His number's showing up on the Stingray."

N's fingers danced across the keyboard. One screen showed Violet's bedroom, and all the others Broadcast Drive. How many drones did he have? Or had he hacked into security cameras? Images flashed across the screen like a slide show, and N's eyes flitted among them, searching for something. It was past one in the morning, and the streets were empty of pedestrians and traffic.

"There," said N abruptly, and Screen 1 locked in on a single shot: a taxi approaching. And there, to its right, was Violet's building. The taxi stopped, and a figure hurried from it. Even from this blurry image, Nga-Yee could tell it was Violet's brother.

"There's no time," said N. "If you want revenge, we'll have to strike now."

Nga-Yee stared at him in disbelief. "Didn't you tell me all that to talk me out of revenge?"

"Why would I want to talk you out of it?" N's eyes were fixed on the screen. "Your sister's reasons for doing what she did have nothing to do with your vengeance. Violet and her brother turned an internet mob against your sister—that actually happened. Your sister killed herself because of Violet's messages—that happened too. And your sister's death caused you untold pain. They hurt you, and if you wanted to hurt them back, an eye for an eye, a tooth for a tooth, I wouldn't try to stop you."

Violet's brother was arguing with the security guard, who wouldn't let him pass.

"When I said you wanted revenge for yourself, Miss Au, that wasn't a criticism. That's just how it works," N went on. "I hate hypocrisy. Absolutely nothing against people doing things for themselves. In your case, if you hate Violet, I'm all for that—look at how coolly she lied to our faces and then burned the suicide note as if it were nothing, as if she'd played no part in Siu-Man's death. Do what you like to her—I won't object. Anyway, I'm only acting as your agent. I'm a tool, like a knife. How you use me, and for what reason, is entirely up to you."

Once again, N had ignited the flames of hatred in Nga-Yee, but she still couldn't make up her mind. She thought again of those messages Siu-Man got before her death, all those poisonous words, the final drops of water that burst the dam. Wasn't it fitting for Nga-Yee to deliver the last straw? One bad turn deserves another. On the screen, Violet's brother had pushed the security guard to the ground. He charged into the elevator and got the door shut before the older man could climb to his feet.

Nga-Yee clutched the mic, her finger on the button. She looked at Screen 2. Violet was at the window, her hair blowing across her face in the summer breeze. Nga-Yee could sense how fragile she was—the slightest nudge, and she would topple like a porcelain doll to shatter on the sidewalk ten stories below. As if playing out her fantasy, Violet clutched the windowsill, her body swaying back and forth, as if to let the cold wind blow apart her existence.

"Elevator's almost at the tenth floor," said N.

Nga-Yee stared at the screen. Maybe she wouldn't need to say a word, and Violet would jump anyway. She looked so weak and defenseless. All of a sudden, she realized something was wrong: Violet was too tall. More than half her body, from mid-thigh up, was visible above the windowsill.

No, she hadn't grown taller, she was standing on a chair.

As the thought flashed across her mind, Nga-Yee pressed the button and spoke the final words she would ever say to Violet To:

"Don't do it!"

Violet's body swayed suddenly, and she looked around in shock. A few seconds later her eyes turned toward the door. She must have heard the doorbell ringing and her brother's frantic cries. She stumbled from the bedroom and disappeared out of the shot.

"Changed your mind?" said N.

". . . gave up. Best to give up." Nga-Yee's palms were sweating as she gripped the microphone. She stared at the empty bedroom on the screen.

"Is this the end of the plan?"

"Yes. We'll let her go . . ."

N shrugged and pressed a button to return everything to the way it was: his drones would come back, he'd relinquish control of Violet's Wi-Fi, and all systems would be back to normal.

A moment ago, as Nga-Yee looked at Violet in the window, she'd seen Siu-Man there. And that was enough for her to realize that no matter how much she hated this person, she didn't want to see her go down the same fatal path as her sister. She recalled Siu-Man lying in a pool of blood, and her own hysterical sobs. She wouldn't want even her worst enemy to be put in that position.

Finally, Nga-Yee could hear the clear, true voice coming from the bottom of her heart.

No matter how much she was suffering, passing her sorrow on to someone else wouldn't bring her happiness.

As N withdrew his drones, Nga-Yee caught her final glimpse of Violet and her brother, and for some reason the famous first line of *Anna Karenina* popped into her mind.

"Happy families are all alike; each unhappy family is unhappy in their own way."

Brother and sister were kneeling at the threshold, embracing each other as the front door stood wide open. Violet couldn't stop shaking. She was probably in tears. If she'd come home ten minutes earlier that day in May, Nga-Yee thought, maybe she'd have been hugging Siu-Man like this, sprawled by their front door, weeping.

Nga-Yee slumped in her chair, and tears started flowing from her eyes. Soon she was letting out choked sobs and then bawling freely. After Siu-Man died, she'd felt hatred every time she cried—vengefulness against the culprit, rage against society, anger at the unfairness of fate. Now she felt nothing but grief, weeping for no reason than that she'd lost her little sister. N handed her a tissue, but she was crying too hard for that, and she looked as if she might fall from her chair. A little reluctantly N knelt before her, allowing her to bury her face in his chest.

Even though Nga-Yee had sworn not to show any weakness in front of N, and even though she couldn't stand him, she somehow felt safe as she put her hands on his stained, wrinkled hoodie.

Perhaps even people who've gotten used to being alone need to be comforted by others from time to time.

Sunday, May 18, 2014

vi, i don't know when you'll see this   03:17

but i want you to know   03:18

i'll always be by your side, i'll never betray you   03:18

even if the whole world hated us   03:19

please never cut your wrists again   03:19

don't die   03:20

i'll share your pain, i'll be a listening ear   03:20

i'll rescue you from that heartless man one day   03:20

please just put up with it for now   03:21

your big brother will always love you   03:22

even if the whole world was against you, i'd still love you   03:23

CHAPTER NINE

Kenneth Lee wrung his hands and paced anxiously around the cramped GT Technology Ltd. office. He knew he ought to put on a brave face in front of his employees, but Szeto Wai was due to arrive any minute, expecting them to present their report. The company's whole future rested on this moment. Yet when Mr. Lee looked at Chung-Nam, it was hard to feel confident. He wasn't great at reading people, but even he could tell from Chung-Nam's dark circles that he hadn't gotten enough sleep.

"Are you okay, Chung-Nam? You're our lead presenter, everything's resting on your shoulders," he said.

"Don't worry, I've got this." Chung-Nam smiled.

He sounded confident, but Mr. Lee wasn't reassured. Only the day before, he'd heard Chung-Nam practicing, and he couldn't make head nor tail of what he was saying—he had no idea what "repeat bonuses" and "G-dollar futures" were, nor how they were supposed to help the business. When he asked, Chung-Nam had come out with even more complicated jargon to explain how these things would entice Szeto Wai into investing. In the end, Mr. Lee gave up. Hao had been benched too, apart from a short segment at the end when he would demonstrate the user experience of a G-dollar transaction.

"Hey, are you really okay?" whispered Hao as Mr. Lee turned aside to ask Joanne if she'd remembered to book a table at the classiest restaurant in Langham Place. Hao had noticed

Chung-Nam's distraction over the last few days, along with the slapdash feeling of the presentation's ending.

"Of course I'm okay," said Chung-Nam.

"You seem preoccupied. What's up?"

"Nothing, just some personal stuff," said Chung-Nam. "Don't worry. Tomorrow we'll be the first Hong Kong firm to receive an SIQ investment. When that happens, we'll be worth ten times as much, and the only thing you'll have to fret about is how to find time for so many newspaper interviews."

"The papers will only want to talk to Mr. Lee—what's that got to do with me?"

"You're our customer experience designer. Obviously they'll want you to say a word or two."

Chung-Nam was smiling, but Hao wasn't sure if this was meant to be a joke. He could tell that Chung-Nam wasn't in the best shape, but at least his eyes were full of energy. By contrast, Mr. Lee wasn't demonstrating any leadership. If someone else from SIQ showed up instead of Szeto Wai, they might assume that Chung-Nam was the boss here.

Ding-dong.

The doorbell rang crisply—the first shot in their final battle. Joanne hurried over to the door, and Mr. Lee rushed over too, never mind his dignity. Chung-Nam and Hao brought up the rear.

"Mr. Szeto! Welcome, welcome."

"Kenneth, sorry to be a little late. The traffic—"

"No problem, no problem at all."

Mr. Lee and Mr. Szeto exchanged more small talk; then the visitors were ushered into the conference room. Chung-Nam beckoned Thomas and Ma-Chai to join them.

"Do we have to?" said Ma-Chai anxiously. "What do I have to do? I didn't prepare anything."

"Just sit and listen," said Chung-Nam. "It will leave a good impression on Mr. Szeto if our office seems united."

Ma-Chai and Thomas nodded, unaware that Chung-Nam had another plan in motion. This report wasn't aimed at Szeto Wai alone; the entire firm needed to be present to witness his coup.

He'd secretly prepared another presentation, which was now on the conference room computer. Hao and Mr. Lee would be surprised by this unexpected turn of events, but they wouldn't dare say anything in front of Szeto Wai. As long as he kept hold of the clicker, no one would be able to stop him from staging his revolt.

The eight of them just about fit into the conference room. Chung-Nam shut the door and walked up to the screen, his insides churning with anxiety and excitement. He looked around, feeling everyone's eyes on him. Szeto Wai looked serious, awaiting an answer to his question: Was Chung-Nam going to play it safe or take a gamble?

Yet something was off. Chung-Nam glanced at the person behind Szeto Wai.

"Oh, I forgot," Szeto said, noticing where he was looking. "Doris had to take the day off, so this is my other assistant, Rachel."

Chung-Nam nodded at Rachel, who tilted her head in acknowledgment. He was a little disappointed—Rachel was good-looking, but Doris was far more enticing. It was also clear that Rachel didn't seem to know what was going on, and it was hard to imagine how she'd ended up reporting directly to Szeto Wai.

Chung-Nam couldn't have known that this woman was just as confused as he was at that moment.

For starters, she was surprised to be introduced as "Rachel"— since when did she have an English name? And what was with this "Szeto Wai" business? As far as she was concerned, his name was simply N.

* * *

A couple of days ago, after Nga-Yee abandoned her revenge against Violet To, she'd come back to Wun Wah House from Broadcast Drive, by which time it was almost three in the morning. N hadn't been unkind enough to send her home alone; after retrieving his drones and other surveillance equipment and restoring everything to its original state, he'd given her a lift. They hadn't said a word to each other the whole way back, and Nga-Yee hadn't been able to tell whether he was happy—after all, many days of preparation had come to nothing because she'd spoken three words.

"Do you think I should have done it?" she asked as she got out of the van.

"Like I said, Miss Au, I'm just a weapon, and it's up to you how you decide to use me. I have no opinion of my own." He leaned forward onto the steering wheel. "Besides, I'm still collecting my fee. You owe me five hundred grand."

She had expected this, but her heart sank.

"And don't ask for a discount because you called it off," said N before she could open her mouth. "Don't think about running away either. You could go to the ends of the earth, and I'd find you."

"I wasn't going to—"

"Let's say I believe you." He looked her in the eye. "If you decide after this to end it all, then please wait till after you've paid off your debt. Ducky and I did a lot for you—don't let it be for nothing. I'll come up with a payment plan that works for you. This Tuesday, July 7, two days from now, don't go to work—come to my place at ten in the morning, and we can do our accounting."

He smiled nastily, and Nga-Yee felt a tremor in her heart. She couldn't complain—after all, she was the one who'd agreed to this back when she was blinded by hatred. The moment she'd let go of her vengeance, she also felt a kind of enlightenment beyond life and death. Her family was gone now, and she was all alone, with no purpose in life. If N's payment plan involved her whoring herself out or whatever to make the money back, she was resigned to it. She just hoped he wouldn't make her sell a kidney—at that point, he might as well have them both.

"Got it," she replied helplessly.

As Nga-Yee walked away, N leaned out the window and called her back.

"I'm not taking one penny less, but I can understand that tonight might have been a disappointment, so I'll let you take part in the second wave for free. You don't get to call the shots this time, though."

"What? Wait!"

But he was zooming away. His expression had been exactly the same as when he'd persuaded her to sign up for vengeance back at the hotel room, his eyes gleaming. Nga-Yee didn't want to have anything more to do with Violet To or her brother, but it seemed he had something else in mind.

On Tuesday morning, Nga-Yee arrived at 151 Second Street. Still hesitant, she walked up the six flights. The front door swung open before she could ring the bell, and there was N in his usual red tracksuit top, cargo pants, and flip-flops. Presumably his Stingray had told him she was here.

"You're punctual," he said, unlocking the security gate.

She didn't respond; her mind was on what he'd said about the "second wave."

"N, let's forget about Violet To, I don't want to—huh?"

She stopped, startled, as he walked out of the apartment and started toward the stairs, shutting the door and gate behind him.

"Where are we going?"

"Hey." He gave her a little shove. "Don't block the way. These stairs are narrow."

Haplessly, she went back down the staircase, wondering what N was up to this time. They walked down one flight, and she was about to continue when she heard N's voice behind her. "Here."

Turning, she saw him take out a key and open the door of the fifth-floor apartment. The setup was the same as his: an apartment that took up the entire level, a wooden door and metal security gate. The only difference was that this one seemed even shabbier. The door showed signs of having had New Year's decorations stuck to it; scraps of red paper still clung to its white surface.

"Huh? This apartment belongs to you too?" said Nga-Yee, confused.

"The whole building belongs to me," he said casually.

Nga-Yee stared. No wonder she'd never run into any other tenants. Property prices these days were rising constantly, and even the tiniest patch of land could be turned into housing. Landlords didn't leave apartments empty, and broken-down ones like this would normally have been sold off to developers by now. Nga-Yee was even more shocked when N turned on the lights. Before them was a small sitting room, empty except for an off-white carpet and a coffee table that matched the wallpaper perfectly. It was minimalist, with no stray objects lying around, and spotless too—the complete opposite of the apartment upstairs. Nga-Yee looked around. There were no windows, and the ceiling was fitted with fluorescent lights and central-air vents, as if this were an office. The vestibule had three doors leading from it; Nga-Yee thought it resembled a doctor's waiting room.

Was there an operating theater behind one of these doors? Perhaps this was where she'd have an organ cut out of her. Instead, N led her through the right-hand door into a room twice the size of the living room, also windowless, but with more furniture: a couch, a long dressing table, several chairs, and a large built-in wardrobe. In the corner was a glass door leading to a bathroom. N pulled open one of the wardrobe doors to reveal a few dozen women's outfits, with rows of drawers beneath them and pairs of high-heeled shoes along the ground.

"This one—" said N, glancing at Nga-Yee as he held up a white blouse, gray jacket, and black A-line skirt. "No. Forget it, your legs are too short." He pulled out a pair of black trousers instead. "What size shoes?"

"Um, thirty-eight," said Nga-Yee uncertainly.

"European thirty-eight—that's a British five or five and a half." N bent and picked up a couple of pairs of black pumps. "See which of these fits you better."

N shoved the clothes and shoes into her arms, ignoring her bewilderment, then pointed at the dressing table. "Put on some makeup and comb your hair. I'll be back in fifteen minutes."

"Hang on!" Nga-Yee protested. "What—What are we doing? Am I . . . am I selling my body?"

N stared at her, then burst out laughing. "Are you serious? You don't have the face or figure for that—I'd be waiting decades for my money. Anyway, who goes whoring at ten in the morning?"

"I thought maybe—AV porn—" She'd seen quite a few books in the library exploring Japan's adult film industry.

"This is Hong Kong, Miss Au, not Japan." N covered his mouth, but couldn't stop laughing. "Anyway, if that's what we were doing, wouldn't I have asked you to change your cheap underwear for something classier?"

That almost made sense. Before she could protest any more, he'd left the room. She had no choice but to change into the outfit he'd picked out, which fit well—how much time had he spent studying her figure?—and get made up. Pulling open the dressing table drawer, she found a profusion of cosmetics: at least forty shades of lipstick and five or six powder compacts. She didn't normally wear makeup other than a touch of color on her lips, so it was an effort to redden her cheeks. She had no idea what would go with her outfit.

Fifteen minutes later, the door behind her opened. She'd been ready to berate N for forcing her to get all dolled up, but it was a stranger who walked in: a rather dashing man in a navy blue suit and red tie, with a pair of rimless glasses.

"Are you—"

"My god! What are you trying to look like, a baboon's ass?"

Only when she heard his voice did Nga-Yee realize who this spiffily dressed man was. Clean-shaven, his hair neatly slicked back, and in decent clothes, he looked like a completely different person.

"N?" she said, staring at him.

"Who else?" He crinkled his brows in amusement. It was definitely N—he still sounded the same. Clothes really do make the man—this was a much bigger difference than she'd ever have imagined. Then again, she wouldn't have recognized him in his old man disguise either.

"But you—"

"Sit. You'll give us away if you go out like that." He pressed on her shoulder, so she sat down, and he pulled up a chair across from her.

"Don't move." He got some wet wipes from the drawer and removed the red rouge. Seeing this well-groomed version of N right in front of her, Nga-Yee felt a little awkward, a little embarrassed, but mostly confused.

"You know how to do makeup?" she said indistinctly, her face in his hands.

"Not really, but I guess I know more about it than a tomboy like you."

His insults were actually reassuring—at least she knew he was the same person.

"Shut your eyes." N dabbed pale bronze eye shadow onto her lids, then some eyeliner. He crimped her lashes and applied mascara, then put on a little of the rouge. Finally he took out a tube of lipstick and put on a tiny amount.

"There's nothing I can do about your hair. Luckily it's not too long, so it won't look too bad if we just leave it." He ruffled it, then put the cosmetics back in the drawer. Nga-Yee looked in the mirror, crying out in surprise. She'd been transformed into an executive. She could have stepped out of an office in Central. She now looked beautiful and, more important, self-confident.

"Stop staring at your reflection, Narcissus." N was heading toward the door, beckoning for her to follow him. "Leave your own clothes and bag here."

N's meanness still made her want to puke, but this whole situation was so bizarre, she couldn't think straight. Why was she in these clothes? Why was N in disguise? Where were they going?

Back in the living room, N led her not to the front door, but the one behind the couch. Over his shoulder, Nga-Yee could see that it led to another narrow staircase. She followed him in; he shut the door and pointed down.

"This is—"

"The back door."

They walked down to the ground floor, where a heavy metal door let them out into an alleyway that ended in a stone wall in one direction and a blue iron gate in the other. Looking up, Nga-Yee could just about make out the sky, but mostly the impression was of being in a small crevasse between tall buildings. N turned right and opened another door; Nga-Yee followed him down a clean, brightly lit passageway. They turned a corner, and Nga-Yee realized where they were: the parking lot of a large residential building on Water Street, adjacent to Second Street.

No wonder she'd never been able to track him down. When she first tried to get him to take on her case, she'd staked out his tenement building—now she knew how he'd come and gone without her seeing him. The saying goes that "the cunning rabbit has three burrows"—for all she knew, N might well have a third secret passage from his home.

N walked over to a fancy black car where Ducky was standing. He, too, was unusually dressed: a black suit and gloves, exactly like a rich man's chauffeur.

"Sorry to keep you waiting." N said. "All her fault—"

Ducky said nothing, just nodded and got into the driver's seat.

N climbed into the back seat. Nga-Yee stood frozen, uncertain where she was supposed to go.

"What are you gawking at? Wake up, okay?" N gestured at the back seat, and she got in resentfully. Ducky started the car, and they set off for the underwater Western Harbour Crossing.

"Where are we going now? What are we doing?" asked Nga-Yee.

"Calm down," said N lazily, his legs idly crossed. He looked like a wealthy playboy. "Didn't I say? You're taking part in an operation."

"Oh!" Her eyes opened wide. Now she knew why they were all dressed up—this was a con job. "N, I told you, I don't want to—what?" Before she could finish, he'd placed a tablet computer in her hands. A picture of a man she'd never seen.

"This is our target," said N nonchalantly. "His name is Sze Chung-Nam."

"What does he have to do with Violet To?"

"Nothing at all."

"Huh?" She stared at him, uncomprehending.

N took the tablet back and tapped at it. "I'm just being a busybody, dealing with this guy. I was planning to work alone, but after the way things ended with Violet, I'm guessing you have some feelings that need to be burned off. Anyway, you were the one who led me to him, and this is all connected to you, so you might as well have a ringside seat."

Nga-Yee didn't understand a word of that, but before she could ask, he'd put the tablet back in her hands. Now the display was cut into four quadrants. Where had she seen this before?

"Oh! This is the security camera footage from the MTR. We looked through it when you were trying to track down whoever sent the messages through their Wi-Fi connections." Nga-Yee remembered it clearly. She'd cleaned up for N that day and made him tea, and when he'd turned on his computer, this crowded platform was one of the images he'd looked at.

"Check out the top left corner."

This quadrant had the numbers 3 and 4 along its bottom, and it showed the MTR train at a station, with passengers streaming on and off. Something odd was going on at one of the doors: several commuters were looking back into the car, and some had their phones out to film whatever was going on inside. Only one man seemed completely indifferent. He walked briskly toward the escalator, not looking back. Nga-Yee looked closely and realized it was the man from N's photo.

"This is that Sze Whatshisname?" She pointed at the screen.

"Correct."

"What about him?"

N tapped to fast-forward, then lifted his finger so the footage went back to normal speed.

"Now look at the bottom left corner."

Nga-Yee did as he said, uncertain what she was meant to be looking for. Perhaps Violet would be there. But no, Sze Chung-Nam appeared again on the platform, standing by a pillar.

"Are we watching him? He came back?"

"Very good. At least you're a little observant," N jeered. "He got off, but didn't exit the station or change lines, just walked around and came back to wait for the next train. He didn't interact with a single person in between, so it's not as if he'd arranged to pass something to a friend or something like that, nor did he use the station bathroom. I've checked the footage all over the station during that time, and I'm certain he was just walking around on his own. I took note of the train he reboarded and saw that he got off at Diamond Hill. Once I'd checked the footage of him leaving that station, I tracked down his identity from his Octopus card. Like you said before, that's easy to do if you know when the person you're looking for left a particular station and have them on film. The problem was there were so many people, I couldn't possibly have known who to pinpoint as the one sending the messages."

"But so what if he returned to the platform? Was he logged in when Violet sent those messages? Looking at the footage now, I don't—"

Nga-Yee broke off, her eyes fixed on something in the background. Something was wrong here. Every station in the Hong Kong MTR system has a different-colored interior, to help passengers tell them apart and get off at the right one. The pillar on the screen was sky blue, but N had said that Violet was at Yau Ma Tei, Mong Kok, and Prince Edward when she sent those messages; those stations were pale gray, red, and purple. As for sky blue, that was Kowloon Tong.

Violet had nothing to do with Kowloon Tong station, but Siu-Man did.

Nga-Yee looked at the bottom right corner, which showed the time and date. How could she have missed such an obvious clue? It was 5:42 on November 7, 2014.

The day of Siu-Man's assault.

N saw from Nga-Yee's face that she'd worked it out, and he touched the screen to send it back a few minutes. This was right after Chung-Nam exited the train. Now Siu-Man, in school uniform, was being helped off by a middle-aged woman, followed by a large man frog-marching Shiu Tak-Ping.

"Here's an easy question." N grinned. "When something like this happens, who do you think is most likely to slip away, wait for things to quiet down, then come back and get a later train?"

"The—the real pervert?" Nga-Yee stared at the screen, then at N.

"You're improving—you got straight to the answer."

"So Shiu Tak-Ping is innocent?"

"You could say that."

"But he pleaded guilty."

"Martin Tong is a mediocre lawyer," N sneered. "He had a good hand but refused to play it. In order to avoid trouble, he advised his client to accept a plea deal. People like that shouldn't be called lawyers. They're basically pinch hitters."

"What do you mean, a good hand?"

"What it said in the Popcorn post! Shiu Tak-Ping's behavior was a bit strange, like when he tried to run, but it makes just as much sense that he was a coward who made the wrong choice."

"A witness said that Shiu claimed he'd touched Siu-Man by accident. Isn't that admitting he did it?" Nga-Yee was finding this hard to accept, having spent so much time thinking of Shiu Tak-Ping as the cause of her sister's suffering.

"Like I said, that lawyer was useless. When you handed me the materials for this case, I looked at your sister's statement, and the answer was there: she said someone touched her ass, that it felt like an accident, but then the hand started fondling her bum and went up her skirt. Why didn't the police and that lawyer ever stop to wonder whether the first touch was by the same hand as the second? There's no way to be sure on such a crowded train. If the defense had brought this up, that'd definitely be enough reasonable doubt to get him off."

Nga-Yee stared at him. "So Shiu Tak-Ping happened to bump into Siu-Man; then, by coincidence, someone else molested her, and he got the blame?"

"It wasn't necessarily coincidence. Maybe Shiu Tak-Ping brushed against her, and Sze Chung-Nam, standing nearby, noticed the way she reacted and started having lewd thoughts." N shrugged. "If you want to talk about coincidences, the main one would be that these two men were wearing similar-colored shirts, so the older woman mistook one for the other. You can also blame Shiu Tak-Ping for being foolish enough to think they were talking about the half second that his hand brushed against your sister and raising such a ruckus that it was the perfect cover for Sze Chung-Nam to get away."

"But . . . you're just guessing, aren't you?"

"Yes." N took back the tablet. "So I went searching for proof."

He pressed play on a different video and put the tablet back in front of Nga-Yee. This was of scenery zooming past an MTR window, though from a lower angle than most people's line of sight, capturing a lot of hands clutching the overhead straps and metal poles. The people seated behind them were drowsing or engrossed with their phones. Close to the camera was a young man holding a pole with one hand; his other hand was out of shot, but he was probably on his phone too. Just as Nga-Yee was about to ask N what this guy had to do with anything, she realized she'd been looking at the wrong person. To the right of the screen, near the door, was that Sze man, looking up at the electronic display at the other end of the car. Between Sze and the door was a girl in school uniform, aged maybe thirteen or fourteen. Her face was contorted, and she was staring out the window. Sze Chung-Nam's right hand was pressed against her buttocks, and moving.

"He—his hand—" Nga-Yee sputtered.

"Ducky's been following him around for two weeks," said N, nodding toward the driver's seat. "Turns out this guy's made quite a habit of it. A new victim every few days, always a girl around this age. He even gets to work and leaves early, to fit better with school hours, and he chooses the most crowded trains to go hunting in. I don't mean to praise him, but he definitely knows what he's doing—the girls he picks are the sort to panic and freeze. He also keeps a close eye on the people around him and stops as soon as anyone starts paying attention. His closest shave was probably with your sister last year, and he still got away scot-free. Ducky had to use a specially made camera to gather this evidence."

N produced what looked like a pair of glasses with thick rims. Nga-Yee noticed tiny apertures on its arms—pinhole cameras. Unlike most secret cameras, these were perpendicular to the user and would shoot what was to the left and right.

Nga-Yee turned her attention back to the tablet. There was a second segment, then a third. These were all virtually the same—only the victim was different.

"Why didn't you stop him on the spot?" she yelled at Ducky, watching Sze Chung-Nam stick his hand up yet another schoolgirl's skirt. These girls looked the way Siu-Man must have, and Nga-Yee felt great pity for them.

"Because he can see the bigger picture—not like you," said N. "My goal wasn't just to catch this guy being a pervert on the train."

"Your goal? What do you—"

"Never mind that for now, we're almost there," N said, looking out the window. The car was on Dundas Street in Mong Kok, approaching Fortune Business Centre, where GT Technology was. The journey here from Sai Ying Pun had taken only ten minutes, thanks to the tunnel.

"We're here? But you haven't told me what we're doing!" Nga-Yee protested. "Are you going to do something to Sze Chung-Nam?"

"What a lot of questions you have." N frowned. "Just follow me, and don't say a word. I'll do all the talking. You just have to stand behind me, pretend to be my assistant, and watch."

Ducky dropped them off on Shantung Street. Nga-Yee followed N into an office building and up to the fifteenth floor, self-conscious about her appearance and the way she walked, hoping she wouldn't give them away.

"Remember, not a word," said N as the elevator doors opened. There was the hint of a smile on his face—he looked like an actor about to go onstage.

"Mr. Szeto! Welcome, welcome."

"Kenneth, sorry to be a little late. The traffic—"

Nga-Yee managed to conceal her surprise at the change in N's accent—he sounded like a foreigner speaking Cantonese, though only slightly. For a moment she even wondered if this *was* N—

Not an actor, but a con man—she corrected her earlier impression.

She followed N into a tiny conference room. That Sze guy was nearby, talking to a couple of his coworkers, apparently urging them to join the meeting.

When she saw Sze Chung-Nam in person, Nga-Yee felt for a second as if she knew him. She told herself this was from the photos and videos, but she couldn't shake the sense that they'd met somewhere before. This momentarily distracted her from her rage. At the end of the day, everything that happened to Siu-Man was because of this bastard.

"Doris had to take the day off, so this is my other assistant, Rachel."

So that was her fake name. Nga-Yee made a mental note.

"Let's get started," Sze Chung-Nam said, moving to the front of the room, smiling confidently. He pressed a button on the remote control, and the words "GT Technology Ltd." appeared on the eighty-inch screen, with his English name, "Charles Sze," and job title. The presentation followed Guy Kawasaki's 10-20-30 rule: 10 pages, 20 minutes, 30-point font. "Hello, everyone. I'm Charles Sze, GT's director of technology. Today I'll speak about our business strategy and plans for development, as well as the benefits we can bring to SIQ."

He clicked to bring up the next slide. Mr. Lee and Hao stared—this wasn't what they'd seen the day before. This ought to have read "We trade more than just gossip," and Chung-Nam was supposed to be talking about the mechanisms by which G-dollars could be traded to create wealth. Instead, the screen proclaimed "The Revolution of News."

"When you were here last month, Mr. Szeto," said Sze Chung-Nam, "we spoke to you about GT Net's basic business model. Now I'd like to say a bit about the company's future, and how we're going to carry out this revolution."

Mr. Lee whispered urgently into Hao's ear, and Hao shook his head to say he knew nothing about this. Chung-Nam knew that his boss must be panicking, but he was also certain he wouldn't say anything. The presentation had to be flawless, and interrupting at this moment would leave a bad impression on the potential investor.

The next slide was about GT Net's potential when it came to the news industry, mostly ideas that Chung-Nam had cribbed from his conversation with Mr. Szeto a week earlier. He'd added in his own research, and it sounded convincing. In order to show that he was more than just a parrot and to bolster his points, he'd spent a lot of time reading the international literature on the subject, analyzing the state of local online media. As a result, he'd been sleeping four hours a night, neglecting his actual work.

Nga-Yee listened to him talk, still unsure what N was up to. She understood that this G-whatever was a Hong Kong web provider, and that they thought N was someone important from an investment firm, which is why they were shilling their company to him, saying it would replace traditional media. But what was N hoping to achieve? This seemed like a normal business meeting.

But the next time Sze Chung-Nam clicked his remote control, the meeting suddenly became anything but normal.

"GT Net already has the characteristics of a news website. For example, we—huh?"

The next slide ought to have been a screenshot from GT Net, but instead the entire PowerPoint system shut down, replaced by a browser displaying GT's website. This seemed like part of the presentation until everyone saw what was actually on the page: a piece of news worth zero G-Dollars, with the heading "[images, video] Preying on Underage Schoolgirls" and a video using Ma-Chai's streaming platform that was still undergoing beta testing.

"Is—is that you, Chung-Nam?" stuttered Ma-Chai.

On the screen, Sze Chung-Nam stood in the middle of an MTR car, his hand fondling a young girl's bum—the first of the videos Nga-Yee had seen earlier, but now the victim's face was pixelated.

It took several seconds for Chung-Nam to come to his senses and frantically hit the remote control, but the video kept playing. After about ten seconds another segment started: Chung-Nam and his next victim.

"There—there must be some kind of mistake—" uttered Chung-Nam. He wheeled around to a keyboard on the rack by the screen and frantically typed in commands—but the video didn't even pause. He tried turning off the computer, but the button seemed to have no effect. He cursed the touch pads, which, unlike old-fashioned switches, wouldn't simply cut off the current. In his frenzy, he thought of unplugging the entire apparatus, but the shelving had been built in front of the sockets, and he would have had to rip them out of the wall.

"I—I can explain, that's not me—"

Nga-Yee glanced at N, who was pretending to be as startled as everyone else, but she could detect the enjoyment in his face. Naturally, even if his expression hadn't given him away, she'd have known this was his handiwork. When Nga-Yee saw these videos in the car, each segment was almost a minute long, but these had been edited to the most crucial thirty seconds. Even after they stopped, Chung-Nam was still pressing the remote control button, using far too much force, so the *click-click-click* echoed through the room.

"Charles, is this some kind of joke?" Mr. Lee would rather have stayed silent, but as CEO, he needed to explain this away.

Before he could go on, Chung-Nam pressed the button again, and this time page 2 appeared.

"Oh!"

That was Nga-Yee, exclaiming in shock. She'd been telling herself to keep quiet, but this next page was more than she could bear. Luckily, she hadn't given anything away—everyone simply assuming that she too was startled by the contents of the page.

A woman's bare torso. Her face cut off. A man's face by her left breast, tongue out. Nga-Yee had seen this before in the Popcorn adult zone, but this time it was the woman's breast that was pixelated, while the man's face was clear. And this naked man was none other than Sze Chung-Nam. Now Nga-Yee knew where she'd seen this short, plump person before. It was his disgusting mouth and rounded chin she'd recognized.

There was a caption beneath:

I am the Marquis de Sade and this is my third little slave.
Aged fifteen—getting too old for me.

Sze Chung-Nam's face was white. He stared in terror around the conference room, his face in stark contrast with the filthy leer on the screen. Nga-Yee couldn't help finding the situation ridiculous, even comical. The room was absolutely silent, and the temperature seemed to plummet. Hao and Thomas glanced uneasily at each other, Joanne was glaring sidelong at Chung-Nam in disgust, and Ma-Chai was looking imploringly at his boss. But Mr. Lee was too stunned to speak, so this hideous silence could only continue.

"What's going on, Kenneth?" asked N in Szeto Wai's voice.

"I—I don't know. Charles, what is this?" said Mr. Lee helplessly. "This—this is—"

"Adult sites may be profitable, but SIQ certainly has no intention of getting involved." N said, sighing theatrically, then turning to Sze Chung-Nam. "I don't know whether your fetish videos ended up in the presentation because you mixed up some files or because someone sabotaged you, but either way, you're clearly unfit for the job. How am I supposed to ever trust you again, Chung-Nam? I'm not going to tell my colleagues that they should appoint a pervert as the new CEO."

"CEO?" Mr. Lee swung around to face N. "What are you talking about, appointing a new CEO?"

"Never mind about that, Kenneth. It's not happening anyway. But if you want to know, you should ask Chung-Nam." N shook his head. "It seems like that's the end of this report. It's a shame I'm leaving for the States tomorrow, so I won't be able to hear attempt number three in person. I'll get someone to follow up, though."

N stood up, shook hands with the dumbstruck Mr. Lee, nodded at Nga-Yee, and left the conference room. At the doorway, he turned to say, "Take care of yourself, Chung-Nam."

Mr. Lee had been about to ask Mr. Szeto and Rachel to stay, in the hopes of rescuing the situation, but now he froze and turned to his employee.

"How did Mr. Szeto know your Chinese name?" That was the last thing Nga-Yee heard Mr. Lee ask Chung-Nam, as she made her exit with N.

Back on the street, they found Ducky waiting for them with the car. They got in and drove off.

"Kenneth's brain doesn't work very fast," said N, removing his tie and looking as if he couldn't wait to be back in his ratty hoodie and cargo pants. "I had to say Chung-Nam three times before he understood that I'd been meeting his employee in secret."

"Was Sze Chung-Nam the one who posted those nude pictures on Popcorn?" asked Nga-Yee.

N narrowed his eyes and peered at her for a couple of seconds as he worked out where she was going with this. "So you actually went through all the websites I gave you?"

"I did. I thought you were making fun of me, making me visit adult websites—"

"There you go again, making an ass of u and me." N laughed. "How much free time do you think I have? I just compiled every website that was part of the case in a single document—it wasn't meant for you, but that's how you saw it."

"So what actually happened? Was this all a trap you laid to expose Sze Chung-Nam as a pervert in front of all his colleagues?"

"Pretty much."

"And that's why Ducky didn't stop him molesting those girls on the MTR?" Nga-Yee was still angry about that—nothing about the plan so far seemed to warrant letting those girls suffer.

"Let me ask you, Miss Au," said N placidly. "What do you think would have happened if Ducky had tried to stop Sze Chung-Nam at the time?"

"The police would have arrested him, of course!"

"Okay, now imagine you're the duty officer. What would you charge him with?"

"Indecent assault." This was what Shiu Tak-Ping had been found guilty of, so Sze Chung-Nam clearly deserved the same.

"Correct. He'd be found guilty, express remorse in court, get a third off his sentence because the offense wasn't serious, and serve one or two months at most. If he's lucky, he might even get away with a suspended sentence," N said, frowning. "That's not what he deserves."

"What's that?"

"Sze Chung-Nam's real crime is sexual coercion. Given that his victims are underage girls, we're talking four or five years in jail."

"Coercion?"

"Like I told you, I found Sze Chung-Nam by comparing station security footage against his Octopus card." N removed his glasses. "At the time, I was just thinking of him as the real culprit who'd framed Shiu Tak-Ping. When I saw how calm and practiced he was, I started to wonder how often he'd done this. All the while you were staking out my apartment and trying to pressure me into taking your case, I was investigating this guy. His browser history told me he'd been posting explicit pictures in Popcorn's adult zone, and though the man's face was blurred out in these images, I could tell it was him from his body."

"He paid escorts to be photographed with him?" Nga-Yee remembered a number of the Popcorn threads referred to local call girls.

N tapped on the tablet and brought up the page they'd just seen in the GT conference room. It turned out that there were five or six more of these. A different girl each time, but the man was always Sze Chung-Nam. All the pictures were extensively labeled; the caption Nga-Yee had seen earlier was only a partial one:

I am the Marquis de Sade and this is my third little slave. Aged fifteen—getting too old for me. I've used her for six months, and although she's still a little rebellious, I've mostly got her under control. Sharing with you all because I know you'll enjoy this.

"I didn't come up with this," said N, looking disgusted. "Every word of that is Sze Chung-Nam's. He actually posted that on the dark web, but I copied it over."

"The dark web?" Nga-Yee struggled to remember. "Oh right—that thing you can only see with an Onion browser?"

"Correct. Sze Chung-Nam is a member of a pedophile chatboard on the dark web, where he calls himself the Marquis de Sade and posts about how he traps and threatens escorts until they submit to being 'corrected' as his slaves. To prove he's telling the truth, he'll also post photos—with his face blacked out. The other perverts love that, as you can imagine. What he did on Popcorn was just the tip of the iceberg. The text and images on the dark web are a hundred times worse."

"But you said it's impossible to identify someone with Onion. How did you—"

"I didn't track him down from his dark web posts, I went straight to his computer, recording every keystroke and downloading every image he saw. I knew what software he used and which websites he'd visited." N grinned, seemingly amused that Nga-Yee was taking an interest in technology. "That's how I discovered this bastard was doing more than touching up girls on the train. He was also adept at choosing young girls who got into escort work to earn a bit of extra money, and he found ways to manipulate them into submitting completely to him so they'd be in his service. They were the main course; the girls on the train were dessert."

"So . . . everything he wrote—"

"All true." N pointed at the first picture. "She actually is fifteen, and that photo was taken without her consent."

Nga-Yee took a deep breath. When she saw that picture on Popcorn, her first thought had been disgust at the girl and how she'd let herself be used like that for the sake of a little money. She'd never imagined how much more there was to the story.

"Sze Chung-Nam is an ambitious, controlling man, and even worse, he's clever," N went on. "He's perceptive and knows how to connect with people—the ingredients of a successful individual. If he'd stayed on the straight and narrow, he'd have become an outstanding figure—but he succumbed to his dark urges. I'm guessing that because he's short, fat, and not particularly attractive, he was ashamed of his looks growing up. Perhaps he was bullied, perhaps he was humiliatingly rejected by women. And unfortunately, the way he chose to get over that was to pick on even weaker targets."

The first time N met Sze Chung-Nam in his office, he'd been surprised at how eager he was to answer questions. If N hadn't already known what he'd done, chances are he'd have been impressed by this enthusiastic, upwardly mobile junior employee.

"According to the *Hunting Manual* he disseminated on the dark web, he used instant messaging services such as Line and WeChat to choose his prey. He would identify individuals with vulnerable personalities, perhaps because they'd been threatened before, and secretly take screenshots while he was chatting with them, which would be the basis for blackmail material later. He was ruthless. Most people would say, "Do what I tell you, or I'll put your naked photos online." He uploaded them directly to the adult zone, then told the victims, "Do as I say, or next time your face will be visible." Most lethally, he knew how to use the carrot as well as the stick. He'd buy cheap gifts for his victims and take them shopping, to give the illusion that he cared about them. That's a form of Stockholm syndrome, I guess. Teenage girls don't know much about the world, so it's easier to manipulate them."

As Ducky tailed Sze Chung-Nam, he frequently saw him out with the very women he'd threatened. They'd go to fairly good restaurants, and Chung-Nam always got the bill. Of course, these dates always ended in a hotel room—Sze Chung-Nam wasn't after fake affection, but actual submission to satisfy his need for control.

"Wait—I still don't understand," said Nga-Yee. "You tricked Sze Chung-Nam's boss into believing you were an investor so you could insert those fake pages in his presentation to expose his crimes—and that's his punishment?"

"Fake pages? What fake pages?"

"The same thing you did to Violet! Taking over their Wi-Fi and inserting fake web pages—" She waved vaguely at the tablet.

"These were real." N chuckled. "Everything you're seeing now, all the pictures and videos actually are on the GT Net home page. And what's more"—N tapped a corner of the screen to bring up Popcorn—"I posted them here too. A thousand views already, so far."

Nga-Yee glanced down to see the following post:

POSTED BY edgarpoe777 ON 07-07-2015, 11:01
FWD: GT Net Pervert Exposes Himself (videos, pics)

Pixelated, still hot! http://www.gtnet.com.hk/gossip.cfm?q
=44172&sort=1

"I'm sure there's an even bigger busybody than I am who's reported it to the police by now, and Sze Chung-Nam will probably be picked up soon. Shame we won't be there to see him getting taken away in handcuffs with a bag over his head," said N gleefully. "The police will check the IP address those photos and videos were posted from and find that it's the GT office. That's my doing, but they won't find any sign of that. They'll probably look for explanations that fit the circumstances, such as that Sze Chung-Nam is a pervert—though he actually is one, of course—and got off on testing the system with his own dirty pictures. They'll say he got careless and accidentally made his crimes public. It's not illegal to post pixelated photos, but in order to investigate this properly, they'll have to check whether the pictures and videos were real or fake, and that's what's going to bring him down."

"So you set up this whole elaborate con for your own entertainment? Why did he have to be exposed during a meeting? You could have put that stuff online and contacted the police yourself."

"Sure, I like a good show. Who doesn't? But that wasn't the main point." N waggled a finger at her. "As Mr. Szeto, I met in private with Sze Chung-Nam. He proposed that after I'd put money into the firm, I'd use my power as an investor to promote him to CEO."

"So what?"

"After Sze Chung-Nam gets charged and convicted, the judge will ask for a background report on the defendant and allow the defense to submit character references to be considered in sentencing. Now that his boss knows he was secretly planning to team up with an investor to launch a takeover, Sze can forget about that. His coworkers will be leery of him. Even better, Sze is probably going to guess that the person who swapped the videos and ruined his big presentation has to be someone from the office, so if any of them offers to put in a good word, he's going to assume they're the culprit pretending to take pity. I don't just want him to go to jail, I want him to be abandoned by his friends and unable to trust anyone, and I want him to be locked up for more than a decade."

"I thought you said the maximum sentence was four or five years?"

"Per offense. He trapped six underage girls into sexual slavery. Even if only three of them are willing to testify, that's still at least twelve years."

Only now did Nga-Yee fully understand that every single girl in those photographs was one of Sze's blackmail victims. She ought to have realized—when he mentioned his "third little slave," that implied the existence of at least another two.

"You could never tell by looking at him," she murmured. "Just now, when he was doing the presentation, he looked like an ordinary person."

"You think hard-core perverts don't look like ordinary people?" N laughed coldly. "Don't be naive. Criminals don't have any special markings. They're very likely to have regular jobs and normal families. We only see one side of them. Mistaking that side for the whole is what lures you into their traps."

"Will those girls be able to get free of him?"

"Let's hope they get help, after what they suffered." N paused for a moment. "You let Violet To off, but I bet you're not going to ask me to show him mercy, are you?"

"Scum like that should be locked up for the rest of his life," said Nga-Yee. She knew she couldn't really blame Siu-Man's death on Sze Chung-Nam, but if he hadn't assaulted her, none of the other stuff would have happened. Violet and her brother had many complex reasons for doing what they did, but Sze attacked girls only for his own animal gratification.

As they talked, the car went through the underwater tunnel and returned to Hong Kong Island.

"Oh yes, you used another man-in-the-middle attack, didn't you?" Nga-Yee said suddenly.

"What?"

"I mean in real life, when you were pretending to represent an investment firm to fool Sze Chung-Nam and his boss," said Nga-Yee. "Rather than making up an investment firm from scratch, I bet you took an existing one and intercepted their communications so you could pretend to be one of their directors. Sze Chung-Nam's no fool, like you said. If you'd invented a company, he'd definitely have seen through that, wouldn't he."

"Hmph. Well you've seen me use this trick often enough. If you *hadn't* realized that's what I was doing, I'd worry you were mentally deficient."

Despite N's studied indifference, Nga-Yee congratulated herself on having seen through him for once. The car pulled up at the parking lot near his apartment.

"Get out, clever clogs," he ordered.

He seemed a bit annoyed, probably because she'd guessed what he was up to and stolen a bit of his thunder. She had no way of knowing that he actually wasn't unhappy at all, but putting up a front so she wouldn't guess what he was feeling.

In N's eyes, Nga-Yee's case was very special. He'd encountered plenty of stubborn clients determined to get their way, but no one had ever been as persistent. She'd even managed to surprise him a few times, such as when she worked out why Mr. Mok had come to visit him, or the way she'd pushed back on his made-up reasons for complaining when she tidied his apartment. When he said she was sometimes bright and sometimes asked moronic questions, given his sky-high standards, that was actually rare praise. And he'd meant it when he said that she, like himself, was a natural-born loner. That's why he'd let her play such a big part in the operations, partly because he was intrigued by this odd woman, partly because he'd found a bird of a feather.

Yet even though N had willingly revealed many of his trade secrets to Nga-Yee—tricks of investigation, methods of fooling people—he would never give up his final secret:

Szeto Wai was his actual identity.

Back when he was establishing himself in America and setting up Isotope Technologies, N was already a hacker. Work took up most of his time, and that was the only reason he never got involved in shadier business. He was a skilled negotiator, able to tell a person's character from the tiniest of details, which made him very persuasive, and he secured plenty of contracts for Isotope soon after it was established. He hated having a job that consisted mostly of bargaining, and this strength of his began to seem like a curse. Then came SIQ, and his wealth grew even further. At the age of thirty-three he'd already earned more money than he could spend in this lifetime. The more successful SIQ became, the hollower this success seemed.

After a certain incident, N made up his mind to bury his real name and return to the land of his birth, where he would carry out an off-the-books investigation and revenge business. He'd always been a lone wolf, and his value system wasn't the same as most people's. By his lights, delicacies worth thousands of dollars weren't necessarily that different from a bowl of wonton noodles from Loi's, and fine wine worth tens of thousands wasn't as good as a beer in front of his computer with Chet Baker crooning over the speakers. The satisfaction he chased was not sensual, but something of the spirit, far harder to grasp. N had nothing against selfish individuals, but if they bullied the weak, if they cared about no one else and thought they could do as they pleased, he took great pleasure in cutting them down.

Yet N was a principled person; he believed that actions have consequences.

The word he hated most in the world was "justice." Which wasn't to say he didn't know the difference between good and evil—but he understood that rather than simplistic morality, most conflict in the world arose from differences of opinion, with both sides raising the flag of justice and claiming to be on the side of reason. This allowed them to justify the most under-handed means as "a necessary evil" to defeat the other side—the law of the jungle, essentially. N had a deep understanding of this. He had money, status, power, and talent, so he could do pretty much whatever he wanted and other people would see him as an avatar of "justice"—but he knew that keeping others down in the name of justice is another form of bullying.

He was clear-eyed about the vicious methods he employed. Even if the people he threatened were triad leaders, even if those he deceived were devious businessmen, he would never let himself believe he was on the side of justice. This was merely fighting evil with evil, turning them all into feral animals.

Because he understood this, he was able to restrain himself.

Whether he was working for a client or just being a busybody, he seriously considered what methods to use and how to dispense punishment proportional to the crime. It was simple to destroy a person. In his eyes, human beings were inferior products, full of cracks and flaws for him to control or manipulate. But too many people enjoyed playing God, and he wasn't going to be one of them.

When someone came to him with a revenge case, he carefully considered the potential client's background and the full details of what happened before deciding whether to accept. N specialized in turnabout, visiting on the perpetrator what they'd done to the victim. When carrying out such commissions, he felt almost carefree—he was no more than a tool, and the enmity belonged to other people. When he interfered of his own accord, though, he had to calibrate his actions more carefully, and was sometimes forced to use cumbersome, roundabout methods in keeping with his ethical system.

While dealing with Sze Chung-Nam, though, he'd encountered a difficulty.

After confirming what Sze had done, N wanted to free his victims, leaving them a chance to seek revenge. He wanted to see this man locked up. He wanted him to suffer the unique torments meted out to sex offenders in prison, so he could live in fear as those girls had every single day. The trouble was, N couldn't find any information about them on Sze's computer, just some photographs with their heads chopped off.

According to Ducky's findings, Sze Chung-Nam had two cell phones—one for daily use, and one for hunting. He got in touch with his victims over the second phone and turned it on only when he needed to speak to them. Otherwise he kept it in his briefcase, powered off. There were no apps on this phone, and he didn't use it for anything except photos of his prey.

Ducky was able to turn up the identities of two of the girls Sze Chung-Nam had been with, but what N wanted was a list of all their names. The picture he'd found online made it clear that there was more than one victim, but he had no idea what the total was. He did know that everyone Chung-Nam targeted would have a similar personality: not bold enough to make a fuss. Even if news of his arrest was reported, they wouldn't necessarily come forward. They might never have learned his real name, nor realize that the person threatening them was the same one in the news—especially if the papers didn't print his photo.

There were many ways for this to go wrong. If Sze ended up getting convicted of the lesser offense—indecent assault—and did only a month or two in prison, he'd be even more brutal and dangerous, and those girls might end up worse off, not to mention all the new victims he was sure to find. Just a year earlier there'd been a terrifying double murder: a foreign financial consultant who was into certain fetishes tortured and killed two South Asian sex workers while high on drugs, then kept their decapitated corpses in suitcases under his bed until he eventually surrendered to the police. This high-stress city could make these sorts of criminals double down on their behavior. N decided that he would strike only when he was assured of success—he wouldn't act against Sze Chung-Nam until he was certain of putting him away for ten to twenty years, so there would be no repercussions for his victims.

"Should we hack into his phone remotely?" Ducky had asked at the time.

"No, too risky. You said he turns that phone on only when he wants to contact his targets. It won't be easy to lure him into this trap, and he's a clever bastard—if he senses something wrong, we'll scare him off and all our work so far will go to waste. I'll think of another way."

When he was looking into Sze Chung-Nam's background, N had noticed that his firm was a part of the Productivity Council's investment program and was seeking a VC. He weighed the risks and rewards and decided to meet Sze using his real identity. Nga-Yee was right—this was a man-in-the-middle attack in real life—except that N actually was the chairman of SIQ, and it was only his motives he was concealing. Everyone at SIQ knew that Szeto Wai was semiretired, but few were aware that he was in the Far East rather than on the East Coast of America—and not even Kyle Quincy knew about his double life in Hong Kong. Whenever they met over Skype, N put on his Szeto Wai getup.

N had quite a few accomplices: con artists, hackers, fighters, jacks-of-all-trades, and he could summon ten or twenty of them at a moment's notice, though only Ducky and Doris knew he was Szeto Wai. In this operation, Doris had been in charge of staying in touch with Kenneth Lee, while Ducky kept tabs on Sze Chung-Nam and searched for his victims.

This is our director of technology, Charles Sze.

On his N's first visit to the GT Net office, he'd left a strong impression on Sze. Five foot three and shaped like a barrel, Sze Chung-Nam was not pleasing to the eye, but he was articulate and full of self-confidence, and he seemed determined to show that there was more to him than shallow people might surmise from his appearance. During their brief conversation N gained a handle on his personality and worked out a strategy for dealing with him. He'd initially planned to "bump into" Sze in the street after this meeting, but now he formulated a bolder plan.

He would lure Sze into seeking him out.

Sze had seemed enthusiastic, so N threw out a difficult question, and sure enough, Sze jumped in to answer when Kenneth Lee fumbled. That revealed how interested Sze was in Szeto Wai. And so, while making small talk, N made sure to mention his fake address, adding that he'd be attending a concert at the Cultural Centre. Sze was enterprising enough not to pass up an opportunity like this.

What N didn't predict was that Nga-Yee would go off-piste.

That day, when he'd returned to Sai Ying Pun from Sze's office, he'd been surprised to find Nga-Yee sitting on his staircase, grimly scrolling through a phone, having left work early. The new information from Siu-Man's phone forced him to turn his attention back to this side of the case. When Nga-Yee insisted on spending the night in order to get an answer as quickly as possible, that put even more pressure on him. He was going to the Cultural Centre the following night to reel in his fish, but Nga-Yee was taking up all the time he'd meant to use for preparation. After the phone call to Miss Yuen on Saturday morning, Nga-Yee finally left, and N summoned an accomplice to act as his date for the evening, then caught up on several hours of sleep. He could go without rest in the course of an investigation or stakeout, but now he was to appear in person, he needed to be fully alert and prepared. If he said so much as a word wrong and aroused Sze's suspicions, it wouldn't just be this foray that blew up, but possibly the entire plan, leaving Sze to get away scot-free.

Sze Chung-Nam hadn't been able to spot Szeto Wai during the concert for a simple reason: N was never there in the first place. Ducky kept watch and told him the appropriate moment to slip into the foyer to engineer their "chance meeting." There, N bumped into a banker he'd met many years ago at a Silicon Valley conference, and he decided to use their acquaintance to make his own deception more convincing. Sze surely had no idea that while he was spouting his nonsense about the orchestra and soloist blending well, N's comments were made up too, pieced together from reviews and past recordings.

For the next week, N burned the candle at both ends, continuing to investigate Siu-Man's classmates while closing in on Sze Chung-Nam. When Nga-Yee bumped into Mr. Mok at

Loi's and charged up to N's apartment to confront him, he'd been preparing for his dinner with Sze the following evening. Nga-Yee kept disrupting his workflow, and unexpected developments kept happening on the Sze front, but N managed to keep things going.

The main reason N wanted to take Sze to dinner was to steal his cell phone.

Not "steal" in the conventional sense, of course. What N was after was the data on the phone: the contact details of his victims, the pictures and videos he'd taken, and so on. If possible, he also hoped to create a back door to his phone, which would give him twenty-four-hour access and perhaps allow him to stop Sze from harming those girls even before the operation was over. Sze being a tech expert meant that he might spot a remote attack, but as long as N had access to the phone, he'd definitely be able to infiltrate it undetectably.

During the dinner at Tin Ding Hin, N realized that Sze was even more capable than he'd thought, and very observant too— although SIQ wasn't actually opening a Hong Kong branch office or making inroads into Asia, these were valid conclusions from the fake clues N had provided. That evening, N had several opportunities to grab Sze's phone, but in the end he decided to leave the hook in the water a little longer before reeling him in, not only to give his target more chances to take the bait, but also to wait till he was exhausted and couldn't fight back. Later, what he heard from Ducky would validate this judgment call.

"The bastard spotted me on the MTR platform," Ducky said on the phone.

"Not you too? How bad is it?"

"Not awful. I gave up tailing him at Mong Kok. Don't think we spooked him too much."

"Just be careful. Wear a disguise if you need to. This guy's sharp."

After this, Ducky kept a good distance from Sze, staying out of sight whenever possible. The surveillance had been going on about twenty days now, and N had already found one of the victims. During this time, Sze was constantly on the hunt for new escorts, at the same time forcing the ones he already had under his thumb into sexual service. The weekend that N was preparing for his second visit to Enoch School to expose Violet's true nature, Ducky witnessed Sze inviting a girl to Festival Walk, after which they went to a hotel. When they emerged, Ducky followed the girl, and once he had her address, he was able to ascertain that she was the "third little slave." He also spotted Sze's coworker Hao nearby and briefly wondered if they were up against a criminal syndicate rather than a lone criminal, then decided that Hao was probably just there by coincidence.

Even with one victim's information in his hands, N didn't change his strategy. His plan from the start had been to get a full list of names, and he wanted to get hold of the unpixelated photos for evidence. The main strike against Sze took place on July 2, the night at the bar.

After taking on Nga-Yee's revenge case, N was forced to continue on both fronts at once. Even as he staked out Violet To's home, he was preparing to grab Sze's phone. Earlier on the day of Nga-Yee's first visit to the mobile unit on Broadcast Drive, N and Ducky had swapped duties, so Ducky kept an eye on Violet while N became Szeto Wai again and visited the bar in Lan Kwai Fong with Sze.

We're here. You can leave your briefcase in the car.

It's okay, I'll bring it with me.

N had been hoping to separate Sze from his briefcase, which contained the cell phone, but Sze declined because he needed to hang on to the report he intended to spring on Szeto Wai. N wasn't flustered—he had a backup plan, and he was working with more associates this evening. Not only were the bar owner and servers among his people, he also had two beautiful women to act as bait: Zoe and Talya. Unlike Doris, these two didn't know what the overall plan was, and they didn't ask questions—they knew it was safer to know as little as possible.

Zoe and Talya's job was to distract Sze Chung-Nam from his briefcase. While he was in the bathroom, another associate took the phone and brought it to another room to hack into it.

The phone security was another headache—it was fingerprint-protected. N had planned three methods to get what he needed: lifting Sze's prints off the car door handle; swiping the glass that Sze drank from; looking for prints on the phone itself. In the old days, this would have meant making a mold, but now even a high school student with the right materials can become a first-rate hacker. N was prepared. One of his associates got the print, scanned it into the computer, inverted the image, and printed it on photographic paper with special electrolyzed ink that the device read as an actual fingerprint. In just a few minutes, they were inside Sze's phone.

After obtaining all his data and installing a backdoor Masque Attack, it wasn't too difficult to get the phone back to him, because all his attention was on baby-faced Zoe. Even though this was a setup, N wasn't willing to let Sze have too good a time, and he made sure to ostentatiously cockblock him, after which Talya could find some reason to further humiliate this "director of technology."

The only mistake that evening took place after N parted from Sze. The associate who was monitoring communications between Sze and his victim accidentally blocked their messages, so the text that Sze sent couldn't reach his "third little slave." Only after N had swung the car around and regrouped with his associates did they realize the error and resend it; luckily, Sze didn't pay much attention to the five-minute outage, and he forgot all about it after the girl replied. After all, he was preoccupied with the takeover. N knew that Ducky would never have made such a mistake, but unfortunately, Ducky had been needed to continue the stakeout on Broadcast Drive.

Once N had the list of names, his job was mostly done. He'd wanted to find the identities of all these victims in order to personally contact them and break the psychological hold Sze Chung-Nam had over them. In addition to suffering from Stockholm syndrome, they didn't have enough information to take a step back and see the big picture. Many assumed that because they were doing escort work, asking the police for help would result in them getting arrested; others were afraid of being shamed by their families if their activities came to light. N simply had to refute Sze's lies. He told them that there is no law in Hong Kong prohibiting women from offering sexual services, but anyone coercing prostitutes could be convicted under the vice laws. Being underage, these girls would be seen only as victims. Although he couldn't do anything about the ones who were afraid of being found out by their friends, families, or lovers, N was confident that he could persuade most of them to come forward and help obtain revenge against Sze Chung-Nam. N was very good at inducing vengeful feelings in other people.

Earlier this day, just as Sze Chung-Nam's evil deeds were being exposed on the GT Net home page, his six victims simultaneously received anonymous emails telling them that Sze would soon be arrested. N didn't tell them about one another's existence, only that he knew they were being threatened, and that stepping forward was the only way to escape their present suffering and also give Sze a good kicking. People are self-interested creatures. If they knew he would be convicted whether or not they spoke up, these girls might well have chosen to stay silent. Leading them to believe that they had only themselves to save could make even the weak among them grow strong. N knew they would all be replying to him later that day, and urging them all to visit their local police stations would be his final move in this protracted game of chess.

As N led Nga-Yee from the parking lot, through the alleyway, back to his run-down tenement building, he heaved a sigh of relief. For the last month, he'd been completely occupied with the cases of Violet To and Sze Chung-Nam, not to mention all the trouble Nga-Yee kept giving him. He'd wondered why he was putting himself through this, but it wasn't his style to give up halfway, so he'd never considered abandoning either case. He did wish he was Satoshi, the true genius of the pair, who would have had more advanced ways of breaking into Sze's phone. He'd witnessed his friend's prowess at college. Satoshi could break into any platform in the shortest amount of time. He was as dexterous as a brain surgeon—one who could rewire the brain. That's why Satoshi wasn't just Szeto Wai's business partner, but also his mentor. His guidance was the reason N had become a hacker.

God knows where Satoshi is right now, or what he's doing.

When N said these words in the guise of Szeto Wai, he hadn't been lying. He guessed that Satoshi, like himself, had grown tired of the moneyed world and was lying low in a small apartment in a big city somewhere, leading a life of freedom.

"Just leave these clothes out," said N to Nga-Yee when they got to the fifth floor. "The cleaning lady will deal with them."

"You mean Heung?"

"Oh, you've met? Yes, she comes twice a week and cleans every apartment except the one on the sixth floor."

Now Nga-Yee understood. She'd been puzzled about why N's pigsty of a home showed no sign of ever being tidied, despite having a cleaner every Wednesday and Saturday—who surely couldn't just have been dealing with his bathroom and kitchen.

N went back upstairs, and Nga-Yee changed into the clothes she'd been wearing earlier. She hesitated over whether to remove her makeup, then caught a glimpse of herself in the mirror and decided it didn't go with her dowdy clothes. She wiped it all off.

After fifteen minutes, N returned, even more sloppily dressed than Nga-Yee. He was back in his T-shirt and tracksuit, and his hair was damp—he'd probably just washed it and hadn't bothered with the blow-dryer, so it was sure to end up in his habitual bird's nest. They went to the sixth-floor apartment, where N got himself a can of iced coffee from the fridge and sat at his desk.

"All right, Miss Au. Let's talk about that five hundred grand you owe me," he said, leaning back.

Nga-Yee swallowed and lowered herself into the chair across from him, sitting very straight.

"Let me ask you—" N absently started tidying the heaps of junk on the desk. "Did you stop to think how you would pay back the money?"

"Can I do it in installments? I can give you four thousand a month, so in ten years and five months I should have five hundred thousand . . ." She'd done the math, and if she pared her expenses to the bone, she could just about manage this.

"What about interest?"

She froze, but understood that this was a reasonable point. "Um—how about four thousand five hundred a month?"

"That's chicken feed." N pursed his lips. "I'm not a bank. Why should I let you pay by installments?"

"Then . . . I guess you'd better cut out one of my organs or take out a life insurance policy and have me die in a fake accident." Nga-Yee had been worrying about these possibilities for a couple of days now.

"Attractive suggestions, but I'm not a gangster. I don't do anything like that."

"You told me I wouldn't make a good enough prostitute—"

"You actually don't have to worry about it. Just give me the five hundred grand you have coming to you."

She stared at him, uncomprehending.

N picked a sheet of paper off his desk and handed it to her; it was a photocopy of a newspaper article. When she realized what it was, her heart flipped over, and a long-buried sorrow rose to the surface. DOCK WORKER DROWNED IN FORKLIFT ACCIDENT.

The headline might as well have been a needle piercing straight into her eyes. This was about her father, Au Fai, and was dated eleven years ago.

"Your family lost its sole source of income as a result."

"Yes." Nga-Yee was shaking, thinking of how hard their life had been, but also that her mom and sister were alive then. "My mother once said that there was a problem with red tape, and the insurance company refused to pay. My dad's boss was kind enough to pay us a bit of compensation—"

"Kind my ass." N was scowling. "That bastard cheated your mother."

Nga-Yee's head snapped up, and she stared at him in surprise.

"Your dad worked for Yu Hoi Shipping. His boss, Tang Chun-Hoi, was just a small-business owner, but later he landed a big government contract, and his company shot through the roof. He got some entrepreneur award last year." N handed Nga-Yee a tablet computer showing Yu Hoi's home page. "His rise was entirely due to underhanded tactics. After your father's accident, he conspired with the insurance adjuster to push the responsibility onto your father. This preserved the company's reputation and also saved the insurer a hefty payout—they would have had to keep paying your father's salary for the next sixty months otherwise."

"Conspired?" Nga-Yee's jaw dropped.

"Your mother probably thought the boss would have sought out the highest possible payout for his employee. Pah—those people are vampires. Slave owners. To them, workers are like spare parts—you throw them out when you have no further use for them." N paused a moment, then went on more calmly. "Your family ought to have received seven hundred thousand dollars in compensation. Even after you've paid me what you owe, there'll still be a fair bit left over."

"Can I still get the payout?"

"Of course not. It's been more than a decade, and all the evidence will have disappeared by now." N smirked. "But I want you to help me take down this Mr. Tang."

"What?"

"I'm giving you a chance for revenge, that's what. Your family's misfortune can be avenged with your own hands. Isn't that a good thing? Tang Chun-Hoi exploited so many workers, leaving them and their families unable to live with dignity while he grew fat on the money that should have been theirs. I heard he plans to buy off government officials so he can rise even higher. Isn't it time he suffers a little?"

There was a picture of Mr. Tang on the Yu Hoi website. He looked coarse despite his expensive suit, and his smile didn't seem genuine. The photograph reeked of money.

"What . . . what are you going to do?"

"I haven't come up with a plan yet. He's made quite a few families suffer, though, so by the law of an eye for an eye, maybe his family should have a hard time too." N grinned. "Is this case of interest to you? In the end, Mr. Tang's one action ended up stealing your entire family from you. It makes sense that he should have to pay for it, don't you agree?"

N's words were stirring up so much rage in Nga-Yee, she almost agreed right away—then stopped herself, because this was a familiar feeling.

When the man at the Housing Authority made her furious, she'd decided to go after kidkit727 come hell or high water. She felt the same way now—hot blood rushing into her brain.

Just as N said when he was persuading her to seek revenge against Violet, she understood the reason for her anger and felt justified in seeking revenge. After what she'd been through in the last few days, though, she was starting to realize something else. There was no reason for her to reject N's offer—it would solve her financial problems and win a measure of justice for her dead parents. Yet something deep inside told her that saying yes to N would mean losing more than she'd gain.

Nga-Yee thought of her mother—how she'd preferred a life of backbreaking work to relying on government handouts.

"No, I don't want this case," she mumbled.

"Are you sure, Miss Au?" said N, looking surprised. "If you're worried about the danger, I promise I'm not going to put an amateur like you in charge of anything important."

"No, that's not why." Now that she understood what was in her heart, Nga-Yee was able to look N firmly in the eye. "I don't want to continue this cycle of revenge. I don't forgive Mr. Tang, but I know if I say yes to this, I'll be led farther and farther along this path. I don't want to lose myself. I need to be true to who I am. I don't care what you do to that bastard, but I'm not going to be part of it."

N looked at her long and hard through narrowed eyes.

"As far as you're concerned, Miss Au, this is the easiest job you could ask for." N's voice was ice-cold, reminding Nga-Yee of his tone when he was threatening the gangsters. "A delicate flower like you couldn't cope with anything tougher."

Seeing how stern he looked, Nga-Yee almost caved, but then she felt her mother's presence. That day at the Cityview hotel, she'd allowed hatred to overwhelm her, choosing the path of revenge without considering what price she would have to pay. Now she would take responsibility for her decision.

"You're wrong. Just give me a chance, and you'll see that I can cope."

Once again, N hadn't expected this answer. He'd dealt with all sorts of nasty characters, but this client was rapidly becoming his most difficult. True, Nga-Yee wouldn't have been much use on the Tang Chun-Hoi case, but he could be just as stubborn as she was, and he wasn't going to take this on without the victim's agreement. If he took on this sort of petty criminal on his own, he'd just be a busybody. N glared at Nga-Yee, his fingers drumming rhythmically on the desk, wondering if he should continue trying to persuade her or just give up.

"If you're not going to work with me," he said eventually, "I guess that leaves whoring yourself out."

"I guess," said Nga-Yee haplessly, taking a deep breath.

"Are you trying to punish yourself? You think you neglected your sister, so—"

"No. I'm doing this for myself. I don't want to become a person I'd despise. Anyway, you've told me not to use Siu-Man as an excuse for my actions."

N scratched his head. It wasn't often that someone was able to throw his words back at him.

"Fine. I can see you've made up your mind." He leaned back.

Nga-Yee sighed, bracing herself for what was to come.

N reached into his drawer and picked up a small object, which he tossed at Nga-Yee. She wasn't prepared for this and barely managed to catch it. When she looked at her hand, it was a key.

"From next week, you'll sweep this place every morning. Also, clean the bathroom twice a week and empty the trash. You don't get Sundays or public holidays off."

"Huh?" She stared at him in confusion.

"Those were simple instructions. Do you really need me to repeat them? From next week—"

"No, I meant . . . you want me to be your cleaner?"

"You think I'm sending you to walk the streets? You're as flat as an ironing board." He shot her a look. "Heung is always mixing up actual rubbish and the stuff I need—that's why I don't let her clean in here. I'll give you a try. If I'm not happy with your work, I'll consider hiring you out to a nightclub. You can clean their toilets."

She didn't mind his insults—but this was an unexpected development.

"And don't bother saying anything about labor law or the minimum wage. I don't believe in that stuff," N went on. "I'll pay you two thousand a month, about half of what a regular cleaner would get, so it will take you about twenty years to pay off the five hundred grand. And if I decide I need you to help me out on a case, you'll have to do that too."

"Twenty years?" Nga-Yee was alarmed.

"Not happy?"

"No, that's fine." Nga-Yee was good at housework, and it wouldn't be too hard to clean a single apartment. "You said every morning—you want me to come here before work?"

"Correct."

"Can I come some evenings instead? If I have the morning shift, public transport can be—"

"No bargaining," he snapped. "I'm a night owl, I work late. Don't want you getting in my way."

"Understood." There was no point pushing any further. She looked around the apartment again, working out how much time she'd have to spend cleaning it every day, and how much earlier she'd have to leave home as a result. Remembering how much effort it was the last time she tidied up here, she couldn't help frowning. This might end up being even before the first MTR train. How was she supposed to get everything done before heading for the library?

"Fine. Have it your way." N reached into the drawer and tossed her another key.

"What's this?"

"The fourth-floor apartment. Third and fourth are empty anyway, you might as well live in one of them. That way you don't need to worry about being late for work." N pursed his lips, as if he found her intolerable. "If you're coming all the way from Yuen Long or Tin Shui Wai, that's an hour and a half. You might be so tired you'd throw away something important, and that's just more trouble for me."

"Yuen Long? But I—Oh!"

Now she remembered, this was the day she was supposed to hear from the Housing Authority about the apartment she'd be allocated in Tin Yuet Estate, Tin Shui Wai.

"But the rent—"

"Oh please. Apartments around here go for more than ten grand a month. If I charged you that, you'd never finish paying me back till your next life. If you can't do something, don't bring it up."

Nga-Yee had no idea if this brusqueness was a front, or if he actually cared about nothing but having her clean his apartment more effectively. In any case, she was due to leave her Wun Wah House apartment soon and would have to start a new life. Looking at the keys in her hand, she thought about it for a while before nodding. She would accept this payment plan.

"Fine, that's settled, then. All right, you can go now, I have things to do." With that, N turned away and switched on his computer.

"Hang on, I have another question—"

"Now what?"

"Will Sze Chung-Nam confess to the police that he assaulted Siu-Man?"

"He's not an idiot, so obviously he's not going to."

"So Shiu Tak-Ping is still carrying the can for him."

"Correct."

"We're the only ones who know the truth. Don't you think we owe it to him to say something?"

"I know you think you're being kind, Miss Au, but actually this is idiotic." N looked at her disdainfully. "If Shiu Tak-Ping had stuck to his guns, I'd consider helping him. But he made the choice he thought would work out best for him and took the plea deal. People like that don't deserve help."

N took a swig of coffee. "If Shiu Tak-Ping hadn't taken the deal, he might have been found not guilty, and Violet wouldn't have been able to use that fake post to stir up all that trouble. Do you really want to help him?"

Nga-Yee hadn't thought of that.

"Um . . . but if that happened, we'd never have found out that Siu-Man wrongly accused him."

"Just give up," sneered N. "Even if Sze Chung-Nam confessed right now and proved that your sister didn't accuse the wrong guy on purpose, people on the internet are still going to say nasty things about how she sent an innocent man to jail."

"No—hang on. Siu-Man didn't even testify. And she wasn't the one who pointed the finger—"

"You think people care about that online? If anything bad happens, they look for someone to blame right away."

"Are people on the internet really so unreasonable?" Nga-Yee frowned. She didn't understand.

"Not just people on the internet—people, period." N shook his head. "The internet is a tool. It can't make people or things good or evil, just like a knife can't commit murder. It's the person holding the knife—or maybe the evil thought animating the person with the knife. You talk about people on the internet as a way of avoiding reality. People are never willing to admit to the selfishness and desire hidden with our human nature. They always find something to use as a scapegoat."

Nga-Yee realized he was right.

"At this point, the internet is the spine of society—" he went on. "We can't live without it. Yet there are those who take a backward attitude. When you see its good side, you praise the net and talk about the great strides human civilization has made; then you see its more negative side, you blame it for causing harm, and you want to restrict it. People think they're being so progressive—but actually these ideologies are exactly the same, deep down, as one or two hundred years ago. The problem isn't the internet, it's us. You heard part of the presentation earlier, so I guess you understand more or less what Sze Chung-Nam's company does?"

"It's a website something like Popcorn? And they also wanted to—what was it—change traditional news media—"

"Their website is called GT Net—it's a chatboard as well as a news exchange site. In an enlightened, mature society, a site like this might well be able to take over the role of traditional media and be a force for good. As it is, it's a terrible idea—it just brings out the dark side of people, allowing them to disseminate unsubstantiated rumors and nasty gossip. And the sheer volume of information in the digital age is more than the average person can cope with. Many years ago, the American writer David Shenk coined the term 'data smog' to describe this. In a fog like this, the data that ought to help us find the truth becomes a mental drug that keeps us in a state of foolishness. Remember the Boston Marathon bombing?"

Nga-Yee nodded. She'd seen it on the news at the time.

"As soon as it happened, the internet worked together to search for evidence, hoping to pinpoint the culprit from footage of the scene and help the police with their investigation." N paused a moment. "The problem is, mistakes in situations like this have serious consequences. One poster found a college student, Sunil Tripathi, who looked like the man in the videos and had gone missing a month before the bombing. He immediately became the prime suspect. Then, when the police had the perpetrator surrounded and there was a gunfight, some netizens listened in on their wireless comms and claimed they could confirm that Tripathi was the murderer. Even mainstream outlets started reporting it as fact. This misinformation wasn't cleared up till the next day. Tripathi's corpse was discovered a week later; the pathology report found that he'd been dead at the time of the bombing. Before the identity of the true killer was revealed, Tripathi's family went through hell. They were already suffering—not knowing if he was alive or dead, being attacked on the basis of these false rumors. The problem here wasn't the internet, even though that's how the news spread, nor was it the websites that were used, but the stupidity of the human mind. In seeking the truth, we choose to believe unreliable sources, and we spread these untruths in the name of 'sharing,' creating a disaster that's hard to undo."

Nga-Yee knew there were innocent people all over the world who'd been smeared on the internet, but after hearing this concrete example, her heart tightened. After what happened to Siu-Man, she could empathize with what this student's family must have suffered.

"The internet is a great place for us to share our knowledge and increase communication." N sighed. "But human beings naturally love expressing their opinions more than they want to understand other people. We always talk too much and listen too little, which is why the world is so noisy. Only when we understand this will we finally see progress in the world. That's when humanity will be ready to use the internet as a tool."

Nga-Yee normally regarded everything N said as twisted logic, but she actually agreed profoundly with this.

"Any other questions? If not, hurry on home and stop getting in my way." N started looking impatient again.

"One more question. Last one." Nga-Yee had been puzzling over this ever since N had explained about Sze Chung-Nam in the car on their way back. "Why did you look at the security footage from the day Siu-Man was assaulted? You seemed to know from the very beginning that the real culprit was out there."

"Correct, I did."

"How?"

"Do you know the categories of sex offenders who target underage victims?"

Nga-Yee shook her head.

"There are basically two types: the pedophiles, who are attracted only to children, and the indiscriminate ones who'll take on any age, young or old. Both of these can be further divided into the introverts and the sadists. The introverts are passive—their crimes are opportunistic, usually flashing or molesting. The sadists are more active—their aim is to make their victims feel pain and fear. That's how they get their kicks. There are also those who use money or other things to lure children into their clutches, but that wasn't relevant here, so I'll skip over them."

"Okay, those are the categories. So what?"

"Both introverts and sadists might touch someone up on a train. The former do it for their own gratification, the latter to terrorize their victims. In a situation like this, neither would choose someone who looked like they might retaliate. Introverts wouldn't anyway, and while sadists like their prey to fight back, they wouldn't do that on public transport—it would attract too much attention. The sadist's goal is to isolate the victim and enjoy devouring her at leisure, the way Sze Chung-Nam brought those girls to hotels. So you see, it seemed strange that Shiu Tak-Ping would commit a crime like this."

"Why? Siu-Man didn't dare say anything while she was being attacked. She didn't struggle."

"But Shiu Tak-Ping wouldn't think so, because he'd had an argument with your sister at the convenience store before boarding the train. When he was arrested, he claimed right away that she'd falsely accused him because they'd quarreled at Yau Ma Tei station. The shop attendant corroborated this. No pervert would be stupid enough to choose a victim he'd just had an encounter with, especially one who'd shown that she wasn't afraid of him. Taking this into account, it seemed likely that Shiu Tak-Ping was innocent—and that's probably why so many people decided your sister had falsely accused him. They may not have analyzed it in that much detail, but they had the gut response that no one would be so stupid."

"So you also thought from the start that Siu-Man was lying?" said Nga-Yee, a little shocked.

"No, because if you flip it around, the chances of your sister falsely accusing him were also almost zero," said N, shaking his head a little. "If Shiu Tak-Ping was right and she really was out to get him, she'd have been the one to raise the alarm, not the older woman. It would have been much simpler for her to just grab his arm and scream. Looking at all the evidence, it was very likely that your sister actually had been assaulted, and also that Shiu Tak-Ping was innocent. Which only left one possibility—"

"That the real culprit had got away," finished Nga-Yee.

"The posters who decided your sister was lying didn't know how they were being manipulated. Kidkit727 was working hard behind the scenes—not to clear Shiu Tak-Ping's name, but for other reasons. When Shiu Tak-Ping took the plea deal, that opened the door for kidkit727 to make more trouble. Meanwhile, Sze Chung-Nam, a repeat offender, got away scot-free." N grinned. "Remember what I said at the start? The only reason I accepted your case was that it turned out to be so much more interesting than I'd expected."

CHAPTER TEN

Christopher Song had just brewed the coffee when he realized that Violet was standing sleepily behind him, still clutching her pillow.

"Sorry, did I wake you?" he asked.

Violet shook her head and sat herself down at the dining table. Christopher had told her the night before that she should sleep in, but for the last three days she'd been up before he left for work, sitting silently as he drank his coffee and then walked out the door. He knew why she was doing this: she was terrified that she would open her eyes and find herself back in the fancy Broadcast Drive condo, all alone, rather than in this shabby two-hundred-square-foot apartment in Cheung Sha Wan.

It had been less than a week since the night Christopher burst into the To household, but their lives had changed much faster than he could have imagined. It was still too early to tell, but he thought this might turn out to be a good thing.

That night, when the security guard summoned the police, Christopher had hardened his heart and decided to fulfill the promise he'd made to his sister: he'd take her away from that awful home. He told the officer that Violet's mother had been missing for many years, leaving Violet with a stepfather she shared no blood ties with. He hadn't mistreated her, but he often left her home alone because of work, which clearly meant he was guilty of neglecting a minor.

Once the courts got involved, they quickly ascertained that Christopher was telling the truth. The Immigration Department confirmed that their mother had left Hong Kong many years earlier and never returned, while Rosalie testified that Violet had slit her wrists a year ago and Mr. To had prevented his daughter from seeking medical help. These were enough grounds for Mr. To to lose custody. In accordance with Violet's own wishes, she was placed in the care of her brother. The judge reached this decision quickly, not only because of Christopher's and Rosalie's statements, but mostly because of the scars still visible on Violet's forearms and her state of near collapse. It was clear that life with her stepfather wasn't good for her.

That night, Christopher had realized that his sister had been about to kill herself, but he had no idea what brought her to this point. Violet said that she knew he was in trouble, and that the only way to get him out of it was to remove herself from this world. It saddened him to hear her talk that way. What a state she must have been in! He was only glad he'd arrived in time to prevent a tragedy.

Mr. To had cut short his business trip and returned to Hong Kong, where he was preparing to appeal the judgment. Sometime in the near future, Christopher would have to face an onslaught from Mr. To's legal team, who'd try to prove that Christopher was even less fit to be Violet's guardian. That was fine. He felt sure he could deal with anything they might throw at him.

He'd promised his sister he would make her happy.

The previous summer, just two months after she slit her wrists, he'd realized that she hadn't given up on the idea of ending her life. One night, she snuck out and they met in the little park between Broadcast Drive and Junction Road. He found her in a state of anxiety bordering on despair, even though it was still vacation time and she didn't have to go to school.

"Violet, promise me you won't do anything stupid," he'd said. "Are you really willing to sacrifice your life just because of those bastards at your school?"

"I'm—I don't want to, but—I can't take it anymore . . ." she sobbed.

"I'll be right here, supporting you." He took her icy hands. "Our society is broken, and the weak are destined to be bullied and exploited. But that just means we have to go on living until we're able to make those scumbags suffer everything we've been through."

"But I don't even know who hacked into the student aide's account and posted that attack on me—"

"I'll find a way to take revenge for you. Whichever bastard did that will get what they deserve. Violet, just promise me you won't try again."

That was last July 27.

From that day, Christopher had known he had to rescue his sister, even if it meant becoming someone he abhorred.

Still, he regretted not having found a better way to persuade her. After Au Siu-Man's suicide, Violet's psychological state had become even more fragile. All he could do to calm her down was insist over and over that the girl's death wasn't Violet's fault.

"Last night's leftovers are in the fridge. Just heat them up in the microwave for your lunch," he now said, putting on his shoes in the vestibule. "I'm sorry I'm not earning more money, or I'd buy you a proper meal."

"No, this is fine," Violet murmured, biting her lower lip.

Christopher said goodbye and headed for the MTR. In the crowded train, he found a spot by the door, standing with his briefcase in one hand, cell phone in the other, distractedly scrolling through the latest news. Should he arrange for his sister to transfer schools? Should she change her surname back to Song? Should he get a second job behind his boss's back so he could afford to rent a slightly bigger apartment? For days now, these questions had been swirling around in his head.

"Huh?"

As his finger flicked along the screen, he saw a familiar face. This was a report about a scandalous case in which the accused blackmailed underage girls into sexual acts by threatening to release nude photos of them. Christopher thought he'd seen this man's face before on some IT chatboard. Even so, he didn't bother reading the whole article, just glanced at it before moving on to the next item.

It briefly crossed his mind that if his sister's delusions were actually true and someone had discovered how he'd stirred up public opinion on the internet to make that girl kill herself, then he'd probably find himself starring in a news item too.

If that day ever came, he wouldn't try to run. He knew that Au Siu-Man's death was on his head.

As long as his sister could go on living, that was enough. For her sake, he would descend into hell without a word of complaint.

He would bear the guilt alone, he thought, until his dying day.

EPILOGUE

"Where do you want these, Nga-Yee?" Wendy held up some cups from a cardboard box.

"Cupboard by the fridge, please."

On Sunday, July 12, Wendy helped Nga-Yee move in. She couldn't afford movers, thanks to N having drained her savings account, and just as she was wondering how she was going to handle this, Wendy had spontaneously offered—she'd overheard Nga-Yee giving their supervisor her new address. Nga-Yee thought of refusing, but she didn't have anywhere else to turn. Besides, she'd already accepted so many favors from Wendy, what was one more?

"Wow, Miss Au, I'd never have thought he'd give you one of his apartments."

That was Mr. Mok, Wendy's uncle, who'd come along to help drive the truck.

"Who are you talking about, Uncle?" asked Wendy.

"Miss Au's new landlord. He's a strange guy." Mr. Mok laughed.

Wendy accepted this without asking any more questions. Nga-Yee wondered at her lack of perception—everything about this situation ought to be setting off alarm bells, but Wendy seemed quite happy to vaguely assume that Mr. Mok had somehow found Nga-Yee a new place in the course of investigating her case.

Mr. Mok helped carry the many boxes up to the fourth floor before he had to leave for work, leaving Wendy and Nga-Yee to unpack them. Wendy was agog at this place—a crumbling tenement building from the outside, a neat, well-maintained apartment on the inside. Nga-Yee had been equally surprised a few days earlier, when she walked in there for the first time. It was obvious that no one lived there—the furniture was under white sheets—but the floorboards and bathroom were perfectly clean. All the furniture and appliances she needed were already there, and she didn't have to bring any of that from her old place. What she had wasn't worth reselling, so she simply gave it away to her neighbors.

She would miss Wun Wah House, but she knew this was a good chance to begin a new life. She read in the papers that many young women came forward after Sze Chung-Nam was arrested, and he was facing a stiff sentence. Yet she didn't follow his case beyond that. Better to forget the past and keep moving ahead. She had to go on living well, for the sake of her parents and sister.

"The last tenant must have been very neat!" said Wendy, inspecting the kitchen. "You've lucked out, Nga-Yee. Sure, there's no elevator, but finding an apartment like this near the city center is incredible."

Nga-Yee smiled but said nothing. She didn't want to explain that there was no previous tenant. The previous morning, while dropping off some stuff, she'd bumped into Heung.

"Oh, morning, Miss Au," Heung had said. She was coming from the stairwell out into the street, just like their first meeting.

"Morning. Just finished cleaning, Heung? You have quite a few apartments to get through—that must be hard work."

"It is." Heung smiled. "But at least I won't have to do the fourth floor anymore."

So N had already told Heung she'd be moving in. Nga-Yee suddenly remembered their second meeting, the morning after she'd spent the night at N's place. And now she was moving into his building—what must the cleaning lady think?

"Um, Heung, please don't misunderstand, N and I . . ."

"I know—don't worry. You were one of his clients too?" said Heung cheerfully. "That guy. He puts up all kinds of defenses, but underneath it all he's a good person."

"Too?" Nga-Yee had been about to disagree with her assessment of N's character, but the word caught her attention. "Heung, are you cleaning the building for free because you owe him money?"

"For free?" She looked puzzled. "No. He was the one who didn't get—"

She stopped abruptly, looked around to make sure no one else was nearby. "Miss Au, you're N's friend and he's letting you stay here, so I don't think it matters if I tell you. N could have taken the ten million dollars, but in the end he wouldn't accept a cent, and he gave it all to me and the other clients. Where else would you find such a generous soul?"

"Ten million!" Nga-Yee gaped. She'd never have guessed that Heung was rich.

"Shh! It didn't all come to me," Heung hastily explained. "I guess I should tell you the whole story. I live in a fifty-year-old tenement building in Sheung Wan. Most of my neighbors are older folk. The government said we had to strengthen the outer wall of the building, so the two dozen households pooled our money and hired a contractor to manage the project. We got cheated. The fees ballooned from a few million, like they'd initially said, to ten million. Sure, you could say it was our fault for not reading the contract more carefully, but the contractor was obviously acting in bad faith. He even took money people were saving for their funerals. My upstairs neighbor Uncle Wong was so angry, he had a heart attack and got sent to the hospital. I happened to mention this to N—I had no idea what he was capable of. He did his thing, and the contractor eventually paid us back twenty million—everything he'd taken, plus interest. I'd been working for N for four years at that point, and I had no idea he was anything more than some software engineer who made apps for a living. We'd have been happy getting the initial sum back, and N could have kept the other ten million as his fee—but he refused to take any of it. He said that was just pocket change, we should keep it for our old age. These days, there are evil people everywhere you look, and then there's N—a modern-day knight in shining armor."

"When was that?" Nga-Yee thought of something when she mentioned the money.

"The work took place last year, but we got the money back only two or three months ago."

Heung kept talking a while longer as they stood on the sidewalk outside 151 Second Street, but Nga-Yee didn't pay much attention to the rest of the conversation. This must be what N was talking about at Cityview Hotel—in other words, he was targeted by the triad because he'd intervened on behalf of Heung. At the time, she'd been impressed by how quickly he dispatched the gangsters, but after spending more time with him, she couldn't help wondering: he could surely have escaped their notice altogether if he wanted. How could he have been so careless as to let them find out his address?

Nga-Yee got the opportunity to ask N this question in the afternoon when she went to his sixth-floor apartment to sort out the utility bills. "Didn't I mention?" he said. "Brother Tiger in Wan Chai had just taken over. I knew the crooked contractor was friends with Brother Tiger. New triad leaders need to be shown who's boss, and I was getting revenge for Heung, so I found a way to do both—and they took the bait. It's better to bundle troublesome things together and deal with them all at once, don't you think?"

His tone was casual, but once again Nga-Yee found this inconceivable. She might never get to the bottom of N. He had the ruthlessness of a hardened criminal, but was more upright than most people, always using his abilities to help the weak. He was more than able to keep himself safely above the fray, yet willing to make himself vulnerable in order to turn the tables and secure victory. N's very existence seemed to go against regular human behavior and psychology.

This led Nga-Yee to have some strange thoughts of her own. She couldn't help wondering if N hadn't predicted from the very start that she wouldn't go through with her revenge against Violet To, and he'd never planned to have her commit suicide in the first place. It was still a mystery to her how Violet's big brother managed to appear at just the right moment that night—unless N had allowed one of Violet's cries for help to actually get through? In which case, the opportunity he'd created was for Nga-Yee to abandon her vengeance completely.

She would never ask N this, of course. Even if she'd guessed right, he'd never admit it.

"Oh wow. Is this your sister, Nga-Yee?" Wendy was holding up the photo frame she'd just pulled from a box: Siu-Man's selfie with Nga-Yee and their mother in the background. After N returned the cell phone to her, Nga-Yee had taken it to a shop to have the photo printed and framed.

"Yes." Every mention of Siu-Man still gave Nga-Yee a jolt of sorrow, but she now accepted that her sister was gone.

Wendy placed the picture on a nearby shelf and clasped her hands, speaking to the photo. "Wherever you are, please protect your big sister. I'll look out for her too."

It was typical of Wendy's brash personality that she would mention Siu-Man so freely in front of her sister, but at this moment Nga-Yee was grateful. And perhaps Siu-Man really was keeping an eye on her from the afterlife.

When they'd put everything away, Wendy put on some music on her phone as they cleaned up. Nga-Yee had no idea that her coworker had such interesting taste—apart from Chinese pop songs, she also had the latest K-pop hits and some Western rock. To Nga-Yee's amusement, she sang along to some of them in her rather dubious Korean.

As Nga-Yee flattened cardboard boxes, Wendy's phone played a familiar tune.

"Oh no, not this one," said Nga-Yee. It was "You Can't Always Get What You Want."

"I didn't know you listened to rock music," said Wendy from the closet, where she was putting away some clothes.

"Rock?"

"This is the Rolling Stones."

"Oh, I just heard it by accident." Nga-Yee pursed her lips, remembering N giving her a hard time. "I hate these lyrics. They say you'll never get what you want."

Wendy stared at her. "What are you talking about? Have you listened all the way through?"

She turned up the volume. Nga-Yee wasn't sure what her point was, but she dutifully paid attention to the words. At the last line—"sometimes you get what you need"—she realized that she'd misunderstood.

"Um, Wendy, I need to head out for a second. There's something I need to take care of."

"Where are you going?"

"To have a chat with my landlord."

As Nga-Yee walked up the stairs, she thought about the end of her conversation with Heung.

"It was Loi who introduced me to N," Heung had said. "The market was bad then, and I'd just lost my job. Loi said he had a friend looking for a cleaner for his tenement building—and that's how N helped me get through the financial crisis. I found him weird to start with—he wouldn't tell me his real name, just went by a single letter. I tried calling him Mr. N, but he scolded me for that. When I got to know him better, I asked why he didn't like being called Mr.—and he said that words like "Mr." and "Miss" are phony. They make it seem like you respect the person you're talking to, even if you despise them. Why not just stop being fake and call people by their names? At least that's honest. He said all relationships should take place between equals."

In the sixth-floor apartment, Nga-Yee found N at his desk, his fingers flying across the keyboard.

"Now what, Miss Au?" He looked up, but didn't stop typing.

"I want you to stop calling me Miss Au. Nga-Yee is fine." She walked up to the desk.

His hands stilled, and he looked steadily at her for a moment, then let out a snort of laughter.

"Have you and your friend had lunch?"

"No, we—"

"I'll have a large wonton noodles, reduced noodles, extra scallions, soup on the side, fried greens, no oyster sauce," he said, handing her a banknote. "Nga-Yee."

She took the cash with a sigh and scowled at him, though actually she wasn't unhappy.

When she left her old home that morning, she'd already been certain this would be the day her life changed completely.

ABOUT THE AUTHOR

CHAN HO-KEI lives in Hong Kong. He has won the Mystery Writers of Taiwan Award for his short stories, and in 2011 he won the Soji Shimada Mystery Award, the biggest mystery award in the Chinese-speaking world.

ABOUT THE TRANSLATOR

JEREMY TIANG's novel *State of Emergency* won the Singapore Literature Prize in 2018. He has translated more than ten books from Chinese, including Chan Ho-Kei's *The Borrowed*, and also writes and translates plays. He lives in Brooklyn.